## "Stop playing with me," Nicola protested softly

"I'm not playing with you." Matt moved closer in the moonlight and squeezed her hand gently.

"Then what do you call this...this act of yours?" She wanted to snatch her hand away. His touch was doing crazy things to her.

"It's no act, Nicky."

"What do you want from me?" she demanded, knowing but not knowing at all.

There was an awful moment of silence, as if they were both frozen in place—Nicola poised for flight, Matt steady, cocksure, compelling.

"I want this from you," he finally whispered, pulling her to him, his mouth coming down hard on hers. She forgot everything, all the inner warnings, the self-promises. Her body leaped in a sweet agitation that wouldn't be denied, and a slow, hot flame kindled within her....

## ABOUT THE AUTHOR

The writing team of Lynn Erickson is back
with another romantic, spine-tingling
Superromance, set in Colorado and
British Columbia. Molly Swanton and Carla
Peltonen report that this book was a joy to
research. Both are avid skiers and enjoyed
unique experience of helicopter skiing. Ca
and Molly live in Aspen, Colorado, and ha
been writing together for more than thirte
years.

## Books by Lynn Erickson

### HARLEQUIN SUPERROMANCE

132–SNOWBIRD
157–THE FACES OF DAWN
184–A CHANCE WORTH TAKING
199–STORMSWEPT
231–A DANGEROUS SENTIMENT
255–TANGLED DREAMS
276–A PERFECT GEM
298–FOOL'S GOLD
320–FIRECLOUD
347–SHADOW ON THE SUN

### HARLEQUIN INTRIGUE

42–ARENA OF FEAR

This book is dedicated
to Dave Hoff,
who came up with the idea
in the first place.

# *PROLOGUE*

IT WAS HOT in the jungle.

Matt Cavanaugh followed the man in the camouflage shirt. The man's shirt was black with sweat, and his pack dug cruelly into his shoulders. The pack was heavy; it had a machine gun strapped on top of it and many rounds of ammunition.

Matt's pack wasn't so heavy, but it still dug into his shoulders, aching, chafing, dragging.

It was hot. It was a lethal heat, and he was too damn old to be doing this sort of thing.

"Señor Smith," the leader of the group said, calling over his shoulder from the front of the line. "We stop here. *Pocos minutos.* A few minutes for a rest."

"And none too soon," Matt muttered thankfully under his breath. Señor Smith. He'd almost forgotten his alias. Of course, he'd had so many over the years: Smith, Jones, Brown. He slapped at a mosquito absently. This was the last one, he thought, the last undercover job. He didn't care what Ned had to say about it. Thirty-eight was too old to be slugging through a crawling, wet jungle. He was losing his edge.

They rested for a few minutes, the men speaking softly in Spanish to one another in the shade of a guanacaste tree.

"One hour more, Señor Smith," the leader said to him, passing Matt a field canteen, "and we will be at the camp. We are lucky this was an uneventful journey."

Yes, lucky, Matt thought, tipping the canteen up, his throat working as he swallowed the tepid, metallic-tasting water. But in the jungle you had to drink, because you lost so much water sweating. In fact, he mused, none of the men, himself included, had needed to relieve themselves— the oppressive heat sapped a body dry. He sat back against the tree and tried to relax. Only another hour. He could make it. The most challenging part of his job was still to come—the meeting with Juan Ramirez.

He leaned back and closed his eyes for a moment, recalling what Ned had said in the briefing about this assignment. Juan Ramirez, a man from a wealthy family of Costa Plata, a rebel leader now, fighting a guerrilla war against the official president of Costa Plata, General Raoul Cisernos, who, as the entire world knew, was a corrupt dictator and a pawn of the Soviet Union via the Cuban connection.

Costa Plata. A tiny Central American banana republic, like so many of the nations in the area, caught in a never-ending spiral of coup and hope and corruption and disappointment.

But this young rebel leader, Ramirez, had been educated in the States. He had, apparently, the brains and determination to lead Costa Plata, but most importantly, he was a firm ally of the United States, a believer in free enterprise and an enlightened populace. He promised his followers a republic, with elected officials, voting rights and an end to Cisernos's brutal police state.

At present, Ramirez was holed up in a camp in the interior jungle of his small nation, surrounded by Cisernos's troops, only venturing out on small hit-and-run missions. The United States could not officially supply the rebels with money and weapons, but they *could* send a representative to assure Ramirez of their support if—and when—he became president of Costa Plata. And to advise him to hang on, that General Cisernos was in trouble and would soon, in all probability, be toppled from his seat of power.

Hence the presence of Matt Cavanaugh, alias Matt Smith, of the U.S. Foreign Service, Section C, for covert operations. C-section, as his boss, Ned, liked to call it jokingly.

It was hot. Matt wiped the stinging, oily sweat from his forehead, pulled the bandanna from his neck, rolled it and tied it around his head.

*"Vámanos,"* the leader said, rising. "Let's go."

They followed a narrow path that snaked through the jungle. It was damp, full of bugs and smelly. The leaves of the undergrowth were limp and faded green like old paper dollars. The jungle screeched and cackled and rustled and wrapped itself around the puny men as if it were not going to let them go. A giant stomach, heaving and grunting, trying to digest them in its hot juices.

Matt stuck his thumbs under the straps of his pack to ease the strain. The skinny guy ahead of him with the RPG-7 machine gun sweated but didn't falter or complain. He trudged in his U.S. army issue boots, the pack a welcome burden, like the gun, a gift for the cause.

This mission was a vital one, vital but unofficial. If Matt was captured by the general's forces and discovered to be an American, the United States Foreign Service would disavow all knowledge of him. He would be on his own, a civilian breaking the law of Costa Plata.

It was a good thing this hike had been uneventful. He always chuckled to himself when Ned repeated the warning about being on his own if he was discovered. It reminded him of *Mission Impossible*, the old television program. "And this tape will self-destruct in five seconds," he would say to Ned, mock-solemnly.

"Get serious, Cavanaugh," Ned would growl.

"Never," Matt would reply with exaggerated insouciance.

But maybe, at thirty-eight, he should start getting serious. Or at least start thinking about it. And he would, after this assignment.

The jungle was a suffocating tangle around him, alive, a mass of hairy green vines catching at him, drooping, criss-crossed, thick with screaming birds and monkeys.

Brightly colored butterflies sat on overgrown hothouse plants, on ferny limbs, fluttering in the seams of green light. The trees grew thickly, stubbornly, viciously, heavy with creepers. Flowers hung like bright rags or had blossoms oddly shaped like shuttlecocks.

The smells. Stink and perfume. The green hum of something gone bad. The glorious whiff of heaven. The tropical brew that attacked the olfactory nerves—too strong, too sweet, too rotten.

The sounds. Cackling and clicking and howling. The buzz of insects excited by the proximity of hot blood. The drumming and ringing of howler monkeys. The rattle of branches moved by an unseen hunter.

It was hellishly hot.

Matt had been in jungles before. In Java and Angola, in Brazil. He'd also been in bitter-cold places: Iceland, Tibet. He'd been in primitive villages and sophisticated cities on assignment. He'd been on yachts in the Mediterranean. He'd been around. And it was time to quit, time to come in from the cold, to get a regular job with the Foreign Service, to take vacations, to settle down.

Alone?

And would the service ever let him come in, knowing all that he knew? But more than that, Matt was good at his job, terrific at it. He'd been recruited straight out of George Washington University, a twenty-two-year-old wise-mouthed brat, a bulletproof kid with a wild reputation already, a lost kid who couldn't have known it at the time, but who was in need of a home and security.

Well, the service had provided it all. And Matt had quickly made his mark in undercover work. Who would have thought a kid with a pocketful of trust fund money was the eyes and ears for the service? In all his travelings, in all those part-time, goof-off jobs he'd taken, not once, in sixteen years, had his cover been compromised. Of course, it had meant no close relationships, not with women, college friends or co-workers. Relationships were luxuries. And his family? Given the Cavanaugh clan, except for his long-suffering mother, they were all too ready to write him off.

"We arrive soon," the leader called to him. "You are very strong, Señor Smith. I was afraid this trip would take much longer."

"Thanks," Matt replied, "but I'm as anxious as you are to get there."

"Yes, I understand." The man nodded, turning away, leading the dozen of them deeper still into the maw of the jungle.

There had been a time, Matt thought, when he would have been thrilled at this assignment. It would have been an adventure. He would have drunk it all in: the discomfort, the heat and bugs and wildness, the wet itch of hairy vines. His job had been a challenge, and an escape, too; an escape from his family, from his alter ego, Matt Cavanaugh—beach bum, trust funder, sometime bartender, apparent drunk, a useless human being.

And all the time he was laughing inside, laughing at those ignorant people who saw only his cover and never knew he was a secret agent for the Foreign Service, a valued employee of the United States government, a man who risked his own life to save their butts.

It was ironic, and he laughed at those ignorant souls. And he cried inside, too, because the one person in the world who needed to know the truth about Matt couldn't be told. But then, his father had disapproved of Matt long before he'd gone to work for Section C, so he guessed it wouldn't have mattered much what he did.

His shoulders hurt, his legs throbbed, he was getting blisters on his feet. And after seeing Juan Ramirez, he had to walk back out of this hellhole. Well, he'd done harder things before, and he supposed he'd do it this time, too, but he was glad they were almost there. He had to be back across the border in three days' time so that the helicopter could pick him up at the rendezvous spot. He'd make it, no problem, and then he'd be flown home in air-conditioned, Pan Am comfort to report to Ned.

If he wasn't caught on the way back across the border, that was.

The leader had stopped ahead and was holding up a hand. He called out something, a password, Matt supposed, then waved his squad on. The clearing appeared miraculously. Matt stepped past some thick brush in the trail and into the encampment. He could have sworn there was nothing ahead except jungle. But there were tents and sandbagged gun emplacements and the entrances to underground bunkers. There were also clothes hanging on lines, rifles stacked against trees, a low-smoke cook fire going in the center of the clearing and lots of uniformed men lounging around, smoking, talking, mending, eating, reading.

"Come, Señor Smith, I will take you to Juan," the leader of the expedition said.

He led Matt across the clearing, waving to individuals, exchanging greetings. He smiled for the first time since he'd met Matt at the drop zone. He was home.

The camp was large. Matt tried to size it up for his debriefing. There were dozens of tents, hundreds of men. And this, he knew, was only one of many secret fire bases the rebels controlled. The soldiers' equipment looked to be well taken care of. Discipline was obviously strict. He tucked the knowledge away for future use.

Juan Ramirez sat behind a folding table in a roomy tent. He was a slim man of Matt's own age, with short, fine black hair and strange hazel eyes that met Matt's when he looked up from the papers he was busy reading. Heavy eyebrows, a thin high-bridged nose and a delicate mouth completed the picture. An ascetic. An idealist with the fire of conviction in his yellow eyes. A dangerous man, so Matt had been told.

"Juan," said the man who'd brought Matt there, "here is Señor Smith."

Juan Ramirez rose, came around the desk, tall and straight and graceful, holding out his slim-fingered hand. "Well, Mr. Smith," he said in unaccented English, with a hint of Boston in it, "welcome to Camp Hiawatha." A thin smile slanted his mouth, mocking his surroundings, himself, even Matt.

"And thank you, Diego," he said to the other man. "You did a good job guiding Mr. Smith here."

"*Gracias*, Juan," the man said, breaking into a smile, backing out of the tent.

"Mr. Smith," Juan Ramirez mused, with obvious emphasis on the "Smith."

"Just Matt, if you don't mind."

"Good. And call me Juan. And please, take that pack off, sit down. You must be exhausted. The camp activities are carried a bit overboard, aren't they?" Juan grinned. "Would you like a drink? Believe it or not, I happen to have a bottle of Cutty Sark. Alas, there's no ice or soda."

"Sure, I'll have a small one. Lots of water," Matt said. He was looking around the tent, taking everything in, preparing all the while for his debriefing back in Washington. There were maps on the canvas walls, a neatly made-up folding cot and a state-of-the-art shortwave radio set.

Juan was filling two tin cups with Scotch and then pouring water from a canteen into them. "Boiled," he said, gesturing to the water, then he handed Matt the well-diluted Scotch.

"To peace," he said, holding his cup up.

"To peace," Matt repeated. The liquid was warm and a bit rusty looking, but it was relaxing, somehow taking the edge off the primitive surroundings.

"So, Matt," Juan began, "you are here. You walked a long way through the jungle to visit me. Your government wanted this meeting. I'm very interested in what you have to say."

Matt studied the man for a minute, his senses alert, his feelers out. Was Juan Ramirez afraid? Overconfident? Hotheaded? Too careful? Was he a liar, only accepting American aid until he achieved power, then condemning the capitalist pigs for interfering? It was Matt's job to report on his intuitions as much as facts. He cleared his throat, felt the alcohol soothe away some of his fatigue and started in. "As you know, the United States has promised to recognize you as the legitimate head of Costa Plata in the event of your victory. Cisernos is a Communist puppet and a bad leader, as well."

"Yes, that we can agree upon," Ramirez said carefully.

"However, the obstacle here is, naturally, your victory."

Ramirez's mouth twisted ironically. "That, too, we can agree upon."

"I was sent here to inform you of a significant development in General Cisernos's status." Matt leaned forward. "Costa Plata is deeply in debt. The economy is falling apart. Cisernos had to take out some enormous loans a few years back. Loans from the World Bank."

Ramirez nodded slowly.

"Those loans will be called in when they come due this fall. Principal *and* interest. The total amounts to several hundred million U.S. dollars."

Ramirez fixed his yellow eyes on Matt intently.

"What that means is that the treasury of Costa Plata will be bankrupt. Cisernos will have no money to pay his army. His regime will fall." Matt paused, then continued. "There must be someone on hand to pick up the pieces, someone to take over from Cisernos. A leader with popular support and, of course, an interest in keeping the United States as an ally. It's May now. Before the new year, Costa Plata will need a new president. My government would prefer it to be you." A droplet of sweat trickled down Matt's cheek, tickling, but he ignored it, holding the rebel leader's gaze in the sultry silence.

"Well," Ramirez finally said, "this *is* news." He smiled thinly, and Matt could almost see the wheels of his mind turning. "And are you a political man yourself, Matt?" All very friendly, mundane, while the man digested Matt's revelation.

Matt gave him his time. "No, not really. I'm merely an employee. I try never to discuss religion or politics."

"Wise of you." He looked Matt in the eye, a sharp glance. "So Cisernos is about to take a fall. Interesting." He leaned back in his chair and turned the tin cup in his fingers. "And what, may I ask, is your source of information?"

Matt shook his head. "Top secret."

"I need to judge whether your information is correct."

"You'll have to take it on faith," Matt said.

"The World Bank is an independent entity. It does not do the United States' bidding. I have heard that the president of the World Bank is nobody's lackey. How can you be so sure the bank will call in these loans?" Ramirez asked skeptically.

"I am sure," Matt said quietly. "Evan Cavanaugh is the head of the World Bank, and he doesn't like red figures in his books. His job is to keep the bank solvent."

"But, still, how do you know what is in the mind of this Evan Cavanaugh?"

Matt smiled sardonically. Oh, he knew all right. What he couldn't tell Ramirez was that the president of the World Bank, Evan Cavanaugh, was his father.

# CHAPTER ONE

NICOLA GAGE LOOKED IDLY out of the bedroom window, out over the misty green expanse of the Cavanaughs' estate in Westchester County, New York. The driveway swept into sight over a hill, past a half-tumbled stone wall covered with dark green, glossy ivy, traversed acres of emerald lawn, then curved into a circle in front of the Tudor-style house.

A lovely scene on this hot, humid June morning: peaceful, secure, bucolic.

The warm breeze wafted in through the open window, fragrant with the smell of newly mown grass and honeysuckle, and with it came the throaty, humming noise of a well-tuned engine.

It was a white Ferrari, a sleek beauty, the top down, the dappled sunlight filtering through the leaves of the locust trees and racing across its shiny hood. The driver pulled up alongside the far wing of the mansion and hopped out of the car without opening the door, a quick, agile movement that impressed Nicola and teased her memory. Somewhere, someplace, she'd seen that movement before.

*My Lord,* Nicola thought, her eyes riveted on the man, *it's Matt, the prodigal son. Well, well.*

She watched as he stood beside his vehicle and removed his aviator-style sunglasses, casually eyeing the old homestead, the multimillion-dollar brick and stucco and beamed house that had once been home to him. Matt Cavanaugh. A face from the past. Oh, she'd seen him briefly—six, or was it seven years ago?—at Thanksgiving dinner. Right here. Thanksgiving had always been a command performance at the Cavanaughs': close family and twenty or so of their nearest and dearest friends. Nicola had been there because she'd just finished hotel and restaurant management school in Michigan and hadn't yet landed her first real cooking job up in Vermont. And Matt had breezed in late, clad in a tuxedo, a bottle of champagne under one arm and a glitzy, half-bombed redhead under the other.

Evan Cavanaugh, Matt's father, had had a fit, Nicola recalled, and the normally reserved, dignified Maureen had held back her tears when the two men, her husband and oldest son, had gone directly and without hesitation at each other's jugulars.

Oh yes, she'd seen Matt that once—if only for ten minutes before he'd left. Just as she'd seen him several times before that, since she'd moved in with the Cavanaughs; although his appearances at the family home had been few and far between. Matt was twelve years her senior. She'd been a tall, gawky kid when he'd graduated from George Washington University's foreign affairs school, come home for two days and had a terrible fight with Evan about his future. Bartending, she remembered. He'd had the nerve to tell his ambitious father he was taking a job *bartending* on a Greek island, and he'd been booted out of the house, Evan yelling after him that he should have expected Matt to pull a stunt like that!

Oh Lordy, Matt was here. Better get ready for the fireworks.

And Nicola had seen him again after that Greek isle scene. It had been one of those few times he'd graced the Cavanaugh home with his presence, around the year Nicola had graduated from high school. He'd shown up on a cold, snowy winter night, when the wind had been howling down the four chimneys and the driveway had just about been drifted over. Matt had sashayed in, back from a skiing trip, or something equally as recreational, out in Squaw Valley, California.

Nicola could almost remember Evan's greeting. "Still bartending? Or are you just plain living off the trust fund my father so unwisely left you?"

"Oh, I take on odd jobs, mostly bartending, but I like to move around a lot. A rolling stone and all that." Matt had shot his father an insolent grin, and the family members, Maureen and Matt's brother, T.J., had winced. Once again the battle lines had been drawn between father and oldest son, and the war had come shortly thereafter.

"You're a bum!" Evan had shouted from behind closed library doors. "The only son I have who's got the brains and the know-how to run the family bank, and you turn out to be a no-good wastrel! Get out of here! I mean it, Matt, and don't come back until you're ready to act like a Cavanaugh and a man!"

Matt had rolled his eyes at his mother, who had been waiting in the living room with T.J. Then he'd smiled at her with true affection, hugged her warmly, and he'd given T.J. a commiserating punch to the arm. As far as Nicola went, he'd grinned at her, too, flicked her heavy dark braid and said, "Hang in there, kid, the old man's not really as tough as he sounds." He'd left then, not twenty-four hours after his arrival. He'd gone back out into the blizzard that raged in the Hudson River valley and had left behind a weeping mother, a confused, sullen brother and Nicola, who could only stare after him and wonder why it was that fathers and sons so often tore one another to shreds.

Nicola stood at the window now and wondered if fathers and daughters fought like that, too. She had no way of judging, because her own father had ignored her so completely that she'd never even had an argument with him. Wentworth Gage, the famous chef, a wealthy and respected and popular man, beloved by all. Beloved by his only daughter, Nicola, even though he rarely saw her.

It never ceased to amaze her, either, that she'd actually enrolled in hotel and restaurant school with the intention of becoming a chef, just like Dad, so the man—who had not even sent her a birthday card in five years—would finally notice that she was alive.

*Dumb, Nicola, really dumb.*

Oh, she'd sent him copies of her grades and letters from professors—she'd sent them to Evan and Maureen, too—but he'd never acknowledged them. At graduation in Michigan, he'd finally, *amazingly*, sent flowers and a note.

Dear baby,
Congrats.
Come and see my new French restaurant on Third Avenue. Dinner's on me.

Love, Dad

*Love, Dad?*

She could have screamed. She could have held a seven-inch chef's knife up to his throat. But instead she beat her pillow and sobbed and missed him so much it ached. If only there had never been the divorce in the first place....

When Nicola was ten, Went had told her mother that he wanted a divorce. Suzanne had had a nervous breakdown over it and had been sent to an expensive private nursing home. Went, good fellow that he was, footed the bill. But he hadn't had time for his daughter, his scared, *terrified*, bereft child, whose whole world had collapsed in a terrible emotional holocaust.

It had been Suzanne's best friend, Maureen Cavanaugh, who had offered to take care of Nicola. Maureen and Evan had become her legal guardians and had provided the only stability in her life from the time she was ten.

It was very odd, too, that Nicola had been able to have such a good relationship with Evan when he was so hard on his two sons. It was as if he could relax his rigid standards because she was not his blood, or was not a boy, or whatever. She saw Evan's faults, but she loved him, anyway. She saw Maureen's too-passive nature, but she loved her, too. And she hadn't stopped loving her own father.

Went Gage never complained that someone else was raising his only child; he loved his freedom and his women too much. Suzanne had been in and out of the private nursing home since the divorce, had been diagnosed as being clinically depressed and even now lived in a Thorazine haze, a pretty, vague woman, who always cried when her daughter visited her in the expensive home.

Some family.

Nicola stepped to one side to cloak herself from Matt's gaze in case he should look up toward her window. But he only began to cross the circular driveway toward the front door. The years had been kind to him, she thought. He'd lost none of those good looks or the indolent grace of his lean, six-foot frame. From what she could see as he approached the front steps, his eyes—those bright blue eyes of his mother's—still sparked with devilry, and his curling brown hair was as unruly and thick as ever. She wondered if he was going to press the doorbell, but he smiled instead and opened the door as if it hadn't been so many years. As if he'd be welcome.

Quickly Nicola realized that she was only half-dressed and was expected—uh-oh, ten minutes ago—on the patio below.

"I don't like Mr. Reyes," Nicola had said to Maureen the day before. "He gives me the creeps every time he kisses my hand and shoots me one of those slick Latin looks."

"Evan can handle him," Maureen had replied. "You know Evan, when it comes to the affairs of the World Bank, he'll put up with worse than Mr. Reyes."

Oh yes, Nicola knew that Evan could handle anybody. He was a powerful man, president of the New York based World Bank, the institution that provided loans to Third

World countries for large development projects. And he was an attractive man, too, who kept himself trim and in great physical condition. He had smooth, tanned skin, regular features, thick salt-and-pepper hair and black eyebrows over large, dark brown eyes.

Oh yes, Evan Cavanaugh had the world by the tail. He also had all the right connections, and Señor Reyes was merely a nuisance, the finance minister of a Central American country, Costa Plata, a small nation that was apparently in deep financial distress. Thus Reyes's visit to Evan Cavanaugh. He was discussing money with Evan, his country's treasury, in fact, which was on the verge of bankruptcy, Maureen had told Nicola. It was all tied in with past due moneys and loans owed to the World Bank that could be called in—unpleasant stuff. Evan, it seemed, was not telling Reyes what the man wanted to hear. But then, that was Evan's job.

As for Nicola, she'd rather cook good food and see folks enjoy it. Basic, simple fun.

Nicola's thoughts drifted back to Matt, and his sudden, unannounced arrival. What a scene *that* would create at brunch, and in front of Reynaldo Reyes, too. Still hurrying, she tossed the sheets up onto the canopied bed, tried to tidy the room, buttoned up her thin, white cotton blouse, tucked it into the matching skirt and slid her feet into open-toed sandals. This was as dressy as she got, as dressy as she wanted to get. She rushed down the elegant, curving staircase and across the floor, her heels tap-tapping on the marble.

Where was Matt? On the patio already? Lordy, Lordy, were *they* all going to be shocked.

She went through the living room, past the wing chairs and across the Persian carpet. She could see the patio now through the drapes, but apparently Matt wasn't out there yet.

Where was he? In the kitchen, talking to Lydia, the old cook? Rambling around the mansion, reacquainting himself? Sprucing up in a powder room? She couldn't see him doing that. Oh no, not Mr. Swashbuckler himself. Men like him didn't need mirrors; they already knew that charm oozed from every pore like hot drops of lava.

"There you are," Maureen chided when Nicola, out of breath, crossed the stone veranda toward the pool. "We're ready to sit."

She wanted to warn Maureen, to shield her from what was to come, but Reynaldo Reyes stood up, his tall, slim, white linen-draped frame bent over Nicola's hand, and Evan was winking at her as if to say, "Put up with his oily behavior for just a short while longer," and T.J. was nodding in her direction—quiet, introverted T.J., who was still, as always, a stranger to her.

Without warning the scene altered. As if an invisible director said, "Places, action," the expressions of the characters and the mood of the setting changed. It was hot out, hot and close with humidity, but goose bumps rose on Nicola's arms as heads turned toward the French doors leading out to the veranda. There was an abrupt, waiting silence. For a split second, just a fraction of time, everything and everyone froze. But then Matt seemed to draw strength from the utter silence and began to move toward the surprised entourage.

"What?" he said lightly. "Have I suddenly grown another head or something?" He kept moving confidently; if a man can be graceful, then he moved gracefully, self-assured, smiling that infernal smile of his, the ironic grin that seemed to lift the corners of his mouth permanently as if he were laughing at the bad joke that was life. And, for widely varied reasons, he caused pulses to quicken.

"Matt," Maureen breathed, tears forming in her eyes.

"Well, if it isn't my big brother," the six-foot-three-inch T.J. offered guardedly.

"Hi," Nicola got out.

"This must be your eldest," Reyes said with less certainty than usual.

Evan remained coldly still.

"Just in time for breakfast." Matt came up to his mother and pulled her into his embrace, kissing her short, blond-gray head first and then her cheek. Nicola could see Maureen's slim, straight body tremble as her firstborn held her close with unaffected love.

Introductions were made to Reyes, of course, who bantered lightly with Matt, while the older son tried out his fair Spanish on the minister. Maureen looked at her husband through pleading eyes, and T.J. stepped nearer to his mother, Nicola noted, and she wondered at the gesture. Was T.J. being protective? Was he jealous of his outgoing, purportedly brilliant brother? Could T.J. actually have thought Matt had come home to weasel his way back into Evan's good grace and usurp T.J.'s position as the future president of the Cavanaugh family business, the First Bank of Westchester?

Once Reyes had released her hand, Nicola had slipped back into the shadows beneath a tree. It wasn't that Matt intimidated her—not at all. It was rather that he was the sort of man who repelled her. Matt Cavanaugh reminded her too much of her father.

From her safe spot she watched the drama unfold. Maureen was still smiling, tentatively and hopefully; T.J. regarded his wisecracking brother without expression but was dragging deeply on a freshly lit cigarette, a nervous habit of his. Evan, too, was staring at Matt, his face closed, suspicious, a hint of anger just showing through. And all the time Matt seemed impervious to the roiling emotional impact his unannounced arrival had caused his family. He kept right on chatting with Reyes, his manner relaxed.

"How's the drought situation in Costa Plata this year?" he was asking. "That's good to hear. And the old El

Libertad Hotel in San Pedro, is it still standing…? Oh sure, I've visited your country. I even had a job there once, on the coast. I bartended for a private party one of your cabinet members was throwing. Quite an affair…. Oh, I got the job through a local man I met." Matt shrugged.

Yes, he was handsome and devilishly charming, and by the sound of it, there weren't many places in the world he'd missed. What an aimless existence, Nicola thought derisively. What a waste of a disarming personality *and* a good brain. And there was T.J.—Thomas John—inwardly motivated, reserved, dull. He was not a bad-looking man at thirty-six, tall and fair and somewhat debonair, but let's face it, she mused, he lacked spark. He was dutiful and capable but so introverted that no one, save Maureen, had a clue as to what went on behind those deep-set blue eyes.

Nicola breathed a sigh of relief when Maureen finally announced that if Señor Reyes was to make his flight back to Costa Plata that morning, they simply had to sit down to brunch. At least Nicola was going to be spared that dose of Matt Cavanaugh charm.

She was wrong, however. She began to move from beneath the shadows of the tree and was heading to her place at the table, when she was suddenly stopped by his hand on her arm, gentle yet firm.

"Nicola." He said her name in a kind of quiet caress that surprised her, taking her off guard. They were barely acquaintances, after all. "Boy, kid, I hardly would have recognized you." He turned her around then and gave her a big brotherly hug, a friendly peck on her cheek.

"Hello, Matt," she said, uncomfortable, aware of the eyes of the others on them. "Nice to see you again."

"I can't get over it," he was saying. "You've really grown into a beauty."

God, thought Nicola, growing more ill at ease by the moment. Why on earth was he trying to charm her, too?

He shot her one of those magic, crooked smiles and continued to hold her. "Little Nicky. The kid."

A beauty, indeed, she thought, smarting. Who was he fooling? Oh, she had passable looks, with long black hair and white skin. And she was trim, able to eat what she wanted, but only because she was so active. But she'd always considered her eyes to be a dull, muddy brown and too expressionless, almost sad looking, she'd been told, and her lips were too full, too pouting to suit her frank, curious nature. Then there were her teeth. A touch crooked because her dad had been too cheap to spring for braces. At five foot eight, her limbs were okay, but as for her small breasts... Height and full bodies didn't exactly go hand in hand.

A beauty. *Take a hike, Matt.*

"And I can't believe you're here," Matt was saying, still smiling despite her skeptical expression.

"It's only a vacation," she replied, wanting to add, *Some of us work, you know.*

"Well, vacation or not, maybe we could get to know each other at last. Heck, you're practically my little sister."

"Um."

"Say, what're you working at now? Weren't you a...a...?"

"I'm a chef. I cook food."

"I knew that," he said with the quirk of an eyebrow and the deepening of a dimple in one cheek. "Where are you cooking?"

"I work for a sportsman's outfitter in Colorado in the summer and a ski lodge in Wyoming in the winter."

He regarded her with interest. "All by yourself, kid?"

"Sure, all by myself." She started to bristle, but he looked impressed and his expression was so winning...

"Are you two going to sit down?" came Maureen's pleasant voice, heightened slightly, Nicola noted, by her barely suppressed anticipation. "Come on, now, Señor Reyes only has a short time left."

Finally Matt released her but kept his warm hand at the small of her back as they walked to the table. She was mildly surprised that she even noticed his touch, that strong hand on the thin cotton of her blouse. His fingers pressed against her gently, guiding her, leading her toward the only two empty chairs—side by side.

She sat down and put her peach-colored linen napkin in her lap and thought, *Boy, is he a flirt.* And that jaunty smile, those flashing white teeth, the blue-blue eyes—a girl could get lost in those eyes of his . . . a naive girl, that was.

Through the years Nicola had heard all the gossip about Matt. If it was Tuesday it must be Paris and Francoise; if it was Wednesday, it was Rome and Maria. She had listened to Evan complain about his eldest son's philandering lifestyle and Maureen's excuses. "You don't know that, Evan. He's just sowing his wild oats. He'll settle down. I'm certain he will. Matt's a smart boy."

But Matt, it appeared, had not settled down. Was this Saturday and Nicola's turn?

A stream of smoke curled up around T.J.'s head. "Put that damn thing out," Evan said roughly. "You're at the table, boy."

Dutifully T.J. crushed his cigarette in an ashtray.

Matt poured himself a cup of coffee. "Hey, T.J.," he said offhandedly, "you running the family bank yet?"

T.J. looked at his father for a breath of time, then back at Matt. "Not yet. I'm into some other ventures right now. Short-term mortgages, that kind of thing."

"He's with a small firm, but he's doing very well," Maureen put in smoothly, and Nicola caught the sharp glance she let fly in Evan's direction. "T.J. has gained more experience on the outside than he ever would if he'd gone straight into the family bank."

"He better be learning," Evan said while the omelets were being served by the stooped and uncomplaining Lydia. "If he thinks he's going into the bank still wet behind the ears—"

"Dad," T.J. said, interrupting, "let's not get into this now."

Evan nodded, then turned to Reyes. "You have children?"

"Ah, yes," Reyes replied in his smooth, well-oiled voice. "I have three sons and two daughters."

"Um," Evan said, "then you know how difficult it is. I don't believe in just handing them a living on a silver platter. They have to earn it. I did. And so can they."

"So true, my friend, so true."

Unspoken words that Nicola had heard too often seemed to hang in the air. What Evan had not said in front of his guest might have gone like this: "Oh yes, I made my own fortune. I built the First Bank of Westchester into what it is today. It was no accident that I was offered the position of president of the World Bank, either. But my father, my very *unwise* father, was shortsighted and left a large trust fund to Matt, enough so that the boy I'd put all my hopes into turned out to be a bum. Thank God," Evan would have said, "T.J. wasn't born yet when my father died, or he would have been provided for, too."

Nicola swallowed her fresh-squeezed orange juice past a lump in her throat. As soon as Reyes was gone, Evan *would* say those things.

"So, Matt," T.J. was saying, "where have you blown in from this time?"

"Here and there. Actually I just drove up from Haig's Point, in South Carolina. I had a good job there, on one of the new golf courses."

"Bartending?" Evan asked, his expression held tightly in control.

"Sure. I met a lot of your old buddies there, Evan. You know, it's a haven for the conservative Washington crowd."

"So what exactly happened to your job?" Again, Evan spoke.

Matt leaned back in his seat and clasped his hands behind his head nonchalantly. "I didn't get along with the boss. He canned me."

"I see." Evan's ruddy color heightened.

"Oh, T.J., dear," Maureen said, "would you pass Señor Reyes the muffins?" Then, "My goodness, *señor*, it's nearly eleven. I don't know where the time went this morning."

"So—" Evan was barely hiding a scowl "—it's been six years, boy. Six years and no more than a dozen calls to your mother here. Don't you think—"

"Hey," Matt said, "the time just gets away from me." He grinned, unconcerned.

"Are you staying?" T.J. asked.

"Maybe."

*That* got a rise from the group, Nicola saw. The idea of Matt coming home for any length of time was inconceivable. Leopards did not change their spots, after all.

Why, she wondered, did it always have to be this way? It was a household swollen with intensity, expectant, ever the apprehensive calm before the storm. Yet it hadn't been that way when she'd first come to live there. Back then Matt and T.J. had been away at college, and Evan had been busy building his Westchester bank into a monumental financial institution. He'd been good to the insecure waif newly come to his home. No, more than that. He'd loved her like the daughter he'd never had. He still did.

Nicola sat there noting the charged air and recalled when she'd had trouble with her algebra in ninth grade. Evan had sat up with her and helped, night after night. And he'd been nicer to Maureen then, too. There had been kitchen and maid gossip in those days of an affair on Evan's part, though, but if it was true, he'd hidden it beautifully. Now, however, Evan and Maureen seemed to be marching to the beat of different drums. They were polite to each other, but gone was the excitement and growth of their marriage. Instead, it appeared that the affection in the home flowed between Maureen and T.J., and Evan stood on the perimeter, looking in with suspicion. Now here was Matt, barging into this already precarious situation. Why, Nicola asked herself, couldn't Evan treat his boys as he did her, with caring and understanding?

Despite the discord she felt so strongly, Nicola believed that this was truly her home. She could talk to Maureen, *really* talk to her, and with Evan she'd been able to laugh and tease and recapture bygone days. Where had her own parents been these past sixteen years? No place that Nicola could reach, that was for darn sure.

Matt moved back to the food, leaning forward in his chair, elbows on the table, his khaki trousers brushing her leg. She inched away unobtrusively.

Matt Cavanaugh. She played with the omelet on her plate, her appetite gone, and glanced at him out of the corner of her eye. He *was* a good-looking guy. And to top it all off, he had charisma; it surrounded him like a circle of delicious candy. She could see the ladies eating their way through the layers just to get at him.

Nicola felt like laughing at herself. Only a chef would come up with a mental image like that! And what did she care, anyway? He was not her type. He was too much like good old Went, her father.

"Ah," came Reyes's accented voice, breaking into her thoughts, "such a lovely home, Evan. So American, many styles borrowed from the Old World, yes?"

"My idea," Maureen interjected. "I couldn't decide on English Tudor or French Provincial. So the outside is English, and the interior more sweeping, more open."

"The gardens are lovely, Señora Cavanaugh. A gazebo on the lawn, so quaint, a small hedged maze... enchanting."

"Thank you," Maureen said graciously.

"Mom sure has a green thumb," Matt put in then, a childish but calculated statement, a rude hand slapping to Reyes, who obviously was polishing the apple.

"Ah, yes," Reyes managed to say, "a green thumb. How clever of you."

"Oh, it's nothing," Matt replied, grinning. "I've always had a way with words."

If looks could have killed, then the one Evan shot his son was lethal. What in heaven's name did Matt have against Reyes? Why, he hadn't even been home long enough to know who the man was or why he'd come. How bizarre, Nicola thought, shooting Matt a look herself.

"Oh my," Maureen was saying as she glanced at the diamond-studded watch adorning her slim, tanned wrist, "Señor Reyes, you did say the limo would be here at eleven?"

"Why, yes. The time has flown." He dabbed at his lips with the napkin and set it on the table, rising. "If you'll excuse me, I'll ready my suitcase. Your hospitality has been most gracious." He nodded courtly at Maureen and Evan, then seemed to hesitate. *"Señor,"* he began, "perhaps you would allow me a moment more of your time? In the library, if you will, in say, five minutes?"

"Of course," Evan replied, and Reyes disappeared across the flagstone terrace and into the house.

"Oh, Evan," Maureen said in a hushed voice, "what can he want now? For three days he's been badgering you so. Doesn't the man know what the word no means?"

"Apparently not," Evan said in disgust.

Matt pushed himself from the table, patted his stomach over his polo shirt and stretched his arms over his head. "What's it all about, anyway, Evan?" he asked, sounding mildly bored.

Evan grumbled something, finished his juice and muttered, "Money, what else? Costa Plata owes the World Bank two hundred million. They haven't made an interest payment on their loans for eighteen months. I'm recommending they be called in."

"You've decided for sure?" T.J. asked.

"I think we're close to a consensus," Evan said. "I'd say there's little chance of renewal."

"What if they come up with some interest money?" Nicola put in.

Evan shook his head. "They won't. They're flat broke. Even the Soviets don't want to throw good money after bad."

"Um," Matt said, "calling in those loans is going to topple the government, isn't it, Evan?"

"Not my problem," the man replied.

"I read terrible things about Costa Plata in *Time* magazine," Maureen said. "It's a police state. Innocents just disappear off the streets every day, and no one has the nerve to question it."

"Since when were you concerned about human rights, Mom?" Matt asked lightly.

"For your information," she returned, "I'm a very informed woman, kiddo. I keep up."

"I'll bet you do," Matt said, then leaned over and kissed her cheek.

"Oh, do stop," she said, but clearly Maureen was delighted. Even Evan had to smile at his son's antics, as did Nicola. But she noticed T.J.'s face then, and was surprised to see open jealousy there. My Lord, Nicola thought, her smile fading, T.J. was too old for sibling rivalry, wasn't he?

"Well, I suppose Reyes is waiting," Evan said, then stood and excused himself.

"Do check on the man's limo, will you, dear?" Maureen asked T.J. "I just hope it hasn't had a flat tire or something, and we're stuck with the man."

"How hospitable of you," Matt said.

"I don't like him."

"And neither do I," Nicola added. "He's been nothing but...but *slimy* ever since he got here. I wouldn't trust him as far as I could throw him."

"Obviously," Matt said, "the Latin lover flopped badly with you two."

Lydia cleared the table with Nicola's help, while Maureen and Matt sat there talking, comfortable, their faces looking young and relaxed. It heartened Nicola to see mother and son reunited; she only hoped that Evan would curb his disappointment in Matt and let sleeping dogs lie.

It wasn't long after the dishes had been cleared that T.J. reappeared, his hands thrust deep in his white trouser pockets as he strode in long-legged steps back to the table. "Well," he said, his brow creased, "Reyes is gone. But I'll tell you, Dad's cooking."

"Oh my," Maureen breathed just as Evan came banging out of the French doors, growling mad.

"Uh-oh," Matt said.

"Can you imagine!" Evan thundered as he began to pace the terrace. "That no good..."

"What happened?" Maureen asked quietly, troubled.

"*What happened!* I'll tell you what happened! That pompous ass offered me a million dollars to renew the loans!"

Matt let out a deep chuckle. "Hey," he said, "it's probably drug money."

"Matt," Maureen warned, "this is not the time—"

"Oh," Evan interrupted, still flaming mad, "the boy's finally using his head. I have no doubt that any money still lying around the treasury is illegal. That pompous..."

"What did you tell Reyes?" Nicola finally ventured.

"I told him exactly where he could go!"

"And what did he say to that?" It was Matt who spoke, and Nicola had to turn and look at him, never having heard such a sober tone of voice come from the man.

"Now *that's* the kicker," Evan replied, pacing even harder. "He had the nerve to threaten me!"

"What exactly did he say?" Again, Matt posed the question.

Evan waved his hand in the air as if in dismissal, but Nicola could see that he was troubled. "It's ridiculous, absurd. Who does that Reyes think he was talking to, anyway?"

"What did he say?" Matt reiterated.

"He said—" Evan turned to face them all "—that if I didn't renew the loans, I was a dead man."

# CHAPTER TWO

NICOLA WANDERED into the kitchen to grab a snack before she was to go horseback riding with Evan and Maureen. Despite the unsettling words between Evan and that ingratiating, calculating Reyes, not to mention the tension caused by Matt's abrupt arrival, she was really quite famished. So what if it was only one o'clock? She hadn't swallowed a bite of solid food since last night.

T.J. had just left for the city. He'd told his parents he had an appointment with a client, and he'd gracefully bowed out of the ride. But maybe there *was* no client, Nicola thought; maybe he was just too uncomfortable around the whole family, afraid the war would break out between Evan and Matt, afraid that he'd be drawn into it. One never knew what went on in T.J.'s head.

The poor guy, she mused, opening cupboard doors, browsing. Trying so hard to emulate his father, waiting to be taken into the family business, wanting to be trusted by Evan, to become financially independent, no doubt. Not an easy life, nor a particularly happy one.

Nicola shrugged, opening the double-doored refrigerator, searching for something that tickled her fancy. Sure, T.J. had his problems, but then so did everyone. Nicola herself had plenty: a load of guilt over her mother, even though her mother's condition was none of her doing, an empty emotional hole where her father was concerned, a certain questioning of her future beyond career, an insecurity that frightened her at times. Well, everyone had their bugaboos, but they lived with them.

Hmm. Salami cut paper-thin, mayonnaise, mustard. Sprouts, lettuce, tomato. Ah, a jar of green chili peppers. She hummed as she layered a fat sandwich on good New York kosher rye. Iced tea with lemon and lots of sugar would be the perfect accompaniment.

Evan hated the way Nicola piled sugar into her coffee or tea, on her cereal. "Use honey," he would admonish, "or nothing. Sugar'll rot your guts and your teeth. Not to mention playing havoc with your blood sugar level!" But she always laughed at him until he subsided, glowering at her from under his thick black brows.

It was affectionate, their teasing, their easy no-holds-barred relationship. Through the years, she'd found she could say just about anything in front of Evan—except swearwords—and get away with it. With him she felt secure. Too bad she couldn't feel that way with more men, but then, considering the way her own father had treated her, that innate distrust and shyness of men was hardly surprising.

*I do okay, though,* Nicola thought. Certainly she was around enough men in hunting and fishing camp and on long horseback rides for the Colorado outfitter service to know that she could pull off being one of the guys. Maybe it was because she had no interest in men sexually. Maybe her body language or attitude or something gave off a loud and clear message: *Hey, fellas, hands off. This girl isn't interested.* Whatever. But they seemed to like her, especially her cooking, and she'd learned to keep a safe distance, holding secret their manly boasts, allowing them their off-color jokes, fading into the shadows when she needed to.

It would have surprised Nicola, however, to learn that the men saw her quite differently; they saw a capable, pale-skinned young woman with gorgeous long black hair and winsome, bottomless dark eyes that challenged a man to probe their depths. They saw a woman who could ride or hike or fish with the best of them, but who required gentling by a trusted hand; a vulnerable woman who only needed the right man to unlock the secrets of her heart and to heal the wounds left by a self-serving father. But then Nicola could hardly recognize these things about herself.

She leaned back against the counter, holding the bone china plate in one hand and the messy sandwich in the other, and took a bite. She chewed thoughtfully. Not bad. It would have been better with a sharper mustard and pickles on the side. Maybe some sliced turkey, too. She'd have to keep the combination in mind for her job at the outfitters. Those men liked to *eat*. No sparing cholesterol, not for them. They liked to play macho hunters out in the wilderness. No nouvelle cuisine, either. Hot and tasty food, sticking to the old ribs, was the ticket.

She pulled an errant lettuce leaf out of the layered sandwich with her teeth, then took another bite. Um, she was starved, and dinner would be late, she knew. Maureen would want them all to go out somewhere to celebrate Matt's being home. Of course, Evan would grumble, T.J. would be so quiet he'd almost disappear, and Maureen would try desperately to make the disparate souls under her care get along. Oh yes, Nicola knew all the games the Cavanaughs played with one another.

She shifted her weight against the counter, uncrossed one booted leg and crossed her feet the other way, chewed, took a quick swallow of sweet-tart cold tea to wash it all down, and was staring unfocused out the window overlooking the green-green lawn when the swinging door from the dining room opened.

It was Matt, looking surprised and glad to have discovered her and casual all at the same time. "Found you," he said. "Do you spend a lot of time in the kitchen, Cinderella?"

The last of the sandwich was posed halfway to her mouth. "Oh." She swallowed. "Were you looking for me?"

He nodded. "Actually I was. Mom sent me to tell you they can't go riding this afternoon. Evan just got a call." He never referred to his father as anything but Evan, she noticed, while T.J. always called him Dad. "Some head of state is in town for a few hours. You know, the usual. They have to meet him for a late lunch in the city." Matt raised his eyebrows facetiously. "'It's an absolute must,'" he said, imitating Evan's intonation so perfectly it was eerie.

"Oh, darn," she said. "I was looking forward . . ."

"Ah, fair maiden, do not despair. I'm going in their stead."

"Oh."

"Hey, kid, it could be worse. It could be Godzilla."

"Oh, I didn't mean that. I just was looking forward to, oh, well, you know. . . ."

"No, I don't know. I can't say I've ever been bereft at my revered father's absence. He tends to go for my throat."

Nicola looked away. "He's not always like that, you know."

"With me he is. But really we don't want to discuss the boring subject of father-son competition, do we?"

"I guess not."

"So, we'll have a nice, long ride and relax, and I'll be so sore tomorrow I won't be able to walk."

"Well, maybe . . ."

He held a hand up. "I promised Mom. You know she hates anyone to go riding alone. Says it's too dangerous."

"You do ride?"

"Let's say I have ridden. It's been a while. Do they still have Brownie in the stables? He was always my favorite."

"Brownie died years ago. He was ancient."

"Hmm, I see. Time flies."

"I guess you really haven't been in touch much," Nicola said carefully.

"No, not much."

She put her plate in the sink and drained the iced tea from the glass. "Well, I'm all set then."

"Good. I'll just run up and change. Meet you at the stables. Pick out a nice calm one for me, will you? No fire breathers."

As she walked out to the stables, Nicola couldn't help wonder at Matt's wisecracking. She used sarcasm at times to mask her true feelings, but not *all* the time. What lay beneath the surface of his mockery?

The stable boy had three mounts saddled and ready when she got there.

"Oh, I'm sorry, Alonzo. Didn't they phone from the house? We only need two horses," she said. "Mr. and Mrs. Cavanaugh couldn't make it. Why don't you put Sally back? I'll ride Lark, and we'll keep Lucky for Matt, okay?"

Lucky was twenty years old and had been a terror in his time, as well as a champion jumper, but now he had settled down, a tall, almost white horse near to his retirement. Perfect for an occasional rider like Matt. Her own mount was a dark bay mare called Lark, a handful but a challenge. She had run away with people consistently, until Maureen refused to let anyone but a selected few ride her.

Nicola stroked Lark's smooth neck and checked the girth for tightness. She looked up to see Matt striding toward her, carrying a grocery sack. He was wearing tall black leather boots and riding britches, as she was, and a white short-sleeved polo shirt.

"Thought I'd dress the part," he remarked. "Country squire and all that." As he said it, he mocked the very concept of rustic squires and the country and himself, but oh, he looked so dashing, slim and straight and young for his thirty-eight years, with a smile that curved adorably. "Here." He held up the bag he carried. "I brought snacks and a bottle of wine. Mom insisted."

She couldn't help smiling back; his good humor was infectious, all-encompassing. Nothing could get Matt down—not his father, not his aimless existence, not even Nicola's apparent reluctance to join him on this ride. "This is Lucky," she said, patting the old gentleman's neck. "He's yours."

"Great. I'm ready if you are. Alonzo, do you have a saddlebag handy? That's it, perfect. This place is so damn well supplied. Makes you sick, doesn't it?" He threw the bag over Lucky's withers, gathered the reins and swung a leg up.

Nicola mounted Lark, keeping an eye on Matt, just to make sure he wasn't going to fall off or something equally embarrassing, but he looked fine on the horse—easy, comfortable and, as always, athletic.

They left the stable yard at a walk, down the lane through the lines of white-painted fences, across the slanted meadow to the bridal path under the huge elm trees along the bank of the Hudson River.

"I wish Maureen and Evan could have come. It's too bad," Nicola said, "isn't it?"

"Oh, I don't know. I kind of like the way things worked out."

She shot a sidelong look at him and saw his mouth twitch a little. Baiting her, that's what he was doing. Lark fluttered her nostrils and shook her head, jingling the bridle. Nicola had put her hair back in a ponytail, but it still clung to the back of her neck in this heat. She tossed her head and swept it aside with a hand. "Hot, isn't it?"

"Not so bad," Matt replied easily. "I've been in worse."

"Like Haig's Point, South Carolina?" she asked. "Or Costa Plata?"

"Maybe."

"You *do* get around."

"This is true. I like it that way. There's a big world out there, and I'm lucky enough to be able to see it. I like new experiences and new places."

"And new faces," Nicola added pointedly.

"That also is true."

She waited for some masculine bragging, but none was forthcoming. She'd have thought Matt would jump at the chance to tell her a few stories, but he didn't.

"Forget my wanton existence. I'll bet Mom talks about me, so you know all the gory details. She does, doesn't she?"

"Well, sure, some."

He nodded and twisted his lips. "You know, kid, you're good for Mom. She needs someone to talk to. She's so lonely, stuck in that great monument to Evan's success. I'm glad you're in touch with her a lot."

She was surprised at the genuine feeling behind Matt's statement, so unlike his usual insouciance, but then, she hardly knew him. Maybe he cared more than he let on.

"I hope so," she said quietly. "I know she isn't happy...."

"Evan leads her a helluva life, doesn't he?" he asked, his words tinged with bitterness.

Nicola couldn't say anything. She knew that Evan and Maureen had a troubled relationship. Divorce was out of the question apparently, due to Evan's position or Maureen's timidity or whatever. And she couldn't really discuss it with Maureen—that was too personal and none of her business, besides.

Matt made a gesture with his hand, causing Lucky to throw his head up and show the whites of his eyes. "Let's talk about you for a change. I'm fascinated. Tell me about your work. Last time I was home, I think you had just finished school. Am I right? And you were skinny."

She ducked her head. "Yes, skinny, and my hair was short that year, not very becoming at all, and you were too busy with the, ah, redhead to notice me."

He threw back his head and laughed. "The redhead. Lord, I forget her name! I thought Evan would appreciate her, but he failed to get the joke."

"You must have known he wouldn't."

"Sure I did. But I keep trying to enlighten him. So—" he eyed her deliberately up and down, his gaze as intrusive as a pair of hands, from her smooth black hair down her neck and over her breasts and waist and hips, down the one leg he could see to the tip of her black leather boot "—tell me more. What exactly do you cook?"

Nicola kept her eyes glued to the path. "Well, I've ended up as sort of a specialty cook. Seasonal. I've worked for ski lodges in the winter, first up in Vermont, then out in Wyoming. And that's how I met Ron Mitchell, who runs the hunting and fishing outfitter in Colorado."

"You just rustle up some grub over the old camp fire, is that it?"

"Not exactly. The ski lodge I work at is four-star, so beans and bacon don't exactly fit the bill," she said dryly.

"I catch a note of irritation. Sorry, kid. I wasn't being patronizing. I'm truly interested."

"Okay. So, in the summer I cook for fishermen or hikers or pack trips, whatever Ron has booked. I'm in charge of everything from ordering supplies to cleaning up. It's hard work but it's fun, and lots of times I get to go along on the trips, so I've learned a lot about the great outdoors. Then in the fall, of course, the hunters arrive. First bow and arrow. Deer, elk, bear, a few, very few, get licenses for mountain lion or bighorn sheep."

"And you're handy with a gun, too?" Matt asked.

"I've gone a few times. Never bagged anything, though."

"A tough lady," Matt said under his breath.

"What?" Nicola asked, not sure she'd heard him right.

"Oh, nothing. You've been around, kid."

"Seems you have, too."

"Just resort hotel to resort hotel. As a matter of fact, I thought I might give Colorado a try myself this ski season. You know, work in a bar at night—something not too taxing—ski all day."

"I seem to remember your mother telling me you were a good skier."

"Sure, we all are. You know Evan. He took us up to Canada every year, come hell or high water, for helicopter skiing. We had to learn."

"He still goes. Every year, in January. He loves it. It must be wonderful up there. All that powder...."

"You ski?" Matt asked, urging Lucky into a faster walk to keep up with Lark. The horse swished his tail in irritation and laid back an ear.

"Oh yes, I love it. I've been skiing at Jackson Hole, since I work near there. It's a great mountain."

"Is there anything you *don't* do, Nicola?" Matt asked.

"Sure, lots of things."

"Hmm." He turned and gave her an inquisitive look. "What, for instance?"

"Well, I don't sing or dance or play the piano. I'm a lousy writer, and I don't paint or draw or act. I don't sew my own clothes..."

He laughed. "Okay, okay."

"And I don't do windows," she concluded.

He was silent for a time. She could see his white knit shirt sticking to him, as her own blouse was. His back was straight and, even under the fabric, she could see the curves of muscle, the lines of his ribs.

"Do you have a boyfriend?" he finally asked.

She stiffened. "No."

"What, a pretty girl like you? And all those men around? Hunters and skiers and such?"

"I'm just one of the guys when I'm at work," she stated.

"What about when you're *not* at work, little Nicky?" His tone had turned soft and fluid, insinuating.

Too long a pause passed before she could find a witty reply, a way to sidestep the question. She should have lied to him, immediately, easily, and told him she dated a few men here and there. Or she could have tossed her head coyly and said it was none of his business. But nothing came out. She could feel his gaze still on her, interested, perhaps amused by her discomfort. She pretended she hadn't heard him and looked down, seeing Lark's muscular neck, her dark shoulders alternating forward and back. A dampness broke out on Nicola's forehead and upper lip. Why was he teasing her? Did he act like this with all females? And how many unsuspecting women had fallen for his charm and good looks?

The path wound down from a hill to the broad, slow-moving Hudson River. Thick greenery lined the way and hung out over the dark, sluggish water. Every so often a monumental granite outcrop, a cliff or hillock of solid gray stone with shiny flecks, would lift from a meadow, the bare bones of the earth breaking through its verdant skin. It was hard to believe that only a few miles downstream lay Manhattan, sweating and convulsing and cursing with seven million tongues.

"You know, it's strange," Matt said, breaking the gravid silence, "but this is probably the longest we've ever spent together. Funny, being raised in the same house by the same parents."

"It is odd," she said, finally able to clear her throat.

"We're strangers to each other."

"I guess so."

"I think we should remedy the situation, don't you?"

Nicola hesitated, then decided to be frank. "I'd say there's not much chance of that. You aren't around. Our paths really don't cross."

He looked at her appraisingly. "Well, there's a rejection if I ever heard one. Hell, Nicola, I'm not used to that."

"I'll bet you aren't."

"Well, well."

"Oh, come on, Matt," she chided. "We're just going on a ride. Don't feel obligated to impress me or...or ask me out or anything like that."

"Whatever made you think I was going to ask you out?"

Oh, what Nicola wouldn't have given to have wiped that sly grin off his face! "You were coming on pretty strong. Maybe I was wrong." She shrugged and patted Lark's neck.

"Just habit." He paused, then added, "*Bad* habit."

"Okay, just so we know where we stand."

"Sure, you're right. I'll practice my big brother routine."

"Come on, let's canter a little. You up for it?" she suggested, not liking the way the conversation was going. She had always been better at action than words, anyway.

"Hit it, kid."

She touched her heels to Lark's sides, and the feisty mare took off down the shaded path so that the bushes whipped by and Nicola had to duck to avoid low branches. Behind her she could hear Lucky pounding along. The wind felt refreshing on her face, the horse surged powerfully beneath her, and she could gallop along forever, free and full of the joy of uncomplicated, pure physical sensation.

But eventually Nicola had to pull Lark up and walk her to cool down. The mare was breathing hard, and her satiny coat was wet with sweat. "That's a girl," Nicola said, patting the horse's damp neck. "Good girl."

Lucky was blowing hard, too, his white hide splotched with dark sweat. "It's too hot to do that today," Matt said. "Us old guys like to take it easy."

"We'll stop up ahead. I know a nice spot. Then you 'old guys' can rest," she said.

They tied the horses' reins to a low branch under an enormous old maple tree and loosened the girths. Matt pulled the saddlebag off and took out a bottle of wine, plastic glasses, crackers and a round of Brie cheese. "Good, the wine's still cool. Want some?"

Nicola sat on the thin grass in the shade of the tree, leaned her back against the trunk and looked at Matt, shading her eyes. "Maybe one glass."

"Good. Live a little, I always say." He sat beside her and poured, handing her a glass. He lifted his. *"Santé,"* he said.

*"Santé."* The wine was cool and velvety, a rosé zinfandel, a little sweet and fruity. A nice vintage. "Um," she said. She closed her eyes and felt the wine warm her belly and the breeze cool her flushed cheeks.

Out beyond the circle of shade insects clicked and buzzed, and the sun came down hard on the tall grass. Nicola could hear the horses swishing their tails at flies and jingling their bridles.

"Nice," Matt said quietly.

"Um."

She heard him moving around then and opened her eyes. He was taking his polo shirt off, pulling it inside out over his head, wadding it up and putting it under his head as he lay down.

"That's better," he said, sighing, closing his eyes, balancing the wineglass in the hollow of his stomach.

She couldn't help looking. He was whipcord thin, his torso ridged with ripples of muscle. He wasn't the weightlifter type at all, being much too slim in build, but he must have done something to keep in shape. A fuzz of brown hair spread across his chest, and a faint line ran down to his navel. She could see his face, too, relaxed, eyes closed, and the stubble of his beard.

It was a good face—a handsome, manly face—his nose generous and slightly curved downward, a bit like Evan's, only larger. But it was that mouth of his, that wide, mocking mouth, that made him appear as if he always had a secret or, perhaps, could read your mind. And then there was that dimple in his cheek, negating the cynicism.

Matt had great eyes, too. Like Maureen's, his were a bit heavy lidded, and they tilted down at the corners, where they met laugh lines. The color, though, set them off from most blue eyes—his were as blue as sunlit tropical waters, clear and almost turquoise.

She studied him from her spot resting against the tree. How could she help it? She could see a drop of sweat from the curling hair behind his ear run down slowly onto his neck, then disappear under his head. Matt Cavanaugh....

He looked young and healthy and in top physical condition. How did his apparently aimless life as a lush and a bartender tally with his glowing health and the obvious care for his body? Shouldn't he be puffy, with circles under his eyes, flaccid muscles and broken veins on his nose?

Strange.

Also, curiously, his face and neck and forearms were very tan, but his torso was pale. A workingman's tan on a beach bum?

Even stranger.

Nicola suddenly had the distinct feeling there was an awful lot she didn't know about Matt Cavanaugh, and what she *did* know was only the tip of the iceberg. Nine-tenths of him was unseen—and dangerous.

She nibbled on a few crackers and sipped her wine. She could smell the dusty aroma of sun-kissed grass, the musk of dry dirt and the faint perfume of wildflowers carried on the soft, damp air. When the breeze blew into her face, she could smell the horses, warm and familiar. And Matt. A vague, foreign scent of male sweat and skin and shaving soap and leather boots. Something inside her belly melted, a soft warmth that curled and sighed in a lassitude of pleasure.

He *was* dangerous, a jarring note in her well-guarded serenity. A man. An attractive man. An irresponsible charmer like her father. And she knew what men like that could do if you let them. They destroyed whatever—whomever—they touched, leaving forlorn lost women behind them, a trail of tears, broken lives, shaky hollow women like her own mother.

Well, it wasn't going to happen to Nicola.

Matt rolled onto his side, facing her, drained his wine and set the glass down. He picked a blade of grass and chewed on it, eyeing her thoughtfully until she looked away.

"You are gun-shy, aren't you?" he asked.

"I'm careful," she said, "about my friends."

"Hmm. And I'm apparently not one of them. Has my father's opinion of me rubbed off on you?"

"I hope not."

"So do I."

"Why should you care what I think of you?"

He shrugged, chewing on the grass, studying her.

She tossed her head, throwing her ponytail off her neck, uneasy under his scrutiny. She would have left if she could have, but there was nowhere to go. Desperately she searched for a neutral subject, but what came out of her mouth surprised her. "Why isn't your chest as tan as your face?"

He looked surprised, then amused, and he glanced down at himself as if seeing it for the first time. "Sunburn," he explained. "I get burned on the beach. I always wear a T-shirt."

"Oh." She shouldn't have asked. Now he knew she'd been looking at him. She felt her cheeks flush. Oh Lordy.

A shrill whistle made her jump. Matt had stretched the blade of grass between his thumbs and blown on it. His eyes met hers over his hands, and they were dancing devilishly.

"Scared you, didn't I? I always was a champ at silly things like this. Always blew louder than T.J. He was a dud at grass whistling."

"I'll bet he tried, though."

Matt laughed. "Until his lips wouldn't pucker anymore. Poor kid."

"It must have been tough having you for an older brother," she said. "Maureen says you were so good at things. Track and skiing and school."

"Oh, T.J. did all right. He's a plodder, but he gets there. We're not real close, you know, so I don't think I bothered him that much. And now, well, he's probably secretly gloating that I'm the black sheep of the family."

"I don't know. T.J. is hard to read. He keeps things to himself."

"He sure does. Sometimes I wonder what goes on under that calm exterior," Matt mused.

Nicola waved a persistent fly away, then she sat, chin on her knees, watching Matt break a piece of Brie off and pop it into his mouth. "How're your folks?" he asked, chewing. "I know your mother's not well. Do you see her often?"

Nicola folded her arms around her knees and stared off into the distance. "She's in a home, not far from here. I don't see her often because I'm not around much anymore. When I visit her, she cries."

"I'm sorry." He said it with such genuine sympathy she was surprised. "I didn't realize..."

Nicola shrugged. "Clinical depression." She still stared out over the bright meadow, but now she was frowning. "And my father, well, he's busy. You know. And I hardly ever spend any time with him." She recalled the last time she'd seen him, having gone to his Manhattan penthouse on an impromptu visit almost three years ago. He was in his silk pajamas, hair mussed, being catered to by a gorgeous brunette who wore his bathrobe. At two o'clock in the afternoon. But she wasn't about to tell Matt *that*.

"Good old Wentworth. Mom told me he was going to get married again last year."

"Guess not. I suspect that he enjoys women too much to tie himself down," she said, trying to keep the bitterness from her voice. And the sadness. She shifted her chin to the other knee. "I really do have to visit my mother before I leave. I've been putting it off. Maureen said she'd take me, but..." Why was she telling him this?

"It's tough, isn't it?"

She nodded, feeling a lump in her throat, the same lump she felt whenever she thought of her mother. And in reaction to that lump of misery, she felt anger as well, anger against her mother, who was too sick, too weak, too helpless to take care of her daughter. Anger, at least, was easier to bear than misery.

She raised her head then and forced a smile. "Let's lighten up, what do you say?"

"Sure. No use dwelling on the bad stuff. When are you leaving for Colorado?"

"In a few days. There's still snow up in the high country until mid-June, so we have a long off-season."

"Heck, maybe I'll see you out there this fall, kid."

"Maybe, but not if you keep calling me kid."

"Sorry, it just slipped out," he said, grinning, his dimple making a shadow on his tanned skin, his blue eyes crinkling. He rolled over onto his back again and stuck another stalk of grass into his mouth idly. An inadvertent thought eased into her mind: he looked as if he'd just woken up. His brown curling hair was tousled, a lock or two sticking up above an ear boyishly. And his eyes, half-closed, had that lazy, sultry look to them, as if he'd...he'd just made love. Oh yes, she knew that look. There'd been the handsome, rakish cowboy up in Wyoming, a rodeo rider. Not surprisingly, he'd had Nicola in Jackson Hole and Laura in Laramie. Too bad it had taken her nearly a year to find out.

Drowsy eyed and languid, smiling slightly and crookedly, sure of himself after a good performance—like Matt right now. Wasn't there a man out there for her somewhere, an honest man?

Lark shook her head, rattling her bridle. The sun sent shafts through gaps in the maple's foliage, mottling the ground. A butterfly settled on Matt's boot tip, bright blue, like a bit of the sky come down to earth. It *was* an idyllic afternoon, Nicola reflected, hot and lazy, tranquil. And despite her better judgment, she found herself still curious about this sexy, philandering man. *Darn.*

She couldn't help liking him when she was with him—he certainly had a way about him. She would dearly love to believe that there was something under his lighthearted surface, something serious, something he cared about other than living it up. Once in a while she thought she saw a sadness in his expression. Wistfully studying his face as he lay there so relaxed, she searched for the truth about Matt Cavanaugh, but she couldn't be sure she saw anything.

The silence lasted a long time. She hugged her knees tighter. "Why are you a bartender?" she asked finally.

He opened his eyes, looked at her from under dark brows and burst out laughing. "I can't believe *you're* going to start on me! Have you been taking lessons from Evan?"

"Seriously," she pressed, "why?"

He stared at her for a moment, making her shift her feet and draw aimless patterns in the dust with a finger. "It gives me freedom. I come and go as I please. It's a great excuse to hit all the world's hot spots. Simple."

"Maybe, but what about the pain you've caused Evan and Maureen?"

Silence came as easily to Matt as laughter. He shrugged and didn't answer, content to lie there, arm behind his head, one foot crossed negligently over the other knee, sweat shining on his bare skin. And he kept watching her, his blue eyes never leaving her face. She crawled with discomfort, frantically searching for a way to change the subject.

"What did you think of Reyes?" she asked. "I didn't like him a bit. He threatened Evan—can you believe it?"

Matt frowned. "Nasty fellow."

"You know about the position Evan's in now, don't you? He's got to make a final decision on calling in those loans to Costa Plata. It'll ruin the country. He's really unpopular, Maureen says. He's had hate mail, calls from congressmen who want to keep the status quo down there. He's gotten threats, too, phone calls, letters. This morning was only the latest."

"Was it?" He looked away, chewing on the stalk of grass.

"Yes. You know Evan. If he thinks it's good for the World Bank, he'll call in those loans, regardless. And he refuses to take any of the threats seriously. Maybe he should have protection. Maureen is worried."

"Is she?"

"Yes. She wants him to hire bodyguards."

"Bodyguards? My father? He's so cocksure, it would never occur to him that anyone would dare try to hurt him." Matt gave a short laugh.

"I know." She drew a spiral in the dust, watching an ant follow the curving line. "Do you think you could talk to him about it?"

Matt tilted a brow. "I am probably the last person on earth Evan would listen to."

She looked down. "I was afraid you'd say that."

"Now, don't you worry about Evan. He can take care of himself," Matt said with finality.

She sighed. "I hope so."

It was a glorious day. They rode back through the slanting gilded light of the afternoon. A few fluffy white clouds slid across the sky, chasing their own shadows along the contours of the terrain. Grasshoppers buzzed, the serenade rising to a crescendo, then falling, as one after another took up the refrain, then dropped it. A perfect afternoon, Nicola thought, except for Matt Cavanaugh's curious, unwanted interest in her and the slight tension between them, as if they were past lovers who had met again after years and still felt a spark of attraction for each other. But that, of course, was ridiculous.

The horses perked up their ears when they turned into the lane between the white fences that led to the stable.

"I'll race you," Matt announced abruptly, grinning a challenge at her. "T.J. and I always used to."

"Sure." She flashed him a smile, kicked Lark and raced away. She heard Matt yell something at her, and then Lucky was pounding along behind her as she lay low over Lark's neck.

There was a ditch across the path; Lark took it, flying, stretching out, but Lucky was there—she could hear him breathing hard at her shoulder.

Nicola won, pulling up in the stable yard in a flurry of hooves and dust, laughing and panting. Matt reined in next to her. "You cheated!" he yelled across the horses' dancing forms.

He dismounted and came around Lucky to help her down, but she was already halfway out of the saddle. "But I won," she said. "Doesn't that count?"

He put his hands on her waist as she dropped to the ground and turned. They lingered there a heartbeat of time too long, scalding and hard on the damp fabric of her blouse, and she felt a deep, shivery exaltation at his nearness. The horses were still sidling and blowing, excited from the race, and she was imprisoned between their hot, lathered bodies, staring, paralyzed, into Matt's eyes as the beasts moved restlessly, pinning them together. She felt him press against her, saw his face close to hers; she smelled horseflesh and leather, dust and hay, Matt's man odor. She felt her own rapid pulse pound in her temples.

"Nicola," he started to say, but Alonzo ran up to take the horses, and the moment was forfeit.

# CHAPTER THREE

THE COLD WATER ran in rivulets down Matt's back and chest, icy, sensual fingers that soothed him while he cooled down and showered off the dust and sweat. He'd be sore tomorrow, he knew, because it had been years since he'd used those muscles sitting astride a horse.

God, but it felt good to be away from the questioning eyes of his family and the *looks* he'd been getting that afternoon from Evan. The bathroom was a safe haven.

He and Nicola had returned from the ride to find everyone home once more. Maureen had complained of a headache, "That DuPlessy woman always gives me one," she'd said, referring to the wife of a French representative of the World Bank, whom Evan and Maureen had gone into the city to meet. So Maureen was napping, Evan had conveniently disappeared into his library, and T.J. was lounging quietly on a float in the pool, sipping on a gin and tonic.

Matt was thinking—and hiding out.

He stepped out of the shower, wrapped a thick blue towel around his middle and searched his shaving kit for his razor.

Sure, he thought, scraping at his whiskers in front of the mirror, it was easy for him to act outgoing, and he'd always had a wise mouth on him. But this charade he was enacting with his family was starting to make his gut churn with doubt. It had been sixteen years that he'd been playing the errant son, the footloose trust funder, the *bum*.

How had it all started? Better yet, why had he let it start?

The answer was right there, staring back at him from the mirror. He'd been recruited by Ned Copple of the U.S. Foreign Service, right out of college, and he'd gone straight undercover for the service, working for the little-known Section C. And from day one, Ned had made his function very clear. "You're to become the playboy, the ex-college kid who's got just enough money to travel on and only needs to take a job when pressed for extra cash. You'll move, on my orders, at a drop of a hat. You'll overhear conversations on golf courses, in swank bars, on yachts that will in due course help your country set foreign policy. The things you'll hear, the circles you'll run in, will provide us with inside info we couldn't possibly get over a negotiation table."

"A spy?" Matt had asked dubiously.

"An intelligence gatherer," Ned had corrected tactfully.

Matt had liked the work. He'd drifted into the "in" circles with ease and grace and moved around the world so many times he'd lost count. And just to make it all look right, he'd taken those jobs occasionally, bartending mostly, overhearing things that made even Ned's head spin. It was truly amazing, Matt had discovered, what a man'll tell his bartender after three martinis.

He'd worked private parties on yachts from the Potomac River in Washington to the Persian Gulf. He'd taken on jobs in the Swiss Alps at exclusive ski lodges, folded towels at the Istanbul Hilton, washed dishes on a kibbutz in Israel, waited tables in Hong Kong, slung gin on a Caribbean cruise ship. You betcha, it was amazing the things a man could overhear.

And there'd been women. Matt had learned how to charm and flatter. There had been senators' daughters and foreign diplomats' secretaries, all needing a sympathetic ear. Oh yes, there had been plenty of them. He had a rule, though. No rolling in the hay with an attached female. There was no better way to blow someone's trust than to bed his woman.

He was tired of it all, true enough. But he'd actually done some good in this old, used-up world of his. There was that time in Beirut when he'd gotten wind of a supposed terrorist raid on an Israeli school. He'd reported in on Ned's scrambled phone line, and the terrorists had been caught not fifty yards from that school. And the time he'd been a tour guide living in Bangkok, Thailand, and been able to quietly arrange the release of some American POWs shot down over Cambodia.

He'd helped, okay. The trouble was, at first he'd enjoyed throwing his purported uselessness in Evan's face. Evan, who had demanded and pressured, presumed and controlled for much of Matt's life. Yep, being a bum had definitely been a tool with which to punish his father and give back some of the man's own. But the years had passed, and Maureen deserved more from her oldest son. It just might be time, Matt thought, to come in from the cold and find out who he really was beneath the carefree, sarcastic facade.

"Jeez," he muttered as he started to get dressed, "why all the sentimentality?" What had gotten into him this past year? And why had he been so eager to take on this latest job for Ned—the Costa Plata Caper, Ned had dubbed it. Had Matt said yes because it meant sticking close to his family for once—particularly to Evan? He'd known immediately when Ned had suggested he gather some information on the meeting between Evan and Reynaldo Reyes that there would be problems in his showing up unexpectedly at home. Yet he had jumped at the chance.

Why?

"You're getting old, man, slipping," he said as he put on his loafers with no socks.

He stood now, dressed in loose, pleated white pants and a black shirt, in the middle of his old bedroom and thought about Reyes. Was the man capable of carrying out his threat? Of course, Evan, the stubborn old coot, would never see the real danger he might be in. Oh no, not his dad; he thought he was above it all, bulletproof.

Coming home hadn't all been bad, though. He'd been expecting the usual recriminations, and instead, he'd discovered a face from the past, a darn pretty face, at that.

Matt heard voices below his bedroom window, around the pool. Idly he pulled back the curtain and glanced out. T.J. was still lounging on the float, drink in hand, and there she was, as sleek and toned as a cat, walking out on the diving board.

Despite himself, Matt's pulse began to pound. She was long limbed and lean, smooth skinned and, oh, that midnight-black mane of hair that swung free over one shoulder...

She was wearing a dark bikini, a string job that left little to a man's imagination. Her hipbones showed, sharp and pointed, and the nice, muscular curve of her fanny. Her belly was flat, the line of her whole upper torso almost as flat, in fact. Small, faintly curved breasts—enough, though, to rev up his imagination. Damn, but those bikinis were provocative. They just about left a woman naked, but not quite; there was only enough material there to drive a guy out of his mind.

She sprang off the board on one foot and did a passable swan dive—not great, but graceful. Then her white body with those scanty dark strips slipped through the clear blue water and came up by the steps. She was laughing and panting and slicking her black hair back with both hands, her breasts straining against the two dark pieces of triangular material.

"You're rocking my boat," T.J. said as his floating lounge bobbed up and down in her wake.

"Oh sorry," Nicola said, and looked as if she might splash him teasingly, but she hesitated; instead she climbed the steps.

*That's right,* Matt thought, leaning against the window-sill, *T.J. isn't the type to take a joke.*

Matt found himself ambling on down to the terrace, fixing himself a light cocktail and heading on over to the pool. He should have stayed away.

Nicola dived in and out several times more, did a few laps, then declared it was enough. And who was there with her towel when she finally came up the steps for good? Just the idea of touching that satiny, glistening white flesh was too tempting.

"Oh," she said, "thanks, Matt." She shivered deliciously and looked away, blinking the water from her eyes. "Wow, it's sort of chilly."

"Um."

"That looks good," she said, nodding toward his drink. "What's in it?"

"Soda. Some vodka."

"Maybe I'll—" Nicola began.

"*Some* vodka?" T.J. interrupted, using his hands to propel himself to the edge of the pool. "Knowing you, brother, it's probably half the bottle."

*Oh boy,* Matt thought, *here it goes, the sibling rivalry.* And he couldn't very well tell T.J. that he rarely drank any booze at all.

He chose to ignore him. "You want me to fix you one?" Matt turned to Nicola.

"Sure. But really light. I mean, just a splash of vodka. I'm a cheap date."

While Matt strode to the outdoor wet bar, Maureen made an appearance. "I thought I heard you all down here," she said.

"Did we wake you?" It was T.J. who spoke, his fair brow wrinkled in concern. "I tried to be really quiet, Mom."

"Thank you, dear," Maureen said, sitting herself down by the pool, "but I was awake, anyway. Lord, but that Claudine DuPlessy gives me a migraine."

"Maybe we should skip dinner in the city," T.J. offered.

"Well..." Maureen began.

"Really, Mom," T.J. said, "we can go another time."

"But Matt's here and..."

"Hey," Matt said, "don't worry about me. I'm happy staying home."

"Are you really?" Maureen asked, and the double and triple meanings dripped from her voice.

"Yes," Matt replied slowly, "I'm as happy as a clam." He let her take his hand and squeeze it affectionately, then he turned back to Nicola with the drink, but not before he noted the envious expression on T.J.'s face before he covered it up. *Whoa there, brother. I'm not the enemy.*

"Oh, thank you," Nicola said, taking the sweating glass, sitting down near Maureen.

"And you won't be disappointed if we stay in tonight?" Maureen asked her.

Nicola shook her head. "No. In fact, maybe I'll drive on over to Fenwick and visit Mom." She shrugged as if it were no big deal at all. "I've been meaning to do it for almost two weeks now."

"Are you sure?" Maureen asked carefully. "Nicola," she went on in a very quiet tone, "I saw Suzanne in May. She's not...clear right now, dear. You might only upset yourself. I'm so, so very sorry."

But Nicola took it like a champ. "Oh," she said, forcing a smile, "I know how it is. Sometimes Mom's very lucid, other times...well, it's those awful antidepressant drugs, you know."

"Yes, dear, I know." Maureen frowned. "You must eat, first, though. I'll have Lydia—"

"Tell you what," Matt chimed in, "I could drive Nicola on out to Fenwick, and then we could grab a bite to eat somewhere."

"Oh," Nicola was quick to say, "I'll be fine. I'll borrow Maureen's car, if it's okay, that is."

"My goodness," Maureen said, putting a hand to her brow. "My car's still in the shop." She straightened and looked at her watch. "Oh, dear, it's five already. Evan was supposed to remind me."

"He was pretty busy today," Matt said. "I can drive you tomorrow to get it. Okay?"

"I guess. Oh, thank you, Matt, that will be fine. So," she said, "you'll still be here tomorrow?"

"Long enough to get your car," he replied evasively. In truth, he had no idea what Ned had planned for him. Maybe, because of Reyes's threat, Ned might want him to hang around and play bodyguard.

Nicola was looking at Matt. "You really don't mind driving me?"

If ever there was an understatement… "Not a bit. I'll see if I can keep the Ferrari on the road for you, too."

"How gallant of you," Nicola replied flippantly.

After finishing her drink, she changed into a red-and-white knit sundress that was sleeveless and midcalf length. It was clinging and sleek looking, showing off her long, elegant limbs and that rather cute bottom he was getting to know. It swung around her legs and hugged her slim waist, caressing all the sensual promise it concealed. He couldn't help watching her, finding new surprises in her face, her movements. She had a fine-drawn, delicate grace, a little sad but wonderfully alluring. She wore little makeup, he saw, just some pale lipstick and mascara, and round white earrings completed her outfit. Simple but suitable.

When Nicola had headed up to change, Matt had done something quite out of character. He'd gotten on the telephone and meddled in her life. He'd told himself that he was just being a friend, that he was only going to be a companion to her during a difficult time. But he'd wondered as he'd dialed the Sansouci Restaurant in the city—Wentworth Gage's place—and made reservations for two. Wasn't he being too pushy, too protective? No, this meddling was not one bit like him. It smacked too much of giving a damn.

He was curious about Went Gage, too, and was indulging his curiosity. What exactly was the man's relationship with Nicola?

They almost made it to the car, almost, before Evan stepped outside and tried to take control.

"We'll eat right here tonight," he said when Matt told him their plans.

"I already made some reservations." Matt stood his ground, holding his slubbed silk Armani sport coat casually over his shoulder.

"Cancel them. Your mother isn't feeling well. We're going to stay in."

"*You're* going to stay in, Evan, we're not."

Nicola cleared her throat. "Evan," she began, stepping between the two men, who faced each other as stiffly as growling dogs, "I'd like to eat out tonight, if it's okay with you."

He gazed at her for moment, grumbled something, then relented. "If it's what you want, Nicola."

Amazing, Matt thought, but he could see now that Nicola was like a late-life child to Evan, a daughter to boot. Apparently Evan did have a soft spot or two. Incredible.

"See you, Evan," Matt said, shooting him a sly smile and helping Nicola into the Ferrari.

Nicola pulled her hair back and fastened it with a clasp while Matt revved up the engine. It purred and sang to him.

"Expensive item," she noted, settling into her seat.

"Hey," he said, putting on his aviator glasses, "what's money for?" The truth was, the service provided it as part of his cover.

"Oh," Nicola said airily, "money can do things like educate kids or buy a home. You know, silly little things like that."

"Why, Nicky," he said, giving her a flashy grin, "you're almost as sarcastic as I am."

A home and family, he mused as he kicked up gravel on the driveway and sped around the circle. What would it be like to have a little house, a little wife and some curly headed little kids?

Nicola would make some man a good wife, he decided. She had always been a cute girl and not a bad teenager, kind of sassy. She was athletic, smart and had grown up to be terribly attractive in an old-fashioned way. Heck, a man could drown in those dark, melancholy eyes of hers.

And there was that vulnerability, too. He liked that. It made him feel all masculine and protective and angry at her folks, who had screwed her up so damn bad in the first place. What right did parents have doing that, anyway? Like Evan, for instance, forcing his sons to be competitive, making them vie for his love and attention, holding himself above them, God-like, unreachable. Evan hadn't learned a thing in the past twenty years. He was still, as ever, an SOB.

*We're one of a kind,* he thought as he drove, *me and Nicola. Messed-up adults because we had parents who never should have brought children into the world.*

Pretty, young, vulnerable Nicola. He'd like to pull off onto that grassy shoulder over there and reach out for her, bring those small, soft breasts up against his chest and stroke the length of that spectacular mane. He'd like to hold her and keep her from pain. He'd like to take her to see her mother tonight and then her father, and when it was done she might cry for a while, but he'd be there all the time, listening, caring, holding her. . . .

Who was he kidding? He'd be willing to bet she was put off by him already, well, by his type, that was. And he couldn't tell her it was all a cover. He couldn't tell her that he wasn't a lush or that life wasn't as funny as he pretended it to be. He couldn't even tell Nicola that he was as worried about Evan as she was. He'd blow his cover to bits. It was all top security stuff, and, if Matt was nothing else, he was loyal to the oath he'd sworn.

Above the Ferrari the trees formed a canopy, that East Coast, lush green ceiling that cooled the roads. Late sun, a golden profusion of shafts, seemed to rush by overhead, spearing the dark green leaves. Tidy stone walls lined the curving road, and beyond them horses grazed.

Matt pushed the Ferrari to the limit when the road straightened, then downshifted and took the narrow curves with ease. His black shirt flapped against his skin in the wind as did Nicola's skirt, rippling against her bare legs. He'd have loved to bend over and run his mouth across that knee or to press his lips to the bone in her shoulder, to taste her—all women tasted differently, some ordinary, some as sweet and succulent as a ripe peach. He already thought he knew what Nicola would taste like.

Fenwick Estates, a very fancy name for essentially a sanitarium, sat east of the Hudson River, on New York's Route 9, not too many miles north of the city. It was a beautiful old place, expensive as all get out, a one-time country manor on thirteen cleared acres behind the ubiquitous stone wall. Dr. Fenwick evidently had decided back in the 1920s that not all mentally disturbed patients belonged locked in cages—especially the ones with bucks.

Matt had no way of knowing just how much Went Gage laid out a year for his ex-wife's comforts at Fenwick, but he'd wager it was twenty-five thousand minimum, on top of a hefty initial investment. Suzanne had been in and out of Fenwick, mostly in, for sixteen years. Sansouci Restaurant had a good reputation—even Evan used Went to cater larger affairs—but it was still a steep bill. Did Went have the grace to feel guilty for driving Nicola's mom nuts?

"It looks smaller," Nicola said when they pulled up to the gate and identified themselves.

Matt turned to her and rested an arm over the steering wheel. "How long's it been?"

"It's been almost two years since I've seen Mom. Oh, I write, and I've called lots, but I never know how I'll find her. I always feel like I make her worse when I come."

"What did the doctor say you could expect this evening?"

Nicola rubbed her arm. "He said Mom was doing very well. What he meant, I'm sure, is that she's on a new drug that's got her less depressed."

"Um." Matt put the Ferrari in gear and drove on up to the parking lot. Maybe this wasn't such a good idea; maybe Nicky should have come alone, after all. He felt out of place. He also wondered if she could bear to see Went tonight, as well.

Nicola insisted that he come along. "Mom doesn't say much," she said. "And, to be honest, I'd like the support, Matt. She'll remember you. You are kind of family."

But not the kind of family he'd like to be.

One thing was for sure: Fenwick Estates spared no cost when it came to accommodations. Every patient had his or her own room and porch, spacious rooms, light and airy. The communal rooms—dining, television, game—could have been those of a luxury hotel. At least Nicola had that knowledge as comfort.

He could see Nicola taking a deep breath as they approached Suzanne's room, a nurse leading the way. Matt was following the women, and Nicola suddenly reached behind her and caught his fingers in hers, giving them a quick squeeze. Touching her hand was like dipping his fingers into a brook of bubbling water, but water that was as pure and hot as a flame. He felt the heat flicker at the root of his being.

Suzanne was sitting, very nicely attired in a lemon-yellow shirtwaist dress, next to her empty fireplace. Behind her, a summer breeze lifted filmy curtains, and Matt noted the scent of lilacs, a sweet, cloying scent reminiscent of bygone days.

Yes, he remembered Suzanne Gage. She'd gone to a private girls' school with his mother, and they'd been close then. Afterward, it had been the University of Rochester for Maureen and a finishing school in Geneva for Suzanne, who was, as Maureen had put it, a dreamy girl, soft and gentle and not terribly in touch. Suzanne had met Wentworth, a native New Yorker, while he'd been apprenticing with a French chef in Paris. It had been reportedly a whirlwind courtship. Later, while Maureen had been busy having her boys, Suzanne had been busy not having children, afraid of the responsibility trying to keep her girlish figure for a husband who already had a roving eye and was trying to save enough cash to open his dream restaurant, Sansouci, the home of the Broadway stars and the New York elite. Twelve years of marriage had passed before Nicola began to grow in her mother's womb, a surprise, disaster. True to form, Went had found other women when Suzanne was occupied with Nicola, kept apartments for them in New York, finally keeping the ultimate apartment right here at Fenwick for Suzanne.

And where had Nicola been all this time? Raising herself, pampering her unhappy mother, doing somersaults in the air to get her dad to notice her.

"Hi, Mom." Nicola walked cautiously to the wing chair and stopped. "It's Nicola, Mom."

Matt was no judge, but this woman's eyes—the same sad, dark eyes of her daughter—were so glazed that a body could swim in them. It seemed nothing short of a miracle that she recognized her daughter at all.

"Nicola," she breathed, remembrance expressing itself on her calm face. "Why, Nicola, they told me you were coming, dear. How nice. Do you like my new dress?" She patted her lemon skirt. "I ordered it from a catalog. I do love the catalogs, don't you?"

It went just like that for a good forty-five minutes. Suzanne, still an attractive woman at fifty-eight or so, with short dark hair and pale skin, seemed to have no sense of time or space. She was not unhappy—the drugs saw to that—but she was so far out in left field that Maureen's description of *dreamy* would have been laughable in any other situation.

Nicola stuck to safe subjects. "Remember the swing set we used to have out back...? Remember Tinker, that big orange cat you found on the road...? I'm in Colorado. Remember, I told you on the phone last summer."

"And you're going back soon?"

"Yes, Mom, I still work for the same people."

"And how is Maureen? Why, I just saw her. She brought me some hothouse flowers."

"She's fine. Mom, this is Matt, her son. You remember him."

Suzanne looked up to where he was still standing near the door. "Oh, my, yes. Of course I know Matt. Why, he was a big, strapping boy when you were just a baby, dear. Come into the light, Matt."

But by the time they were saying their goodbyes, Suzanne stared at him as if for the first time and said, "Oh, Matthew, has it really been twenty years since I've seen you?" And she started crying silently, tears oozing out of her eyes.

"It's those drugs," Nicola said as they walked back outside. "If they'd quit giving her so much, then maybe—"

"Hey." Matt caught her arm. "They give her the drugs because she's clinically depressed. You can't have it all, kid. Without the little white pills, she'd be..."

"I know. Suicidal."

"That's right. This way she just looks at her catalogs and stays out of harm's way."

Nicola seemed to tremble then with the chill of her misery. "Damn," she said, trying to gather herself.

By then, Matt had decided that Sansouci was a terrible idea. No way was he putting her through any more of this hell. She probably wasn't the least bit hungry as it was. He wished to God that he could take this lady up to his room and lie down on the bed and hold her all night. She was so precious to him at that moment, so in need, that he could almost thank the Gages for giving her all those insecurities—it had kept her, so far, from finding happiness in the arms of another man.

Matt led her over to the car and opened her door. "Want the top up? It's getting cool out."

"Sure," she said, but her voice was threatening to crack. "What a mistake I made coming here. What did I expect? A miracle cure?"

"You expected love."

That got her attention. Suddenly Nicola looked up through glistening, dark eyes and stared at him. "Why, Matt Cavanaugh," she said, "of *all* people to figure that one out."

"Hey," he said, getting into the car, "I'm human, you know. Well, almost."

Surprisingly Nicola declared that she could use something to eat. "I really don't want to go home yet."

"You sure?"

"Yes."

It was time to come clean. He felt like ducking his head. "Listen," he began, "I did a stupid thing. While you were changing, I made reservations at, ah, Sansouci. Dumb, I know. You can bite my head off, if you want."

Nicola turned and studied him for a moment. He'd expected anger from her but instead got curiosity. "Are you trying to play big brother or what?" she asked. "I mean, if I want to see my own father while I'm here, Matt, I don't need a bodyguard, you know."

"Well, I . . . Hey, I slipped. It was a lousy idea. So," he said, "where would you like to eat?"

"You said you had reservations."

"Yes, but after seeing your mother, you may not want to go there."

"Why don't you let me be the judge of that," she said.

"You really want to see him?"

"Sure, why not? Who knows when I'll make it east again? And one thing's for certain, he'll never come see me."

"You've got guts, kid, I'll say that for you."

"Nicola. Nicky, if you must. But quit calling me kid."

Matt drove the parkways and crossed the river into Midtown Manhattan, enjoying the ride, enjoying the comfortable silence between them. At that hour of night, eight-thirty, there was little traffic heading into New York City, and they made good time.

He was thinking a lot about this woman sitting next to him, her eyes staring straight ahead. He'd like to know her better. But he had no right to even approve of his own thoughts. What could he offer her at present? He couldn't even tell her that he wasn't quite the bum she thought he was. And yet a part of him wanted to woo and charm her that night, to catch her with her guard down. He felt like a single cell dividing itself, tearing apart, as if he were becoming two separate entities, conflicting beings. And all because of a job and an oath he'd sworn many years ago. Well, he was fed up with the work, with the question bobbing around in his head continually now: *If I weren't the footloose trust funder, then who would I be?* Maybe he really was playing himself; maybe he really was a wise-cracking wastrel. He owed it to himself and to his family to find out.

He parked in a secure garage a block from Sansouci, took his jacket from the back and locked up. It had rained lightly in the city earlier, and the air was as soft and tangible as spun silk. There was something special about dusk, a feel to it, a peaceful ending to the day.

"It's pretty out," he commented, and took Nicola's arm. "I love it after an evening shower."

"Me, too," was all she said as they crossed Third Avenue and headed east.

Just touching her, seeing the last light catch in her hair, smelling the faint scent of her honey sweetness, lent him a kind of shaky elation. It couldn't last—he wouldn't do that to either of them—but for now he'd accept those feelings and enjoy them.

Nicola stopped beneath the striped canopy and took a deep breath. "Boy, I think I'm just asking for it tonight," she said.

"You want to find another spot?"

She shook her head, determined.

Inside Sansouci it was dark and elegant. The gold damask walls were covered with signed photos of the rich and famous. The booths were plush red velvet, the linen the finest. Chandeliers twinkled, waiters flourished, soft classical music hung on the air. Even the carpet seemed to give beneath their feet.

"Nice," Matt said, then gave his name to the headwaiter.

"It looks the same," Nicola breathed. "I guess Dad's done pretty well for himself."

"Even better, I'd say."

On their way to the table, Matt touched her arm lightly. "Would you like me to tell the maître d' who you are? I'm sure your father..."

Nicola smiled. "No. Went always makes the rounds of the tables. You know, 'How is the sauce? The veal?' That kind of stuff. He won't be able to miss us."

They had a cocktail, then ordered their meals and chose an expensive bottle of Bordeaux. Nicola studied the menu carefully, commenting on this and that, the new items, the always popular entrées. No nouvelle cuisine for Went's place; every dish was swimming in his famous sauces, lots of clarified butter and garlic and heavy cream. The vegetables, lightly steamed or sautéed, were as rich as the entrées.

Wonderful tasting foods did not go hand in hand with limited calories.

"I thought everyone ate light nowadays," Matt said, leaning his elbows on the table and catching her eyes over the candle.

"Not Dad's customers evidently. I guess they still splurge once in a while."

"Maybe he's smart," Matt said, "and lets everyone else in the business lighten up their menus. This way, he's the only game in town."

"No one ever said Went was dumb." Nicola sipped her drink casually, but he noticed her eyes kept glancing over his shoulder toward the swinging kitchen doors.

"How long's it been?" Matt asked a few minutes later over their tender Bibb lettuce salads.

"Since I've been here? Well, I'll bet it's been six years. The place wasn't even that established yet."

"Nervous?" Just then the wine steward arrived, the white towel over his arm. Matt sniffed the cork on the bottle, nodded, then tasted the wine. "Excellent," he said.

Dinner arrived. Nicola had ordered scallops in a white basil sauce with baby carrots and summer squash, while Matt had opted for pork tenderloin medallions that were dripping with mushrooms and a Dijon sauce. The bread was hot and yeasty, the butter molded into little seashells, the silverware heavy. But Nicola looked the best of all. Her hair was clasped to one side and fell over a milky shoulder; her eyes, those lovely dark eyes, looked at everything tentatively, and her mouth . . . Each bite she took she tasted carefully, her lips parting for the fork, closing, moving slowly. Forget the food; Matt could have nibbled on those lips all night.

"Is yours good?" he asked.

"I can't fault Went for the cuisine."

"Mine's passable," he teased.

Nicola's dark brows raised. "Isn't it good, Matt? Went's food is usually the very best."

Ah, yes, he had her there; he'd caught her off guard. She still cared. She still looked up to the creep and idolized him. A sharp spear of jealousy knifed through him. What had Went ever done for her?

The man himself finally came popping out of the kitchen. Matt hadn't noticed, but Nicola was a dead giveaway. She seemed to stiffen in her seat, and her cheeks grew rosy in anticipation and apprehension.

Matt glanced over his shoulder. Wentworth Gage was older now, but still just as lean and tall, just as craggy faced and effusive. He was not at all the picture of the fat, jolly cook, being much too hyper to ever gain weight. He'd lost none of his charm, either, as he moved from table to table, just as Nicola had said he would, bowing, exclaiming, kissing a hand or two.

He looked the part. He wore his tall white hat, loose black-and-white checked pants, the white jacket open at the throat and his coveted European chef's badge pinned properly to his breast.

"Oh God," Nicola said, as if poised for flight, "he's coming our way."

"I think it's a little late to run."

"My Lord!" came the man's voice seconds later. "But, can it be? Can it be my *Nicola*?"

The charm and polish oozed from him as if he'd rehearsed it. He held Nicola's shoulders, kissed the air next to each cheek, stepped back and grinned proudly.

"My darling Nicola, *chérie*," he kept saying, "you should have called. You should have asked for the best seat in the house! But this is amazing, finding you here!"

Nicola could not have been more embarrassed by the fanfare. Heads turned in their direction, whispers abounded. "Who *is* she?"

She looked down at her lap. "Dad, you're making such a fuss," she said, flustered. "I wrote you last spring. I said I might come."

"Of course you did! Didn't you get my answer in the mail?" He looked positively outraged.

"Why, no..."

Holy Toledo, Matt thought, suddenly wanting to punch the guy's lights out, she swallowed the old letter-in-the-mail routine—hook, line and sinker!

"But I can't imagine why you didn't get it," Went was saying, the consummate actor. "Now, you must let me take you out tomorrow, Nicola, darling. We'll do the town!"

"Well...I..."

Matt cleared his throat. "We already have plans," he said, grinning at Went wolfishly.

"Matt..." Nicola began, confused.

There was no way he was going to let Went, that phony, French-accented New Yorker, court her for a day and then dump her out in the cold again. No way. "I'm afraid," Matt said, shooting her a look, "that Nicola and I are tied up. Our plans are firm."

A moment of silence stretched out like a thin thread ready to snap. Nicola looked uncertain, Went was gauging his adversary—whom he hadn't yet recognized after so many years—and Matt glared at him with unbending determination and a charming smile.

Went finally sighed. "Well, then, perhaps the next day. I do want to spend some time—"

"I have a flight," Nicola said, and her voice was sad. "I'm off to Colorado again."

"Oh," Went said.

"I have to be there, Dad."

"But this is unfair. It's been too long."

"You could visit her in Colorado," Matt said pointedly as he poured himself and Nicola more wine.

"I'm afraid," Went said, "I didn't get your name."

"Cavanaugh. Matt Cavanaugh." He could have added, *My folks raised your daughter, remember?*

"Of course! I should have... And how are Evan and Maureen?"

The atmosphere lightened a bit after that, and Went seemed eager to please. He mentioned always wanting to travel in the West, and wouldn't it be grand if Nicola could find a week sometime to spend in the city? He never mentioned Suzanne, however, and neither did Nicola, who had fallen quite silent, still obviously uncertain, still hurting and sad and adoring and slavishly grateful.

"Well, I must be off to the kitchen before my new *saucier* curdles the hollandaise. You *will* write, Nicola? And you must find that week to visit sometime." He kissed her again and held both her hands in his. Surprisingly Matt thought he detected a slight hesitation, a faint regret, perhaps, in the man's dark eyes.

"Phew," Nicola said, utterly unnerved by the time Went left. "I didn't expect all *that*." Then she seemed to collect herself and looked up at Matt sharply. "Why did you lie to him like that? I could have spent tomorrow in the city." Her tone was accusing.

Matt framed his answer carefully. "I thought I was helping. I assumed that Went would either call and cancel out on you, or he'd have painted the town with you and then let the years pass...."

"But it's my problem, Matt, not yours."

He held her eyes in challenge. "So go on into the kitchen and tell him you're free for the day."

Suddenly there was a feeling of suspense, a wedge forcing itself between them as they sat there, each poised to do battle. It was finally Nicola who relented. "Okay," she said, "you're right. Dad would have given me those hours, then so long Nicola, see you around."

"Mad at me?"

"Yes. Very. You acted like Evan."

"Whoa there! Evan? Me?"

"Yes. Like father, like son. How do you like that?"

"I don't."

It was as if she'd thrown a bucket of cold water in his face. He'd really let himself slide that time. He'd been angry, jealous, stubborn and controlling. Wow.

He couldn't believe it; he'd let his facade drop and hadn't even recognized it. He'd compromised his cover. And for what? To protect a girl he liked, to keep her from getting hurt.

What was wrong with him?

She was watching him across the expanse of exquisite linen and silver and crystal and congealed rich sauces on fine china. She was seeing something unexpected and wondering about it. And it occurred to him to just give up and tell the truth, tell her that he cared about her feelings and that he wasn't a superficial, irresponsible cad. Of course, he couldn't do it.

"Misguided romanticism," he quipped. "Sorry, kid. Just call me Don Quixote."

"Well," she said, mollified, "maybe you were right to do it. But don't do anything like that again, ever. I mean it, Matt. You're not my big brother, you know."

Comically he crossed his heart like a kid. "Never, I swear. Each to his own bad end, I always say. I don't know what came over me."

When the bill arrived, it had Went's note scrawled across it: "Compliments of the house."

"Nice guy," Matt said, "your old man."

But Nicola said nothing; her soft, childish mouth, her pretty, full lips tightened into a line and she frowned slightly.

Outside it was sultry. The city once again oozed the smell of hot pavement and car exhaust, and the carousel it was on vibrated and whirled to a tinkly tune as they walked to the garage to pick up the Ferrari.

"You wouldn't let me drive it, would you?" Nicola asked wistfully as the attendant pulled up, braking with an echoing squeal.

"Sure. You want to?"

"Could I?" Her eyes were shining, those huge dark eyes that he could drown in. He'd do anything to keep that happiness on her face, even let her drive the service's hundred-thousand-dollar toy.

"I'm a good driver," she assured him.

"Get in, kid." He opened the driver's door for her with a flourish. "She's all yours."

Nicola *was* a good driver once she got used to the sensitive clutch and special racing gearbox. She grinned and her long dark hair flew around her head and through the open window, whipping strands across her face as the wind of their passage buffeted her.

"Oh! This is fun!" She gunned it on the West Side Highway, where the traffic thinned out, and the Hudson River flashed by along their left, the battalions of uniform apartment buildings skimming by on the right.

"Take it easy. Cops," he said mildly.

"Oh? Am I going too fast?"

"A little.

He relaxed back against his seat and watched her profile, her open mouth, her black veil of hair. He was giving her pleasure, and it felt good, really good.

Sometime later she pulled into the driveway at home, stopped in front of the door and, reluctantly, turned the car off. "Thanks," she said. "That was a treat."

All the lights were out inside the house by then, and only the yellow porch light guided their way to the door. They both walked slowly, side by side, companionably. Matt wanted to be a decent fellow with Nicola; he wanted her to really like him. Yet if he continued on this path, she'd see right through him to the truth—she almost had back at the restaurant.

"Well," she said at the door, fumbling for her keys in her purse, brushing at the insects that buzzed around the yellow light, "that was nice of you to go along with me tonight. Thanks."

She was adorable, shy and a little uneasy, so young, a world younger than he was. "You're quite welcome."

She found her key and was inserting it into the lock, but he put his hand over hers, stopping her. She looked up swiftly, with a jerk.

"I've got a great idea. Let's go skinny-dipping in the pool," he said, knowing what he had to do, hating it. "I used to do it all the time when I was a kid."

*"Matt."*

"Sure, come on. It's a hot night. Perfect."

"I don't think so." She was stiffening up; he could feel it in her hand, in the sinews of her arm.

Slowly he turned her to face him. "Why not?"

"Please, this is ridiculous and you know it."

"Then we'll wear suits."

"No, I'm going to bed."

He put his hands on either side of her, leaning against the front door, imprisoning her. "You're chicken, kid."

She had pulled back as far as she could, and he could tell she was trembling a little, trying to put up a brave front, but uncertain and totally unable to play the games that other women did.

"Maybe I am chicken," she said breathlessly.

He let her go, of course. He couldn't hold a woman against her will. "You sure you don't want that swim?"

"No." She slipped away, opened the door and was inside in a moment, closing it in his face.

He stood there, staring at the shiny black paneled door and elegant brass knocker and artful fanlight at the top. He sighed then and turned away to go around the side of the house to the pool. She was something special, something valuable, not to be toyed with like his other ladies. Yes, he'd need that swim, with the cool, soothing water sliding against his hot skin.

He unbuttoned his shirt as he walked in the darkness and yanked it off, angry with himself suddenly. Angry with himself for caring.

# CHAPTER FOUR

THE CRACK OF A GUNSHOT split the air, echoing off the walls of the surrounding mountains, repeating itself until, weaker and weaker, it died off. Startled, Nicola looked up from the skillet she was holding over the black iron wood stove.

"A little early, isn't he?" Ron Mitchell remarked dryly.

"It isn't even dawn yet. Is he crazy?" Nicola said. The late elk season this year started promptly at sunup on Saturday, November 3, and a hunter could lose his license if he was caught shooting before that time. Everybody knew that.

"Sure, there're lotsa trigger-happy crazies out there, Nick," Ron said, throwing another piece of wood into the old cookstove.

"Someday a fool like that's going to kill someone," she said, turning back to her home fried potatoes.

She and Ron were the only two stirring in the main log cabin at five o'clock that morning. As guide and owner of the Colorado outfitter service, Ron was checking on the supplies for lunch, the water cans, the ropes in case someone had to drag his kill out, and looking at the topographical maps of the McClure Pass area, searching out new places where he'd locate elk for his customers, who'd paid a bundle to bag a nice trophy this week.

Nicola was, of course, cooking. She had to get up very early to start the fire in the wood stove until it heated up the room and until it reached the right temperature for cooking. No turning the knob to Low or Medium or High. The old stove was a challenge, but once it got going, it cooked like a charm. She had potatoes frying on one burner, a batch of buttermilk biscuits in the oven and French toast stuffed with cream cheese browning in butter in another skillet.

Outside it was still pitch-black, and cold, too. Dawn in the Colorado Rockies, at ninety-five-hundred feet of altitude, often produced subfreezing temperatures. When Nicola arose in the morning in her own tiny, unheated cabin, she threw on long underwear—tops and bottoms—jeans, wool socks, a heavy wool plaid shirt and a bright orange hunting parka before she even brushed her teeth. She made her way across the clearing to the main cabin, where the kitchen and rec room were, and rustled up a huge breakfast for the six hunters who habitually booked Ron's service for this same week every year.

Ron was whistling, feet up, sipping at the coffee in his own personal mug, the one with the lady's face on the side and her nether parts on the bottom so they could be seen when he tipped it up to drink. The aroma of brewing coffee filled the big room, along with the mouth-watering scent of the cooking food.

"I get fat every summer, Nick, you know that? And it's all your fault."

"Sorry." She flipped the French toast adroitly with a spatula. "Just doing what you hired me to do."

"Too damn well." Ron lit up his first cigarette of the day and sighed. He was a middle-aged man, an ex-rancher, who'd found it more lucrative to run a hunting-fishing-guide service than to punch cows. He worked like a demon from June to November, then retired for the winter with his wife on his considerable spread down in the valley near the town of Redstone. He had jug ears, rough features and big gnarled hands, but he could tie a fishing fly to catch the most elusive trout, climb a sheer mountainside, gentle a skittish packhorse, track an eight-point buck across rock or fix a broken Jeep with nothing more than a screwdriver and the roll of duct tape he always carried.

Nicola had been working for him for three seasons. She made a lot of money—two thousand dollars a week during hunting season—but she earned every penny of it, she figured, cooking, washing up, ordering supplies, wrestling with the stove, which she'd nicknamed Old Bertha. and it wasn't easy to cook in high altitudes. Water boiled at a lower temperature due to less atmospheric pressure, and everything took *much* longer to cook: beef roasts an hour longer, a roast chicken half an hour more. Four-minute eggs took six, pasta took half again as long as the directions called for, and all baked goods took longer, too. Carrots never seemed to cook. The first year it had been a guessing game, but now Nicola had it down to a science.

Ron had other guides in his outfit, but this week he was leading the group; he always took his best clients out himself. Most of the six men who were hunting now were old customers, men who came every year at the same time, and they came not only for the hunt and the glorious autumn scenery of the Rockies and the great food, but also for the male companionship, the time to swap stories, see familiar faces and catch up on the past year.

Nicola checked the biscuits. Two minutes more and they'd be done. The checkered oilcloth was spread on the plank table and set with plain, heavy crockery and stainless steel flatware. The coffee was brewed—lots of it. Cream and butter were set out, along with homemade preserves that Ron's wife made: local chokecherry jam, tart and garnet red; clear pink crab-apple jelly; wild raspberry. And homemade salsa, too a mixture of onions and garlic and tomatoes and jalapeño chilies, without which no right-minded westerner would think of settin' down to the table.

"Smells good," was Ron's comment.

"You always say that."

"You got those sourdough pancakes on the menu this week, Nick?"

"Tomorrow," she said, covering the French toast and setting it on the warming shelf on the top of the stove.

Ron grunted and stubbed his cigarette out. "Your friend Evan is mighty eager. Is he gonna be one o' them-there angry types if he doesn't bag a bull?"

"Don't worry about Evan. He's hunted all over. He knows the odds." Evan had finally kept his promise and made it out west to hunt, and Nicola was thrilled; she'd been nagging him to do it ever since she'd started working for Ron. There were men he knew who came every year, two of whom had booked the same week as Evan, so he fit in as if he'd been coming regularly. The old boy network reached even to McClure Pass in the high Rockies.

The front door opened then, and Dave Huff walked in. "Gosh darn, Nicola, that smells good! I'm starving." He came right over and kissed her on the cheek, a lighthearted, fair man who lived fifty miles away in Aspen, an old skiing buddy of Evan's. "Um, sweet smelling and a good cook to boot. What more could a man ask for?" Dave always had a kind word for everyone, a joke or a funny story to tell.

The other men were starting to straggle in. Terry Swanson from North Carolina, a hard drinker, a man's man and a very good hunter. Eric Field, a tall, rangy Californian, who claimed he'd been mauled by a bear once. Fred Henn, a businessman from Denver, who was very quiet and did not know the others well. Evan came in then, shook Ron's hand and said pointedly that he hoped they had good luck that week.

Jon Wolff was the last man to arrive. He was the owner of the ski lodge in Canada that Evan and family frequented each January, so they were old friends. He was from Austria originally, a widower of around sixty, weathered but straight as a ramrod, with a hawklike profile. He and Dave Huff were also acquainted, as Dave and his wife met Evan and Maureen at Jon's Bugaboo Lodge every year without fail.

There were, however, no women at hunting camp. Except for Nicola—Nick—who was perfectly happy to be one of the guys, ready with a quip, accepting of bad jokes, a sexless creature who carefully kept her relationship with Ron's clients on a professional basis. Only once had one of Ron's hunters knocked on Nicola's cabin door in the night; Ron had talked to him the next day, and it had never happened again. And Nicola liked it that way.

"Nicola, have you met my old pal, Dave? Of course, he was here last year," Evan was saying. "Isn't she a grand girl?"

"Stop it, Evan, you're embarrassing me," Nicola said.

"And do you know Jon? Jon, come over here. Sure, you know Jon, don't you? How does the season look, Jon? Kept my week in January open for us?"

"Ya, sure, Evan."

Evan rubbed his hands together gleefully. "It's cold as a witch's, uh, bottom out, men. Great hunting, great day."

"There could be more snow, though," put in Terry Swanson. "They'd be down lower then."

"Say, did anyone hear a shot a while ago?" asked Eric Field.

"Yeah," Ron said, "somebody was what you might call overeager. O'course, he couldn't see his hand in front of his blamed face in the dark, much less an elk."

"Crazy," Fred Henn murmured.

"I hope he's long gone when *we* get out there," Evan said.

"Dangerous," Jon agreed, shaking his head.

"There's always one in every crowd," piped up Dave Huff.

"Breakfast," called Nicola, setting the biscuits on the table, then the aluminum coffeepot, a bowl of home fries and a platter heaped with thick, crispy French toast sprinkled with powdered sugar. "Chow's on, men."

They ate quickly, greedily, excited by the hunt to come, gabbing and telling tall tales, bragging, throwing out off-color jokes. Cups of coffee, sweetened with thick cream and sugar—or honey, in Evan's case—were swallowed. Biscuits were split and loaded with sweet golden butter and gobs of jelly. Forks cut into French toast, letting rich, melted cream cheese ooze out. Murmurs of appreciation rose from the table, slurps and "Pass, please" and the clink of forks and knives and "More coffee." The talk was also of the best spots to sit and catch an elk off guard, the times of day that the huge beasts lay down in the protection of the forest, hunting rifles, telescopic sights, the difficulty in packing out a kill without horses handy, how to get a Jeep with a winch in close enough to drag out an animal.

"Not like deer," Terry Swanson said, his mouth full of food. "Elk are some kind of heavy critters."

The talk was all hunting, hopes for the day to come, past experiences. "Damn fool shot himself in the foot trying to load his gun," Ron was telling Eric.

"Dumb horse stepped into a gopher hole and went lame. I almost had to carry him out," Terry Swanson said.

"In Kenya, I got a wildebeest," Evan told Fred Henn, "but I'll bet an elk is as big."

"Have you ever hunted at Tigertops in India?" Fred asked. "Not as many animals as East Africa, but more exotic."

Nicola had heard it all many times. She ignored most of what the men said, busy refilling cups, passing biscuits, pulling another batch out of the oven. The room grew warmer from Old Bertha, and Nicola took off her wool shirt and cooked in her bright blue long-underwear top, sleeves pushed up, neck buttons undone.

The men finished eating, thanked Nicola, gave her outlandish compliments and got ready to leave. It was already 5:40, and the stars still shone, but everyone wanted to be in their spot at first light when the game would be moving around, feeding, drinking, dark shadows against a quickening sky. Opening day.

"We'll take the Jeeps as far as Silver Ridge," Ron said, taking his Winchester from the gun rack, pulling on his bright orange parka and cap. "Everybody got jackets and hats? Jon, give me a hand with the box of lunches, will you? Thanks."

They were ready, each man in heavy walking boots, thick wool socks, heavy pants, long underwear, wool shirts and sweaters. Parkas and hats in fluorescent orange, as prescribed by law to prevent accidental shootings, were greatly in evidence. Nicola followed them outside into the cold morning as they shouldered their favorite rifles, their Remingtons, their Savages, their Weatherbies and Winchesters, checked their pockets for ammunition and checked their sheathed gutting knives.

"Good luck," she said to them all. "Good hunting, guys." She gave Evan a thumbs-up and an encouraging smile, and he grinned back at her like a boy and winked broadly as he climbed into one of the two awaiting Jeeps. Nicola noted the excited chatter of the men, the nervous energy that made them ready to pop. They'd go on like that for a mile or so up the dirt road, the two Jeeps bouncing and lurching, the headlights making crazy, blinding tunnels deep into the forest, then the men would grow quiet and expectant as they neared the spot where they'd wait for dawn in silence.

Elk, Nicola thought as she stood there, were wily and elusive animals. Only hunters with the best guides would even see one this week. In September, though, when it was rutting season, and men could buy a bow and arrow license, the bugle of the bulls could be heard echoing in the valleys, affording a hunter greater odds of bagging one. It never ceased to amaze her that a nine-hundred-pound animal could hide so well in the mountainsides.

Shivering, she went back inside the toasty warm cabin. The men, hungry and sleepy eyed, had stormed the place, and in the space of twenty minutes, laid waste to it. She straightened and stacked dishes, swept the mud from heavy boots out the front door and restoked the fire in Bertha, as she planned on having a nice breakfast herself.

Outside, the dark was grudgingly giving way to a mother-of-pearl glow. The men would all be in their places by now, cigarettes extinguished, hunching down on rocks or fallen logs on the edge of the cold forest or overlooking gullies, ravines, streams. They'd be spaced out, the six of them, a couple of hundred yards apart, waiting, hushed, their hot, nervous breathing forming white plumes in the frozen air. And then maybe a branch would be heard snapping deep in the bowels of the forest, and hearts would begin to pound. At first, in the half light, an animal would only be a slow-moving shadow merging from the dark trees, scouting the open meadows. Probably it would be a female—a cow—because the few bulls lingered safely behind, rarely showing themselves. And a trophy bull elk... It was going to take a lucky man to even glimpse one this trip.

Dawn spilled into the valley while Nicola filled the sink with cold water, using the single hand pump in the camp. That there was even one source of running water was a luxury to find in a cabin in the Rockies. Ron's idea. He'd dug the well out back himself.

The men wouldn't be cold out there despite the frigid temperatures. No. They'd be sweating, each hoping for a first shot before the game on the mountainside was spooked. Then hunting became purely a matter of chance. Oh, Ron knew where the spooked elk herds would most likely be, running through the ravines, crashing through the thickets. But to get a *safe* shot at a fleeing animal was quite another thing.

Maybe Evan would get a chance....

She put the remaining biscuit dough in the oven for her breakfast, then slipped back into her parka. In a minute or two more, she knew, the shooting would start. Then it would sound like World War III out there for an hour, the gunshots bouncing off canyon walls, off rock escarpments, rumbling down through the valleys.

Gunshots like that crazy shot earlier. The fool.

Standing out in front of the cabin, the chimney smoke behind her spiraling upward in a long, thin line, she hugged her arms around herself and turned to take in the panorama around the hunting camp, a view that was familiar to her by now, familiar but still awe inspiring. To the east there were mountains, dark green and gray up close, fading away into the distance toward the white-peaked Continental Divide. The pale morning sun sat on a saddle between two far-off peaks, as if resting there before undertaking its day's work, pinkish, huge, extending long fingers of fragile light to where Nicola stood, touching her with golden warmth.

She turned again, to the north. A long slope of brown grass and spruce climbed away from her, up and up, until she tipped her head back to see the dark hump of the mountain covered with early snow. To the west was a deep cleft that fell away beyond the farthest log cabin in the camp. She couldn't see it from where she stood, but she knew there was a narrow, verdant canyon down there, with a bubbling stream that flowed down over rocks, twisting and turning, to empty into the Crystal River, which emptied into the Roaring Fork River, which finally joined the immense Colorado River, which fed a good deal of the great Southwest before it flowed on into the Pacific.

The south. She turned once more. An alpine meadow spread before her, dissected by the dirt road, studded with brush and shaded by a giant blue spruce, an ancient patriarch. The field was brown now, but in the summer, she knew, it was full of wildflowers: blue harebell, red Indian paintbrush, daisies, tiny purple asters, magenta elephant head, lupine, pink owlclover. A riot of color and variety.

This was her world for half the year, this high mountain beauty surrounded by cool, clear light and sparkling dry air.

The sun had risen a little since she'd been standing there, throwing long shadows across the meadow. It was peaceful, still, utterly silent, and Nicola was the queen of all she surveyed. A pity that the shooting would soon begin.

There was a sound, though, a faint noise, barely perceptible but there—a man-made noise—and it was growing louder, coming closer. A Jeep, grinding up the dirt road. Could Ron have forgotten something? Could Ron's wife down in the valley have sent someone up, a new arrival? But Nicola was positive everyone who'd had a reservation was already there. Well, then, who could it be? Maybe T.J.? Evan had said his son had flown into Denver with him, but T.J. was supposedly staying in the city, a business deal. Well, whoever it was, she'd be stuck with him until the men returned.

The odor of biscuits, on the verge of burning, stirred her out of her reverie. Oh, darn! She hurried back inside, snatched up the pot holder, pulled down the heavy oven door, grabbed the pan and blew on the golden tops.

*In the nick of time,* she thought.

The cabin door swung open then, and she turned around, cocking her head. The light was behind him, and his face was in shadow. But something in that carriage, in that stance...

"Hey, kid," came a familiar voice, "smells good. Got enough for me?"

*"Matt?"*

He unslung the rucksack he was carrying over his shoulder and tossed it on the plank floor. "Who else?"

"But what on earth are *you* doing here?"

"I paid my fees, rented a Jeep, followed the map Mrs. Mitchell gave me..."

"You know what I mean." She could still hardly believe it. Matt, here.

"If you'd fix me up with some coffee and maybe one or two of those biscuits, I'll tell you my life story, anything. I'm tired and I'm hungry."

"Well, sure." Nicola hesitated, still wondering, barely over her surprise, then put down the pan and fetched him some leftover coffee. She set it down on the table. "There you are. Sit. I'll get you some biscuits."

"Thanks, Nicky," he began, when abruptly the war started in the distant mountains, gunshots splitting the air, one after another. "Um," Matt said, "the boys are certainly having a good time."

She wondered momentarily at his mocking tone, then dismissed it. Good old Matt, sharp-tongued, too quick with a clever remark.

He ate like a starving man, she noticed as she sat down opposite him and folded her arms on the table. Once in a while he talked with a mouthful, then swallowed coffee, then took another huge bite of biscuit laced with jam and butter.

"Great rolls," he said at one point.

"As soon as you're done feeding," Nicola said, one eyebrow arched, "I'd just *love* to hear why you've come."

"Sure, sure."

Well, he hadn't lost any of that seductiveness, she saw, or his good looks. It had been almost six months since she'd seen him. But she remembered that night after dinner at Sansouci as if it had been only yesterday. He'd put his two hands on the door at either side of her head, and he'd leaned close, imprisoning her, making his play, his blue eyes all soft and sultry, sending an undeniable message.

Nicola sat there feeling heat prick the back of her neck as he ate and watched her intently. Was he remembering, too?

Oh yes. She'd almost, *almost*, let him kiss her. She'd let him move in on her like a wolf on its prey, press himself against her dress lightly, but just enough so that there was no doubt as to his condition. Her eyes had locked with his, and her lips had parted, and she'd felt wildly, insanely dizzy with a powerful, awakened need.

Oh, brother.

But it had been Matt who'd moved away from her, saying something like, "You sure you don't want that swim?" Yes. And she'd felt mortified, and afraid, because she'd darn near let him con her. Well, it wasn't going to happen again.

"More coffee?" she asked, rising abruptly, hiding her face.

"Sure. And the rolls were wonderful."

He'd been gone that next morning. Maureen had told Nicola something about his finding a place to live near the city and a job. Then Nicola had left for Colorado. Six months, and now this. Out of the blue.

"Well," he said, patting his lean, muscled stomach over the yellow-and-brown wool shirt, "bet you never expected me."

"No, I didn't. Does Evan know?"

Matt shook his head. "Mom told me he was up here this week. You know, I'm working down in Crested Butte right now."

"Crested Butte?"

"Right. I told you I might be out in Colorado this winter."

"How long have you been there?"

Matt took another sip of coffee, then shrugged. "Not long. A couple weeks."

"You have a job?"

"At a bar. But it's still off-season, so my boss gave me a few days to get acclimated."

"Crested Butte's a ski area, isn't it?"

He nodded. "That's right. It's only a few miles from McClure Pass here, as the crow flies. An hour's drive."

"I see."

"No more questions?" Matt gave her a crooked grin.

"Oh, sorry. I was just curious. I mean, you're the last person on earth I expected to see here." And she wondered at the reception he'd get from Evan.

"Well," he said, "I made an effort to see Mom and Evan at home last summer when I was in New York, and I thought I might join him up here in camp. You, know, father-and-son hunting trip. Spend some quality time, and all that, with each other."

"Come on, Matt," Nicola said sarcastically.

"Hey! I'm a changed man. Why the third degree, anyway? It's a free world."

She eyed him warily. "Yes, it is. Well, I guess I better show you the spare bed. You'll bunk in with Dave Huff."

"I've met Dave. Funny guy. I skied with him one winter up in Canada."

"You did?"

"Many, many moons ago, kid...Nicky."

"Um." She walked outside while Matt shouldered his pack and followed. "It's next to the last cabin," she said, pointing. Then, turning to him, she asked, "Say, didn't you bring a gun?"

He smiled. "I never shoot anything except with a camera."

"Then why are you here?"

"To have that quality time with Evan. I told you." He walked on ahead, carrying his rucksack easily, his strides long and self-assured. Nicola watched that jaunty male sway, the tight buttocks beneath the faded blue jeans.

"What a waste," she breathed.

Doing the dishes in cold water was impossible, Nicola had learned, so she habitually boiled a big pot of water, soaked them in it, then scrubbed and rinsed with cold. It took forever. She filled the big kettle from the pump at the sink, took a deep breath, then lifted it, starting toward the stove.

"Here, jeez, that's too heavy for you."

Oh, swell, he was back. But any man who wanted to help with the dishes . . .

A few minutes later, Matt rolled up his sleeves and stuck his hands in the hot water and scrubbed away. Nicola rinsed and dried.

"Hot in here," Matt said, and she saw him wipe his brow on his forearm. She pushed open the window. "Thanks," he said, shooting her a quick smile. "That's what I love about Colorado. Freezing in the morning, hot by noon."

"Not always," Nicola said, taking another dish from him. "You know you don't have to help. I'm used to it."

"I like helping. Well, helping you, that is."

"Really?" she replied dryly.

The dishes were stacked and put away in no time. And all due to Matt's good-natured assistance. And she really didn't have to peel potatoes or anything till two or so. The beans were soaking . . .

"Hey," Matt said, "want to take a hike?"

"With all those gun-toting maniacs out there?"

He was standing in the doorway, a casual shoulder against the frame. "Sure. We'll wear our orange and stick to the clearings. Come on, it's a glorious day."

"I don't know," she said doubtfully. She wasn't sure she wanted to go anywhere with him. A girl could lose herself in those laughing blue eyes or want to smooth down those stubborn curls around his ears. He should have brought a lady friend with him if he didn't want to find the guys and go hunting. Why pick on her? And then she wondered as she stood there, uncertain, and eyed him, was this how Went behaved with women? Helpful, gentlemanly, *friendly*? Was this how her own dad lured them into his trap?

"Well?" Matt said.

"I guess . . . just an hour or so. I have work to do." *You idiot!*

Matt carried a water bottle and two ham-and-cheese sandwiches in a small day pack, and they headed out across the south meadow toward a sloping hillside that was spangled with dark firs. It was a glorious day, just as Matt had said, and she was perfectly content to follow his footsteps through the brown grass and the wet patches of snow. Over logs they went, across rivulets and marshy ground.

"Watch it," Matt said, indicating a muddy pool beneath a clump of skunk cabbage. "Here, give me your hand. Okay, now jump."

She came up against him, her hand still gripped in his tightly. The sun, warm on her parka, was in her eyes, and she couldn't see his face, but she knew her cheeks were flushed, and she was breathing a whole lot harder than she should have been. He seemed reluctant to let her go, but then an errant gunshot somewhere off to their left intruded on the moment, and Matt dropped her hand. "Let's go," he said.

Puffing, Nicola followed him up the steep hillside, along a deer trail, across a field of boulders. At the top of the rise, they could see the tall, white-capped mountains beyond them, and the valley below seemed minuscule.

"Phew," Nicola said, "my legs are tired."

"Mine, too. Let's rest a minute."

The earth smelled of autumn that day, of snow melting on dead brown leaves and marshland, fecund. There was another odor, too, mingling with the soft decay—a male odor, sweaty yet sweet with soap. Matt's odor. Why was it, Nicola wondered while she glanced at him, that some men smelled so sensual while others left her cold?

She'd been resting on a log near him, nibbling on her sandwich, silent, when suddenly Matt went "Sh," reached over and put a finger to her lips. "Over there, across the valley. Sh." He moved closer to her on the log, put his arm over her shoulder and pointed, sighting her eyes down his arm. "See him?"

"No," she whispered, all too wary of Matt's nearness. "What?"

"Bull elk. A trophy size, too." He edged closer. "Look, see that outcropping of rock? There?"

"Yes..."

"Okay. Now, about a hundred yards down. Just in that stand of aspen. A little to the right."

"Yes!" Nicola gasped. "I see him. He's looking right at us!"

"You bet he is," Matt said in a hushed voice, his arm still extended over her shoulder. "He knows we're here. He's downwind and can smell us. But he thinks if he moves, he's dead."

"But elk don't *think*."

"Sure they do. Not like us, but they're damn smart animals."

The huge beast, a splendid bull with six points on his rack, stood in the golden light with his head held high and still, alert, his neck massive, swollen, and he carried his antlers parallel to the hump on his back, as if poised for flight. He blended right into the background, his tan-and-dark-brown hide a perfect camouflage against the trees and rock.

"Beautiful," Nicola said.

"Magnificent."

"I hope none of the hunters spot him."

Matt looked very somber and very intense. "That old boy's been dodging them for years. He'll make it."

"But if we had a gun?"

"We wouldn't have seen him, then."

Nicola did not question that curious statement. There was something magic, mystical, in the idea.

The big beast stood there unmoving for a full ten minutes before he turned slowly and calculatingly and vanished into the dense forest on the far hillside.

It was a time before Nicola spoke. "I never thought I'd see one," she said. "I mean, the guys all talk about the big old bulls. But you know if they'd seen one, they'd have shot at it. Wait till I tell them.''

But Matt shook his head. ''Let's not. Let's keep the old guy our secret.'' And something in his voice, some uncharacteristic, singular need to share, stirred her so deeply that it was almost a physical pain.

It became one of those silly things—who's going to make the first move?—when either of them inched apart. It seemed the most natural thing in the world to sit there with Matt's arm around her shoulders, natural and comfortable, and yet there was a charge there, a current that Nicola felt flowing between them. Oh yes, it was just like that night six months ago. It seemed that all he had to do was touch her, smile at her, acknowledge that *kid's* existence, and her limbs turned to jelly and her head began to grow light.

''Well,'' Nicola said, ''that was exciting.'' She stood up and stretched. They started back.

He lazed the afternoon away, or so she surmised, because he'd disappeared into his cabin, and she had not seen him since. Maybe he was out on another walk. Maybe he was reading.

She shrugged and bent back over the pile of potato peelings and scraped away. He'd acted that morning as if her company were the most important thing in the world to him. He'd done dishes, helped shake out bedrolls in the sun, gone on that hike. He'd even made the grandfather elk their own special secret. He'd held her hand walking back to camp after she'd tripped once, and he'd smiled and laughed, tipping his head back, the strong cords in his neck working. Yes, he'd behaved as if she mattered. And then he'd simply vanished. Oh well.

Darn him! Why did he have to ignore her like this? Disappointment settled in her stomach like too big a meal.

It was five-thirty by the time the Jeeps came lumbering into camp. Over the front of one of them, strapped to the hood, was a young bull. Someone had been lucky. Evan, she hoped.

And speaking of Evan, Nicola thought, where in the devil *was* Matt? What if the two of them began that one-upmanship routine and the battle raged? Everyone's week would be ruined.

The hunters were dog tired and starving, dusty and scratchy eyed, but undaunted by the long day.

"Hey, Nicola!" Dave Huff's voice. "Come and see what the greater white hunter here bagged!" It was Dave's elk. They strung it up in between the trees—tradition—and told tall tales as to how Dave had tripped over it sleeping in the woods. "Don't believe a word of it," Dave told her, and patted her so hard on the back she jumped. "Oops, sorry," he said. "I forgot you were a girl."

Where was Matt?

Should she warn Evan?

The men tromped inside the main cabin, put their feet up, lit cigars—three of them coughed—and poured themselves stiff brandies. If they behaved like this all year long, Nicola knew, they'd all be dead of strokes.

"Great animal," Evan said to Nicola. "Did you see it? Damn, but I'm jealous. Tomorrow's my turn, boys," he said, brandishing the cigar. "You bet it is."

"Want to put a hundred on it?" Terry Swanson asked, his hunter's eye challenging.

"Sure," Evan said. "A hundred it is."

"Long day," said Eric Field. "My back hurts like crazy."

"I have some liniment," Jon Wolff suggested. "Goot for the muscles."

"I'll try anything."

"Yup," Evan said, "it was a good opening day. We passed a couple other camps on our way back, and no one had a thing hanging. Good work, Ron." He saluted the guide with his drink. "Here's to tomorrow. Cheers."

Down went the brandies, fast.

Where *was* Matt?

She'd have to warn Evan. This wasn't fair, to either of them. She'd pull Evan aside and tell him that... The door opened then, and in he strode. Oddly, Nicola noticed, his boots were muddy. So he hadn't been napping, then....

"Hiya, Evan. That your elk outside?"

"Why," Dave said, "it's Matt! Well, I'll be damned! Matt Cavanaugh!"

"Matt," Jon exclaimed, "goot to see you again. Such a surprise."

"Hello," Ron said, "I'm Mitchell. I take it my wife sent you up? I wondered about the Jeep out back."

"Well," Evan said finally, the wind gone out of his sails, "this *is* a surprise."

Matt nodded. "I couldn't call or write, so here I am."

Evan looked at Ron. "Is there room?"

"He's got the spare bunk in Dave's cabin," Nicola said from the kitchen. "I hope that's okay."

"Glad to have him," Dave said.

"Well." Evan put the cigar down in an ashtray. Clearly he was no longer feeling his oats. "I hope this trip isn't jeopardizing a job or anything like that, Matthew."

"Naw. I took a few days off."

"You going to hunt?" Evan asked.

"Now, Evan," Matt said, picking up the brandy bottle, eyeing the label, "you know I'm squeamish about that stuff."

"You gotta be kidding," Terry Swanson said under his breath, disgusted.

The atmosphere had changed dramatically just since Matt had entered. She'd expected something like this. It wasn't that the guys minded the new face or a nonhunter, really. No. It was the tension, a palpable thing, running like a high-power line between father and son. Everyone felt it.

Nicola could hear a chill wind kicking up dust outside. She threw another log on the fire while the men began to talk among themselves once more. But Evan was silent now. Wary. And Matt was unusually quiet, as well.

She brushed off her hands and caught herself glancing at Matt. Gone was the jaunty, carefree demeanor. Instead, she saw a grimace on his face when he stared at his father, almost as if he were in pain.

Why, she asked herself, had he really come here?

## CHAPTER FIVE

THE NEXT MORNING at five-thirty, over the sourdough pancakes, it started.

"So, Matt, how're things going with you?" Dave Huff asked jovially, helping himself to more maple syrup.

"Pretty good."

Nicola poured Fred another cup of coffee and checked the diminishing pile of pancakes in the middle of the table.

"You been working anywhere interesting lately?" Dave winked. "Oh, you young kids, footloose and fancy-free."

"Well, I was working at—" Matt began.

"*Kid*. He's no kid," Evan snorted. "And he hasn't *worked* a day in his life."

Nicola felt her heart contract in her chest. *Oh no*. She bustled over. "More coffee, Evan?"

But he was glaring at Matt, tight-lipped, and only shook his head at her query.

"Oh, come on, Evan," Dave said, one of the only men in the world who could josh Evan Cavanaugh and get away with it. "I'd like to hear where he's been."

Matt was looking down at his plate, his expression hidden, but Nicola could see a muscle in his jaw tighten.

"Now, where were you, Matt?" Dave pressed, seemingly oblivious to the tension between the father and son.

Matt raised his head, and Nicola could see that his expression was bland. She whispered up a silent prayer of thanks. "Oh, you know me, here and there. I worked at

Haig's Point until last June. It's a great place. My golf game
sure improved."

"I'll have to try the courses there sometime," Huff said.

Evan muttered something under his breath.

"Und so, you are verking out here in Colorado now?"
Jon asked. When Matt nodded, he said, "You vill not find
so much powder skiing as ve have in Canada."

Matt laughed, his carefree self once more. "Maybe not,
but I've got a job and a place to live. And Crested Butte's a
small, friendly town. I think I'll have a good winter."

"Go on," Evan interjected, "ask him about his job."

Jon looked uneasily from Evan to Matt. He was quite
aware of the enmity between the two men, having seen their
act on their ski vacations years before. "Und vat is your
job?" he asked.

"I'm a bartender at this place called the Wooden Nickel.
They say it's real busy during the season. Good tips."

*"Good tips,"* Evan said scornfully.

Nicola went over to him and, under the guise of refilling
his cup, laid a hand on his arm gently. Evan switched his
eyes up to hers and saw the message there. He looked away
quickly, and she hoped he understood her silent plea.

"Hey, Fred," Terry was saying, "you hear the one about
the traveling salesman who stopped at a farm? Well, see, this
farmer's got three daughters..."

Then Eric had one of his own. "Now wait, fellas, I've got
one. Now, let me see, I have to remember the punch line. Oh
yeah.... Well, see, there was this traveling salesman stopped
at a farm, and there was this crippled pig..."

They all laughed at that one, too, even Evan, and Nicola
relaxed. The Coleman lantern hissed and the cabin smelled
of freshly brewed coffee and wood smoke and bacon frying,
a masculine, congenial atmosphere.

"Well, Dave, my good man, are you gonna let someone
else bag a critter today?" Ron asked, blowing smoke across
the table.

"You bet your butt! It's somebody else's turn. Who's gonna be the lucky guy?" Dave asked, grinning.

"I feel lucky as hell," Evan said. "I even dreamed about an elk last night. I could see him in my sights, a big buck, turned sideways so I could get a perfect head shot off. You bet, I'm as good as a hundred dollars richer." He sighted along an imaginary rifle barrel and squeezed an imaginary trigger. "Pow."

"Let's go, men," Ron said, heaving himself up, "and see if we can get Evan that elk. Good breakfast, Nick."

"Great pancakes," Dave said warmly.

The others agreed, complimenting her, and she liked their polite, gentlemanly ways with her. She liked cooking for people who appreciated her efforts; it must be her need for reassurance, she guessed, that made her work so hard to get those compliments.

"You're an awfully good cook, Nicola," Matt said. "I didn't realize how talented you were."

"Thanks." Flushing, she looked down. "But it's not talent, it's just hard work."

He looked at her and smiled. "You would say that, wouldn't you?" He pulled on his orange parka. "You take care today and don't work too hard."

"Oh, I'll be fine, don't worry. Enjoy the hiking today."

He started toward the door, ready to follow the other men, then turned back to her.

"Sorry if things got heated up just now."

"Oh, you mean you and Evan," she said after a second. "I guess it was bound to happen, and, uh, don't mind your dad too much. He's just surprised to see you."

"Sure, Evan's surprised. I saw you give him a look at breakfast. Thanks, but I can fight my own battles."

"Maybe the rest of us would rather not have those battles fought in front of us," she said quietly.

"You've got a point there." His curved, guileless grin came back then, and he seemed to swagger a little as he went through the cabin door into the predawn darkness.

Some of the men returned early that afternoon, while Nicola was putting the last ingredients into the beef Bourguignonne: the wine and chopped onions sautéed with bacon, the mushrooms and tomato paste. But they only grabbed some snacks and went to their cabins for naps. A solid week of hunting was grueling business.

Dinner was another round of off-color jokes, cigars and liquor and a detailed discussion of a near miss by Eric Field. "Goddamn, I had him in my sights! I was waiting until he turned just a bit, then he musta heard something, and just as I squeezed the trigger he jumped and took off. It was so close!"

"Sometimes it's good to wait, sometimes it ain't," Ron said. "Those're the breaks."

"Yeah, tough break," Eric agreed.

"There's always tomorrow," Jon pointed out.

"Sure, tomorrow."

"Yeah."

After dinner, Evan paid up on his bet good-naturedly, and they sat around the fire, stocking feet up, balancing brandy snifters on full bellies. Nicola heated water on Old Bertha and washed up. As she was finishing, Matt got up and started drying dishes.

"You don't have to do that," she said.

"I know." But he kept on drying.

"I'm used to doing it."

"I like to keep my hands busy. Bartenders have to wash and dry glasses all night, you know." He held a glass up to the light, squinted and rubbed a spot over again.

"I guess they would," she said. His hands were lean, like his body, capable, dexterous, his movements sure and efficient. She watched him work out of the corner of her eye. His red plaid shirtsleeves were rolled up; his forearms, swelling from strong wrists, had cords in them that stood out as he reached for a bowl and dried it.

When she was done, she turned away from the sink, leaning back against it, still holding a dish towel. "Thanks," she said.

"My pleasure."

Laughter burst from the group around the fire. Terry stood up and began pantomiming some funny happening. "And then he..." Nicola heard him say. The fire crackled in the old stone fireplace and spat a spark up into the darkness.

"This is a great place," Matt commented.

"It is, yes. Ron does a good job."

"So do you."

"Matt..." She hesitated, looking down at her feet, which were thrust out in front of her, crossed at the ankles.

"What?"

"Well, I was just wondering...why you came up here. Really."

His gaze met hers steadily. "For a little camping and hiking. R and R."

"Oh."

"You don't sound convinced."

"I'm not."

He shrugged. "Why else would I come up here?"

"I don't know."

"Don't be so serious. I'm here to have a blast, to hear a few new jokes, to enjoy the mountains. And now, kid, I'm one beat guy. I'm going to bed. That cold and lonely bed in my cold and lonely cabin."

She frowned. "See you in the morning, Matt."

"That was an opening. You were supposed to take me up on it."

"I'm just one of the guys, remember?"

He raked her with an outrageous leer. "Not in my book, kid."

The next morning was blintzes, tender crepes wrapped around a cheese and cinnamon and vanilla mixture, topped with sour cream. And blueberry muffins and home fries again. It had snowed a little in the night; Nicola had walked through the light dusting on her way to the main cabin.

Fred, losing his reserve finally, was hopping with delight. "They'll be easy to track this morning! Oh boy, it's my day! I can taste success already. How sweet it is!"

"If it snows too hard, we'll have to come back early. These storms can be real bad. Somebody gets caught in one every year," Ron said.

"Let's hurry then," Fred suggested.

"Chow's on," Nicola called.

It didn't snow that day, and Nicola got some hand laundry done in the sink with water she'd heated up. She also washed her hair, then sat with her back to Old Bertha to dry it and read a little more in the novel she'd brought along, not that she'd had much spare time to read.

That evening the hunters returned empty-handed once again, but they'd seen a herd of cow elk in a secluded valley and were going back the next day in search of the bulls. Dinner was pork loin, roasted and stuffed with prunes, and a linzertorte for dessert: ground nuts and butter and sugar in the crust and Mrs. Mitchell's raspberry jam baked in the center.

"Oh God, I'm going to burst," Eric Field said, and everyone laughed at him enviously because he was so skinny.

Matt pushed himself back from the table and set down his coffee cup. "Nicola, that was great. Worth walking twenty miles uphill and freezing all day."

"I'm taking you home to Aspen with me," Dave teased. "Ruthie won't mind. She'd love not having to cook."

"I might ask you for some of your vunderful recipes," Jon said. "So delicious. I could serve them at the lodge."

"I'd be glad to give them to you," Nicola said, flattered.

"For a free week of skiing," Evan advised jokingly.

"Maybe ve could verk something out," Jon replied, not seeing the humor, and everyone laughed again.

"You going into town tomorrow?" Ron asked Nicola.

"Yes, I think so." Town was the tiny, picturesque hamlet of Redstone, fifteen miles away in the Crystal River Valley. "I'm getting short on a lot of things."

"Can you get me a carton of Marlboros? I'm about out," Ron said. He glanced at Jon. "Some of these ex-smokers this week have been bumming my packs. Right, Jon?"

Jon grimaced.

"Sure."

Everyone was tired that night, sitting around sipping drinks, talking desultorily. Terry dozed off, jerked awake, swore, got up and said he was going to bed.

Nicola was checking her supplies and making a shopping list for her foray to the grocery store.

"So, Matthew," she heard Evan say, "doesn't your new boss expect you back at work?"

"Oh, I have the whole week off," Matt replied easily.

"You just started, boy. How can you have the whole week off?"

"It's not busy yet, not until Thanksgiving, when the skiing starts," Matt said evenly.

Nicola looked up. Evan had been tolerating his son for the past couple of days. Things had been going along relatively smoothly—until now.

"Some sense of responsibility! I can tell you, no employee of mine would take a week's vacation when he'd just been hired."

The other men avoided one another's eyes.

"And that job last spring. You got fired. Probably for drinking too much, if the truth be known."

"Lay off, Evan," Matt said lightly. "No one wants to listen to family quarrels."

"You can't keep a job."

"My boss at Haig's Point was a jerk."

"They all are, according to you."

Nicola closed her eyes.

"Boy, am I bushed," Eric said, rising. "See you in the a.m., guys."

Carefully Nicola wrote: butter, milk, parsley, lasagna noodles, oh, and cigarettes for Ron. Her back was bowed to the inevitable onslaught.

"I suppose you've gone through your trust fund," Evan continued. He was like a bulldog; once he had his teeth into something, he couldn't let go.

"Oh, there's a little left," Matt replied offhandedly, as if he hadn't a care in the world, as if his father's argumentative abuse didn't faze him.

He was disappointed in Matt, Nicola told herself. He was hurting and he couldn't help taking it out on his son, but oh, he *could* wait until they were alone.

"Well, Evan," Matt drawled, getting to his feet, "I think we've provided enough entertainment for the evening. Good night, all."

"Take it easy, Matt," Dave Huff said kindly.

*"Guten Nacht,"* Jon said.

"Goddamn kid," Evan muttered when the door was closed behind his son.

"Ah, let him be, Evan," Dave said. "You're not going to change him at this late date."

"I guess not. But, hell, the least he could do is pick up a gun and hunt with it."

Nicola pulled her parka off a wall peg and threw it over her shoulders. "See you in the morning."

"See you, Nick."

Once in her chilly room, she turned on the Coleman lantern, debated whether to build a fire in the potbelly stove but decided not to. She was too tired. She stripped down to her long underwear, shivering, ready to crawl under the down comforter but realized she'd forgotten to turn off the lamp. She stepped gingerly across the cold floor, up to the dresser where the lamp stood, and happened to glance out the window.

She froze. There was a man across the way, leaning against a wall of the main cabin. She only saw him because the moonlight glistened bone white off his face, casting gaunt shadows on his handsome features. She drew in her breath and totally forgot the cold floor.

He looked so different out there alone, stripped of his insouciance, his clever remarks, his dazzling smile. Had the argument with Evan affected him more than he'd let on?

If he was not enjoying himself, why was he here? Why had he come in the first place? He could have hiked around Crested Butte. But if he came to bug Evan, he should be pleased—he'd certainly done *that*.

She studied him as he stood there in the darkness, and she knew it was a terrible thing to do, to intrude on a person's privacy, but she couldn't stop herself. There was something so lonely about the figure out there in the cold, something she recognized, as if he were suffering the same sort of bereavement she herself had so often felt.

Without considering the consequences, without her usual caution, without her promise to herself to be wary, Nicola pulled on her jeans, stepped into her boots and shrugged on her parka. Letting herself out of her cabin, she went out into the cold night and moved silently across the clearing.

The stream in the canyon burbled, muffled male laughter came from the main cabin, and he must not have heard her approach.

"Matt?"

He stiffened, startled, and whirled to face her.

"Sorry, I didn't mean—"

"What are you doing out here?" he asked.

"I meant to ask you that."

"Just getting some fresh air."

"I thought you might be...upset at Evan," she said carefully.

"He's quite a bully, isn't he?"

"Not to me."

"No, not to you."

"There's good in Evan, really there is. I just wish... I mean, why is it that you two are always at each other like that?" She searched his face in the darkness, but the shadows hid any expression that might have enlightened her.

He gave a short, bitter laugh. "What can I say? Evan is so damn competitive, he feels threatened by his own sons. One he chased away, the other is his slave. Poor T.J."

*Poor Matt,* Nicola thought. Aloud she said, "It's a shame."

"Thanks for the thought, kid," he replied nonchalantly.

"I just wondered... when I saw you out here... Well, I guess I shouldn't have bothered you."

There was a pause then, a split second of awareness between them that held Nicola immobile. Matt shifted forward, reached out to touch her cold cheek with a finger, and she felt a tremor of excitement, bright and breathless, rippling outward from his touch. He dropped his hand, started to say something, then gave up and strode away into the night shadows.

TUESDAY MORNING'S BREAKFAST was whole-grain waffles covered with sliced bananas, chopped walnuts and maple syrup.

"Sorry, no home fries today," Nicola said. "I've got to buy more potatoes."

"We'll forgive you this time," Dave said, his pale blue eyes twinkling.

"Let's get going," Evan said impatiently. "We only have a few days left."

Matt leaned back in his chair and stuck his thumbs in his belt. "I don't think I'll go out hiking with you guys today. You mind, Ron?"

"Suit yourself."

"Too tough for you?" Evan asked, prodding.

"Too intense," Matt replied, shooting him a glance. "I think I'll get a ride into Redstone with Nick here."

She looked up, surprised.

"Is that okay with you?" Matt asked her.

"Sure. Why not?" But there was hesitation in her voice.

The other men were on their way out. "Maybe he's got the right idea," Eric said. "Warm and cozy and good company."

"I'd rather bag an elk," Evan muttered.

"See you later, kids," Dave called over his shoulder.

There was silence when the hunters left except for their voices outside and the growl of the Jeeps starting, then dying away. Nicola stayed deliberately busy, filling the big pot with water from the pump, starting to lift it.

"Here, let me," Matt said at her shoulder, very close behind her. She was afraid to move, afraid she'd touch him, but he stepped in front of her and lifted the pot onto Bertha.

"Ron'll have to start paying you," Nicola said too brightly.

"Perhaps we can *verk* something out," he replied, imitating Jon so comically that she couldn't help laughing.

"You really want to go into Redstone?" she asked, looking at him.

"Well, to tell the truth, I have to check in with my boss. I promised." He leaned close to her and whispered conspiratorially, "I just didn't want Evan to find out I really am responsible. It would ruin my image."

"Oh, I see." She stood there, hands on hips, dishrag in one fist, studying him. He meant it; he really meant it. He wanted his father to think the worst of him. He wanted to punish Evan. "Won't you two ever grow up?"

He grinned. "Hey, where would the fun be then?"

She began to clear the table, wiping at the spills of sticky syrup, turning her back to him. *Men.* They never grew up, not any of them. They never seemed to suffer any sort of sadness for long. They just used women and important words but meant nothing by those words. They didn't even know the real meaning of them. If Nicola ever found a man who meant what he said, who didn't play juvenile games, she'd probably fall in love on the spot.

"You're mad at me," Matt said from behind her.

She shook her head silently, piling dirty dishes up.

"You are, I can tell. You think I'm immature and irritating, like Evan does."

She carried the dishes to the old tin sink and checked the water on the stove. "What if I do?"

When she turned to retrace her footsteps to the table, he was there in front of her, blocking the way. "Don't be mad. It's not worth the effort, kid." Then he tilted her chin up and stared down into her eyes. He was so close she could feel his warm breath and smell the fresh scent of him. His expression was serious for once, his mouth a straight line instead of a curve, his dark brows drawn together. They stood that way for too long, and her heart pounded in her chest as if it would fly through her rib cage. She could feel her cheeks flushing and heat crawling up her neck.

"Matt," she finally whispered, her mouth dry.

"You're as pretty as a picture, Nicky," he replied softly.

"Matt, don't."

He dropped his hand, then gave her an impudent smile. "And a damn good cook, besides."

The spell was broken, and maybe he'd meant that to happen. She cleared the table, scrubbed it clean, soaked the dishes, all in silence. And she washed them while Matt dried, in silence, too, except that he whistled popular tunes while he worked, leaning one buttock against the counter, casual and lazy and much too good-looking.

More than an hour later, her chores done, Nicola checked her shopping list, added a few things and took her coat off the peg. "You ready?" she asked.

"Sure. We can take my Jeep. Or would you rather drive?"

"You drive." That'd keep his hands and his eyes busy, she figured.

It took thirty minutes to reach Redstone, a two-block-long village down in the valley, a tiny place right on the banks of the Crystal River, its main road overhung by giant cottonwood trees. The stores and houses were all fixed up in quaint Victorian style, and up on a hill overlooking the town was the famous haunted mansion called the Redstone Castle, built by coal baron John Cleveland Osgood at the turn of the century. Redstone had been planned originally to house workers for the old coke furnaces just outside of town, but it was now mainly a tourist haven.

"Where can I find a phone?" Matt asked as soon as they turned off the highway and crossed the river on a rickety old bridge that gave onto the one and only street Redstone boasted.

"I guess the tourist information building would be the easiest." It occurred to Nicola momentarily to wonder at this uncharacteristic single-mindedness of Matt and his telephone call, but she directed him to the small log building that was also an art gallery and souvenir shop. It was open because of hunting season but would close soon, as no one ventured to Redstone in the winter, preferring the opposite end of the valley, where the ski resort of Aspen was located.

He parked in front and they went in. "There's the phone," Nicola said, pointing.

"Oh, good, I'll just be a second."

She nodded to the girl behind the counter. "Nice day," she commented.

"It's been a good fall." Which Nicola took to mean lots of hunters buying beer and ammo and postcards.

Idly she looked at the postcard displays. Matt had his back to her, but he was dialing a number on the old-fashioned black wall phone. She could hear the dial whirl, and it whirled too many times, as all of western Colorado used the same area code, 303, and you didn't need to dial that code at all to reach Crested Butte.

She kept looking through postcards, not even seeing the scenes of the Maroon Peak or Redstone Castle or the Hot Springs Pool in nearby Glenwood Springs. She wondered who Matt really was calling and why he'd lied to her, why he'd *bothered* lying to her. So maybe it was a girl, not his boss. Did she care? *Big secret*.

She listened to his voice, low and urgent, and couldn't help straining to hear. He was probably trying to convince this femme fatale to come out and meet him here, or something like that. And Nicola bet he could be persuasive, very persuasive. However, he had a hand up to the receiver, muffling his voice, and she couldn't really hear a thing. Not that she'd wanted to.

He hung up finally, looking a little thoughtful. Probably the woman had turned him down. Smart girl. "Okay, that's done," he said. "I'm not needed yet."

"Hmm. Well, that's good." She'd better play along. No sense embarrassing them both. Still, the idea that he'd lied to her, the notion that he'd just been talking to another woman, was more unsettling than she cared to admit.

"So, onward to the grocery store, right?" he was saying.

"Right."

She bought five big bags full of groceries, paid with one of Ron's signed checks, and they carried them all out and wedged them in the back seat of the Jeep.

"There," she said, "that'll be it for the week."

He shut the flimsy Jeep door, latching it after three tries. "Now, after all that hard work, how about a beer?"

"A beer? Isn't it a little early?"

He checked his watch. "Hell, no. It's after eleven. Tell you what, you get a beer *and* a burger for lunch. What do you say?"

"Well, I have to get back and start . . ."

"Come on, take a break. I'm starved myself."

"Okay, a quick one."

There was only one saloon in town, in the Redstone Inn. They sat at the bar, and Matt ordered two draft beers and two burgers with the works. And French fries.

"Not as classy as your cooking," he explained, "but you need a break from time to time."

They could see themselves in the mirror behind the bar, the only customers in town this time of day: a handsome man in a hunter's plaid shirt who looked utterly at ease, and a dark-haired girl who was a little tense, a little distracted, halfway between laughter and tears.

*Why did I agree to this?* Nicola thought, switching her eyes away from the mirror. *What's wrong with me?* Matt was not the kind of man she liked or wanted to like. Why did fate keep throwing them together? Or was it fate? And why was he pursuing her when it was that woman on the phone he really wanted?

But Matt was talking to the girl behind the bar, a snazzy blonde dressed in tight jeans and a satin cowboy shirt. "Oh, it sure does liven up in here come evening," the girl was saying. "All those hunters away from Big Mama and rarin' to go."

"I'll bet. And you're the belle of the ball. You work here all winter?" Matt asked, turned on his charm like a well-oiled motor.

"No, I work in Aspen in the winter."

"You don't say. You know, I'm bartending in Crested Butte myself. Are the skiers big tippers?"

The blonde rolled big blue eyes. "Are they ever!"

"Maybe I'll come up to Aspen skiing this winter. I'll look you up. Where do you work?"

"The Red Onion."

"Sure, I've heard of it."

The girl leaned on the bar, her satin-sheathed breasts resting on the polished wood. "Hey, you do that. Ask for Sunny."

"I'll do that . . . Sunny."

*Oh boy,* Nicola thought. She was getting to see him in action. And as far as Sunny was concerned, it wouldn't have mattered if Matt had been with a girl or alone. All's fair in love and war was Sunny's motto, obviously. Nicola sipped at her beer and ate the hamburger, which wasn't at all bad. Matt ate and drank, still talking to Sunny. He did draw Nicola into the conversation, she had to admit, but the blond girl behind the bar barely noticed her existence. Not that it mattered.

Sunny was sending off signals, loud and clear, embarrassingly clear.

"Matt, we have to go," Nicola said quietly. "I have dinner to fix."

"Oh, sure. Well, Sunny, it's been fun. My sister here has to get back. Take care."

"See you on the hill this winter," Sunny cooed coyly.

Matt waved, stuck a bill under a plate and turned to go, but not before Nicola noticed two things: the bill was a ten-dollar one, and his beer glass was still half-full.

Strange, for a lush. The large tip, on the other hand, wasn't a bit odd.

"What was with the sister routine?" she asked once they were outside.

"I didn't want to hurt Sunny's feelings," he said. "I didn't want her to realize I like you better."

"Oh, Matt."

"There I go being immature again, right?"

She got into the Jeep and folded her arms across her chest, and he climbed in beside her. "Nicola, I was just being friendly. I like to talk to people."

"Your *sister*."

"Jealous, kid?" he asked impertinently.

She whirled to face him. "The only thing I might have to be jealous of were her oversized mammary glands!"

"Yés, they were considerable, weren't they?" Chuckling, he started up the Jeep and rumbled toward the highway.

They bounced in silence for a time, until Nicola felt foolish and unfolded her arms. "Let me ask you one thing, Matthew Cavanaugh."

"Sure, anything."

"Why do I keep running into you? I mean, I have barely seen you since I was ten, and all of a sudden, wherever I turn, there you are."

"Coincidence."

"No."

"Luck?" He laughed, then and laid a hand on her knee. "Didn't I say we should get to know each other better? I think I said that."

"Why?"

"Because I like you."

His hand was on her knee, warm and solid, but then he had to steer around a large pothole on the road and took it away. The spot still felt warm, though.

"Come on, Nicky, relax. Aren't I allowed to like you?"

She was confused. It would be easy to believe him, pleasant and flattering, and what harm could come of a simple friendship? On the other hand, her instincts, her experience, told her that he was dangerous. He could hurt her. Better safe than sorry.

"Well, can't I?" he pressed.

"You can if you want to," she said flatly, "but it may not do you a bit of good."

He laughed at that, throwing his head back, a free laughter that made her want to laugh with him. But she didn't.

They climbed up the highway to McClure Pass, and Matt turned off onto the dirt road to the hunting camp. It was cooler up here; a few clouds were scudding in from the west, but the good weather still held. Matt maneuvered the Jeep over rocks, around potholes, up hills, jouncing along the rough terrain. Nicola was thinking of what she had to do first: boil the rice, as it took forever at this altitude. Stuff the capons. *They'd* take all afternoon. It was a moment before she realized that the Jeep was at a standstill. She glanced over at Matt only to find him turned toward her, his left arm resting on the steering wheel, his right arm resting on the back of her seat.

"Is something... I mean, is the Jeep broken?" she asked.

"No."

"Then . . . ?"

"Nicola." He said it caressingly, and abruptly she was afraid. She froze, holding her breath, knowing what was coming, terrified but knowing and perversely longing for it. The moth flying into the flame.

His right hand moved a little, going to the back of her head, creating a small, insistent pressure that she gave in to. Closer. Their lips met softly, then, harder. Inside Nicola was a new sensation, a wonderful, wild sensation, as if she were for the first time in her life free of all restraint, feeling pleasure in a purity she never knew existed, a white-hot shaft of wonder that scalded her all the way to her belly. She felt a frantic desire to touch every part of him, to pull him close, to fuse herself with him, to lose herself in the sensations, in him, for a moment of oblivion.

They broke apart finally, and reality came flooding back to her. Her breath came in great, shuddering gasps, and she felt dizzy.

"Nicola," he said again, his hand still on the back of her head.

She wanted to run, to hide from him, from her own response. She felt the desperation of a hunted creature, the deathly confusion of the prey, but she could only sit there rooted to the spot, held there by pride and Matt's knowing blue eyes.

# CHAPTER SIX

THE ACCIDENT HAPPENED at dawn.

Most of the men, all but Evan and Eric and Fred, had already gone up in the first Jeep to their hunting spots, but the second Jeep, it was discovered, had a flat. The three men quickly changed the tire.

Nicola saw it happen. She was out in front of the main cabin, waving goodbye to the men. "Too bad about the flat," she said, lifting her hand to see them off, when abruptly and without warning there was a whooshing sound, and a puff of dust kicked up in the dirt right next to Evan's foot. An instant later came the crack of the gunshot echoing through the valley.

The tableau remained stationary for a split second—everyone paralyzed in whatever position the shot had found them, like one of the lifelike dioramas in a natural history museum. The pause seemed to last forever, yet it was over in an instant, the very instant Eric shouted, "Hit the ground! Holy—"

They all reacted immediately and mindlessly, dropping to the earth, covering their heads, waiting for another shot to whistle by and plow itself into a solid object.

Nicola lay there, too, stiff, her skin quivering, waiting for that shot, that high-powered bullet that would rip into Evan or Fred or Eric or her. It was an endless wait.

Eventually someone let out a pent-up breath, someone else moved, someone whistled, a long, low, shaky sound.

"I think it's okay," Fred said. "We can get up now. God, that was close." He climbed to his feet, dusting himself off, staring in the direction from which the shot had come.

"Evan," Nicola breathed, still shocked and breathless, "are you all right?" She hurried to his side and took his arm.

"Hey," he said, trying to laugh, "that was a close one. I'd like to get my hands on the idiot who fired that rifle."

"How in God's name," Eric was saying, "could someone mistake a man—a man in bright orange standing next to a Jeep in the middle of camp—for a goldarn elk?"

No one had an answer to that one.

Nicola gave the near miss a lot of consideration that morning as she worked, but another subject kept intruding into her musings, too: Matt and the Jeep ride back from Redstone. What a blind, pathetic thing she'd done, letting him see her out of control, panting after him, clinging to him, mindlessly in need. Stupid, stupid, stupid!

Yet she had responded. And where there was smoke, there was fire. Darn him with those magic blue eyes and that all-knowing grin of his. For a moment, she'd really felt that Matt cared about her, that he was trying to tell her something, or show her something, by that kiss. For a moment... Darn, he was a puzzle to her! Why, why did he keep turning up like a bad penny?

She shook her head and sighed and went back to work. Evan. He was the one she had to think about. Eric Field had, of course, put it in a nutshell. Evan had been climbing into a Jeep, the main cabin directly behind him, his orange coat and hat on. How had that hunter mistaken him for game?

Or maybe, just maybe, it had not been an accident.

She was folding cloth napkins, sitting at the table, when suddenly she stopped cold and dropped the linen.

Hadn't it been only days ago, around November 1, that Evan had announced to the press that he was definitely calling in those Costa Plata loans? And the political experts had given the president of that country, Cisernos, just a short time at the outside for his junta to collapse. Had someone from Costa Plata panicked? Was someone seeking revenge?

She recalled with utter clarity Reynaldo Reyes's threat: call in those loans and Evan was a dead man.

*Come on, Nicola, that's crazy.*

But was it?

Anyone could have found out Evan's whereabouts this week. And wouldn't a hunting "accident" be convenient?

Everyone who'd been in camp when the shot had narrowly missed Evan, knew the general direction from which it had come. She wondered, as she began to fold napkins again, if the hunter, the would-be hunter, had been sitting in his spot just waiting. And if so, wouldn't there be evidence, like broken branches or flattened down grass, a discarded Styrofoam coffee cup, a chewing gum wrapper, *something*? If a man had been there for a long time, waiting, then maybe he'd left some kind of evidence behind—especially after missing his target. He'd have run, and quickly. And he could have been careless.

Nicola knew she was really reaching when she laced up her heavy boots and put on her parka and gloves. She'd never find the spot. She didn't even know what exactly she was looking for. Nevertheless, she headed out of camp on foot and hiked to the northwest, having sighted a couple of high spots where a man might have waited and watched, staring toward the camp.

It was slow going. Hiking around in the meadow was one thing, but the path she took, a sort of crisscross game trial, led her through unbroken territory. Lots of thicket and buck brush, lots of hidden holes she turned her ankles in, lots of fallen logs. And she was climbing, to boot.

Figuring that a hunting rifle with a good scope could have an accurate range of a couple hundred yards, she pushed on up the steep mountainside, zigzagging the area, her eyes to the ground. It was not only tedious walking, but seemingly futile, as well. Sure, it was easy standing in front of the cabin and looking up, deciding where the shot might have originated, but actually searching the rough terrain...

*This is useless,* she thought, breathing hard. Maybe it had been an accident, after all. And even if it hadn't been, she wasn't likely to find a darn thing.

She was ready to head back to camp, when she crossed an old mining road that hadn't been used in years. Brush and weeds had inched down the embankment over time and obscured the way, and a part of the road had even slid over the cliff, probably in a spring mudslide. Curious, she followed it, finding the way much easier than breaking ground through the woods. If she followed it downward long enough, she thought, it might even bring her out in the meadow somewhere, and she'd be home free. What a waste of an hour this had been.

She'd been following footprints for nearly thirty yards before the fact even registered in her head. The old road was muddy from the recent snowfall, and the prints were as fresh as some of the deer droppings she was seeing.

"Wow," Nicola whispered, realizing that she might just have come across the intruder's path. "You don't suppose...?"

She followed the tracks for a few more yards, then lost them. Backtracking, she could see where the man had left the trail and headed off into the woods. She glanced at her watch. It was getting late, and dinner still had to be prepared. But she might be onto something here.

She trudged through a dark stand of firs, the pinecones crunching beneath her boots, the fallen needles smelling fresh and damp. Then she broke out into a clearing, a small, steep hillside, at the bottom of which were some rocks. Was this the spot she'd viewed from the cabin? Trying to keep from breaking into an uncontrolled run down the hill, Nicola stepped carefully, keeping her balance. In an unmelted patch of snow, she saw a single footprint and her heart began a rapid beating. *Someone* had come this way. And recently.

The rock escarpment, three massive boulders balancing on a perilous cliff, kept its secrets. There were no prints, no signs of anyone having ever been there. She looked around the area, careful to stay away from the edge, and was disappointed to see nothing whatsoever. Shrugging, figuring she'd been following a perfectly innocent hunter, and angry that she'd wasted so much time, she turned around sharply, ready to beat a quick path home.

She saw it then. The sunlight bounced off the metal and struck her squarely in the eye. Nicola walked over to the grassy spot, leaned over and picked up the shell casing. She was no rifle buff, but it sure looked like a 30-06, a very common caliber of ammunition. Excited, she scoured the area. Yes! There were some depressions in the grass. Someone could have been sitting or kneeling right there . . . and, oh wow, a cigarette butt. No, three of them! On the paper just below the filters was stamped the name Marlboro.

Several thoughts invaded her mind at once. First, to smoke three cigarettes took time. Whoever had been there had been there for a while. Waiting for a clear shot of Evan? And secondly, hadn't she just bought Ron a whole carton of Marlboros? He'd said something about people bumming his cigarettes . . . But who? Who had he meant? They were all smoking cigars every night, but who was smoking cigarettes?

"It's amazing," came a voice that made her jump out of her skin, "the people you find roaming the woods."

Nicola's hand flew to her heart. "Damn it all, Matt Cavanaugh, you scared me out of my wits! Darn you!"

"Sorry," he said, smiling, striding up to her. "But I didn't see you."

"I bet."

"Honest. I came along the ridge. Anyway, what in the devil are you doing up here?"

Nicola eyed him carefully. "I might ask you the same thing."

"Now what does it look like I'm doing—swimming?"

"Ha, ha." She watched as he took a long drink from his water bottle, then passed it to her. "Thanks." She drank, thirstier than she'd realized, and wiped her mouth on her sleeve. "Well," she said, gazing up at him boldly, holding her own, "you left with the first Jeep this morning, so I guess you haven't heard yet."

"Heard what?"

While he rocked back on his heels and listened, hardly believing, she told him the whole story. Then she stuck out her hand and unfolded her fist. "A shell casing," she said, "and these cigarette butts. They're Marlboros," she concluded, satisfied.

"Right you are, Marlboros," he said, taking them from her. "This *is* Marlboro country, Nicky. Plenty of people smoke the things."

"You aren't taking this one bit seriously, are you?"

"An assassination attempt on Evan?" he said, trying to hide a smile. "Come on, kid, that's kind of farfetched, isn't it?"

She shot him a disgruntled look. "You were there when that Reyes character threatened Evan. And don't you think it's a little too coincidental that Evan nearly gets shot just days after he tells the world he's calling in those loans?"

"So he is going through with it?"

"Don't you read, Matt?" she asked.

"Hey, Crested Butte is one laid-back town, Nicky. We hardly get up in the morning and run out front to get the *New York Times*."

"So you don't even care about Evan's safety, do you." It wasn't a question. "And here I've got evidence, right in my hand, and you ignore it."

"Really," Matt said, trying to sound contrite, "I just don't see what's got you so fired up."

"I don't suppose you would."

They hiked back to camp in silence, and Nicola could not help but question his complacent attitude. How could a son possibly be so unfeeling, so out of touch with a parent's troubles? She glanced at him several times, then shook her head in wonder.

NICOLA WAS LATE putting dinner on the table, and the men, some of them, at least, were in a foul mood. Two had missed shots at a bull elk, and one had sprained his ankle, Terry Swanson, the avid, gung ho hunter from North Carolina.

"How am I going to hunt like this?" he said, chewing on his cigar in disgust, his swollen ankle up on a chair.

"You could find a good spot and sit there," Eric suggested.

"That's how much you know," Swanson spat back. "Californians."

Jon Wolff was quiet, as well, barely exclaiming over Nicola's fare; evidently he'd spent the whole day hiking the harder terrain and had been one of the men to miss a shot.

"There's tomorrow," Ron suggested, casting Nicola a helpless glance. "We'll hang another in camp tomorrow. I can feel it. Weather's turning, too. Snow in the air. Right, Nick?"

She was serving up second helpings of creamed carrots. "You bet. We're in for a real blow. That'll move the animals around." She caught Matt's eye then, inadvertently, and looked away too quickly. How *could* she have kissed him? But worse, far, far worse, he knew she'd responded like a lovesick spinster. He probably felt sorry for her. *Here, let's throw the lady a bone or two, it doesn't have to mean a thing. Do her a favor.* Oh God.

Where had those promises she'd made herself gone? How could she have done that? A time machine, that's what she needed, a way of getting another chance. Given that second chance, she'd repel his advance, say all kinds of right-on things and ease out of the situation like a pro. But he knew she was insecure and hopeless around men. Sure he did. And he'd taken advantage.

"Carrots?"

"What?" Nicola said, shaken from her reverie.

It was Dave. "I asked for more carrots, Nick. Earth to Nick, come in Nick." He got a laugh from the group.

"Very funny," she said, spooning Dave a heaping pile. "Eat them. They're good for your eyesight. Maybe you'll hunt better tomorrow."

"Got me!" Huff said admiringly.

How could Matt take everything so casually? How could he not care about Evan's safety? No matter their relationship—and half the fault was Evan's—Matt should at least have responded with...with alarm, with worry, at least with concern when she'd told him about the shot. She fixed him with a dark glare.

So far, Nicola had kept secret her find up in the woods that day. She'd been planning to show everyone immediately, but something held her back, an invisible hand of warning. All evening she kept thinking about those cigarette butts and about the other Jeep having left at least a half hour before Evan's. Anyone could have hiked to that place on the escarpment, and some of them were smokers, too.

Eric, the Californian? No one knew much about him. Was he a...a hit man? Oh my gosh....

Or that Terry Swanson, the drinker who never got too drunk, with his thick, North Carolinian accent. He'd had plenty of experience with guns. How had he really sprained his ankle—running from that spot after he'd missed? Nicola glanced over at him from the kitchen, eyeing him speculatively.

It was Jon Wolff, though, she suddenly remembered, who'd been bumming cigarettes. She looked at him, at his sharp, German features, his tall, lean build. Maybe Jon had taken that potshot at Evan. For money? For political reasons? There certainly were a lot of Austrians who had emigrated to Central America, maybe to Costa Plata. Did Jon, or someone close to him, have interests there?

*Whoa,* Nicola thought. She was sure letting the old imagination fly. Next thing, she'd be thinking Ron did it—a prearranged payoff from a Costa Plata source. *Sure, Nick.*

Regardless, she had to get Evan aside and show him what she'd found. He had to be warned. Just in case.

The men were, needless to say, discussing hunting safety when she served dessert. No one had forgotten the near miss that morning, apparently. And maybe it was just that, after all, an accident—a stupid, half-blind hunter, a bullet that had ricocheted.

Casually she tapped Evan on the shoulder and nodded toward the door. No one paid him any mind when he stood, stretched and put on his coat. Nor did anyone think about Nicola's departure, or so she thought. What neither she nor Evan saw was Matt's somber gaze following them out the door.

"My, Nicola," Evan said, zipping up his parka, "you're looking awfully mysterious."

Nicola, too, zipped up and thrust her hands in her pockets. "I had to talk to you alone," she began, pacing back and forth in front of him, stomping her feet in the cold. "It's about that accident this morning."

"Come on," Evan said, shaking his head, "that's all I've listened to today."

"Well, I'm sorry," she said, "but you have to listen again. There's something I've got to show you."

The cabin door opened and closed then, and one of the men stepped into the shadows toward them. "What's going on?" It was Matt.

Darn. He'd only make light of everything. "I'm having a private conversation with Evan," she stated, wishing he'd go away.

"Don't tell me," he said, "it's about 30-06 shell casings and Marlboros."

"That's right," Nicola said, "and I intend to have my say."

"What's this all about?" Evan asked.

"Oh, Nicky here'll tell you," Matt replied. He looked her in the eye then and nodded. "Go ahead."

Nicola produced the casing and cigarette butts from her pocket and handed them to Evan. She told him how she'd found them and gave him a detailed summary of her theory. "It's just too coincidental," she said, "your calling in those loans, that Reyes's threat, and now this."

Evan sighed. "Nicola, I appreciate your concern, honestly I do, but the whole thing's preposterous." He handed the things back to her.

"It's not!" she insisted.

"Television," Evan said, scoffing, "and all those thrillers you kids read. It's making you confuse fantasy and reality."

Nicola shook her head in frustration. "Why are you so stubborn, Evan?"

"Me? I'd call it sensible. Some nut made a mistake this morning. That's all. Hunting accidents happen every day."

"I'd tell you I think Nicola's got a point, but you always know best, Evan," Matt said sarcastically.

"Well, well," Evan said, turning to him. "I'd almost think you give a damn."

"Don't read too much into a simple statement," Matt replied.

"Come on, you two, *please*. This is serious," Nicola begged, but they were ignoring her.

"Look, Evan, I'm really not in the mood to argue. Do whatever you want, stay and get shot, it's none of my business."

"You know what you are?" Evan said. "You're a coward, boy. It would be just like you to turn tail and run when the going got tough. You're a wet-behind-the-ears kid, not to mention a bum. Don't tell *me* what to do when you can't even get your own act together."

They faced off like two snarling dogs, neither giving ground. Nicola, afraid to move, stayed in the shadows and felt utterly helpless. Evan's face, turned to the light from the cabin, was diffused with red, and Matt's profile, partially obscured, looked pale and ghostly.

"Well?" Evan was saying, "none of your smart-alecky remarks, boy? Nothing to say?"

"Oh," Matt replied coolly, bitterly, "I have plenty to say, Evan. But now's not the time or place."

"I think the timing is perfect, boy. This has been coming."

Matt folded his arms across his chest. "You really want to hear it, don't you?"

"Please," Nicola tried, her voice a whisper. Oh God, why did they have to do this to each other?

Neither seemed to have heard her plea. Evan thrust his face toward Matt's. "Why don't you get what's eating you off your chest, boy?"

"Okay, fine. I don't mind at all telling you what a lousy father you are, Evan. You drive me out of the house every time I see you. You always have. Even when I was a kid, you pushed and pushed. 'Say, Matt, a B's decent, but let's try for an A next time.... Oh, Matt, I know you won that swim meet, but you could extend your arms more.' Yeah, Evan," Matt said, boiling now, "you're the reason I'm a bum. And as for my brother—"

"What about T.J.?" Evan was in a rage. "What right do you have to criticize him?"

"Plenty. You've driven the guy half out of his mind. You've held the presidency of the family bank over his head for ten years now, dangling it like a carrot. And Mom, she's been in the middle of it all. Just look at how T.J. has to cling to her skirts because he can't talk to you. You're driving them both nuts, Evan!"

"Go to hell."

"Maybe I will. But I'll see you there, Evan, you can bet on that." Matt stormed back into the cabin abruptly, his face ashen, his hands held at his sides in white-knuckled fists. Seconds later he emerged, a bottle of Wild Turkey tucked under his arm, and strode toward his own cabin.

"Go ahead," Evan yelled after him, "get drunk! You couldn't possibly act like a man, could you?"

All the while Nicola was standing there, hugging herself with her arms, shaking, trying not to cry. The door of the main cabin was open, a rectangle of light spilling out onto the ground, silence coming from within. They'd heard. They'd heard it all, and to a man, they were embarrassed. How could Evan and Matt have done such a cruel thing—not just to themselves, but to everyone?

Dutifully, quietly, she went in and cleaned up the kitchen. Slowly the men began to talk again, their voices low, their eyes avoiding Evan, who sat apart from them, brooding, still hot under the collar. And all the while, she kept seeing Matt's face, pale with rage, beyond frustration. Why did she feel so badly for him? He'd get over it, probably already had, in fact. Why, he probably wasn't even as upset by the fight as *she'd* been. But he'd been so pale; she'd never seen anyone white with fury before, she'd only read the term in books.

Oh Lord....

Dave Huff was talking to Evan. He didn't look as if he were ready to turn in yet. That meant Matt was alone in the cabin, alone with a bottle of Wild Turkey and his thoughts. Alone with the aftermath of a terrible anger and no one to talk to. She took up her parka again, said good-night and headed out along the line of cabins.

"Matt?" She rapped lightly on his door. "It's me. Can I come in?"

"Suit yourself."

She pushed open the door and found him sitting on his bunk, his back to the wall, his knees up, arms hanging loosely over them, the bottle in one hand.

She forced an encouraging smile. "You aren't going to drink that whole thing, are you? I mean, it won't help."

"Don't play shrink with me," he said tightly. "I'm not in the mood."

She sighed, still poised half in the door, half out. "Okay, I won't. But I think you should consider that Evan is probably frightened. But you know how he is."

"Oh yes, I do know that." He took a long swig. At least, when he tipped up the bottle, she could see that it was still nearly full.

"Well," she said, shifting her weight to the other foot, "do you want to talk?"

He hung the bottle over his knee again, negligently, but his face, for once, looked all of his thirty-eight years. For a long, uncomfortable moment, he stared at her, as if deciding. Finally, when she was crawling with tension, he spoke. "Come here."

Tentatively Nicola closed the door and walked to the bed. She sat down gingerly. Her back was to him, and she could sense his reaching out, his fingers touching her long hair lightly—she could feel the need oozing from him like blood from an open wound. Where was the carefree Matt now?

Slowly he pulled her back until she rested in the crook of his arm, her head against his chest. She could hear the heavy beating of his heart. This was how it should have been between a man and a woman, she thought, open and honest, sharing the good and the bad.

Nicola knew he was going to kiss her. The long, corded muscles in his chest and arms were tightening, rippling, anticipating. He'd press her to him, turn her face to his and cover her mouth with those warm lips. She could almost taste him, and she prepared herself.

"Nicky," he whispered, his arm flexing, his hand rubbing her fingers, "this isn't going to help."

Her heart squeezed. Did he think she'd come there to offer herself as if she were some kind of a pill or something?

Sensing her alarm, he laughed lightly. "Said that badly, didn't I? What I meant, what I should have said, is that I need to be alone right now."

"Oh."

"Hey—" he ruffled her hair gently "—I know I must be nuts. I'll get over it, and I'll rue the night I let you go so easily."

"Will you, Matt?" she asked, easing away from his hold. "Will you?" But she never got an answer.

THAT NIGHT, sleep, which normally came to her quickly, was elusive. She couldn't help lying there beneath her down quilt in the cold darkness and wondering about the parallels of their lives. At times, hers seemed worse. At least Matt didn't have a mother who was unable to cope with life, an unhappy woman who had nothing left to offer but tears. And sometimes she'd have given anything to have a good, sound argument with Wentworth. *Something* was better than nothing. But she had her work and her independence, and maybe someday Went would slow down and have time for her. There was always hope.

But Matt. Half his life was already gone, and he'd made nothing of it. And one thing was for sure: a man did not so easily find opportunity in his middle years. He had to already know how to go out into the world and make things happen. Matt had no experience with success; he deliberately avoided it.

Conflicting emotions buffeted her every time she envisioned him. She'd felt wonderfully alive in his arms, trembling with awakened sensation and need. And yet the very pleasure he'd brought her also scared her half to death. To be so dependent on someone else, on a man, when previously she'd stood up, strong and self-sufficient, facing life unencumbered—it was frightening.

She decided that night in the cold silence of her room. She decided that this game she was letting herself be drawn into—the male-female game—was no good. She didn't know how to play it, nor did she want to. She'd made a dumb mistake going to him that night, playing the expected role, but she wouldn't repeat it. A moth might fly into a flame and die, but *she* had another chance.

The next morning she made her way through the cold darkness to the main cabin and lit the Coleman lamps, determined. She wouldn't have lost anything—there hadn't been anything between them to lose. This was it. They were only acquaintances, after all. It wasn't too late.

She lit the wood in the stove, pulled out her pots and pans and then saw it: a small, folded, white piece of paper propped on a burner. She opened it, a hand of foreboding brushing her heart.

Nicky,
Sorry, but I had to get back to work. Say my good-byes, will you?
                                        Matt

She looked at the note once more, staring at it, blinking away the moisture in her eyes. Then she crushed it in her hand, pulled open the door of the firebox and tossed it in.

## CHAPTER SEVEN

MATT BOUNCED ON THE SEAT of the Jeep. It was still dark out, and he was driving too fast, but he felt the powerful urge to put the hunting camp behind him as quickly as possible.

A hideous thought prodded his mind as he steered: his old man deserved everything coming to him. Yet a part of Matt loved Evan; a part of him still remembered when he'd been a small boy and his father had taken him riding and skiing and camping and they'd had great times, father-and-son stuff. So what had happened?

Things must have degenerated during Matt's teenage years, the time a boy had to struggle to rid himself of his father's control. The old king against the young one. In primitive societies, the young king had to kill the old one. In civilized ones, they were only allowed to quarrel. Some fathers, Matt guessed, were able to accept the independence of their sons, but Evan never had. He wanted to run their lives. He *did* run T.J.'s.

Matt pulled the steering wheel sharply to the left to avoid a deep rut. He wondered what Evan would think if he knew what Matt actually did for a living. Would he respect his son then? Or would his present censure merely attach itself to this new information?

*Ah, hell,* Matt mused, *who cares?*

But then he recalled, without a bridging thought, as if so many years had not gone by, the pain and wild frustration of being powerless against his father, the injustice of it. It was an old story, a cliché, but that didn't lessen the suffering a boy went through. His estrangement from his family had begun long before Ned Copple had gotten his hooks into Matt. What bothered him was that it still hurt so much.

It was well past first light when Matt made the summit of Kebler Pass. Crested Butte was a nice little town, hidden away from the hustle and bustle of the real world. Too bad he'd be leaving it so soon.

Matt had gotten a room in an old painted Victorian bed-and-breakfast place called the Brass Horse. It was inexpensive and strictly for transients, young college types taking a semester off to work and ski in the Rockies. He made his way up the steps quietly and turned the key in his lock, letting himself into his room, tossing his duffel bag onto the bed. He picked up the phone and dialed without even taking time for a much needed shower.

The call was answered on the second ring. "Copple here."

"It's Matt. Listen," he said, kicking off his muddy boots, "we've got real problems."

"Your father?"

"Exactly. Someone took a shot at him yesterday morning, and I couldn't get to the guy before he took off."

"Damn. I take it Evan's all right?"

"Fine. The person missed. Trouble is, Evan's not taking it seriously."

"He wouldn't."

"I had to leave the camp and get in touch with you. And I'm going to have to dump this cover and head back to New York, pronto."

"I don't like it, Matt. Evan's going to catch on."

"I don't have a choice, Ned. It's bad enough that he's up there in that camp unprotected as it is."

"You're in Crested Butte?"

"Right. And tomorrow I'll be in New York. I don't have the slightest idea *what* I'm going to tell my folks, either. I just know that Evan's going to be in twice the danger there, and plenty hard to cover twenty-four hours a day."

"I'll put a couple guys on the case to spell you."

"Do that."

"But what about the next few days?"

"I don't think the man'll try again, Ned. A second attempt would look too coincidental. Whoever took that shot is probably gone."

"And the group of hunters?"

"Could be one of them. I want you to check out a few names for me. You never know. Got your pencil?" Matt gave him everyone's name at the camp, their home cities, anything and everything he'd noted in his head. He never mentioned Nicola, though; it just didn't seem right to even share her name with Ned.

"Okay," Ned said, "call me the minute you get back to New York. Oh, and don't forget to leave your job there in the usual manner. Evan, God bless his determined soul, might just pick up a phone one day and check on his son."

"Got ya." He hung up and went straight to the shower.

Evan sure had gotten into a pickle this time. It had only been a few days since he'd made his announcement on the Costa Plata loans, but Matt was betting on that finance minister, Reyes, having taken immediate action. With Evan dead, the World Bank might take a new, less hard line, on those loans. Just the possibility would have been enough to cause Reyes, with Cisernos's blessing, to act quickly.

What excuse was Matt going to use when he got home? And just how in the devil was he going to stay close to Evan—especially after that fight last night?

Showered and changed he bundled up his dirty clothes and shoved them into a plastic bag—they'd get washed in New York. Then he packed up his few belongings, checking the room for anything he might have forgotten, and headed back down the stairs and out into the bright autumn morning.

Crested Butte was a small, funky ski area, an old mining town with only one paved street, the century-old mining shacks and false-front stores only recently spruced up with new paint. It was a town that had seen its share of battles between labor and management in the old days, and battles between the huge AMAX mining conglomerate and environmentalists in the more recent past. It was cozy and charming, and its inhabitants were stranded back somewhere in the idealistic, freedom-loving sixties.

Matt had only just come to this mountain retreat, and now he was leaving. He'd known all along it wasn't going to last, but he'd needed a cover job, an excuse to be in Colorado to show up at hunting camp. And while Evan had been brooding over his oldest son's latest bartending job, he'd been too busy to see through the cover and to question why Matt had been comfortably working in a restaurant in New York then suddenly up and gone to Colorado. No, Evan wouldn't possibly suspect anything fishy, because he'd been too mad at his son. But then, that was the whole idea of a cover in the first place.

He ambled on down the main street and felt his stomach growling. It was well past ten now, and a bite or two would hit the spot. He eyed a favorite locals' spot, Penelope's, a two-story fern-and-stained-glass eatery in one of the old false-front buildings still left standing. The house's famous tenderloin hash sure would hit the spot.

Matt knew a couple of the employees there; they were regulars at the bar where he worked. He took a seat at the counter, pushed aside the menu and smiled up at the waitress. "Hi, Suzy. Tenderloin hash, please, and a couple of eggs, sunny-side up. Coffee, too."

"Where you been?" Suzy was twenty at the outside, blond, short and round and sassy; her old blue jeans beneath the apron were faded and torn in spots—suitable for Crested Butte.

"Hunting," he said.

"Catch anything?"

"You don't *catch* the game, Suzy, you shoot at it. And no, I'm not really much of a hunter."

"I'm glad," she said, then bounced off to put in his order.

Suzy, he thought, like several of his other acquaintances here, was going to be buzzing with the news tomorrow. He could just imagine it. "Hey, did you guys hear about Matt? He got fired. Poor old drunk."

Matt drank his coffee and let his thoughts settle themselves. And as soon as he had a perspective on what he needed to do in the next few days, he took a moment to think about Nicola and the cool, impersonal note he'd left. He sighed. If he closed his eyes, he could see her black swatch of hair swinging over her shoulder as she leaned over the monstrosity of a stove. Ah yes, her cheeks were flushed, her dark eyes bright... Too bad there hadn't been time to unpeel all her layers, every lamination she'd built up to protect herself. Too bad he couldn't have come clean about himself, but then, would she—like Evan—merely shrug and think, so what? The knowledge of his real job didn't change a thing about his personality. Was that what she'd think?

Nicola. An amazing woman. He'd been nosing around on that ridge yesterday morning, looking for the spot where the bullet had come from, and he'd run into her. Uncanny. And too close for comfort. He hadn't been able to tell her that he'd hiked back to keep his eye on Evan and heard the shot, so he'd come up with some lame excuse for his presence.

Nicola.... She was even more appealing in jeans and a plaid shirt than in her city duds. A woman of the outdoors. Lean and hard muscled, competent. But sweet and vulnerable, too. A combination that was irresistible. It was uncanny how she'd found that spot. Uncanny, as well, how she'd gotten under his skin and muddled his thoughts. It was a new experience, at his ripe age, to feel like that because of a woman. He'd felt like that in high school, even in college once or twice, but not since. He stayed too tightly in control to ever let himself feel like that about a female.

"Tenderloin hash and eggs sunny-side up," came Suzy's voice, and she plunked the plate down on the table. "Get you anything else?"

"Just some more coffee."

So why, he wondered as he broke the yolk of an egg with a corner of his toast, hadn't he found the right woman? Was it really because of his unusual line of work? Maybe. Or perhaps he *was* a coward, hiding all these years behind his cover. Nasty thought, that.

Okay then, Matt decided, maybe he was a chicken at heart, but he still had this job to complete for the service. He could hardly march into Ned Copple's office and announce that he was through, at least not until the Costa Plata Caper was over.

"Hey, Cavanaugh!" came a voice from across the aisle, an old-timer who was fond of calling everyone a flatlander.

"Hi, Gary."

"Ya got anything to show for yer huntin' trip?"

Matt shook his head. "I got skunked, old buddy."

"Told you ya would. Now if you'da let me guide ya . . ."

Matt barely listened, although he nodded at appropriate moments as he chewed pensively. What a lousy assignment this had turned into—watching his own father. Normally Ned would have handed this one over to the FBI or even the National Security Agency, but since Matt had the expertise and the inside edge, it had fallen to him. Here he'd been, hanging around his parents since last summer and having to come up with the wildest stories as to why he'd taken a job near New York, why he'd moved on to Colorado just a couple of weeks ago, and now, why he was going back to New York. Ned was really going to owe him for this one—retirement from Section C, maybe. Although, Matt recalled grimly, Ned was fond of saying that you never retired from the field, you only got buried.

"Yessiree," old Gary, the plumber, said, "I got me a six-point trophy bull back in '52, I did. And I ain't hunted since. Course, I could find ya a big ol' bull if I wanted, mind ya."

"Sure you could, Gary," Matt said.

A picture of Juan Ramirez flew into his mind. The rebel leader was sitting behind his desk, his yellow eyes alight with the fire of reform and revolution. It wouldn't be long now, Matt guessed, before the hopeful and idealistic Juan readied his guerrilla troops to free the downtrodden people of Costa Plata from Cisernos. And then the good-hearted U.S. Congress would vote on aid to that war-torn country, to Ramirez, its new president, and on it would go, the cycle of idealistic young men replacing the older, jaded, corrupt ones. And maybe, just maybe, this one would turn out to be a good guy.

"So, ya wanna take a ride on up to Harvey's Ridge there, Matt?" Gary grinned, showing darkened teeth. "Might jist get ya an animal today."

"Say," Matt said, "that's really nice of you, but I probably have to work."

"Yer misfortune," Gary said, shrugging.

Evan, Ramirez, Reyes—the images flew around in Matt's mind as he paid his check and headed back out to the street. And who *had* taken that lousy shot at Evan? An amateur, that much was evident. Would Reyes have sent an amateur, though?

And Nicola. Oh yes, she was whirling around in Matt's head, as well. One thing was sure, he'd been an idiot to have kissed her. Everything had been just fine after they'd left the bar in Redstone; that was to say, Nicola had been plenty put off by his flirtation with the buxom Sunny. Then he'd gone and spoiled it and kissed her.

Why did she always have to be around, complicating matters?

Nicola, tall and lean, graceful, competent. *And smart*. But on those sad, melancholy eyes, those questioning, judging eyes that made him look deep inside himself despite all the warning sirens in his head. Nicola....

ALTHOUGH MATT WASN'T DUE BACK to work at the Wooden Nickel till the end of the week, it was no trouble switching shifts with one of the guys so he could work that night. He kept a beer on the bar next to the cash register, taking drinks from it in full sight of the handful of locals who patronized the place that quiet Thursday evening.

The talk ran to the usual stuff: gossip, what kind of ski season it was going to be, who was getting married, who was knocked up, who'd gotten arrested for driving under the influence last Saturday, and, because the snow hadn't flown yet, how the hunting season was going.

"So, how was the hunting?" a steady customer of the bar asked Matt.

"Didn't see a damn thing."

"Too many guns out there nowadays."

Matt nodded, agreeing, taking a swig from his glass. "Too darn many easterners, too."

"It's not a sport anymore. It's a freaking shooting gallery."

"Ah, shut up, Abner," someone else called over. "You been sayin' that ever since I kin remember."

Matt laughed with the rest of them, maybe a little louder, and tilted his glass again, then served a new couple at the bar, mixing their cocktails adroitly.

"I can see you been a bartender a long time." This was from an older man with a familiar face, who sat at the bar next to Abner.

"Yeah, I've been around." Matt shrugged.

"Where you from?" The man pushed his beer glass toward Matt, who refilled it automatically.

"Lots of places."

"Crested Butte ain't a bad town. You might like it here."

"It's as good as any. I hear the tips are great during ski season."

"That they are."

Matt drank again, then knocked over an empty glass when he reached for it. "Slippery," he said to the older man, winking broadly.

By the end of his shift, he was slurring his words and spilling drinks. When he ambled out at 2:00 a.m., the bar was three-deep in dirty glasses, and he'd left the cash register jammed.

The following morning he awoke at ten, eyed his already packed duffel bag, showered and brushed his teeth. Afterward, carefully, he poured the bathroom glass full of bourbon from a bottle he'd borrowed from the bar and gargled with it, grimacing and spitting it out. Then he slapped some bourbon on his unshaved cheeks, dressed and, whistling jauntily, went to work.

He arrived at the Wooden Nickel at eleven, just in time for the day shift. Someone had gotten there before him, though, and had cleaned up the mess. The barroom smelled of stale smoke and flat beer, but the bar was clean as a whistle now. The manager, Jay, sat on a stool, counting last night's take and making out a deposit slip. He looked up when he saw Matt.

"Hello, hello, hello, Jay buddy," Matt said, approaching the bar. "Up with the birds, I see."

Jay looked him over and sniffed, wrinkling his nose in disgust. "Hell, Cavanaugh, you smell like a brewery. I like you, man, but you've only worked here a couple of weeks, and you can't stay sober. This place was a disaster area when I got here."

"Sorry, it was a busy night."

"Busy?" Jay tapped the pile of bills he was counting. "With this take?"

Matt stood there, waiting.

"I'm gonna have to let you go, Cavanaugh. I hate to do it, but business is business. Pick up your check. I'll take your shift. Sorry, man, but that's the way it's gotta be."

Matt grinned carelessly and shrugged. "It's been fun."

"Yeah, I'll bet," Jay said bleakly.

Only ten minutes later, Matt threw his stuff onto the back seat of the rented Jeep and swung into the front seat. By the time he was halfway to Denver he'd forgotten all about the check, the job and the humiliation he always felt. He was thinking only of his assignment—protecting Evan Cavanaugh—and furiously trying to think up some half-baked excuse for arriving, yet again, at the old Westchester homestead.

# CHAPTER EIGHT

NICOLA COULDN'T have been more surprised or pleased when she'd opened up an envelope from Evan and Maureen and found a round-trip airline ticket to New York.

Hope you'll have time to use this. We'd love to see you at Thanksgiving this year. Consider the ticket an early birthday present.

Love, Evan and Maureen

Her job with Ron's outfitter service had been through for the year, and the job she hoped was still available in Wyoming was not due to start until close to Christmas, so she had decided to go ahead and fly east. And, Nicola had thought as she'd packed, the employment at the ski lodge near Jackson, Wyoming, was no real plus in her life—it didn't pay very well. Maybe she'd stay in the East this winter, find a good-paying position and tuck a little money away in her savings account. One thing was for sure, she'd learned, and that was that good, dependable cooks were hard to find. All she'd had to do was look through the want ads in the papers to discover that.

In fact, she was sitting in the kitchen at the Cavanaughs', talking to Lydia and leafing through the *New York Times* help wanted section discussing just that.

"You know, Lydia," she was saying, "I could find a place to hang my hat in the city right here and have a job in a day." Nicola ran her finger down a long column. "It's tempting."

Lydia sipped from a coffee mug that read This Is My Kitchen, Find Your Own, and snorted in derision. "Sure you could, Miss Nicola. Jobs in the city are a dime a dozen. But finding a place to live, now, there's the hitch."

"Um." She flipped the page.

"Always been that way in New York. Take Mr. T.J., for example. He still has to live at home and commute."

*He doesn't have to,* Nicola thought. He lived at home because of Maureen and because he intended to stay highly visible, so that when the time came for Evan to retire from his spot as president of the family-owned bank, T.J. would be readily on hand. The trouble was, Evan was still going strong.

"Here's one," Nicola said, tapping the page. "'Assistant chef for large hotel, East side. Excellent pay, benefits plus. Send résumé.'"

The kitchen door swung open and Maureen walked in. She looked positively radiant in a shimmering green robe and matching slippers. "Good morning, Nicola, Lydia. Is the coffee ready?" She ran an affectionate hand across Nicola's shoulder and sat down. Morning routine at the Cavanaughs' never varied. Breakfast was served at eight, promptly, in the formal dining room, but Maureen and T.J. habitually invaded Lydia's territory every morning early and read sections of the paper—T.J., finance, Maureen, the society page—then disappeared to shower, dress and prepare for the day. Evan never showed his face until fully dressed, at eight sharp.

"You know," Nicola said, "it's tempting to try and find a place to live in the city and snatch up one of these jobs. It would be different, anyway."

Maureen raised a thin brow. "Now, you know you wouldn't be happy, dear, unless you could hike or ski or do something outdoorsy."

"I could do all that on vacations and on days off. Same as I do now."

"Well, I suppose you could. It would be wonderful having you close. You could even live here."

Nicola's head came up from the paper. "And commute? Ugh. What I should probably do," she said lightly, "is tell Went that I'm moving in with him."

Maureen made no comment. It was understood that the subject of Nicola's relationship with her parents was best left alone. "My, the coffee's strong," Maureen said. "Have you switched brands, Lydia?"

"Twenty years ago I did," Lydia replied pertly, and went about her work, squeezing fresh orange juice using an old-fashioned metal contraption with a handle.

T.J. came in. "Morning." He still looked drowsy and shuffled his slipper-clad feet. His light brown hair was mussed.

"My," Maureen said, "but you look like something the cat dragged in." She accepted his kiss on her cheek. "Sleep badly?"

"Not great." He fetched himself a coffee mug and sat down, pulling out the financial page, burying himself in it.

"So, Nicola," Maureen said, "I'd love to take you shopping today."

Nicola had confessed that she hadn't a thing to wear for the Thanksgiving gala—tomorrow night—and she'd been putting off the search for two days. She sighed, grimacing. "I guess I better take you up on it. It's either that, or I show up in jeans."

"This afternoon, Dave and Ruthie Huff are due in. So we'll have to make it this morning."

"Okay." The prospect of shopping with the exacting and untiring Maureen was intimidating. Of course, Nicola was thinking, she'd like to look her best. Went was catering the affair, as always, and, much as she hated herself for it, Nicola would love to impress him, make him really notice her.

"The Huffs are coming?" T.J. rattled his paper, hunching his shoulders over it.

"Yes. And they'll stay in the yellow room. They missed their shopping trip last year, and Ruthie insisted on coming early."

"Old Dave probably went duck hunting, instead," T.J. commented.

"Something like that," Maureen put in. "And, Lydia, if Nicola and I aren't back by noon, you tell Margaret to dust the yellow room, won't you?"

"Margaret," Lydia snorted, still squeezing oranges, "wouldn't know a dust rag from a mop."

Maureen went back to the society page, and Nicola held in a giggle.

It took them the entire morning at the Scarsdale Mall to find just the right creation for Nicola. Maureen rarely did her shopping in the city, preferring the small, exclusive local boutiques. It was always embarrassing shopping with Maureen, because she insisted on buying Nicola gifts, with Nicola protesting futilely. Generally there came the moment of compromise: Maureen paid half, a future Christmas or birthday present, and Nicola picked up the tab for the rest. This trip was no exception.

"This way I'm only half as mortified," Nicola said, putting her credit card back in her wallet.

"I don't know why you won't let me just buy you something."

"You took me in, you fed me and cared for me all those years. It's enough."

"Well, I got a daughter that way, didn't I? And I skipped the diaper stage. It was my pleasure, I assure you."

Yes, Maureen got her daughter, ready-made, eager to please. And, Nicola supposed, she got a mother.

Suzanne's face popped into Nicola's head unbidden. That sad, ethereal face that was still unlined, the dark, bottomless eyes. For many years, Nicola had prayed that one of the drugs her mother was given would be the miracle cure. Other people's depression had been controlled so that they led normal lives. But one drug reacted much the same as the next for Suzanne. If the medication kept her mother from weeping at the drop of a pin, then it made her drowsy or caused unbearable headaches or some other insidious side effect.

Oh yes, Nicola knew all about the antidepressants on the market. She'd read everything written, kept up on the latest pharmaceutical research—she still did. But what she'd discovered was that for every action, there was a reaction. There was no complete cure for clinical depression, not for Suzanne, anyway, but she kept hoping that a new drug would work or that her mother would wake up one day cured. She couldn't stop the hoping or the pictures in her mind of her and Suzanne doing things together. Like shopping for a dress. Considering everything, though, she'd been fortunate. She had Maureen's love, and Evan's—and how many people had been given a second chance like that?

Maureen was driving, heading back home, taking the curves slowly and cautiously. Cars kept passing; one driver behind her beeped.

"Oh, bug off!" she said under her breath.

Nicola laughed. She herself would have been doing the speed limit or better, but then Maureen had never been a confident driver. Evan, she knew, was terribly impatient with his wife in the car, refusing to understand that some women of Maureen's generation were still a bit behind the times and that they preferred it that way.

Yes, Evan could be a bully. The way to handle him, though, was to let him vent his steam, then regain lost ground when he was in a more receptive mood. His bark, at least to Nicola, had always been worse than his bite.

Curious, she wondered if Evan had mentioned to Maureen the near miss up in hunting camp. Probably not. And she wondered, too, if Maureen knew about the fight between Evan and Matt and Matt's sudden departure.

"Heard from Matt lately?" she ventured.

"Why, yes, in fact I did. A couple of weeks ago. He called to say he was back in New York, of all places, and job hunting again. I don't know why he hasn't been out to visit. My, but he moves around so much I can't keep track." She sounded blasé, but Nicola knew better. Nicola wondered if Maureen even knew that Matt had been to hunting camp at all. Maybe it was best she didn't.

The memory of Matt's visit still hurt Nicola. It seemed that every time Matt breezed in, he left behind wounded hearts. Hers was no exception. But then she'd let it happen, hadn't she?

So Matt was somewhere nearby. That great winter he was going to spend in Colorado had obviously turned sour. Had it been the fight with Evan? Or had Matt lied about having time off from his job? Maybe there never had been a job. She wouldn't put it past him. . . .

In the East. He'd made that long-distance phone call from Redstone, she remembered. Had he telephoned a lady and the woman had convinced him to leave the West for a visit? Maybe he'd left camp so abruptly because he had made other arrangements.

It killed Nicola to be constantly plagued with thoughts of Matt, with mental pictures of his sparkling blue eyes and that easy, dimpled smile. It killed her to know that she'd pegged him right all along—a man too much like her father to be safe—and yet she'd fallen for his charm, just like all those other women before her.

"Flight gets in at three," Maureen was saying.

"What?"

"Dave and Ruthie get in at three. Knowing Dave, it'll be Chinatown tonight. He *always* wants Chinese. Can you imagine, driving all the way into the city just for a cheap dinner?"

"I like Chinatown," Nicola said. "It's . . . funky."

"Um. Well, I'd rather eat locally, thank you, but Dave, bless his heart, is always insistent. And he's one of the few men who can hold his own with Evan."

"They go back a ways, don't they?"

"Twenty-five years. This winter is the anniversary of our first trip to the Canadian Rockies, in fact. We met Dave and Ruthie that year, and Dave hit it off instantly with Evan. They're like kids together, always challenging each other. Someday—" Maureen shook her head "—one of them is going to overdo it."

"Is that why Jon's coming to Thanksgiving dinner this year? Is it a kind of reunion?"

"I suppose. Jon's got family in New York. He's got family all over the place. He visits us every so often."

*Family all over the place,* Nicola thought, remembering her notion about Jon and those cigarettes. Casually she asked, "Does he have family in South America?" She would have said Central America, but then Maureen might have gotten too curious.

"Now, that's a funny question. I'm not sure I know. He might. Why do you ask?"

"Oh, no reason." But Nicola filed the information away in her mind. *He might. . . .*

As so aptly predicted, Dave bounced into the Cavanaughs' house that afternoon insisting that everyone dress casually. "It's the annual trip to Chinatown," he announced cheerfully.

"Must we?" asked Maureen as she and Ruthie embraced.

"Did you ever try to say no to Dave?" Ruthie made a face.

Like Dave, Ruthie Huff took excellent care of herself. In her mid-fifties, she didn't look a day older than forty-five. She wore her brown hair short, but not old ladyish, and she had it frosted regularly. Her five-foot-five figure was trim and fit; she skied, hiked, bicycled—one of Aspen's beautiful people. In many ways, Ruthie reminded Nicola of Maureen. The difference was, Ruthie held her own with her husband—and then some.

"Well, hello, Nicola," Dave said, turning to her in the living room. "I didn't know you were going to be here."

"Neither did I."

"Oh, Ruthie," he said, "you remember Nicola from years ago, when she lived here. Say, is Went, that old charmer, catering the *grande affaire*?"

"I hear he is," Nicola said easily.

"The way you cook, kiddo, he's a fool not to put you right in his own kitchen."

Dave, Nicola thought, was never one for tact. "Oh, he's got a stable of sous-chefs already. Who knows, maybe someday." She shrugged. *Sure.*

It was a Wednesday night, a work night, and Evan had gotten tied up in the city, something about an African diplomat and a World Bank loan to see the man's country through a drought crisis. They were all to meet Evan in Chinatown.

Somehow, Nicola got dragged along, as did T.J. She'd have preferred to have spent a quieter evening at home, maybe to have had dinner with Lydia in the kitchen and then to have curled up with a good book by the fire. But when Dave was persistent, Ruthie was right: he just would not take no for an answer.

They all ate at Dave's favorite restaurant on the edge of Chinatown, on Canal Street. And did they *eat*. The six of them ordered the whole gamut, the Imperial Dinners. There was Mandarin lobster and Szechuan beef, hot and spicy, and twice-cooked pork, sweet-and-sour shrimp, Oriental vegetables and chicken lo mein, mountains of steamy hot rice, delicate pots of fragrant tea. Everyone exchanged dishes. Dave and Evan, of course, had to bite into the red peppers, both exclaiming emphatically that they weren't hot in the least. And then T.J. tried one and nearly choked.

"There's steam coming out of your ears," Nicola teased.

It *was* a good time. But somehow, Nicola had gotten paired up with T.J., and—she hated to be so critical—he was his usual, quiet, boring self. He watched his father and Dave and all their silly, boyish antics, and he looked as if he were somewhere between disapproving and jealous. She wondered if he had any real friends, male friends, or if there was a woman in his life. If so, he sure kept her a secret. Now, Matt, on the other hand . . .

Oh, brother, there she went again, letting him crop up in her thoughts at the most unwanted times. And yet if he was there at the table, he'd be holding his own with Evan and Dave. He'd be dropping those hot peppers into his mouth like oysters and telling everyone that they weren't as bad as some he'd had. He'd make his mother smile and irritate Evan, and he'd woo Nicola, catching her off guard, making her laugh with his good humor and spontaneous remarks. She'd feel all glowing and warm inside, and her cheeks would get flushed. If he was there, that was.

"More tea?" T.J. asked her.

"Oh, sure, thanks."

They walked the twisted streets of Chinatown after dinner, slowly, complaining about eating too much, laughing about how they'd all feel after Thanksgiving dinner tomorrow. Ruthie bought a silk kimono with brilliantly colored parrots on the back, and Dave got them all paper fans with dragons on them, made in Taiwan.

"Now, what am I going to do with this junk?" Evan asked.

"Oh," Dave said, "use it when your temper flares, Evan. Although, God knows when I can recall anything like that happening to you."

They were easy people to be with, and they laughed a lot, the men cracking terrible jokes, making even worse puns. All but T.J. Around Evan, he paled.

The city, the lights and sirens and exotic odors, the myriad people, the thousands of shops and restaurants and street hawkers, delighted Nicola. New York was exciting, vibrant, *alive*. There was a pulse to the city, a beat like a steady drum, unique, compelling. It wouldn't be so bad to work there. She could see shows and walk the streets, leap into the melting pot of the world. And on days off, she could drive up into the mountains; in the summer she could hike and in the winter, ski. She'd see Suzanne more often that way, and maybe even Went—if he could spare the time. Then, of course, Evan and Maureen were nearby. And maybe she'd run into Matt once in a while.... *Do yourself a favor, kid, and forget him*.

They got home late; it was past eleven, but Dave and Evan stayed up in the living room and chatted over brandies. Nicola said her good-nights and headed to her room, yawning. Country girls hit the sack by ten. Lord, but bed looked inviting. The bag from the boutique was still sitting there, however, the shiny, dusty-rose bag with twisted ribbon handles. She'd better hang up her dress.

Idly Nicola wondered if Went would even notice her tomorrow. Would he make his rounds through the throng of guests? When everyone was served, would he sit down to a glass of wine? She'd be in her dress, with its calf-length swirling skirt of dark green velvet and its draped top. A little old-fashioned, not daring or anything, but elegant. And expensive—Maureen had seen to that. And maybe Went would put a hand over hers and tell her how terrific she looked. Then maybe he'd say, "Gosh, Nicola, honey, I wish you'd stop by more often. I really meant it about showing you the town. I know I've never been there for you, darling, but I've changed. Give me a chance. Let me show you. I love you, baby, I always have."

Nicola changed into a nightgown, turned out the lights, frowned into the dark and crawled into her warm, safe bed.

THE ROLLS-ROYCES AND MERCEDESES and long black limousines started arriving at 6:00 p.m. but by then everything was ready.

Went had been in the kitchen since early that morning, so early that Nicola had still been asleep, and when she'd finally gone downstairs, she'd been afraid to do more than poke her head in and say a quick hello.

When Went worked, he *worked*. He'd brought two helpers with him, and all day long there were rattles and bangs, arguments and swearing in French and English, coming from behind that swinging door.

"It's always like this," Maureen said, waving her hand. "Don't pay any attention."

Just before six the Huffs and T.J. and Nicola and the Cavanaughs gathered in the living room to drink a glass of bubbly and toast the holiday. The men were all dashing in their tuxedos; even T.J. had a kind of flair in his formal clothes. The women were lovely—Maureen in gold lamé and Ruthie in a suede skirt and elegant beige sweater of feathers and angora.

"You look beautiful," Maureen whispered, leaning close to Nicola. "I wish Suzanne could see you. She'd be so proud."

Nicola had twisted her hair on top of her head. Her neck was long and white and graceful, the dark velvet of her dress showing up its smooth texture, and she wore a cameo her mother had given her. She flushed at Maureen's words, noting the men's appreciative glances, ill at ease under the attention, unaccustomed to it. It was a heady feeling, being dressed up and glamorous—flattering but discomfiting.

Then the guests began arriving, and the entire, sparkling house was filled with beautifully dressed women, men in dinner jackets, chattering, waiters circulating with champagne and hors d'oeuvres on silver trays.

Nicola was introduced to so many people her head spun, and she gave up trying to remember who and what they were, or which sensationally dressed woman belonged to which distinguished man. There were many faces that looked familiar, either because she'd met them before at the house or because their visages had graced the pages of *Fortune* or *Time* magazine.

There were Wall Street magnates, World Bank officials, the head of the Federal Reserve Bank, even a senator from the Midwest and his wife. Jon Wolff was there, wearing a rusty old tuxedo that must have seen performances at the Staatsopera in Vienna before World War II.

Maureen was gracious, Evan jovial and avuncular, T.J. quiet, as usual, nursing a glass of champagne in a corner, watching the gathering silently.

Dinner was announced. At each setting was a card with a name. Maureen had worked for hours arranging the seating, worrying about who was having an affair with whose spouse, who was quarreling, who would be comfortable with the rather strange wife of Nigeria's World Bank representative, and who spoke French or Italian or German. Nicola was seated to the right of Evan, at the head of the long table, and to *her* right was an empty chair with a card in front of it. She looked over at the attractive woman sitting beyond it, the wife of the Midwest senator, she thought, and they both shrugged and smiled at each other. But Nicola knew who had been meant to sit in that empty chair; she knew whose name was on that card. Matt. Probably he'd had to work that night, or perhaps he'd simply chosen not to come.

The feast was worthy of Wentworth Gage. Roast turkeys, each stuffed with a different dressing: pine nut, oyster, old-fashioned bread and egg. Yams in brandy and butter, trays of relishes, whipped potatoes, five different vegetables to choose from. Cranberry jelly, orange-cranberry sauce. Rolls hot out of the oven, celery sticks stuffed with caviar, cranberry bread. And each dish had Went's touch—a shade of difference in an herb of a spice or a texture, a special, mouth-watering flavor that made even the most jaded palate crave another taste.

Nicola was proud of her father's expertise. He was more than an expert, he was a genius. She was proud and almost jealous. If *her* reputation matched Went's, would he notice her then? Or did he simply not care?

Did he consider Nicola at all? Was he ashamed that he spent time with other women instead of his daughter? She rolled his delectable yams over in her mouth and wondered at the mystery that was her father's mind. She'd tried everything to get him to notice her. So far nothing had worked, not even following in his footsteps. Damn him.

He emerged from the steaming kitchen when dessert was being served: pecan pies, pumpkin pies, pumpkin chiffon cake. Oh, he was charming when he wanted to be! He was tall and lanky, elegantly slouched, his face rawboned with a big nose. But his expression made his homely features attractive in a quirky way. He was smiling now, grinning, bowing to the long tableful of guests. Applause greeted his bow, and he accepted the homage due him with regal modesty.

"Thank you, thank you. I hope everything has been satisfactory. No one's going to leave with an empty stomach, I assume?" he said.

Laughter greeted this sally, and groans and pats on many full bellies.

"There is someone here tonight ... Oh yes, there she is!" Went said, searching the crowd. Then he stalked, long legged, straight to Nicola. She stared up at him open-mouthed as he reached down and tugged at her hands, pulling her upright. "I want to introduce my daughter to you all, my beautiful daughter," he said, smiling warmly at her. "And, ladies and gentlemen, this child of mine is a talented chef in her own right! My daughter, Nicola Gage!" And he drew her close, his arm around her as the entire assemblage oohed and aahed and clapped.

She blushed; she hung her head; she laughed in embarrassed pleasure. At that moment she adored her father. "Thank you," she said, her cheeks burning, but her voice was too low. She cleared her throat and spoke up more loudly. "Thank you." And Went squeezed her tight.

He finally let her go and waved to everyone, disappearing back into the kitchen. Nicola sank into her chair, half laughing, half crying. Oh yes, Went could be charming.

The senator's wife leaned across the still empty seat between them and said, "I'm Irene, Nicola. I had no idea you were Went's daughter. How proud you must be."

"Oh yes, of course," Nicola replied.

Nicola wasn't certain exactly when she became aware of a stir at the entrance to the formal dining room. Maybe it was when Evan turned in his seat to look, or maybe it was the eyes of the secretary's wife, which lifted to the door. Whatever. A few more heads turned, curious, as waiters walked around unobtrusively, serving coffee and liqueurs. A voice could be heard. "Well, well, Clyde, I'm late again, as usual, aren't I? Happy Thanksgiving!"

And the butler, Clyde, came into the dining room, ushering in the new arrival, ushering him directly toward the empty seat next to Nicola. She heard Evan grumble something under his breath, and the crowd buzzed and whispered. Heads bent, people wondering, guessing.

But Matt was oblivious to the quiet commotion he'd created. He was self-assured and roguishly handsome in his tuxedo as he strode toward Nicola, his smile perhaps a bit too broad. Or maybe she was only imagining that.

"Nicola? Well, fancy finding you here," he said a touch too loudly, and she wondered, for a split second, if he'd had a few too many drinks before arriving. "Has it been a wonderful Thanksgiving dinner?" he asked insolently, raising a goblet of wine as soon as he sat down.

"Yes, delicious."

He leaned across Nicola and spoke to his mother. "Sorry I'm late, Mom." Then he nodded to T.J. and his father, raising his glass as if in a toast to them.

It was quite an act, Nicola thought. Errant son, wastrel, ne'er-do-well. Debonair but irresponsible. Why had he come? Why had he bothered? And did anyone else but Nicola notice that it *was* an act? She wasn't quite sure how she knew, how she recognized the falsity of his routine and knew it wasn't the real Matt.

"I'm Irene," the woman on Matt's right was saying, holding her slim, beringed hand out to him.

"How delightful to meet you, Irene. Better late than never, as they say."

Nicola had time to catch her breath, to steel herself. Matt, unexpected, his black-clad thigh touching hers as he leaned toward Irene. And then he was turning toward her, his head bent close. "Nicola, you look gorgeous. I didn't know you were going to be here."

"Maureen sent me a plane ticket."

"Well, isn't that nice?"

The food in Nicola's stomach felt like lead. Her heart pounded too hard. She was irritated at her reaction; Matt only had to appear and she fell apart. But his head was still bent toward her, and an invisible current flowed between them, so intense that it would begin to spark in a moment....

"Quite a collection," he whispered sarcastically.

"Yes." Her heart fluttered ridiculously, and that awful, exquisite slow melting began in her stomach as his breath fanned her cheek. He'd kissed her, this man, pressed his lips to hers. And his hands had stroked her body, moving on her skin, the same hands that turned the crystal wineglass right now, letting the light sparkle on its facets.

She felt trapped, frightened, her senses sharpened to fever pitch but concentrating on one thing alone. She raised her coffee cup, drank, tasted nothing, felt Matt's eyes on her, and she knew she was defenseless.

There was dancing after dinner. A five-man combo played old tunes, Lester Lanin style, danceable music. It was better then, away from him, and she relaxed a little, tapping her foot to the music. T.J. took her for a requisite dance. "Moon River," she thought it was.

"Don't move too fast," she said. "I'm so full I'll pop."

But T.J. didn't laugh at her attempt at humor. "I'll be careful," he promised, utterly serious.

Then Dave Huff grabbed her for "Chances Are," hummed in her ear, made absurd, lewd suggestions that she laughed at. Then Evan took her for a spin, leaving Maureen in the grasp of the vice president of the World Bank. "What's that son of mine up to?" he asked her. "Did he give you a hint?"

"'Up to'? What would he be up to?" she asked innocently.

"I don't know. Showing up late like that. Why'd he bother to come at all?" muttered Evan.

"Forget it. Have fun. Are you having fun, Evan?" she asked.

"Sure, *fun*. When this crowd goes home, I'll have fun," he groused good-naturedly, and she was glad to have nudged him out of his bad mood.

Then an official of Evan's family bank, whom Nicola already knew, asked her for a dance. He was a nice man, only a little shorter than she was. Oh well. But he danced like Fred Astaire, and he made Nicola laugh and blush with his compliments. Oh, this glitzy life could become a habit, she thought. And then she felt like Cinderella, disguised as a beautiful princess, with the clock ticking closer and closer to midnight.

When the band broke into "On the Street Where You Live," Nicola was talking to Maureen, the flushed and successful hostess. A hand touched her arm, a voice said,

"Excuse me, Mom," Nicola turned, and Matt pulled her out onto the floor.

"I've been patient," he said, looking down at her.

She couldn't breathe. He was holding her too close, one hand at the small of her back. His breath was wine sweet, his blue eyes held her hypnotized, seeing into her innards, unlocking all those carefully controlled emotions.

"Patient?" she asked faintly.

"Your dance card was full. I was getting into a jealous snit."

"Matt."

"I wanted to apologize for leaving hunting camp like that."

"You don't need to apologize."

"I thought you might be insulted."

"Why?"

He laughed, his dimple deepening, and pulled her close, whirling her around. "You're the best-looking female here." He grinned down at her. "Not the richest, not the oldest, but the best looking."

They spun by Evan, who scowled at Matt, then past T.J., who stared wordlessly, his face a mask, unreadable. Did T.J. ever *enjoy* anything? She felt light in Matt's arms, and she wondered whether he could feel her trembling. She wanted to go on forever in his embrace, but at the same time she couldn't wait until the music was over, the dance ended, her gown turned back into rags.

"Matt, my dear boy," came a voice, "vill you please let me have the pretty lady for a minute?" It was Jon Wolff, looking a bit like Count Dracula in his rusty black.

Thank heavens. She was saved. But when Matt reluctantly handed her over to Jon, she felt suddenly cold and naked. Ridiculous.

"Later," Matt whispered huskily, and then Jon was stepping around the floor with her, stiff and formal and so very proper.

"I am so glad to find you, Nicola," Jon was saying, and she had to force her mind back to reality. "I have a problem up at the lodge, the Bugaboo Lodge, you know."

"Oh dear, is it serious?" she replied politely.

"Yes, very serious. My cook has left me. He got married and his vife must live in Calgary, so there I am. It is Thanksgiving and I have no cook."

She looked at him quizzically.

"Would you be interested?"

*"Me?"*

"I pay very well. Christmas to April. The verk is very hard, long hours, but sometimes you can ski, too."

"Are you really offering me the job, Jon?"

"I am begging you, Nicola. You see before you a desperate man."

A crazy thought skimmed through her brain: a desperate Jon, bending his face to her neck, with his vampire fangs bared. She stifled a giggle.

"Vill you consider the offer, at least? I have put ads in the Calgary and Edmonton and Vancouver papers, but it is very late for a fine chef to change plans," he was saying.

"Do you want my résumé?" she blurted out.

"Ah, no, Nicola. That veek at hunting camp was résumé enough."

"I'll take the job," she said impulsively.

"Just like that?"

"Yes, why not? I'd love to."

Jon had stopped and was regarding her in utter amazement. "You vant to know the details? Now?"

"Tomorrow. I'll call you tomorrow. All right?"

"Fine, perfect. *Gott in Himmel*, I am a happy man."

"And I am a happy woman, Jon!" Nicola said, delighted.

"Come on, Jon, tear yourself away from Nick. I've got to tell you about these new powder skis I just bought!" Dave Huff said, coming up to them. "You don't mind, do you?"

"Tomorrow. You vill call?" Jon said as Dave grabbed his arm.

Nicola laughed. "Don't worry, I'll call you."

The band was taking a break. Nicola wandered across the floor, smiling automatically, nodding, returning comments. But her mind was busy. The Bugaboos! She'd heard Evan talk about helicopter skiing in Canada for years. There were no ski lifts out in the wilderness of the Bugaboo Mountains of British Columbia, only helicopters to transport the skiers to snowy peaks, then pick them up at the bottom and spirit them away, up to another untouched piste.

Jon's Bugaboo Lodge had been one of the first places established for that kind of skiing. Oh Lordy, but she had a million questions for Jon tomorrow! She didn't even know how to *get* there or how many people she'd be cooking for or where the supplies came from! What an adventure! What an opportunity!

She had to get away somewhere and think. Questions teemed in her brain. Wow. The patio. Slipping to the far side of the room, to the French doors, Nicola let herself through. It was cold and damp out, with a breeze whirling dead leaves into corners. She hugged her arms and walked back and forth, smiling to herself in the moonlit darkness.

The Bugaboos. She knew a few things about Jon's lodge, from Evan. It was very expensive to spend a week there, about two thousand dollars per person. It was totally isolated in the winter, except for the helicopter and a radio-telephone. The food, he'd remarked often enough, was superb. Uh-oh, better get out the old recipe books.

She marched back and forth, planning, thinking, excited. Oh yes, she'd have to ask Evan what kind of skis were best in that bottomless Canadian powder.

"Nicola." The voice startled her, and she turned toward it, stopping in midstride. A shadow detached itself from the dark bulk of the house and approached her. "I saw you come out here."

"Matt."

"Who else? What're you doing, marching around in the cold?"

"I've been thinking." She laughed, wanting to share her news. "I've had the most wonderful offer! Jon wants me to cook up at his lodge this winter!"

"Does he?"

"Yes. Isn't that wonderful?"

"I suppose so."

"Well, it is." She wouldn't let his casual attitude spoil her happiness. "Just think, I'll be able to see Evan and Maureen when they come up in January. Won't it be fun?"

"It's pretty isolated up there," Matt said.

"I'll be so busy, I won't even notice."

"Will you?"

"Aren't you glad for me, Matt? This is the opportunity of a lifetime!"

"Hmm. Right. Come here, Nicola, and stop talking so much."

"Why?"

"Okay, I'll give in." He moved close to her, so she could see his face and his formal white shirt in the moonlight, then he took her hand and held it, playing with her fingers. "I don't want to talk about your new job."

"What do you want to talk about?" She longed to snatch her hand back, but she couldn't. Her mouth suddenly went dry; heat radiated up her arm from her hand, and that awful, helpless melting started once more.

"You. You look beautiful tonight, but I told you that already." His voice was soft, soothing, and he wouldn't let go of her hand.

"Why are you doing this?" she asked in a low voice.

"Doing what?"

"Playing with me."

"I'm not playing with you."

"Then what do you call this act of yours?" She finally pulled her hand away.

"It's no act, Nicky."

"What do you want from me?" she asked, trembling, knowing but not knowing at all.

There was an awful moment of silence, as if they were both frozen in their stances, Nicola poised as if for flight, Matt steady, cocksure, compelling.

"I want this from you," he finally said in a whisper, and he pulled her to him, his mouth coming down hard over hers. She forgot everything, all her inner warnings, her self-promises. Their flesh spoke for them, the only reality she knew at that instant, the only reality she wanted to know. Her body leaped in a sweet agitation that wouldn't be denied, and a slow, hot flame kindled in her, warm and throbbing. She felt his lean, hard body against her, flattening her breasts, and his arms were like iron bands holding her, and she wanted to be held.

Then he lifted his head, and the cold touched her face. "I'd like to do that again. What do you say, Nicky?" He was smiling, holding her lightly.

"No," she said, realizing how she'd been taken in. "I don't think so." She was breathing hard, her heart thudding in her chest as if she'd run a race.

"You didn't like it?" he asked.

She backed out of his embrace, shivering suddenly from the cold. "Yes, I liked it."

He reached out for her once more. "You're cold. Want my coat?"

"No, I don't want your coat. I don't want your kisses, either."

"Nicola, I swear..." He sounded sincere, but she knew how good he must be at *that*.

"No." She held up a hand. "Don't touch me. You're like my father. I know about men like you. You don't mean a thing you say."

"Don't equate me with your father." His voice was tight.

"Why not, Matt?" she asked breathlessly, turning and moving toward the French doors, toward the light and heat and noise inside.

But he had no answer; he just stood there, a slim, straight figure in stark black and glistening white. And Nicola hurried away from him, hurried inside to mingle and smile and drink another glass of champagne, to compliment Maureen and tell Evan the news about her new job.

And all the while she felt the pain of leaving Matt, the pain of his dishonesty, the pain of his agonizing similarity to Wentworth Gage.

It struck her suddenly, like cold fingers running along her spine, and she stopped in her tracks in the middle of the crowded room. She was afraid of what Matt represented, and she distrusted him just as she did Went—yet didn't she love her father with as much passion as she hated him?

# CHAPTER NINE

IT WAS SATURDAY. That meant it was the day that the old guests left, spent, sated with skiing and good food and conversation—and the new guests arrived. A crazy day, what with the Bell helicopter buzzing between the helicopter pad in Spillimacheen, fifteen minutes over the mountains, and the lodge, taking out the old, ferrying in the new.

It was the day, too, that Jon Wolff turned into an old lady, fretting and worrying and checking the supplies that came in on the helicopter, checking the guest list, the linens, the menus, the thousand details that made the Bugaboo Lodge run smoothly.

This job had turned out to be the most challenging of Nicola's life. She cooked for around twenty people per week, connoisseurs all, wealthy folk for the most part, who knew the difference between beluga caviar and fish eggs, and what year was the best one for Burgundy.

That Saturday in January was special, though. The Cavanaughs were coming for the week. Evan always came, Maureen sometimes, but this week both T.J. and Matt were making the trip, as well.

"All of them?" Nicola had asked Jon.

"Yes, they haven't all come together for years. Isn't that nice? But I vill have to put the young men in the same room."

Matt and T.J.? Here? Was this some sort of attempt at family reconciliation? It smacked of Maureen's doing; she wanted her sons to get along with their father so badly.

Matt. Why? He knew she was there, but she didn't flatter herself that she constituted reason enough for him to suffer the proximity of Evan for an entire week. And how would he react when he got there? Would he be his usual flippant self? Would he treat her casually? Would he pursue her again?

Well, she would stop that, just as she had at Thanksgiving.

She prepared the beef tenderloin that would be the main course for dinner that night, readying it for the oven. Her kitchen was a dream—no Old Bertha to stoke up. Electricity from the lodge's own generator, the best in commercial stoves—a Vulcan—and a huge refrigerator and even a walk-in freezer. She kept a week's worth of supplies on hand—a lot of food—but the fresh produce came in on Saturdays the same way the guests did: by bus from Calgary to Spillimacheen, two hundred miles, then by helicopter to the lodge.

The Bugaboo Lodge was isolated. In the summer there was an old logging road that connected it to the outside world, but in winter the road was closed by snow and by the very immediate danger of avalanches that regularly slid off the slopes above the road. The place was linked to the outside world only by the radiotelephone set to Banff, where the Canadian Helitours' main office was, and by the helicopter—tenuous links, especially when bad weather prevented the chopper from flying. None of these facts, though, kept people from all over the world paying top dollar for a week of blissful skiing and gourmet meals.

There were two girls who helped in the kitchen, the helicopter pilots, who doubled as mechanics, three guides for the skiing, several maids and Jon and herself for staff. And they were busy every day from Christmas to mid-April, working hard and skiing when there was room in the helicopter. Nicola was given a week off once a month, when Jon's former cook would fly in and take over, and she needed that week.

Matt. She hadn't heard from him, but then she hadn't expected to. Maureen wrote that he was working in a bar in Tarrytown, nearby, and that she saw quite a bit of him. *How nice for Maureen.*

Her first reaction to Matt had been correct—he was dangerous. He was too attractive, too much fun, too free and easy. He tugged at her emotions in a way against which she couldn't defend herself. And he'd be here soon, right here in the lodge, and she'd have to see him every day, talk to him, be polite. Well, maybe she could stay extremely busy right here in the kitchen.

Jon bustled in. "*Mein Gott*, Nicola! Vill you have enough raspberries for tonight? You ordered a lug, didn't you?"

She smiled to herself. Jon was always like this on Saturdays. "Yes, don't worry."

He poured himself a cup of coffee and sat down hunched over the kitchen table. "I need a rest—I am exhausted. I have made ten beds this morning. Those lazy girls."

They weren't lazy, and Jon didn't need to make beds, but you couldn't tell him that, not on Saturdays.

"Vat a veek! It is the vorst. *Mein Gott*, I mean the best. Such a mixture, so many important people." He sighed and gulped half the coffee. "The Huffs and the Cavanaughs, you know them. But the others. Do you know the name Helga Gantzel?"

"No."

"Ach, you young folk. A once famous actress. So beautiful. Of course, she's my age now, sixty or so, but ven I vas young she vas the toast of Germany, of all Europe. And she's coming with Werner Bergmann. He is young, very young, but vith a voman like Helga..." He snapped his fingers. "And there's a Japanese man, a Mr. Yamamoto, and Carlos Santana, who is from Spain. A financier. It's no coincidence those two are coming this veek. They snatched up last-minute cancellations, to talk to Evan, you know."

"Why would they want to talk to Evan? Do they know him?"

"No." Jon leaned forward. "These two have set up an auto plant in Central America, in Costa Plata. You understand vat's going on there? Evan has told you?"

"Yes, I know. But how would you know about these men and their auto plant?"

"I have family in Managua. Nicaragua is so close. You see, my cousin has been so vorried about the political problems there. Such a nightmare for him. And he tells me these things. He is thinking of moving his family to Canada, even."

"Oh, I see."

"These men, they vill lose everything when Cisernos falls. And Evan is here this veek. They vant to talk to him."

"Oh Lordy, how awful. Evan will have a fit. He hates to be bothered by business when he's on vacation."

"I know, I know. Vat a week this vill be." Then he bounced up and put his cup in the sink. "So? Everything's okay here, Nicola? Dinner vill be fine?"

She smiled reassuringly. "I've got it all under control, Jon."

He went out mumbling under his breath, *"Gut, gut. Mein Gott."*

There wasn't much to do until later. Nicola checked everything once more, then let herself out the kitchen door. It was a clear, bright day, sunny and cold. A beautiful day. Thank heavens the chopper could fly to bring the guests in. There had been Saturdays when the old guests had been stuck here while the new ones were twiddling their thumbs in Spillimacheen, a tiny crossroads boasting nothing more than a general store, a post office and the helipad. But, still, the skiers who insisted on untracked powder put up with the inconveniences to get it.

She walked along the snow-packed path toward the building where the staff lived, which was separate from the main lodge. Nicola was lucky; as chef she had her own bed-room, which was very nice, but not in the least luxurious. And she shared the bathroom.

Even the main lodge was not fancy. It was a plain square edifice of stucco and wood and windows, two stories high, but its setting was spectacular. It faced a glacier and the famed rocky Bugaboo spires. A long mountainside flowed upward from the building, covered with snow-laden spruce, and all around rose the peaks of the Bugaboo range, sharp and white and pristine under the sun.

Nowhere else in the world was there skiing like this, Nicola thought, letting herself into her room. She'd been up, oh, maybe a couple times a week since December, whenever there was room in the helicopter. Paying guests, of course, came first, but sometimes a skier was injured or too tired or wanted an afternoon off. Then Nicola could go skiing—and it was heaven. Into the chopper, crowded, everyone laughing and excited. Up to the top of a mountain, the chopper's blades kicking up a whirling maelstrom of snow as it landed and disgorged its anxious passengers. Then on with the skis, the goggles and following the guide down, carving turns in the untouched snow until her legs were as weak as jelly and her heart was content.

She combed her hair and redid her ponytail, put on mascara. She tucked her bright pink turtleneck into her corduroy slacks and thrust her face closer to the mirror, clucking her tongue at the white "racoon eye" marks on her face—from wearing goggles while skiing. Everyone who skied had them all winter long.

She sprayed perfume behind her ears. Oh yes, she knew why she was doing it. For Matt. But she couldn't help it. A girl had her pride. She wanted to be attractive; she wanted him to notice her. She wanted to have the choice of saying no.

Or was she just playing games with herself? That night on the terrace... She shivered again, right there in her toasty-warm room, remembering. Sometimes she thought she'd been cruel, turning him away like that. Sometimes, as she lay in bed awake and wondering, she questioned whether Matt might not have meant what he said. Maybe he *did* like her. Maybe he was old enough to want more than a one-night stand. There were times—isolated moments—when she thought there was a sadness behind Matt's mocking blue gaze and curving smile. A loneliness. But maybe she was just kidding herself, wanting him to have a weakness, wanting him to be a nice guy deep down inside.

She gave one last look at herself in the mirror, felt her heart give a thump, then she turned and went outside just in time to see the helicopter landing on the pad, returning from Spillimacheen.

Jon was there to greet the group. He was dressed in his usual Saturday outfit: his wool knickers and hand-knit knee socks and a boiled wool Bavarian jacket. He greeted everyone graciously, with heavy, Germanic courtesy, clicking his heels, bending over the ladies' hands, shaking the men's somberly. Nicola stopped at the corner of the lodge, watching, wondering, preparing herself for the sight of Matt.

A young honeymooning couple got out of the helicopter, then an older man—most of the guests were male. No one she knew. A pair of college boys on break. Then a woman. Oh Lordy, she was wearing a full-length sable coat, and she dripped with jewels. It had to be Helga Gantzel. Was she going to *ski* in that coat? Helping Helga down was a gorgeous young hunk—blond, pale blue eyes, shoulders like Hercules and a smile like the Cheshire cat. Werner.

Then a slim, dapper Japanese man got out. The one Jon had mentioned? And a swarthy, handsome fellow. The rich Spaniard?

She waited, but no Cavanaughs were on that trip. She sighed with relief, feeling as if she'd had a stay of execution. But it was only for a few minutes more, until the chopper made another flight.

She should go into her kitchen, but that would be hiding. She couldn't let Matt govern her actions, and she did want to see Maureen and Evan. So she stood there in the sunlight with Jon, chatting with the new arrivals, introducing herself, answering questions, acting the part of the hostess, which Jon liked her to do.

"Oh yes, wonderful skiing this week," she said, answering one of the college boys. "We've got ten feet of snow so far this year."

"Awesome," he said. "When do we start?"

The helicopter was returning, floating toward them through the clear air, glinting in the sun. Then it was settling down on the pad, causing a whirlwind, whipping Nicola's hair into her eyes. The small blizzard died down, the snow settled, the door slid back. Oh yes, there was Maureen! And Evan. She waved and grinned. T.J. got out, looking around as if assessing the place, comparing it to his memories. His face showed no emotion; he smiled at Jon, but it never reached his eyes. Poor T.J.

The three Cavanaughs ducked under the rotors, and Jon greeted them. Nicola hugged Maureen, kissed Evan's cheek, then impulsively kissed T.J.'s, too. "I'm so glad to see you!" she said.

Other people were ducking and moving toward them—strangers, a couple of young women obviously on the prowl, another pair. Oh, it was the Huffs!

Matt was right behind them. Nicola kept up her facade, joking with Dave Huff, saying hello to Ruthie, asking questions, answering dozens of queries about the skiing. But something inside her sighed and rolled over, and she had to take a deep breath.

He wore a bright blue parka and jeans; he moved so well, so fluidly. The smile was on his face, telling the world that he refused to bow to the rules, that he didn't care what anyone thought.

"Hello, kid," he said.

"Hi, Matt." She kept her voice even, unaffected.

"Don't I get a kiss, too?" He mocked her, challenged her.

"Sure." She stepped up and brushed his cold cheek with her lips, but even that brief touch was like fire. The memory of his taste and smell came rushing back to her. "That okay?"

"For now," was all he said.

The Bugaboo Lodge was done on the inside in cheery cuckoo-clock, Bavarian-style knotty pine, with utilitarian furnishings. There was a cozy bar by the huge stone hearth, and that was where everyone met before dinner for wine and hors d'oeuvres and animated conversation. All the guests there naturally wanted to size up their companions for the week, the people with whom they'd be skiing all day, drinking and eating at night, their best friends for the charmed time they spent in the lodge. Introductions flew around thickly, as did questions. "Where are you from? Oh, do you know the Johnsons?" And offhand remarks of other places visited, backgrounds, jobs, the vital facts they needed to know about the strangers they were with to place them.

Nicola came out of the kitchen for a while before dinner, having promised Evan to have a drink with them.

The first person she saw when she walked into the room was Helga, leaning against the fireplace in tight black velvet pants and a shiny gold sweater. Her shoulder-length blond hair, still glamorous, fell over one eye, and Helga had a habit of pushing it back behind an ear. Diamonds flashed from her lobes, her wrists, her fingers. She was holding a glass and smiling up at Werner, smiling tightly and a little desperately.

"There she is!" Evan called. "Come over here, Nicola."

"All settled in?" Nicola asked brightly.

"Oh yes, Jon always gives us the same room," Maureen said. She looked wonderful in tan slacks and a pale pink ski sweater, but then Maureen always looked that way.

Evan thrust a glass of *Gluwein* into her hand. "Oh boy, it's just like old times. I can't wait. Hope the weather holds."

"So, how is your job?" Maureen asked.

"Wonderful. Lots of hard work, but I've skied quite a bit."

"You going to ski with us this week?" Evan asked.

"I hope so."

T.J. came over. "I haven't been here in years. It's all the same, Dad, isn't it?"

"The cook's new," Evan said, "and that's what matters."

"You better tell me if the food's good," Nicola said. "I mean it. You're the only ones I can ask."

Maureen pointed at the tray of appetizers on the bar. "Well, those were delicious."

"Better than Went's," Evan agreed. "Everyone was saying how good they were."

Nicola blushed. She never wanted to be *better*, for goodness' sake. She only wanted to be noticed by her father. "Don't tell him that, please," she said, treating the whole thing like a joke.

A burst of laughter made her turn her head. The college boys had latched on to the single ladies. They must have been telling naughty stories. She noticed Matt then, in the corner with the dark Spaniard; he was listening to the man, his eyes bright, the curved smile on his face. Was he avoiding her deliberately? Or was it Evan he was avoiding?

He noticed her looking at him and held his glass of wine up in a brief salute, then turned back to the Spaniard. Nicola was angry at herself suddenly and ashamed that he'd caught her watching him. *He* obviously didn't wander around mooning over *her*, craving a word of greeting, wondering, hoping, despising his own weakness. No, he kissed a girl, flattered a girl until her insides melted and her head spun, then he forgot her.

"Nick! What's up?" It was Dave, slapping her on the back, full of fun. Her spirits rose instantly.

"Beef tenderloin and new powder," she said.

"Oh, I'm going to gain weight," Ruthie moaned. "I know it."

"No, you won't. You'll ski it off," Nicola said.

"Unfortunately, I can eat more than I can ski," the woman replied.

"Hey, Evan, old buddy. You up to the steep and the deep?" Dave asked, poking Evan in the gut with a finger, taunting. "Can you keep up?"

"Don't worry, Dave, my boy. I just had my yearly physical. I'm fit as a fiddle, 110 percent. You just better watch your tail."

The conversation was light and easy, the guests bubbling with expectancy, geared for having the best week of their lives, lubricated by Jon's famous *Gluwein*. On everyone's mind was the same anticipation, the same excitement, a togetherness that crossed international barriers—the love of powder skiing, the thrill of that first glorious untracked run in the morning.

Nicola and two helpers served the meal family-style in the dining room. Everything had turned out well, and even Jon relaxed for an hour, joining the guests at dinner.

There was cream of asparagus soup, butter-lettuce salad with Nicola's special vinaigrette, thinly sliced beef tenderloin in mustard sauce, lightly seasoned zucchini and wild rice with pine nuts.

"Oh my God, I'm going to just stay here and eat all day. Forget the skiing," said one of the guests, a man from Toronto.

"This is *wunderbar*," Helga said. "Don't you think so, *Liebchen*?"

"Excellent," Werner said.

"Marvelous!" someone else agreed.

Dessert was raspberries, the ones Jon had been worried about, in peach liqueur.

"Sit down for a moment, Nicola," Jon said. "Everyone vants to meet you."

So she joined the entourage for a small glass of brandy.

"To our wonderful cook," Ruthie Huff said, raising her glass.

Nicola was embarrassed at the praise, liking it, but discomfitted by the attention. She sipped the smooth brandy and felt her cheeks grow hot as the roomful of people toasted her.

She smiled, and she must have replied something witty, because the group responded with laughter. And when she looked across the table, there was Matt, gazing at her. It seemed to her that the laughter and conversation died away and the room was empty except for the two of them. They stared at each other that way for an unending moment, for too long. Then the world jerked back into place, and Nicola heard the buzz of conversation again, the clinks of forks on dishes, and she excused herself quickly, too quickly, and beat a hasty retreat to the kitchen.

The drinking and introductions and conversation continued after dinner, after Nicola had overseen the cleanup and the breakfast preparations. She could have gone straight to her room; she considered it seriously, but Evan and Maureen would have wondered. They expected her to spend some time with them.

The flames undulated and hissed and spat in the big fireplace. Conversation eddied and flowed, jokes were repeated, stories compared. Skiing was discussed, fervently, intently, knowledgeably. What kind of skis were best in warm heavy powder as opposed to cold light snow. Which ski boots were warmer or gave more support. When the weight should be shifted in a turn. Whether to keep your weight equally on both skis in powder. Whether to make big swooping turns or tight ones. What kind of wax to use.

Nicola sat by the fire, surrounded by the guests, the strangers who were already getting to know one another, gravitating into cliques, feeling one another out, just as they did every week all winter long.

She was tired from her long day, on edge, feeling Matt's presence too keenly despite the fact that he was ignoring her. She could see him across the room, talking to the Japanese man, Rei Yamamoto, and to the Spaniard again. Then Jon, ever the perfect host, joined them, introducing the three men to Werner and Helga at the bar. Helga seemed always to be at the bar. She didn't even ski, Jon had told Nicola; she was there to be with Werner, and young Werner adored powder skiing.

Helga liked Matt immediately, Nicola saw. The woman moved her shoulders provocatively under the glittering gold sweater, and the blond hair fell over her eye as she talked animatedly to Matt. She still had charm, a trim body and a carefully nurtured beauty—from a distance—but it must have been her life's work to keep herself that way. Nicola felt the bite of jealousy as she watched Helga zero in on Matt. Werner must have felt the same way, because he was glowering, but then Matt said something to the young German and Werner smiled, was charmed, gave in to Matt's friendliness.

"Great group, isn't it?" Evan asked her . "Some good skiers."

"Gee, Dad, I sure hope you don't get anyone in your group who'll hold you up," T.J. said.

"Oh, Jon will see to it that nothing like that happens," Maureen was quick to say, "won't he, Evan?"

"Sure, he'll put me in the fast group. We have to get our vertical feet in, you know," Evan replied complacently. Every skier was promised one hundred thousand vertical feet of skiing for the week. If they went over—a feat to brag about—they paid extra for the privilege; if they didn't make enough runs to reach their hundred thousand, they got credit for their next visit. It was set up that way, because the largest expense in the operation was the helicopter—the more it flew, the more it cost.

"Señor Cavanaugh," came a voice. "I am Carlos Santana. May I introduce myself?" It was the swarthy Spaniard, a handsome man in his mid-forties, dressed in stunning Continental style, wearing a cashmere turtleneck sweater and pleated wool trousers.

"Mr. Santana?" Evan shook his hand. "My wife, Maureen, my son T.J. And you know Nicola."

Carlos bent over Maureen's hand, then Nicola's. He smelled of brandy and cigarette smoke and heavy male cologne. "A dinner fit for the gods," he said to Nicola. *"Absolutamente perfecto, señorita."*

He turned to Evan again. "Imagine my surprise at finding you here in this remote spot, *señor*. Perhaps you would have a *momento* sometime? I have a small point I wish to discuss with you." He took out an ostentatiously ornate cigarette case and lifted a cigarette from it.

As he searched in his pocket, T.J. held his own lighter up. "Let me," he said.

"Please have one," Santana offered, holding the case out to T.J., then to the rest of them, but only T.J. took one, lighting Santana's cigarette, then his own.

"'A small point'?" Evan repeated dryly.

"I assure you, it is nothing. Just a moment of your time." Santana waved his cigarette negligently.

*Darn him,* Nicola thought. *Can't he leave Evan alone? The man's on vacation.* She should warn Evan about Santana and Yamamoto, but Jon would already have done that, she was sure.

Helga was leaning on the bar, her mascara smudged, her voice growing thicker. When Nicola went to the bar to get herself a soda water, she could hear Helga talking to Werner and the man from Toronto. "I've been around," Helga was boasting. "I speak five languages, did you know? Yes,

Werner, *Liebchen*, you know, but Harold didn't know. And I have made films in twenty countries, yes, twenty. Once I was dubbed in Chinese. And I'm telling you both something. *Bitte*, darling, can I have another drink? What was I saying? Oh yes. That man, Santana, that oh-so-elegant Spaniard. From Madrid, he tells me." She leaned conspiratorially toward Werner and Harold. "I *know* Madrid. He is no more *madrileño* than I am. His accent is Central American, pure Central American. He thinks he can fool me, Helga Gantzel? I lived in Madrid for three years with my fourth husband, who was the Count of Salamanca."

"Is that so?" Harold asked.

"Yes, dahling. It would be like Paul Newman pretending to be English, you understand. So, Señor Santana is an imposter. I'll bet my last mark on it."

A Central American, Nicola thought, abruptly alarmed. Was he from Costa Plata? Was he only pretending to be a European investing in that country?

She glanced over to where Santana stood talking casually to T.J., both of them puffing on their cigarettes.

And then Nicola recalled the cigarette butts she'd found at the hunting camp. Whoever had tried to shoot Evan was a smoker. But lots of people smoked. Many Europeans still seemed to. And so did T.J., for that matter. Even Maureen had smoked once, but Evan, the health nut, had made her give it up. She still stole a puff or two from T.J.'s cigarettes occasionally.

Was there any significance to Santana's pretending to be from Spain? He had his reasons, she was sure. But what were they? And what was the "small point" he wanted to discuss with Evan? Something related to the World Bank, she'd bet.

She glanced back across the room at Evan, who was talking to one of the helicopter pilots, Junior. Evan loved all that technical stuff: lift and horsepower and fuel consumption and RPMs. He noticed her gaze and mimicked her troubled frown and smiled at her, then went on asking Junior about the chopper.

Well, she wasn't going to let Evan ignore this new information she had. She took her glass of soda water and went over to him.

"Hi, Junior," she said, "mind if I talk to Mr. Cavanaugh for a minute?"

"Go ahead," Junior said, "I was just on my way to the bar. See you tomorrow, Mr. Cavanaugh."

"What's this serious look of yours?" Evan asked. "Someone criticize the menu?"

"Evan, I really think you should get serious yourself for a minute and listen to me."

"Go ahead, whatever it is." He rolled his eyes and up-ended his glass.

"Did you know that Santana and the Japanese man, Mr. Yamamoto, have an automobile plant in Costa Plata?"

"Jon told me. It figures, doesn't it? You just can't get away from them. Don't worry, I can handle it."

"But I just heard Helga saying that Santana's accent was Central American, *not* Spanish. What if he's from Costa Plata? What if that awful Reyes sent him here to hurt you?"

Evan shrugged.

"Are you sure he's just a businessman, Evan?"

"Listen, Nicola, I'm here on vacation. Frankly, I don't care if he's Elvis Presley returned from the dead. I'm here to ski powder."

"But, Evan, what if he's here to influence you or threaten you . . . or even worse?"

Evan patted her head with affection. "Now, don't you worry about those kinds of things. Tell me, how's the skiing? That's what I'm really interested in."

She sighed. "Oh, Evan, I wish you'd take this less lightly."

"Not this week, Nicola." And he patted her head again, smiled and went over to join Dave Huff, who was telling a group the story of the time he'd been caught in an avalanche just above the lodge on a steep run.

"It was like swimming. I couldn't breathe," Dave was saying to his spellbound audience. "All I thought was, 'this is it, Dave, old boy.'"

"And who pulled him out?" Evan broke in, slapping Dave on the back cordially. "Yours truly!"

"Were you hurt?" one of the college boys asked.

"Banged up a bit. But I got in my hundred thousand vertical that week, anyway," Dave bragged.

"Sure, if you count the distance he slid in the avalanche," Evan retorted.

They made a great pair, those two, Nicola thought. Old friends, good buddies. They'd hunted together for years, skied together, visited each other. It was a good thing they had no business interests in common; where business was concerned, Evan had no friends at all.

She was aware of something then, as if there were a cold draft on her back. She turned, thinking to find a window open, but she met Matt's gaze from across the room. He was watching her, a glass in his hand, his dark brows drawn together.

She was suddenly uncomfortable, too hot in the smoke-filled room, her skin prickling. The allure was still there; she couldn't escape it. What did he want from her? Why did he run hot then cold? Why did he alternately pursue then ignore her? It wasn't fair.

She turned away deliberately and sat down, nursing her soda water, listening to Dave's funny stories. She wished she could just leave, go to her room, go to bed, forget Matt Cavanaugh and his games. But she'd turned stubborn; she'd outwait him. She'd sit there until everyone was gone, and then she'd confront him. She rehearsed the confrontation in her mind. *What is your problem, Matt? Pick on someone else, will you?* Oh yes, she could be stubborn and determined when she wanted to be!

People were starting to drift away to their rooms. Bedtime was early in the lodge. Breakfast was at seven, and then the chopper fired up, and the first group had to be ready to go. And almost everyone, except Helga and Maureen, wanted to be in shape to hit the slopes tomorrow.

The fire still crackled, the college boys had their women pinned into corners, Helga swayed out of the room on Werner's arm, waving a glass around. *"Guten Nacht,"* she said to everyone graciously, slurring. *"Guten Nacht,* my friends."

And then Nicola turned to face up to Matt, to toss him the gauntlet. She'd make him leave her alone; she'd tell him just where he stood in her book. She'd tell him.

She swiveled around, ready for the challenge. She searched the room, her heart pounding. But he was gone.

# CHAPTER TEN

THE LODGE, which had been silent and expectant that Sunday afternoon, burst into life. Suddenly there came the sound of ski boots thumping outside, the front door banged open, and the living room and bar swelled with happy, flushed, animated people, with high-pitched chatter and laughter and a lavish amount of boasting.

The day of skiing was over, the guests had returned home from the hills.

"What'd you think of that new bowl we did today?" Dave Huff slapped Evan on the back. "Now, that was a run!" He was weary but elated, his blue eyes dancing.

With the help of one of the maids, Nicola set out trays of hearty snacks: cheeses and thin, crispy Finnish crackers, wedges of her own pizza bread, cut vegetables and dips. Everyone crowded around the bar, where Dave was standing mixing drinks, his enthusiasm spilling over into the crowd. Helga and Maureen, the only two who had stayed behind that glorious day, awakened from their naps and appeared downstairs clad in après-ski attire: wool slacks, hand-knit sweaters and ankle-high boots of soft suede.

Maureen touched Nicola on the arm. "Noisy, aren't they?"

She nodded. "But happy as larks. Oh, what I wouldn't have done to have been up there in that fresh powder."

"Will Jon let you ski?"

"It's up to me, really. If I have my work done and there's room in the chopper..." Nicola shrugged.

"Ah," Evan said, joining them, "there you are." He gave his wife a kiss on the cheek.

Even Maureen looked mildly surprised, and she smiled warmly. "You must have had a good day."

"Wonderful." He beamed. "And don't listen to Dave. I outskied him every inch of the way."

Yes, Nicola could see, everyone was cheerful, though exhausted. But it was a good tiredness, a healthy one, and it glowed on the red-cheeked faces.

She glanced around the room. There was that young honeymoon couple, off in a corner by the fireplace, totally lost in marital bliss. And T.J., over there, chatting quietly with the Japanese man, Rei, and his pal Carlos. An odd couple, she thought again, wondering at their true motive for this skiing vacation. And there, near the bar, was Ruthie, taking a glass of wine from Dave, casting around for a place to sit, flushed and pretty in her bright pink one-piece suit.

Nicola checked the trays of food, set out some more crackers and wiped up a spill. Idly she looked around the room, telling herself it was to see if anyone needed anything, but knowing that she was really searching for Matt.

Why did the mere knowledge of his presence in the lodge make her stomach feel hollow with excitement?

She thought back to that time she'd seen him last June, stepping out of his Ferrari, the easy, ironic smile on his lips, and she recalled the way the morning sun had struck his hair, lighting it. She'd been unable to keep her eyes off him since. And if she was being thoroughly honest with herself, she'd have to admit that her thoughts were constantly invaded by images of him, by the little nuances of caring she'd caught him at, by his mannerisms, his walk, the sway of his hips and shoulders.

"Here." It was Evan, handing her a glass of wine. "I feel so bad, up there all day having a ball, and you down here cooking in a hot kitchen. Have a wine, relax a bit."

"Thanks," Nicola said, taking it, trying to collect her thoughts. "But I'll just *bet* you were thinking of me while you were up there." She nodded toward the peaks outside.

"Well..."

Matt appeared finally from upstairs, and Nicola watched him out of the corner of her eye. He'd showered and changed into jeans, a white turtleneck and a dark green sweater. His hair was still damp, combed back over his forehead and ears, and he looked around the room briefly as if checking out the lay of the land.

"So Dave fell right above me," Evan was telling her and Maureen, "and I swear, I thought the snow was going to give."

"A slide?" Maureen asked, alarmed.

But Evan shook his head. "Oh, I don't really think it would have slid. That guide of ours today, Hans, was real careful. And can he ski! You should see him in the bottomless stuff in the bowl."

"Are you going to ski tomorrow, Maureen?" Nicola asked, trying desperately not to follow Matt with her gaze.

"Tomorrow, yes. A few runs."

"Good, good," Evan said. "The snow's dynamite." He leaned against the wall, eyeing the roomful of skiers. "Look at that kid," he said, gesturing toward Matt. "Fits right in, doesn't he? But I guess he's had lots of experience in resorts."

"Evan," Maureen warned.

Matt sauntered over. "Hi, folks." His greeting was general. He did not look at Nicola.

"Did you have a good day?" Maureen asked.

"Great skiing," he answered.

Nicola glanced down at her wine. She wished she could escape to the kitchen, but Evan would make a remark about it, and Maureen would beg her to stay and...

"I've seen you ski better," Evan said abruptly to his son.

"I guess I'm out of practice. Give me a day or two," Matt replied easily.

"You just don't understand about taking care of your body," Evan began.

"Sure, I know, the body's a temple." Matt gave a short laugh.

Evan bristled. "Well? It is, and if you'd take better care of yours—"

"Please," Maureen began, but Matt had already turned his back on the three of them and was heading toward the bar.

At least Matt hadn't risen to the bait tonight, Nicola mused. In fact, he seemed distracted, as if Evan could have said just about anything and it would have rolled right over him.

"That boy's just downright rude," Evan said, disgruntled. "He didn't even say hello to Nicola."

"He's tired," Maureen said doubtfully, as if she herself knew that wasn't quite it.

"Tired from doing *what*?"

Finally Nicola was able to make an excuse. She edged her way through the crowd, picking up empty glasses, soggy cocktail napkins, broken crackers. She disappeared into the kitchen, stirred the pots, checked the oven and the bread that was rising on the shelf above the stove.

Why did Evan continually hound his children? He treated her so kindly, but with his boys he was relentlessly hard and controlling. Sometimes, she thought, she could shake Evan. But he'd never listen to her.

Nicola's pity for Matt was short-lived, however, when she returned to the throng and saw the act he was putting on. Only minutes before he had been distracted and remote, but now he was the epitome of the garrulous barkeep, serving drinks from behind the bar, talking to two people at once, laughing, toasting the great day on the hill with Dave. What a charmer!

She stood in her tracks and watched him from across the room. *Was* it an act? Or was this the real Matt Cavanaugh? How thoroughly, disarmingly attractive he was. No one could resist him. He was busy telling an acceptable, mixed-company joke, something about a mouse and an elephant, and leaning close to Helga's ear. Helga was lapping it up, holding her glass high for Matt to refill, smiling broadly, her makeup a touch too loud for the rustic setting.

On and on the joke went. The elephant fell into a pit, and the mouse rushed for help. "Oh," Helga exclaimed, "the dahling little mouse!" And as the older woman pushed her heavy blond hair off her face, Nicola could see that her eyebrows were raised as if she were permanently surprised.

The crowd thickened around the bar, and all Nicola could see now was Matt's handsome head, still bent toward Helga, while his hand, seemingly with a mind of its own, poured drinks with a flourish. He was laughing and talking a mile a minute; his eyes shone with joie de vivre. His lips curved in that smile she was growing to know so well.

He'd pressed those lips to hers . . .

So the mouse returned to the pit where the elephant was stuck, but he hadn't found a rope. "Well, how are you going to get me out?" Matt asked in his deep elephant's voice. The mouse squeaked, "I've been keeping this a secret. I didn't want to hurt your feelings." Suddenly the mouse produced his male adornment, dropping it over the edge . . .

The crowd roared its approval. Nicola folded her arms across her chest tightly.

"He's incorrigible," Maureen said at her ear, but she was smiling. "I don't know how Matt does it."

"Years of practice," Nicola said coolly.

"He was an outgoing little boy. It seemed as if he got all the charm in the family. . . ." She paused, uncertain, then went on. "T.J.'s so serious-minded. I just wish he'd relax."

"Maybe here he will," Nicola put in.

"Ah! There you are!" Jon hurried over to Nicola's side. "I vas vorried...."

"Dinner's all set."

"Of course it is." He mopped at his brow. "The beginning of the veek is always so tense."

"Everything is wonderful," Maureen assured him, winking at Nicola.

"Oh yes, yes, I know, and my poor dead vife, Greta, she used to say I vorried too much. Maybe she was right."

"I think she was," Nicola replied. "Have a glass of wine. Dinner will be on the table at seven sharp. I promise."

Jon nodded distractedly and headed off into the group again.

"Phew," Nicola said, smiling ruefully.

"Is he always this bad?" Maureen asked.

"Always. Until Friday, then he calms down. But Saturday morning it starts all over again."

"I never noticed."

"You never knew anyone who *verked* for him before," Nicola said, and the two of them laughed.

One by one the skiers climbed the steps to shower and change for dinner. A few of the hard hitters, though, stayed at the bar, where Matt continued to tell amusing stories and pour stiff drinks. Ruthie dragged Dave away, while Evan went up with Maureen in tow. T.J. hung around, leaning against the fireplace, and the honeymooners stayed where they were, entwined and oblivious. The college boys stuck around, pumping one of the guides on how he skied the powder. Carlos left, but Rei had another drink and sat down next to Werner on the couch. Werner wasn't paying any attention to the man from Japan, though. No. Werner was watching Helga with an acute eye.

*Now, if I had drunk all that liquor,* Nicola thought of Helga, *I'd be facedown on the bar.* But old Helga was going strong. Only that veil of hair that hung over her eye had slipped a notch or two.

Matt held up a bottle of schnapps. "One more?"

"Oh," Helga said, breathless, "I mustn't. Well…perhaps a wee bit on the ice here." She batted false eyelashes.

Red-hot jealously spurted through Nicola. Quickly, unable to bear another moment of Matt and Helga, she went into the kitchen, picked up the nearest thing in sight, a pot holder, and threw it against the wall.

Dinner was a success. Like hunters and fishermen, the skiers ate huge amounts of food. The difference was, Nicola tried to lay off the butter and cream sauces, the high-cholesterol items.

Jon popped into the kitchen when the tables were cleared. "Excellent," he exclaimed, "excellent!"

"Thank you."

"I don't know vat I would have done this season vithout your expertise."

"Oh," Nicola said modestly, "you'd have found someone."

When she returned to the living room, Hans was counting heads for the after-dinner activities—cross-country skiing and snowmobiling—for those who still had the energy.

Rei Yamamoto and Carlos chose the snowmobiles, and T.J. opted to join them. At least, Nicola thought, T.J. had made some new friends, even if their motives were a bit questionable. She wondered if those two had befriended T.J. just because his father was head of the World Bank. Oh dear, maybe they were going to try to get at Evan through his son. Or maybe, she thought, ashamed of her cynicism, they just enjoyed T.J.'s company.

"Come on, Nicola," Evan coaxed. "Come cross-country skiing with us. Get some exercise."

"Well…"

"Come on, you'll sleep like a log!"

It wasn't a bad idea, she decided. It'd take the edge off, chase the weariness from her bones. It would also spare her the sight of Matt playing games with Helga.

Several of the other guests were getting ready, trying on the low leather boots, propping skis from the storeroom against the walls in the living room, choosing long poles.

Nicola hurried over to the bunkhouse and pulled on a pair of knickers and long woolen socks, a heavy turtleneck and an oversize Scandinavian sweater. Grabbing a hat and warm gloves, she rejoined the group.

"Oh, good," Evan said, seeing her attire, "you're going."

There was Evan and a guest from California and Dave. Werner was tugging on his boots and surprisingly so was Helga. Nicola would have thought the woman too inebriated to stand, much less ski. The guide was that cute young man from Vermont, Skip.

Yes, it would feel good to work out the kinks, push herself a little, get some fresh air. She felt better already.

It was just then that Matt clattered down the stairs, with his parka and cross-country ski boots on. Her heart sank.

It occurred to Nicola to back out of the deal then. Enough was enough for one evening. But she wasn't going to let Matt spoil everything for her. She wasn't going to cower or run away. She'd just ski ahead of him—or lag behind. She didn't want to play his game anymore; she'd be darned if she could figure out his rules, and the stakes were much too high for her.

The moon was full, sitting lightly on a jagged peak, as they all pushed off from in front of the lodge. It was surprisingly bright out, but all the color was leached out of things, so that the scene was akin to an old black-and-white film, all silver and jet and shades of gray. Skip led them toward the summer logging road, which was well packed for a few miles from previous cross-country skiers.

Behind them, heading out from the lodge, were the snowmobiles. Their engines growled and whined as they approached the skiers, then passed them, disappearing around a bend ahead until they could no longer be heard.

"I don't know why T.J. likes those things," Evan said, puffing along beside Nicola. "Too damn noisy."

"They're fun," Nicola said, "once you get the hang of them."

"No exercise involved, though," he said critically.

The group moved in a line now, silent for the most part, following the silvered path through the pines. It was a beautiful night, the stars diamond sharp in the black sky, the air fragrant with pine and wood smoke from the chimney of the lodge. She was aware of Matt behind her; she could hear his breathing as he slid across the packed snow, one ski, then the other, his poles moving in even rhythm with his legs. It was a nice evening, true, but she'd have preferred to go it alone.

Up ahead of the column was Skip, keeping an easy pace. Directly behind was Werner, then Helga, Dave, Evan, and in front of Nicola was the Californian. Matt held up the end. If she could drop behind a bit, wait a few minutes, then she'd follow on her own. It would be peaceful....

Nicola skied over to the side of the road and stopped, bending over as if to retie her boot. She could feel the smooth rise and fall of her chest, her even breathing, the dampness on her brow under the wool hat. In a minute or two they'd all be around that curve that led into a steep-sided canyon. Matt had said nothing when she'd pulled aside, merely taken up the slack and gone on with the others. Good.

She waited, gazing up at the heavens, tipping her head so that the face on the moon righted itself. There was nothing in the world like a night sky in the mountains—sharp, crisp, utterly delineated from the horizon. She was immensely glad she had decided to go along.

She pushed off after a suitable time, moving from side to side to gain momentum, poling, pushing, pulling, pumping. She kept a comfortable pace, listening to her breathing, feeling that perfect rhythm and the slight burn in her arms and thighs. She was really going to sleep like a baby tonight.

He came at her from beneath a tall pine, a shadow detaching itself from the forest. At first she was startled, then irritated.

"Can't you take a hint?" she said, skiing on.

But Matt quickly closed the gap she was purposefully creating between them. "I thought maybe you had trouble with your skis," he said, breathing hard.

"Well, I didn't."

He was abreast of her now, slowing his pace to match hers. "Great night, isn't it?"

"It *was*."

"Come on, Nicky. We're here to have fun, aren't we?"

"You're the one paying for fun. I just work here. Look, Matt, you don't have to be nice to me. Go play your games. Go on, catch up with Helga."

He chuckled. "Why, Nicola Gage, you're jealous."

She flushed and was glad he couldn't see it in the dark. "Don't be ridiculous."

"I'm flattered, kid."

"Don't be."

They skied in silence for a while then, until they could make out the group ahead.

"We may as well catch up," she said.

"I kind of like it back here."

That was the only excuse she needed. She knew it was spiteful and childish and that he'd probably laugh at her, but she did it anyway, forcing her pace, pushing herself to the limit.

But he kept right up, as if he'd anticipated her move. "You're mad because of Thanksgiving," he said, sucking a lungful of air. "You're mad because I kissed you."

Nicola was really panting now. She wouldn't give him the pleasure of an answer; she'd just keep skiing until he left her alone.

But he kept up, and she could hear his hard breathing behind her, close behind. Darn him!

"Will you slow up?" he finally said.

Nicola felt sweat dampening her back and chest, and her hair beneath her hat was wet. Still, she shook her head. "Just leave me alone, why don't you?" But her pace slowed inevitably, and soon he was beside her.

She heard it then, ahead of them, an angry voice, no, more than one. Matt had halted and was listening.

"What?" she said, sliding to a stop.

"Someone sounds like they're ticked off," he said lightly.

Still breathing hard from their skiing, they came upon the group moments later. And they both stopped short at the tableau that presented itself, a black-and-white picture etched into the pale silver snow.

Helga was stamping one ski, furious, not altogether sober, and Werner was by her side, his square jaw thrust forward pugnaciously, his features harsh in the moonlight. And Evan faced them, his expression hard. The others stood around in stiff discomfort, unwilling spectators.

Skip cleared his throat. "Say, uh, we better be going back."

But Helga was livid with rage.

"What's going on?" Matt said, catching his breath.

"Ah!" Helga hissed between her teeth, lifting a pole and brandishing it dangerously close to Evan's face. "This man, this father of yours is a cheat! A liar!"

"Now, see here, Helga," Evan said, his face as contorted and pallid as hers, "put down that pole. It was just business, for God's sake."

"Business!" she shrieked. "I came to you for help and you . . . you insulted me!"

"Helga," Evan said, "what do you want from me? Put down that damn ski pole."

Nicola watched it all, caught somewhere between wonder and embarrassment and fear for Evan. What in heaven's name was Helga talking about? And shouldn't they get that pole out of her hand before she really did hurt him?

It was Matt who made the first move. "Helga," he said, his voice demanding and hard, "give that to me. You're acting like a child."

But Helga swung around abruptly. "You stay out of this!" she cried, poking at Matt, almost catching his thigh with the sharp tip of the pole. "Everyone is trying to destroy me!"

"Helga," Evan said, "you've gone crazy."

"Ha!" she cried, beside herself.

The group held its breath collectively. Finally Evan tried to maneuver his skis backward, and Nicola could see he actually was taking the woman quite seriously.

"Yes," Helga said, her voice as shrill as fingernails on a blackboard, "someday you will pay for this, Evan Cavanaugh. Someday I will kill you!"

## CHAPTER ELEVEN

"NICOLA! Ach, *Mein Gott*, Nicola!"

She rubbed her face and tried to rouse herself. "What is it?"

"Ve are in terrible trouble!" Jon's face was drawn; he was jumping with nerves. "Did you know half our food order vas missing? From Saturday. Did you know?"

Nicola sat up and tried to think. "I had Jenny check the invoices. She said everything was okay."

"Ach, *Mein Gott*. She knows nothing, that girl. Half the lettuce is missing and only one lug of tomatoes came in. And the case of Riesling I ordered to go vith the salmon!"

"Oh Lordy."

"This is vat I have nightmares about. Maybe I should go to Calgary and run a normal hotel. *Gott in Himmel*, then I could go to the store myself or phone the delivery people! This place, I am getting too old for it, Nicola."

"Look, we can manage. We'll have vegetable salads, instead."

"No, no. That is not good enough. And the vine. And the salmon, too! No. But I have fixed things, I think. That is vhy I'm getting you up so early. I have persuaded Junior to fly you to Spillimacheen in a few minutes. Then you vill see, probably the stuff is still sitting at the bus stop. Or, if it isn't, then you call Nobel Food in Calgary and have them ship it on the next bus, so ve'll get it tomorrow."

"Oh. But who'll do breakfast and pack the lunches?"

"I vill. Me and Jenny, that careless girl. You vill be back soon, anyway. How long can it take? As soon as the groups stop for lunch, Junior vill pick you up in Spillimacheen."

"Darn," Nicola said, "I *knew* I should have checked those invoices myself."

"Yes, yes," Jon said, agreeing. "The other cook before you alvays did."

She felt a stab of guilt. This was so different from her previous jobs, so isolated here, and she should have realized... In Colorado, of course, you could always drive to a grocery store and pick up missing items locally. But not here. Jon was probably wishing his former cook hadn't married and moved to Calgary—he'd probably double the man's wages at this point to have him back.

"Now, you hurry to meet Junior. He vill have to make this a fast trip."

"Sure," she said, looking down at herself, "but I better get dressed, Jon."

"Oh yes, of course...."

She dressed quickly, pulled on her parka and ran along the snow-packed path to the back door and into the kitchen. Jon and Jenny were already busy cracking eggs and brewing coffee.

"It's omelets this morning," Nicola reminded them, feeling that awful guilt again. "With coffee cake. Figure three eggs per person."

"Okay, ve do fine. Just get that stuff for us."

"And for the lunches, I've got it all written down in my book. Don't put bananas in the lunches. Sometimes they freeze and turn black."

"I know, I know. Go get in the helicopter so Junior can get back quick."

Reluctantly Nicola left the kitchen. She should have reminded Jon about the honey for Evan's coffee, but Jon knew, she was sure. And a hundred other details. She *should* have suggested Jon go to Spillimacheen, but under the circumstances, she'd best let him work off his agitation in the hot kitchen.

The big Bell helicopter was sitting on the helipad, its rotors drooping. Junior was leaning against it, smoking a cigarette. He stubbed it out in the snow when he saw her coming and waved, then headed toward the cockpit door.

"Thanks, Junior, this is a big favor." Nicola said as she reached him. "Jon's going nuts."

"I know. He almost cried when he woke me up this morning. The guy needs a course in stress management," the pilot said over his shoulder.

She climbed in. Surprisingly there was another person there, sitting in the middle of the forward-facing row of seats. She blinked and stopped short, half in and half out.

"Hello, kid."

"Matt?" She pulled herself in hesitantly and sat on the bench facing him. "Are you leaving or something?" she asked, busying herself with the seat belt.

"No, just going along for the ride. I have to make a phone call," he said casually.

Another one of his mysterious phone calls, Nicola thought, remembering the one in Redstone, the one he'd lied about.

"It's for a bartending job in Palm Beach. I was supposed to call last week, but I forgot," he was saying.

Junior started the helicopter, and snow flew around in a white cloud outside, obscuring the lodge. The engine whined, warming up, and quivered, like a creature coming alive.

"All set, folks?" Junior called back to them, lifting his earphones, and Nicola raised her thumb.

The chopper rose straight up, defying gravity, tilted crazily and turned east, toward Spillimacheen. If Nicola twisted around, she could look through the Plexiglas bubble and see where they were going, over the Bugaboo Mountains, straight east, down into the Spillimacheen River Valley. The morning sun filled the interior of the machine, lighting Matt's face but leaving hers shadowed. He looked tired, as if he'd been up late. Maybe he had—with Helga or one of the single ladies. She switched her eyes away from him, looking out of the side window, watching the white peaks flit by below.

Matt's eyes were still on her, however. She could feel them, touching her like fingers. She wouldn't look; she wouldn't. It wasn't far to Spillimacheen, fifteen minutes over the mountains. She would just sit there and take it, and then they would land and she could get away from him.

The mountains fled below, giving way to lower peaks, then foothills, and then she could see the river, winding black and shiny along the valley floor. Almost there.

"Not having much of a week, are you?" Matt said over the noise of the engine.

She didn't take her gaze from the window. "No. Frankly, I'm tired of trying to figure you out."

"I know."

His reply surprised her, and she turned her gaze to him. He looked sincere.

"Mom begged me to come on this ski trip. I wouldn't have been here otherwise. And T.J. She wants us to be friends, all her menfolk. Believe me, it's not much fun for me, either. Evan rags on me and humiliates T.J. He won't meet either of us halfway. Hell, Nicky, I'd rather be lazing on the sand in Palm Beach."

He meant it. No joking, no devil-may-care pretenses, no sarcastic cover-up. He felt *something* then.

"Nicky, can we call a truce? Just be friendly for this week?" he said.

"I'm not at war with you," she said carefully.

He gave her a rueful smile. "I wonder." Then he leaned across, took her hand from where it lay on her lap and started playing with her fingers. "You have pretty hands," he said. "Small and pretty."

She pulled it out of his grasp. "I thought you wanted to be friendly."

"I *was* being friendly."

The chopper was descending, tilting, vibrating.

"Too friendly," she said.

"A guy can't win."

She sat quietly for a minute, gathering her thoughts. This was the perfect time to bring up the subject. "Matt, can you be serious for a minute?"

He looked at her questioningly.

"It's Evan. I'm really worried about him. There was that business with Helga last night. What on earth was that all about?"

Matt laughed. "Helga. Evan's known her for years, ever since she was a big star. Our bank helped her finance an apartment building in New York years ago. Then she came to him last year and wanted him to invest in a movie. She would be the star, of course. Her comeback. He wouldn't. Part of the trouble was she was going to play the part of a thirty-five-year-old. You know Evan. If he thought it was a bad investment, he would have told Helga so—brutally."

"Oh."

"I knew all that. So does Mom. It's no coincidence Helga's there this week. She's still trying to convince Evan. She's harmless. Sad, but harmless."

"Are you sure? Isn't it awfully odd that she's here this week? She doesn't even ski. And those two smoothies, Yamamoto and Santana. Did you know they have business interests in Costa Plata? Santana wanted to talk to Evan. Jon told me all about them. They stand to lose a lot of money if Costa Plata goes bankrupt."

"Jon? How does he know all that?"

"He has a cousin in Nicaragua who's worried, too. So worried he may move to Canada."

"Jon? A cousin in Nicaragua?"

"That's what he said."

"Small world, isn't it?"

Nicola looked at him sharply. He wasn't the least bit surprised about Jon's cousin—it was as if he already knew. She furrowed her brow. "I'm really concerned. What if one of those men is working for Reyes? Do you remember that threat? Oh, and I forgot. Carlos Santana has a Central American accent, not Spanish. So that could mean—"

"Since when are you an expert on Spanish accents?"

"I overheard Helga say that. She had a Spanish husband—she speaks the language. I mean, *you* could tell that Laurence Olivier was English and not American or Canadian, couldn't you?"

"You're in earnest about this, aren't you?" he asked.

"Yes, darn it, I am. I tried to tell Evan, but he poohpoohed it. He's on vacation. He refuses to pay any attention to it."

"Little Nicky, you're really getting worked up, aren't you?"

"Don't patronize me, Matt. I think you should be concerned, too. He's your father.

He was studying her, watching her too closely, a strange expression chasing itself across his features, a narrowing of his eyes, but then, as if he thought better of it, he wiped his face clear and grinned roguishly. "Don't worry, kid, Evan can take care of himself."

Spillimacheen was a tiny crossroads. There wasn't much snow on the ground here surprisingly, not like in the mountains. Junior let them off on the curiously incongruous helipad.

"I'll be back whenever they take their lunch breaks," he said, leaning out of the cockpit door. "You better stick around and watch for me. Around one, maybe. And I'll be in a hurry."

"Okay, thanks. See you." Nicola waved at him as he pulled his head in, closed the door and took off, rising, tipping, blowing snow at them, buzzing away toward the mountains like a busy insect.

"So, business first?" Matt asked.

They walked to the general store, whose plate glass windows were so cluttered with dusty displays that they were opaque. Spillimacheen, B.C., read the sign over the door. Bus to Calgary Loads Here.

"A thriving metropolis," Matt said as he opened the door for her, and the bell that announced customers tinkled in welcome.

The man behind the counter was smoking a pipe. When they entered, he took it out of his mouth and studied it intently as he spoke. "I heard the helicopter. You folks from the lodge, eh?"

"Yes," Nicola said. "I'm checking on our produce shipment that came in Saturday on the bus. We're short several things, and we wondered if they got left off the helicopter." It was somewhat disconcerting, talking to the man while he directed all of his remarks to his pipe.

"I don't think anything got left. You go on and check around here. I'll ask my wife. She's in back." He gestured with his pipe.

They looked around the store, but there was nothing except the usual stuff sold there: cans of food, guns, fishing rods, kerosene lamps, gasoline cans, axes and hand tools, snack foods. They looked outside, but there was only the bench by the door and a hitching post, presumably for horses in the summer.

"They never sent it," Nicola said to herself.

"Does this happen often?" Matt asked.

"Not since I've been here. Let's go see if his wife found anything."

She hadn't.

"Darn," Nicola said. "I'll have to call Calgary. What a hassle. And the helicopter will have to come pick it up tomorrow. Oh, is Jon going to have a fit."

The public phone was outside, an open booth that was very chilly in this winter weather. Nicola called Nobel Foods in Calgary and, in her sternest voice, demanded to know why three cases of produce, fifteen pounds of pink salmon on dry ice and a case of Riesling had been left off the bus to Spillimacheen.

"We'll have it up there tomorrow," the man promised. "On the bus that gets in at two. Okay?"

"Not really, but we can't do anything about it. Are you sure it'll be here tomorrow? We can't just phone and ask, you know."

"I'll put it on myself, first thing in the morning," he assured her.

"Inefficiency," Matt commented when she hung up.

"You'd think by now, after all these years of dealing with the lodge, they'd be more careful, wouldn't you?" She gestured to the phone. "Go ahead. Your turn."

He reached for the receiver, then hesitated. "While I make this call, maybe you could see if the fellow inside sells coffee. I didn't get any this morning."

"Me, neither. What do you take?"

"One sugar. Please."

It was pretty obvious that Matt was trying to get rid of her. Who was he calling? she wondered, opening the door and tinkling the bell again. If it was a man about a prospective job, why would he care if she heard or not? She'd bet his call wasn't about a job. What she couldn't figure out was why he bothered acting so mysterious about it, as if everyone didn't already know his reputation with the ladies.

"Sure, we have coffee. The machine's right over there. Help yourself, young lady," the store owner said to his pipe.

When she got outside again, Matt was leaning against the wall of the building, hands in pockets, shoulders hunched against a stiff breeze. He took the Styrofoam coffee cup from her. "Thanks. This'll really hit the spot."

"Did you reach the man?" she asked deliberately.

"No, he wasn't there. I'll have to try later."

"Um. Too bad."

"So." He looked at his watch. "What now?"

Nicola turned full circle, taking in all of Spillimacheen, what there was of it. She gave a little laugh. "We've got until at least one this afternoon."

"Can we take in a quick movie? An art gallery? Botanical gardens?" he asked dryly.

She had to smile, even though being stuck for several hours in Spillimacheen with Matt Cavanaugh was not her choice of a way to spend her morning. And they *were* stuck together; there was nothing to do, not even any place to sit and wait inside where it would be warm. It was as if Matt had planned it that way. "We can wait here, I guess," she suggested.

"Or we could take a walk." He slapped his arms. "Warm up a bit." He finished his coffee and tossed the empty cup into a trash can.

There was absolutely no choice unless she wanted to wait there all alone. "Okay. Where to?"

He pointed down the country road. "That way."

They set off at a good place, attempting to warm up. The road followed the floor of the river valley, and mountains rose on both sides of it. The wind blew on and off, chilly gusts that picked up dead leaves and dust devils where the ground was not covered by snow. A farmhouse, white and Victorian square, sat back from the road to their right. Brown stubble poked from the light dusting of snow in fields on either side of them.

They marched in silence, side by side, a fair distance between them. Nicola tried to think of a safe subject, but everything that came to mind seemed artificial and forced, so she just let the silence continue. And so did Matt.

They passed a barbed wire fence enclosing an empty field in which some sort of livestock had once grazed; it was bordered by a line of tall, denuded oak trees, planted long before as a windbreak by the pioneers to this remote valley. A farm dog, shaggy and bristling, raced, barking, to the end of his territory bordering the road.

"Quiet, Spot," Matt said.

"He isn't spotted."

"But does he know that?"

They continued on, leaving Spot watching after them suspiciously. "Do you like dogs?" Matt asked.

"Sure, I like dogs. I never had one, though." She kept her eyes straight ahead, determined to appear neutral in all ways.

Matt pulled the collar of his blue parka up and stuck his hands in his pockets. "There's a lot I don't know about you."

She shrugged.

"And finding out is like pulling teeth."

She said nothing.

"A hard nut to crack, is that it?"

She kept walking, lifting her hand to push back a strand of hair that was blowing into her eyes.

"All right," came Matt's voice, "I apologize. I'm duly punished. Now you can let down and answer my questions."

"I thought we were going for a walk," she said mildly.

"We are. Damn it, Nicola." He stopped short, right in the middle of the road, took her arm and pulled her around to face him.

She stumbled, her forward motion stopped too suddenly, and put a hand out to steady herself, touching Matt's arm. She drew it back as if stung, then stood there, breathing hard, held face-to-face with him.

"I'm not your enemy," he said finally, softly.

"Then let me go, Matt," she said quietly.

He dropped his hand. His eyes were sad. His dancing blue eyes . . . She focused somewhere over his shoulder, knowing he was still staring at her. A gust of wind ruffled his hair and batted at her parka. She sniffed, her nose dripping and red from the cold.

He made an angry gesture, a cutting motion with his hand. "Okay, you win. We'll play your game—"

"I'm not playing a game," she interrupted swiftly.

"No," he said, eyeing her from under dark brows. "I forgot. You don't know how to play games."

"Can we continue our walk now?" she asked coolly. Inside, she was exulting at the power she had over Matt when she was cold to him. Exulting and a little scared, and then it came to her that she *was* playing a game. She'd lied and not even known it. Because what she really wanted to do was to go to him and feel his strong arms around her, his mouth on hers, his hard, lean body pressed against her. She wanted to rest her head on his chest and feel his hands stroke her and calm her fluttering heart and whisper into her ear that he'd be so very careful with the delicate love she offered him.

Matt turned and strode away, his shoulders tense. She kept up, apart from him, hating what she was doing, but knowing no other way to protect herself.

An old pickup truck came toward them, the only vehicle they'd seen. It slowed, then stopped, and an elderly man stuck his head out of the window. "You folks got a car broken down out here, eh?"

"No, we're taking a walk," Matt replied. "Thanks anyway."

"A walk? Saints alive. A walk, eh?" The man shook his head. "It's going to snow, don't you know? This afternoon. My old knees told me. Don't be out walking too long."

"Thanks," Nicola said. "We won't."

"Snow," Matt repeated when the truck had gone on. "You think he's right?"

"Oh no. If it snows, the helicopter won't be able to pick us up," Nicola said in a worried tone. "Oh wow, that'd be awful. Dinner..."

Matt searched the sky. "It isn't bad yet. Junior will be back before any weather rolls in."

"I hope so," she said fervently. Stranded in Spillimacheen with Matt, not only for the morning, but until a storm blew past? She *couldn't*. She couldn't bear being around him all that time, fencing and parrying and having to watch what she said and did. And wanting him all the time, craving his touch as a person dying of thirst craved water. Oh no. It couldn't happen, it would be intolerable. Junior would have to make it back!

They reached a curve in the road and an old apple orchard. A split rail fence ran alongside the trees, and a flock of pretty birds with cherry-red heads were pecking at the few withered old apples still clinging to the gnarled branches. Matt stopped, put a foot up on the lower rail of the fence and leaned crossed arms on the top one.

"Cute birds. Do you know what kind they are?" he asked, as if nothing had happened, as if she hadn't made him angry.

"They're called pine grosbeaks in Colorado."

"I like birds. They're so uncomplicated," he said idly, watching them. They twittered and flapped, busily eating the apples, hopping from branch to branch, scolding one another.

She stood beside him, feeling foolish, cast in the role now of sulking youngster. "I like birds, too," she said.

"You see?" he said, turning, leaning his elbows against the fence. "We do have something in common."

"That we like birds?" she asked.

"It's a start."

# CHAPTER TWELVE

MATT RIPPED OPEN THE CANDY BAR, shoved half of it in his mouth, then dialed Ned's private line in Washington. He was well aware of Nicola standing close by, chewing on her own snack from the general store, eyeing him.

Had she seen the numbers he'd dialed?

He swallowed, took another mouthful and turned slightly in her direction. Not only could she have seen his hand, but if she'd wanted, she could have made out the numbers, as well. He gave her an innocent grin.

The phone rang and rang. No answer. At this point he had two options: either stall the helicopter pilot somehow and try again later, or dial directly into the Foreign Service switchboard, using an unscrambled line, and give his instructions to Ned's secretary. He opted for choice number one. Wait. Choice two would have Ned murderously furious; an agent only used the open lines in case of a dire emergency.

"No one home?" Nicola asked from her spot leaning against the wall. She was suspicious. Oh, Nicky hadn't clue one as to what he was up to, but just the fact that she was curious was enough to tell him that he'd started making mistakes.

*So what?* He was fed up with his line of work, anyway. Either Ned brought him in, or Matt was going to take his chances and quit. They wouldn't really, ah, terminate him, would they? Heck, Jennings, one of the other Section C agents, had been brought in after thirty years in the service, and now he had a cushy job, working for the Paris office as a translator. Naw, Ned wouldn't give Matt too hard a time....

"Well," Nicola said, sighing, "guess we both struck out today."

"Looks that way." He noticed the sarcastic note in her voice—she thought he'd been trying to get a lady, no doubt, but he couldn't tell her otherwise. He watched as she crumpled up her candy wrapper and tossed it, a basketball-style bank shot, into a nearby trash can. "Good eye."

"For some things."

Dust was kicking up across the road and swirling around the building. It was going to be a hairy ride back to the lodge. "You want to go inside and wait?" he asked.

"Sure, why not?"

What really hurt, what twisted his gut into knots, was how much he cared for Nicola. He wanted to plunge into that bottomless pool of sensations with her, delve into his true feelings, really live, for once. But that meant coming clean. And even if he told her everything, even if he showed his real face, what would that face be? He had no way of telling; he'd lived this charade too long. He was a coward, he guessed, afraid that there was no real Matt Cavanaugh behind the cover identity, or afraid that if there was a real man there and he spilled the beans about himself, he'd find out that she didn't like him, anyway.

Now *that* was a scary proposition.

Nicola leaned her elbows on the counter inside the store and chatted with the owner. "It's really starting to blow out there," she said.

"Looks bad," the man agreed, staring gravely at his pipe.

"I sure hope the helicopter makes it here soon," she said.

"Bad" was an understatement. Matt could see outside from where he stood, resting a shoulder against the front window. The dust was now mixed with icy pellets of snow, dashing itself against the glass, obscuring the street. During the moments between gusts, he could see dark and threatening clouds scudding across the peaks to the west. They were in for a real storm. The prospects of the chopper returning to pick them up were getting dimmer by the second.

He turned, folded his arms and watched Nicola. She tossed her head, laughing at something the shopkeeper said, and he could see the long, delicate line of her neck. He wondered vaguely if they were stuck here for a night, where they would sleep.

"Getting worse out there, eh?" the man was saying.

Nicola turned and glanced out the window, looking straight past Matt, as if he didn't exist. "Darn," she said, frowning, "the helicopter will never fly in this now. Darn."

Not that she wanted his reassurance... "Look," Matt said, "I'm sure Jon can handle things. This isn't your fault, Nicky."

She only stared at him, then turned away again, stiff, upset. "Well," she said to the man, "can you put us up somewhere for the night if we have to stay?"

"Not here," he replied. "But the bus is due in at two. You could catch a ride to Radium Hot Springs, about an hour away. There're a couple of hotels there."

She let go of a breath. "What do you think, Matt?" Her eyes didn't meet his.

"I guess we'll have to if Junior doesn't get here by two," he replied distractedly. *Swell.* Now Evan was left totally without protection. Murphy's Law. First he couldn't get hold of Ned to have the guests checked out, now this. And what if one of the guests—Rei, or Carlos, most likely—made an attempt on Evan's life tonight? The thought chilled him, almost made him physically sick. And there was only that damn radio contraption back at the lodge, a tenuous link with the outside world in the event of an emergency. Matt had no control of the situation; he was stranded, without even a radio link to the lodge from here.

"You don't look too pleased about this," Nicola was saying.

"I'm not. Sorry," he added quickly, "I meant about being stuck here." That didn't help, either.

The trouble was that he was worried sick about Evan, and just being near Nicola made him feel vulnerable, unable to trust his own reactions, his own judgment. His carefully constructed world was crashing down around his ears, and there wasn't a thing he could do to stop it.

They waited until two, unable to do a thing, both ill at ease—for vastly different reasons, Matt knew. Poor Nicky, stuck with him. He wondered just how much she disliked him, just how strong her antipathy to men like her father really was. And yet she still loved Went, didn't she?

"Bus is here," the man said, startling Matt out of his dark reverie.

Of course, they sat together in the nearly empty bus. But it was a silent ride. He tried to make small talk with her; he tried not to notice her thigh pressed up against his on the narrow seat.

"Really coming down hard out there now," he said, staring out the window as the daily bus sped along the country road.

"Yes," she said. "I hope it stops by morning."

"Me, too."

All so polite, so careful, as if one of them might shatter the precarious wall of civility that had gone up between them. What he really wanted to do was spend his precious, difficult time they had together pouring out his problems to her, telling her about his confusion, his disillusionment, his gut-wrenching concern for Evan. He could, for instance, tell her that he'd been living at home since Thanksgiving, a thankless chore at best, and bartending at a glitzy steak house in nearby Tarrytown. And all to keep an eye on Evan. There were the other agents Ned had sent; Matt usually checked in with whoever was watching the place at night on his way to work in the evening.

Maureen had been bewildered at the rather weak excuse he'd given her—"I couldn't find an apartment, Mom"— but happy to have him around. Evan growled and grumbled about his no-good bum of a son, but so far had let him stay. Oh, how furious Evan would be if he knew Matt was his bodyguard!

And T.J. wasn't real happy about having big brother on the scene, either. He never said a word; he held whatever jealousy or resentment he felt about Matt inside, but Matt sensed those pent-up feelings, close under T.J.'s skin, ready to erupt someday. He just hoped he wasn't around when T.J. let loose. He pitied his younger brother. Yes, he pitied him, but he didn't really love him.

He could push the limits of security and tell Nicola all that, or he could tell her just enough to wipe that barely expressed distrust off her face. He could. But, damn, the very notion of baring his soul like that was unthinkable.

"I hope one of the hotels has a room, *rooms*," she said, correcting herself.

"Me, too." *That is, if we get there at all,* he thought to himself as he glanced out the window into the worsening storm. He knew it would be even worse up in the mountains at the lodge, a real old-fashioned blizzard.

Radium Hot Springs, down the river from Spillimacheen, wasn't much larger, but it did have a couple of hotels and restaurants and, naturally, the popular hot springs. There were shops for tourists, gas stations, a post office— the essentials.

They got off the bus and stared up and down the street through the sheets of falling snow. About a half a block away, right in downtown, was a small, clean-looking hotel.

"Shall we try it?" Matt asked.

"It's as good as any, I guess."

They got rooms, but they were lucky, the desk clerk told them, because this time of year was popular with the tourists from Calgary. "On a weekend," he said, "we'd be full up." Then he glanced at their empty hands.

"We got stuck up in Spillimacheen. We're at the Bugaboo Lodge," Matt offered in order to save Nicola any embarrassment. He heard her laugh at his shoulder. Well, at least *she* hadn't lost her sense of humor.

"Thanks," she said as they climbed the steps.

"Oh, that. Yeah, well, I forgot we took two rooms, and all I could see was that guy staring at our empty hands."

They dined around eight but might not have eaten at all if Nicola hadn't phoned his room and suggested it. He'd been lying on his double bed, staring at the unmoving ceiling fan, brooding, feeling frustrated and helpless. How unlike him. But then, he'd never been assigned to watch his father before. And he'd never had to lie to a woman he cared about before, either.

"I think there's a restaurant right down the street," Nicola had said. "I'm really hungry, and I thought you might want to join me."

He'd leaped at the opportunity to be with her again, to take in that special, honey-sweet scent of hers, to forget those bugaboos hiding in the recesses of her mind. "That sounds great. I'll be in the lobby in three minutes."

The restaurant they ate at was strictly Western in flavor, right down to the sawdust floor. Wagon wheels hung on the walls, the lighting was old, converted oil lamps, the tablecloths red-and-white checked oilcloth. Country-and-western music drifted through the air from a jukebox. Nicola ordered salad and barbecued chicken; he settled for a steak, on the rare side.

"You want it practically walkin', eh?" the waitress said.

"Well, not quite."

They both had Canada's own Moosehead lager, and then there was nothing to do but wait for Nicola's salad to arrive. She gazed around the room; he gazed at her face.

"Would you stop that?" Nicola finally asked.

"Stop what?"

"You know, staring at me."

"Oh, sorry."

Silence. And then they both said something about the Willy Nelson song that was playing, and they both shut up and smiled self-consciously. He picked up the glass sugar dispenser and turned it slowly in his hands; she straightened her silverware for the fourth time.

"Um," he said, "snow's letting up."

"Yes, it is." She poured the rest of her beer into her glass.

"You want another one?"

She shook her head. "Booze makes me say things I regret."

"Like what?"

Nicola laughed. "Oh, you know. You've probably seen your share of tipsy women."

"Oh, I've seen plenty. But you're not like that."

She seemed to be deciding something as she sat there with her brows drawn together. Finally she sighed, as if giving up. "Okay," she said, dropping her gaze, "if I'm not like the ladies you meet in bars, what am I like?"

She'd opened the door a crack, albeit reluctantly, but he was ready to go in. *Take it slow. You're both new at this trusting stuff,* he cautioned himself.

"Well, for one," he said, his voice low and sincere, "you don't play games."

"Go on." She picked up her fork and turned it over in her hand.

"You know what you don't want ... but then again, and maybe I'm dead wrong, you don't know what you really *do* want."

"Very observant."

"You aren't mad yet?"

She smiled and shook her head. "Not at all, I'm fascinated. I didn't think you ever thought about this kind of thing."

"Well, I know what you think about me," he remarked dryly. Then he said, "I think you idolize your dad, and I know you love your mother, but I think you put too much stock in your hopes that she'll recover someday."

"Um."

"Phew," he said, smiling broadly, "I thought you might have slapped me by now."

"Not me."

"Good enough. Well, I honestly believe that you think I have it better with Evan and Maureen than you do with your folks. Let me clarify that." He cleared his throat and swallowed some of his drink. "You need to take a good, hard look at Went and Suzanne and accept reality. The way it is, I think maybe you scare Went off."

*"What?"* Her salad had arrived, but suddenly she wasn't very interested in it.

"Well," Matt said, "with your dad, it's got to be slow and easy. He ran away from family commitments years ago, and if you really want his friendship, you'll have to prove to him it won't be a demanding relationship."

"You know," Nicola said, picking up a lettuce leaf thoughtfully, "maybe you're right. Maybe every time I see him, I'm too eager. You might have something there."

"Maybe there's more to me than meets the eye," he ventured.

Her glance came up sharply.

"Anyway," he said quickly, "I have my intuitive moments, I suppose. For instance, I think you're real vulnerable with men...."

"Oh?"

"I do, yes. And I was rotten to have taken advantage of that."

"I'm *not* afraid of men."

"I never said 'afraid.' But you are sensitive. Oh, I see you holding your own with the old boys, like at hunting camp, but it's different with me, isn't it?"

Matt sat there with his elbows on the table, his fingers steepled in front of his face. He watched her and he waited. He watched her duck her head, not so much in embarrassment as in thought. And he saw the delicate curve of her neck where her hair was swept back, and her capable, slim white fingers holding the fork. Her lips were parted, expectant, lovely.

"I think I went too far just now," he said as much to himself as to her. Did he really want to continue this probing of their souls? Yet, to let these moments pass, to dodge the risks, was equally reprehensible.

Finally her eyes came up. "You hurt me, Matt. I thought I was ready for you, but obviously I was wrong."

The food arrived; the waitress was talkative and lively. But Matt barely noticed her. He felt as if he were on the edge of an abyss, ready to either step back out of danger or to plunge in.

The waitress left, returned to fill their water glasses, shrugged, then disappeared for good.

He took a very deep breath and pinioned Nicola with an intent gaze. "If I hurt you," he said, "I'm sorry, more sorry than you know or will even believe."

She shook her head, wondering. "What's with you, Matt? One minute you're Mr. Playboy, the next you're like this.... You're thoughtful and caring and...and, I don't know. That's the trouble, I keep thinking you're someone else. You confuse me."

"*You're* confused!" he said, then laughed ruefully. "I'm the one in the fix, Nicky."

"What fix?"

He cut into his steak, took a bite, tried to find a way out. He could tell her everything, but that was just not possible considering the oath he'd sworn those many years ago. And yet he felt cheated. If only he could somehow convince her that he wasn't the useless jerk he appeared.

"Look," he said, "there are some things about me you don't know. Let's just say that things aren't always as they appear."

"You're talking in riddles, Matt." Her dark, melancholy eyes held his.

"I know I am, but it's the best I can do. I care for you, Nicky, I really do."

"I wonder."

"Hell. What more can I do? I'm not lying. I want you, kid. I want you in every way. And I've wanted you since that day last summer, since we went riding. Remember?"

"Oh yes," she replied carefully, "I remember."

"So that's it. I haven't cared about a woman this way for a long time, Nicky. Maybe never. Either you believe me or you don't."

Like him, she sliced into her chicken and took a bite, but she swallowed hard, nervously, and then had to wash it down with half a glass of water. He waited, having no idea whatsoever how she was taking this revelation of his or if she was even believing it. He could hardly believe it himself.

Finally, in midbite, she stared at him in earnest. "What do you really mean, Matt?"

"I mean forget the dinner, forget the lodge. Let's take tonight and grab it. I can't promise you more than that, Nicky, but I can promise there'll never be another one like it. Not for me, anyway."

"Just like that?"

"Just like that."

"And if I want more? If I become a clinging, jealous, screaming harridan?"

"It won't change the way I feel."

"So...it's a proposition. Plain and simple, isn't it? No, don't answer that. I get the picture. We both want to...to go back to the hotel together. But there are no strings attached.''

Matt leaned back in his seat, slumping. He'd blown it. He couldn't promise her more than tonight, and he'd blown it.

"Okay."

"What?"

She was looking at him, her face pale and dead serious. She put her napkin on the table. "I said, okay. Let's go."

It was as cold as ice outside. The snow had let up, but the night sky was inky black and a bitter wind swirled down the nearly deserted street, slashing at them as their boots crunched in the newly fallen snow. He walked close to Nicola's side and hunched into his coat. "Cold?" he asked.

"Freezing."

*But not for long,* he thought, toying with a smile.

They walked up the hotel steps holding hands, and Matt could almost feel the flood of her conflicting emotions streaming through her fingertips. She was understandably on edge. Nicola obviously had never made a habit of this. In her touch was anticipation; she was wondering if she'd be any good at it, if she could live up to his expectations. He could help her with the nervousness, but as for the rest, she'd have to discover for herself that he wasn't some kind of international bed hopper who slept with every pretty lady he could get his hands on. There was warmth at the tip of her fingers, though, and that came from desire, from need, from the bottled-up wellspring of love deep inside her. He'd have to nurture that, treat her like a precious treasure. The last thing on earth he wanted to do was to see her hurt.

*But don't ask for more, Nicky. I'll give you all I have while I can.* Would there be a way of holding back the dawn?

He tried to lighten the situation, squeezing her hand, smiling down into her eyes. "Your room or mine?" he asked softly as they approached their doors.

"Oh," she said, "mine."

He took her key, pushed it into the lock, swung open the door. She seemed hesitant.

She took a deep breath. "I'm a wreck, Matt. Isn't that ridiculous?"

"No. In fact, it's part of what makes you so special to me, Nicky. Just never change, promise me that."

Kicking the door closed gently with his foot, Matt caught her arm and pulled her to him, imprisoning her against his chest while he locked his fingers together at the small of her back. He kissed her then, slowly, moving his mouth over hers, carefully parting her lips, exploring, tasting. He pressed against her and felt the tautness below her waist straining against him, and his own need, a red-hot bar of desire. He pushed his knee between her soft thighs and felt her quick, indrawn gasp. Finally, with his lips still on hers, he reached up and unfastened her long dark mane and spread it lovingly over her shoulders.

And then he smiled with his mouth pressed to hers. "I've wanted to do that for so long," he whispered.

Nicola put her hand against his stomach and nudged him away a little. "Would you mind if I, you know, take a quick shower? It's been a really long day and, well... Don't laugh at me."

"I won't," he replied, and ran a finger across her chin lightly. "But I could use one, too."

She looked puzzled for a split second, then shook her head. "Oh no. I know exactly what you're thinking, Matt, and..."

"Why not?"

Nicola looked completely ill at ease, in a quandary. "I, ah, I've never..."

"Then now's the perfect time to start."

She was difficult to convince, but in the end he won out. With only a small lamp turned on by the bed, she let him unbutton her shirt and toss it aside. Then, while he undressed, she unzipped her pants and stepped out of them.

But he got to take care of the bra and her panties, grabbing her hand and pulling her toward him, even though she protested all the way. She was lovely, all long, lean limbs and slim, curved hips, her breasts small and firm. Yes, she was beautiful to him, just as she'd been that time on the diving board when he'd studied her from afar. But now she was his, and it was all he could do not to have her instantly, right there on the bed, quickly, without preliminaries. But he held himself back; it would only make it that much more pleasurable when they finally joined.

Before they even stepped into the shower stall, Matt turned her around and crushed the full length of her body to him, feeling those small breasts against his, the length of her hips and thighs molded to his own, her breath hot and quick now, full of expectation but a little uncertain still.

Finally he reached inside the stall and turned on the water. "Warm enough?" he asked.

She stuck her hand in. "Perfect."

"I want my back scrubbed," he said.

"No way, me first," she replied as she stepped in, laughing, the spray from the shower head striking her dark head and her slender shoulders.

Matt moved in and faced her, blinking away the water, spanning her waist with his hands. She was all soft and warm and slippery, and his desire to know her fully quickened.

He rubbed the bar of soap along her spine and kissed her thoroughly, deeply, bringing his head up once to shake off the water before his tongue probed the moist inner warmth of her mouth again. And all the while he ground his lips to hers, his hands lathered her back and hips, her soft belly up to her breasts. Oh yes, those wonderful, pert breasts, whose crests grew hard at his touch.

Nicola leaned back against the wall of the shower and raised her arms, running her fingers through her hair, pushing the heavy, slick mass back over her shoulders. But he caught her hands and held them to either side of her head, then lowered his mouth to her bosom, flicking his tongue from one breast to the other, over and over, drinking in the shower spray again and again, until she moaned and twisted and bent to put her mouth to the top of his head.

"Oh God, Matt...."

He moved lower, tasting the underside of her breasts, her stomach, making her squirm when he nibbled on a hipbone. She tried to stop him when he lowered his head further, but his mouth and tongue were strong persuaders, and he savored her, sinking to his knees, until she twisted her fingers in his hair and cried out, her whole body rocking, sagging, clinging to him.

Barely toweled off, he led her to the bed and pressed her dripping wet body onto the sheets. She must know, of course, that he had yet to find his own release, and she took the time to run her hands along the ridges of muscle on his back and chest, his thighs, until he groaned, almost losing control. He rolled onto his back, breathed deeply and asked her if she was ready.

"Yes," she said softly, running a finger down his chest until he quivered. "I can't believe it," she said, "but I am."

Matt stayed on his back. He wanted Nicola to remember this night, to find the greatest fulfillment possible. With his hands he positioned her above him, her knees straddling his hips, and then he guided her to him, feeling the soft, warm flesh enfold his hardness. Moving his hands from her hips to her waist, he entered her fully and deeply, and they both gasped together at the hot, pulsing pleasure of the union. Thrusting upward to meet her movements, Matt caressed her breasts with his hands, kneading them as she arched her back and her head lolled from side to side.

"Oh God, Matt, oh God," she whispered, and he spoke as well, unintelligible things, endearments, encouragement, until they were both panting and clinging and thrusting, harder, deeper, their flesh pounding and grinding. He let himself float on the cloud of white-hot passion, knowing that her desire was reaching a crescendo, waiting for her, pacing himself. Their movements became frenzied as they sought the same moment of release. It built and it promised, beckoning; it built into a fever pitch of gasping and thrashing, and then finally, they both cried out into the night and shuddered, holding each other and trembling.

At three in the morning, Matt awakened, and he touched her cheek with his lips, half thinking to awaken her as well, to begin the odyssey anew. But she was sleeping so peacefully, so beautifully. In the darkness he could just make out her profile, and he smiled to himself. She'd said their lovemaking was the most wonderful thing she'd ever known, and he'd kissed her and said the same. Amazingly it was true. And now there was no doubt left in his mind that this was the woman he wanted to share his life with. Yet, lurking like a shadowed creature in that corner of his brain was the knowledge that the time wasn't right. There were things to be done, ends to be tied up. And there was his father, over that tall ridge of snow-clothed mountains, in danger. How could Matt forget that fact and wallow in this newfound love? In the morning he had a job to do, a commitment to fulfill. And Nicky wasn't going to like it. No matter what she'd said last night, they both had known it was all sweet lies—there were *definitely* strings attached.

If only, Matt thought as wind rattled at the windowpanes, the dawn would never come....

But it did. Scratchy eyed, he slipped out of bed and dragged the telephone into the bathroom, closing the door as far as he could without pulling the wire out of the wall. He switched on the light quietly.

"Be there, Ned," he said in a low whisper as he dialed.

On the third ring, Ned answered. "Matt, for God's sake, what's going on?"

"Things are getting sticky. Here's a list of possibles." Matt rattled off the names of those he wanted checked out. "Got it all?"

"Yes," Ned said. "But when will you be in touch again?"

"Damned if I know. It's not so easy. All there is in the lodge is the radio telephone to the Helitours office in Banff. I could use it, but only in an emergency. And when I'm gone from the lodge, Evan is left unguarded."

"You should have talked him out of this trip, Matt."

"Sure. Ever try to reason with Evan?"

"You want some backup?"

"There's no way to get them here. No, I'll handle it."

"Okay. I'll get right on this list," Ned said. "Later."

"Sure, later." He hung up and sat for a moment, thinking, rubbing the stubble on his chin. What if something had gone down last night?

But he couldn't consider that. *Stick to the facts, Matt.*

He rose from where he'd been sitting on the closed toilet seat, snapped off the light and opened the door carefully, trying to keep it from squeaking. In the darkened room he didn't see her at first, though, not until he was putting the phone back in place.

But she was sitting up in bed, the sheet pulled up to her chin. Their eyes met and locked, and in that instant he knew, undeniably and irrevocably, that he'd compromised his cover.

# CHAPTER THIRTEEN

MORNING BROUGHT WITH IT a pale winter sun, but gray clouds still clung to the surrounding peaks. They caught the bus back up the valley to Spillimacheen, but the highway was icy and the going was slow. Matt's body was there on the seat next to her, his thigh in the faded denim touching hers, rubbing against it with every jounce of the vehicle, but his feelings and his attention were elsewhere.

Nicola wondered who he had been calling so early in the morning. Who was so important that he'd missed one—now two—days of skiing to fly to Spillimacheen to use a telephone? A prospective employer? No, not likely. A woman? No, not really. She just couldn't believe he'd go to all that trouble for a woman.

Who, then?

She turned her head slightly to study his profile. He wouldn't notice, because he was looking out the bus window at the gray-brown river valley sliding by. His brows were drawn, his mouth curved down at the corners, so unlike his usual expression. Something was on his mind, an all-consuming problem that had to do with that illicit phone call this morning.

It certainly wasn't Nicola he was worrying about.

She felt betrayed. This wasn't the same man who'd loved her in the night. That man had been warm and passionate and giving, intent on her pleasure, caring about her. She felt a hard lump of pain in her belly, and she wanted to double over with it, curl up and hug the ache to herself. Nausea rose in her throat, and she turned her head away quickly to hide the burning tears in her eyes.

She'd let herself in for it; she'd done exactly what she'd sworn not to do. Like a moth, she'd flown directly into the flame, eyes wide open, wings fluttering in an ecstasy of fulfillment. Why, then, was she so surprised to be burned?

He'd been withdrawn all morning, neither the insouciant playboy nor the rebellious son nor the happy sportsman nor the tender lover. He was an entirely new person, one she couldn't touch, not even physically. He'd given her a lame excuse for the phone call, the bartending job in Palm Beach, but it was such a manifest lie that he'd barely even tried to convince her.

The phone call was the key to Matt Cavanaugh. The phone call. She had to know about that, then she'd understand him. That was what she focused on as the bus rumbled up the valley of the Spillimacheen River toward the distant mountains. She could bear it, she could function, if she just held on to that one idea: the phone call.

Matt shifted in the seat, inadvertently pressing a shoulder against her as the bus lurched around a curve. "Sorry," he said.

"Um." She couldn't fit her brain around the reality of his detachment. He'd loved her last night. His lips had loved her, his hands, his whole lean, hard body had worshiped her.

"The ride seems longer than yesterday," he remarked idly.

She looked at her hands. He'd said he liked her hands once. Last night she had touched him intimately, held him, stroked him with them. "Matt." Her voice was very low, and she didn't even know what she was going to say, but she needed some sort of communication with him, some proof of her own self-worth.

"What?" He turned his head, as if noticing her for the first time.

"I just said your name."

He sat, politely expectant and maybe a little impatient, wanting to get back to his private thoughts.

"Matt, I...uh... I think I should... I think you owe me an explanation...."

He waited.

She plunged in. "Who were you calling this morning?"

His faced changed, chameleon-like, lighted up by a jolly, slightly embarrassed smile, punctuated by his adorable dimple. "I told you, the man in Palm Beach. For the job, you know."

"That's not good enough, Matt. It's a lie."

He changed again, his mask turning to one of utter neutrality, mild, sincere. "Okay, so it wasn't anyone in Palm Beach. But it wasn't important. It has nothing to do with you, Nicky."

"Yes, it does. It changed you, that phone call. You're different. It's as if I don't exist anymore. Something happened," she said in a low, harsh voice, not looking at him. Then she noticed that one of her hands was clenched into a fist.

"Look, I have some problems. Nothing serious, but I can't talk about it." Now he was peeling down through another layer to the nice guy, the affable, thoughtful pal.

"Matt, you can tell me. Please, whatever it is, you can tell me."

He put a hand on her fist, stroking her fingers so they relaxed. "Take it easy, kid. There's nothing to tell."

"Is it another woman?" she threw out, knowing he'd deny it even if it was. "All those calls? Redstone and now here. Where does she live? It must be on the East Coast if you call from here so early... and she's never home, is she? Is that your problem, Matt, that your girl is cheating on you?"

Then he did the first genuine thing he'd done all morning—he laughed.

"Don't laugh," she said brokenly.

"Oh, Nicky, I'm sorry. Is that what you think? Another woman, oh my God."

"Well?"

He took both of her hands in his; his expression was earnest, and she knew it was the real Matt now, the one she loved. "No, there's no other woman."

"Then tell me about the phone call. What's going on, Matt?"

"I can't." His face was sober; it suddenly struck her that there was a look of Evan about him—in his eyes and in the lines that bracketed his mouth—a look of a man who carried a great responsibility and had learned to live with it.

"Matt?" she whispered, frightened by this revelation, this truth she'd just seen.

He squeezed her hands. "I can't tell you, not now. Trust me."

"Matt, what is it? Is it . . . is it something about Evan?" The words had flown into her head; she didn't even know where they'd come from. "I don't know. . . . It seems that you've been around him so much. Is he in danger, is that it?"

"Nicola." His eyes were shadowed as he searched her face. "Please, Nicola. I love you. Please trust me."

Her heart leaped at his words, and joy burst within her. *He loves me.* And then, in the same breath of time, the joy whirled inward upon itself and turned cold and hard and dropped like a stone to her feet. "That's probably what my father says to all his women, but they make the mistake of believing him," she said.

"I'm *not* your father."

"No," she said miserably, "no, you're not." For the rest of the ride, Nicola could only stare out of the window feeling a knot of uncertainty grow in her chest.

It was the other helicopter pilot, Bernie, who picked them and the food up later that afternoon at Spillimacheen. If he wondered at the bleak silence between Nicola and Matt, he said nothing about it. "Guess you were stuck pretty bad, huh? What a mess. Jon was going bananas, you can imagine. Will he be glad to see you!"

"Everything okay at the lodge?" Matt asked casually. "Good skiing today?"

"Great. There was a foot of new powder this morning from yesterday's storm."

"Sorry I missed it," Matt said, not sounding very sorry at all.

THE NEXT DAY the weather was perfect: cold and clear, with a blue sky and all that new powder that everyone had been skiing the day before.

Jenny, who'd tweaked an already bad knee skiing in the previous day's fresh snow, offered to clean up after breakfast and take care of the box lunches so that Nicola could go skiing—if there was room in the helicopter. She said she'd get Cindy to help her, so Nicola didn't feel too guilty.

"Go on," Jenny said, her plump, freckled face concerned. "Then I'll feel ever so much better. Skiing yesterday was fantastic."

Nicola looked around the kitchen at the mess left from the breakfast of Belgian waffles with strawberries. Then she checked the menu for dinner: baked salmon steaks with white wine sauce, glazed baby carrots, saffron rice.

"Okay. I'll get the salmon out to defrost. Could you cook the rice for me, in case I get back late?"

"Sure. How much?"

She thought. "Better make it four pounds. I'll add the herbs later."

"Fine, got it. Look, I'm writing it down on this note to myself." Jenny waved the paper in Nicola's face. It read, Rice 4 lbs.! "Now go, have some fun."

Nicola could use some fun. Those two days with Matt had exhausted her mentally and emotionally. She'd been carefully avoiding him since their return to the lodge, or had he been avoiding her? At least she didn't have to see him constantly or be so near that it took all her willpower to keep from reaching out and touching him. She wondered if everyone at the lodge could tell by looking at her that she and Matt had made love. Did it show?

Oh, there had been the expected joke when they'd returned. "Why couldn't it have been me?" Dave Huff had wailed comically. There had been raised eyebrows and funny comments and innuendos.

"Ach, *Gott in Himmel*, are you all right?" Jon had cried, and everyone had laughed at that.

Evan had stared at Matt impatiently, as if disliking the attention his son was receiving, and Maureen had been a little bewildered at Nicola's silence.

Oh yes, Matt had handled everything perfectly. She was grateful to him for that, because it would have been beyond her. He'd put on the disarming, convivial mask, held up a hand to everyone and announced loudly, "Sorry to disappoint you, folks, but we got two rooms. Count 'em, two. Here's my receipt. Where's yours, kid?" And he dangled the hotel receipt from his fingers.

"Oh, *Liebchen*," Helga had called out, "I'm so glad you're saving yourself for me!"

Everyone had chuckled and accepted Matt's statement, and that had been that. How useful his many faces were, and how very practiced he was at putting them on, at choosing the right one for the right time.

Nicola found Jon in his office, booking reservations. "Do you think there's room for me to ski today? I could use some exercise."

"Yes, you poor thing. Stuck down there in the valley." He clucked his tongue and checked the day's schedule. "I think so. Ask Bernie to make sure. There are only nine going in his machine today."

"Oh, good. Thanks, Jon. Was it too awful when I was gone?"

"'Ve managed." He sighed, taking a long drag on his cigarette. "It's always something like that. I'm going to retire, I tell you."

"You'll never retire. You like the skiing too much," she said.

"Sure, sure." He waved her away. "You go now. Take care."

She ran to her room to change. Everyone would be gathering in groups now, putting on ski boots, gloves, goggles, sunscreen lotion. She had to hurry. Her red ski suit, flattering and comfortable, warm. Long underwear, cotton turtleneck, sweater, wool socks. Wool hat, Smith goggles—tinted dark enough to protect the eyes from the reflected sun—her ski boots, left unbuckled for now, although it made it hard to hurry along the path to the helipad. Her skis, a pair of specialized powder skis, short and wider than normal to plane up in the bottomless powder, and very soft to make turning effortless.

The helicopter was already warming up, ready to go. Hans, the guide, was loading the skis and poles into the outside basket of the machine. Everyone stood around in bright-colored ski clothes, bursting with excited anticipation, exuberant, full of suggestions for Hans. "Let's do the North Col first thing, it'll be great," Evan said.

"Wrong exposure," Dave said. "We want to ski it in the afternoon."

"Oh, be quiet, you two," Ruthie said. "Hans knows where he's going."

Werner was there and T.J. and Carlos Santana and Helga. Was she going to ski? But no, Nicola saw, she didn't have ski boots on; she was just going along for the ride.

Nicola clumped up to Bernie. "Is there room for me?"

Bernie looked over the skiers and counted heads. "Sure. There're only seven here and you. I think there's one more coming."

"Great."

Evan was making a boisterous comment to Werner. "You young kids, you could probably ski all day and you-know-what all night! I envy you!"

Even Werner had to crack a wintry smile at that. "I am not so very young, you know," he replied modestly.

"He's just the right age," Helga said defensively.

"I'll bet," Ruthie said, winking at Dave.

"Nicola! Great! You're coming along," Evan said. "It's too bad you were stuck in the valley."

"We've had wonderful skiing," T.J. offered. "Haven't we, Dad?"

*"Fantastic."*

"All right, folks. Is everyone here? I think we're ready," Hans was saying. "Oh, here comes the last one."

Nicola looked and bit her lip. Darn it. Matt was hurrying along the path, skis over his shoulder, looking as if he didn't have a care in the world. He was so handsome and debonair in his bright blue parka, which matched his eyes perfectly, his goggles pushed up on his forehead and his tight ski pants with bright red racer's padding on the knees and shins.

"Sorry," he panted, "sorry I'm late."

"For God's sake," Evan grumbled.

"Okay, let's go," Hans said.

They all climbed in the door of the helicopter, arranging themselves on two bench seats facing each other. Bernie stuck his head in, counted them all, then pushed the door shut.

"It's going to be cold up there this morning," Dave said.

"Then the snow will be lighter," Carlos said. "Much better than warm sun."

"He's right," T.J. put in. "It'll be good this morning."

Nicola had managed to sit as far away from Matt as possible, in the corner opposite Hans. She would pretend he wasn't there, that's all. She'd have her day of skiing and enjoy it.

The helicopter let them off at the top of a shining white peak. Hans unloaded the skis and poles, everyone took his own and put them on, stepping into bindings with neat clicks, gloved hands grasping poles, pulling goggles down. Everyone stamped and took a deep breath, getting ready.

"Skadi check," called Hans. Skadis were the electronic rescue beacons that every skier wore on a cord around his neck. They sent out electronic beeps that could be detected by a receiver, so that if someone was buried by an avalanche, that person could be found rapidly. No one was allowed to ski the untracked Bugaboos without one turned on to send a signal. Hans had each person move past him while he listened for beeps in his earpiece to make sure the Skadis were working. "Okay, all set."

The group was poised, expectant, at the top of the run. Below them was a glistening, pure white bowl of powder snow, a blank piece of writing paper, and each skier was desperate to inscribe his own perfect message upon it, his own gracefully carved words, linked one after the other, endlessly, down the face of its purity, until the wind covered the tracks or new snow filled them in. Above was the clear, cold blue sky to witness their descent and the yellow sun that cast their elongated shadows ahead of them. The chopper was gone now, its faint thumping still audible, returning to the lodge to pick up another group and deposit it, also, on the top of the world.

"Oh my God, heaven!" Dave breathed, sucking the thin air into his lungs.

"Let's go," Evan cried, stamping his skis.

"You will all stay behind me," Hans cautioned.

"Yes, yes," they chorused, impatient.

"Be careful of the cliff there." He pointed with his pole, a compact, fair Canadian, young and wiry, sober with his responsibility. "We'll stop and count heads just above the trees, there."

"Come on!"

War whoops split the air as Hans aimed his skis downhill first, sliding off easily, relaxed, then Evan and Dave, T.J. and Matt, Carlos and Werner. Nicola watched them go for a second. She and Ruthie would ski together, the buddy system being in effect. The men were all marvelous skiers, carving round turns down the fall line, leaving their twisting trails behind to testify to their passage. They flew like brightly colored birds, rooster trails of snow streaming behind them, only their arms and heads visible in the snow churning around their bodies.

Nicola pushed off with Ruthie. Ah! She felt the resistance of the snow, shifted her weight, turned to the left, rose, then shifted again, sensing the inert acceptance of the snow under her pliable skis. She was free, skimming down, swooping, the cold wind hitting her face, her chest heaving like a bellows. Left then right, the snow boiling up around her; she sucked it into her lungs and felt like coughing, as if she were breathing in dust, ducked her chin to breathe more easily. Down, down, her legs aching, but she couldn't stop— that would be a betrayal of herself and the mountain.

Pure sensation engulfed her, a perfection of movement and balance and strength that drove all thought from her except the next turn and the next. And then she was aware of the group stopped in front of her above the line of trees that stood like old women in snow-encrusted shawls, and she leaned on one ski, came around in a perfect curve and stopped.

"Oh Lordy!" she cried, full of joy.

"That was great!"

"Terrific!"

"¡Fantástico!"

"My poor legs!" somebody lamented.

"Okay, everyone here? So now we'll make our way through these trees. Carefully. There's another snowfield below. Try not to fall into any tree wells, please," Hans said.

Tree skiing was another story entirely. You needed to make tight, perfectly controlled turns, and you needed a good eye for choosing your path, snaking between the trees without hitting any. It was slower, more demanding, but requiring greater skill.

"Oh boy," Ruthie said, "don't leave me to climb out of a tree well by myself."

"Okay, we'll stick close together," Nicola replied, pushing off with her poles. The air in the belt of frozen trees smelled of pine, fresh and cold, and the snow was stippled with shadows. Nicola dodged under an overhanging branch, brushed it and felt it release its load of snow onto her. The pitch was steep; she had to work her legs harder, make quicker, more complete turns to keep her speed under control. She felt the dampness of sweat on her skin under her suit, felt her chest going in and out, her legs working, shifting, weight to one side, lifting then shifting to the other.

She came out into the bright sun below the trees, Ruthie right behind her, and stopped by Hans. Beyond them stretched another snowfield, thousands of feet in altitude.

"What's this run, about four thousand feet altogether?" Evan was asking.

"That's about right, Dad," T.J. said.

"Okay, so four or five runs like this, and I'll make my quota for the day." He meant that his week would add up to the promised hundred thousand vertical feet, Nicola knew.

"Too bad you missed those two days, Matt," Evan went on. "We did twenty thousand vertical each day."

Matt was leaning negligently on his poles. "Those're the breaks, I guess," he said carelessly.

Then they were off again, slicing down on the smooth, white, flawless surface, letting out inadvertent cries and shouts of pleasure at the precision of movement, breathing in the tickling crystals. Pole plant, lift to that perfect moment of suspended weightlessness between turns, pressure the snow, lean into it, carve the turn, pole plant, lift again to hang above the powder, shift to the other side, *press*.

Nicola pulled up to a stop halfway down the slope to help T.J., who'd taken a tumble. "You okay?" she asked, handing him his hat and snow-packed goggles.

"Sure, I'm fine." He untangled his skis and stood up, slapping his hat against his leg to dislodge the snow.

"That was a good one!" Ruthie said, laughing, as she stopped beside them.

"When you do it, you should do it right," T.J. said, smiling for once.

They all arrived down at the spot in the valley where the helicopter was going to pick them up and stepped out of their bindings, waiting.

"Let's do that again," Ruthie said.

"Yes, we will. If we all go to the right a little, we'll have another untracked run," Hans agreed.

Bernie came for them shortly, the thump of the rotors announcing his approach.

"Good run?" he called, leaning out, pulling his headphones away from his ears.

"*Wunderbar,*" Werner shouted back, grinning widely, waving a ski pole.

"We're going to do that one again," Hans said. "Can you meet us right here with the lunches?"

"Sure thing."

The skis and poles were loaded, they all climbed in and the chopper tilted, beat at the air, surged, and they were up, on their way to the top of the mountain again.

Matt was sitting next to Ruthie, teasing her. Nicola looked away, but she could hear what he was saying. "You've lost weight, Ruth, you know that? You look terrific. And you haven't forgotten how to ski, either.''

"Oh, shush, Matthew. I have sons almost as old as you!'' And she poked him in the ribs with her elbow.

Helga sat next to Werner. "*Liebchen*, was it good? But I like the scenery so much better from up here. And Bernie is such a gentleman.'' She held Werner's arm, clinging to him, wearing too much makeup to withstand the revealing light of day. She was deliberately rude to Evan, turning her back on him. Was Nicola being as obvious as that in her snubbing of Matt?

Everyone talked, joked, complained about tired legs or shortness of breath. Nicola could have been with a group from the week before or the week to come. Everyone was red cheeked, red nosed, stimulated by the thrill of adventure.

"Oh, Werner,'' Helga said over the loud din, "you are enjoying yourself, yes?''

And he smiled, replying in German.

"Well,'' she said, snuggling against him, "it was hunting in the autumn, and now skiing. Perhaps we shall fly to a beach in Mexico next month.''

But Nicola only heard the part about hunting. In Colorado? she wondered, her brow furrowed. "So, Werner,'' she began, leaning across the aisle, "you're a hunter, too. Tell me, just where do you like to—''

"All right!'' Dave cried. "At the top of the world again! Everyone ready?''

Bernie let them off in the same place. They clicked into bindings, grabbed poles, looked to Hans for direction. Then down they went once more, on the other side of the bowl. Werner and Carlos crossed each other's tracks in figure eights, a long precise line of connected loops. Down, down, until their legs burned and they had to sniff back the cold drips from their noses.

Nicola and Ruthie were in the middle of the group, off to one side. The white slope lay ahead, seamed by a gully. Nicola turned aside to avoid it smoothly, putting pressure on her ski, totally forgetting about Werner and hunting, loving the pleasure of the power, the exhilaration, the challenge. The hill dropped off suddenly in front of her skis, a ten-foot cliff, but she was going too fast to stop. She sailed off the cliff, horrified, her heart lurching, but she landed softly, easily, with a whoomp. "Oh Lordy!" she cried to no one in particular, stopping to catch her breath.

Ruthie appeared around the side of the cliff. "God! I thought I'd find a wreck," she said.

Nicola laughed in relief and triumph. "I did it! I jumped that cliff! Did you see that?"

Over lunch she told the others the story of her surprise flight.

"You're lucky you didn't break your neck," T.J. admonished, blowing a stream of cigarette smoke out into the pristine air.

"Aw, she can handle it. Who taught her, after all?" Evan said. "And will you put that cancer stick out, T.J.?"

"Sure, Dad," T.J. said, stubbing his cigarette into the snow.

"Take it easy, Nick," Dave said. "If something happens to you, our gourmet delights are finished."

Matt watched her closely while she replied to these remarks. She was too aware of his scrutiny, oversensitive. It probably meant nothing. But her mouth was dry, and she couldn't seem to swallow her sandwich. Hans opened a bottle of wine, handing plastic glasses around to everyone, and they toasted the day, one another, the runs, Bernie, Hans, anything and everything.

"Oh, look," Helga said. A Canada Jay was stealing a crust of bread from Werner's fingers. "Even the birds love you, *Liebchen*."

The afternoon went too fast. Nicola wanted it never to end. It flashed through her mind briefly that Jenny should be cooking the rice, but the thought fled just as quickly. The only reality was turning and turning, writing her story on the snow, breathing and flexing and descending flawlessly, feeling the mountains, knowing them. She wished suddenly that her mother could share this pleasure with her. Maureen could share it with her children. So could Ruthie, whose sons and daughter often came to Canada with her. Suzanne would come alive under the influence of the immense sky and the mountains and the clear, cutting air. Maybe she should write Suzanne's doctor and ask if her mother could come up to visit her at the lodge. Yes, she'd have to do that....

They were on their last run, a thousand feet above the valley where Bernie would pick them up, when Nicola saw that Evan had stopped below her. He was leaning forward on his poles, head down. Evan *never* stopped; he prided himself on his endurance, she knew. She halted just above him, sinking up to her knees in soft snow. "You okay?" she asked, panting.

Evan looked up. He appeared tired, the color drained from his usually ruddy cheeks. "Yes, sure, I'm fine. Just catching my breath."

"You sure?"

"Go on, I'm fine. Where's that son-of-a-gun Huff? He left me, didn't he?"

"Up ahead, I guess. Are you sure..."

But Evan was getting angry. *"I'm okay."* Then he pushed off with his poles, turning nicely, easily, without any problem.

Nicola decided to keep him in sight. He'd be furious if he knew she was watching out for him, but he hadn't looked well. Altitude sickness, possibly. It could come on very suddenly. She skied behind him, keeping well back. They were almost down. The helicopter was already there, waiting for them, a silver bug squatting on the snow, its antennae circling idly.

Maybe Evan was tired, maybe he'd had too much wine at lunch, she thought.

Five hundred feet above the valley, Evan careened forward, sprawling in the snow. Nicola felt her heart catch, then she was racing down to him, snapping off her skis, kneeling in the snow next to him.

"What happened?" she heard, and looked up. It was Matt, stepping out of his own skis. "I saw him fall. Is he hurt?"

But Evan was sitting up, growling something. "Damn binding was loose." He stood, brushing off snow, swearing under his breath.

"You all right, Evan?" Matt asked.

"I'm…" began Evan, then abruptly, as if alerted by some internal alarm, his eyes grew huge and knowledgeable, and he fell over backward into the snow, unconscious.

## CHAPTER FOURTEEN

NICOLA CRADLED EVAN'S HEAD in her lap as the helicopter's right ski touched the landing pad, the big machine tipped crazily, and then the left ski settled down hard amid the crowd gathered there, waiting anxiously. She fought the panic welling up inside her. Panic wasn't going to help Evan.

Matt, who sat across from Nicola, looked at her gravely. For a brief moment she saw a flood of emotions flickering across his face: fear, helplessness, anger, regret. So much turmoil seething inside him, she thought, just like her. So he was human, after all. *Oh, Matt,* she wanted to cry, *what's happened to Evan, what's happened to us?*

Jon was the first to open the sliding door, and Matt leaped down to the pad.

Then Jon was up inside the helicopter, beside Dave. "How is he, Nicola?" Jon asked, stooping over.

"He's still unconscious," she said, putting her hand to Evan's brow. "I just don't know."

Maureen climbed into the helicopter then, and Dave put his arm around her shoulders. "He'll be okay," Dave was telling her. "I think he overdid it today."

"Oh God," was all Maureen could get out.

"Vat if it's his heart?" Jon turned to Dave.

But then Matt was back, issuing orders, dragging in the stretcher. He worked with amazing efficiency considering it was his own father lying there ashen-faced and unconscious, and in moments Evan was being carried across the snow toward the lodge.

"He ought to go straight to the hospital," Ruthie Huff said to Nicola.

Maureen, who was walking with them, her hand clutched in Ruthie's, wasn't so sure, though. "I don't know," she said. "What if he's only got altitude sickness?" She looked at the two of them for help. "It couldn't be his heart. Evan's so healthy."

"Of course not," Ruthie said reassuringly. "I only meant that he should be checked out by a doctor. He's as strong as a horse."

Inside the lodge, everyone seemed to be talking at once, offering opinions to Maureen, who was trying to follow the men with the stretcher up the stairs.

"Too much exertion," Rei said, rushing up, bobbing his head.

"The flu," said another.

"I don't think it's his heart," came the guide's voice, "I've seen heart attacks before. Their lips turn blue."

"Look," Nicola finally said brusquely, making a path for Maureen to the stairs, "let's just let Mrs. Cavanaugh go on up and see. Excuse us."

The men had gotten Evan from the stretcher onto his bed, removed his boots and parka and put a blanket over him. Nicola stood in the doorway and tried to see if Evan was any better, if he'd regained consciousness yet.

"Fill this, will you, T.J.?" Matt handed his brother the water pitcher and turned back to Evan, bunching a pillow under his neck. "Hey, Evan," he said in quiet voice, "Dad. Feeling any better? Hey, come on."

Jon rattled into the room then, nudging past Nicola, carrying a portable oxygen bottle. "I think he needs air, yes?"

Then Matt began to place the mask over Evan's mouth and nose, but Evan stirred, pushing the contraption aside. "Get that . . . away."

Nicola's heart leaped. For a brief moment the grouchy old Evan had reappeared.

T.J. moved past her then to Maureen, who was sitting on the edge of the bed, and handed her the pitcher and water glass.

"See if you can get him to take in some fluid," Matt suggested.

"What's all this?" Evan was drawing up his knees and trying to throw off the blanket.

"Oh, darling," Maureen said, reaching out to still him, "do lie there calmly, won't you? You've had a terrible time."

"That's right," Matt agreed, hovering over the bed, "do what Mom says. We don't even know what happened to you yet."

Within a very few minutes, Evan seemed much himself again, grumbling, complaining about all the fuss, insisting that he'd gotten a little light-headed and taken a bad spill. "Huff's probably laughing his head off," Evan said angrily.

Oh, but it was good to see him like this again! Never had Nicola welcomed more gladly one of Evan's irritable moods. Everyone seemed relieved, too, and smiled at his comments.

Jon put away the oxygen. "Ve von't be needing this, I think."

"You didn't eat enough breakfast," Maureen declared. "I warned you, darling."

"I ate plenty."

Within twenty minutes of returning to the lodge, Evan's color was better, and he seemed completely lucid, if tired and complaining of nausea.

"Dad's going to be fine," T.J. said, putting a hand on Maureen's shoulder.

"Of course he is," the woman breathed.

Nicola felt her heartbeat settle into an even pace finally and went out unobtrusively, letting her breathing return to normal, remembering that she had work to do. She answered questions from the guests who were waiting below. "It looks like he'll be fine.... Yes, that was a close one.... No, he's talking and sitting up.... No, he says there's not any pain." She made her way into the kitchen and hurriedly pulled out pots and pans, checked the cooked rice, turned on the oven, grabbed things out of the fridge and tossed them on the cutting board. How long would the salmon take?

"Is everything all right here?" It was Jon, standing in the door, his brow furrowed.

"All's well. Dinner will be at the usual time. Not to worry," she called over her shoulder.

"That Evan," he said, "a strong man, yes? But still, I think maybe he should be seeing a doctor."

"He insists he's fine."

"Ah, yes, he vould. But everyone is still very vorried, you see." He mumbled something else and then headed back to the guests.

Everyone was worried, Nicola thought to herself as she reached for the wire whisk and a bowl. But *was* everyone? Or was there one guest who was merely berating himself?

She called the maids to serve dinner at seven then returned to the kitchen and began to clean up. Evan was reportedly doing much better, resting comfortably, and Matt and T.J. had come down to dinner while Maureen had taken hers in the room with Evan. Probably, Nicola told herself, Evan had overdone the skiing. He was no spring chicken, after all. And yet his boast to Dave the day they'd all arrived nagged at her. Evan had bragged that he'd just had a complete physical and was as fit as a fiddle. It seemed unlikely to her that he would have just collapsed like that.

Too many coincidences, she thought, becoming unsettled all over again. First Reyes making that threat, then that near miss in hunting camp, then Helga's tirade, and now this, a perfectly healthy man keeling over for no apparent reason.

Was Reyes behind all this? Or how about those two, Rei and Carlos, both heavily invested in Costa Plata? They'd practically jumped Evan the minute he'd arrived. She remembered her thought about Reyes having sent them.

Then again there was Helga. Nicola pictured the woman's expression when Evan had been carried in on the stretcher. Not surprisingly, she'd looked awfully smug. And Nicola guessed it would be a mistake to underestimate her. Of course, her lover, Werner, with those frigid pale eyes of his, might be protecting Helga's interests. Or *was* he a lover? Maybe she'd hired him to come along and—

"Hello, am I disturbing you?" It was Maureen, poking her head in. "I wanted to get Evan some tea."

"How is he?" Nicola opened a cupboard and pulled down a box of herbal tea and a jar of honey.

"Thanks," Maureen said. "Oh, he's his usual self, grouchy. But he still feels sick to his stomach. I thought some tea . . ."

"Poor Evan," Nicola said, thinking. "Maureen, could I come up and talk to you and Matt and T.J. for a minute?"

"Why, of course." She looked at Nicola suspiciously, then smiled. "I'll tell the boys to go on up to Evan's room. Is everything all right, dear?"

"Oh, probably," was all she said.

The atmosphere in the bar was hushed that night when Nicola walked through. Everyone was still up and about, but conversation was low and lacked the usual animation. They were all subdued, each wondering about the isolation of the lodge, questioning his or her strengths and weaknesses, probably wishing there was a doctor handy, just in case. On her way up to Evan's room, Nicola spoke to several of them, giving reassurances that Evan was going to be fine.

"You know," Dave said, stopping her on the bottom step, "Evan's never been sick a day in his life. Try to persuade him to fly into Banff in the morning, will you, Nick?"

"I'll try."

She found the Cavanaughs already there, Maureen and
T.J. both in chairs, Matt lounging against the dresser. Evan
was propped up in bed, looking tired and drawn but alert.

"I feel like a complete fool," he said to Nicola when she
closed the door behind her. "I'm not an invalid."

"We know you aren't," Nicola was quick to say. Already she knew Evan was not going to like her little speech,
not one bit.

"Well," she said, coming to sit on the foot of the bed,
forcing a smile, "I guess everyone's wondering why I wanted
to see you all." She glanced around at the faces nervously;
they all looked as troubled as she was feeling, all but Evan,
that was.

"What's on your mind?" Maureen asked softly. "You
can tell us, dear, we're family."

Nicola sighed. This wasn't going to be easy. "I don't think
Evan's sick," she began, and looked them each, one by one
in the eye. "What I'm saying is, I believe someone here at
the lodge is responsible for what happened to him today."
She met Matt's intent gaze and held it for a long moment.
"I think someone's trying to . . . kill him."

Maureen was the first to react by gasping, her hand flying
to her throat. And then T.J. let out a long whistle and fum-
bled for his cigarettes.

"Now see here," Evan began, pushing himself up.

"*Listen* to me," Nicola said, feeling Matt's eyes scruti-
nize her, "this can't be a coincidence." She turned to Evan
abruptly. "You've got to tell Maureen about hunting camp,
Evan. You have to now."

"What about hunting camp?" Maureen asked.

They told her then, and T.J. as well, because he hadn't
been there.

"Damn, Dad," T.J. said, "you should have told us before! Are you *trying* to get yourself killed?"

Maureen was practically in tears. "Oh, Evan," she said, clutching his hand, "darling, what if Nicola is right? This Costa Plata business. And that horrible man, Reyes, who threatened you. And now you're telling me someone took a shot at you? Evan, how could you have kept that from me? What's happening to us? Maybe you should listen to Nicola."

"Ridiculous," Evan said, storming. "She's got one hell of an imagination."

"No," T.J. put in, "she's right. Something strange happened to you today."

"Like what? I fell. Big deal."

"You passed out," Nicola said, getting frustrated, "and you know it."

"And how did someone make me pass out?" Evan snorted in derision.

"I don't know," Nicola said. "Poison, something."

"Poison!" Now Evan was really angry, red suffusing his cheeks and neck. "Are you crazy, Nicola?"

"Now, wait a minute," T.J. said, stepping forward, taking his mother's hand, "maybe she's not so crazy. I think you should fly into Banff first thing in the morning and get some tests taken."

"The hell I will!"

"Evan," Maureen said, "*please*, listen to the children, they might be right. Oh God."

"I'm not going anywhere! You've all lost your minds!"

T.J. put a hand up as if to silence his father. "What about Rei and Carlos? Don't they have a joint venture in Costa Plata? An auto plant?"

"So what?" Evan asked, steaming. "I already talked to both of them. They admitted they came here this week to find out exactly where I stood on those loans."

"Well," T.J. said, "there you are. You told them face-to-face you were going to be the instrument of their financial ruin."

"He's making sense," Nicola said. "Please listen to him, Evan."

"Hogwash."

"And Helga," Maureen said. "I wouldn't put anything past that...that *woman*."

"There's Werner, too," Nicola added. "We only have Jon's word for it that he's her lover. And in the chopper today, Helga mentioned that Werner had gone hunting this fall."

Evan laughed harshly, but the act seemed to drain him. He sagged back onto his pillows. "Next you'll be telling me that Werner is a hit man," he said, trying to sound amused. He waved his hand in the air. "You're all letting your imaginations run wild," he said. "I could tell you about Jon's family, too, you know. He's got relatives in trouble in Central America. They stand to lose a lot. The problem is, my concerned family, everyone could be after my hide. It's not the first time, and I assure you, it won't be the last."

"But Evan..." Nicola protested.

"*Enough.* I was perfectly fine until you started all this tonight, young lady, and I won't hear another word. Men in my position make enemies. It's the name of the game. Now, why don't you all disappear and let me get some rest. Tomorrow's going to be another fabulous powder day."

Disheartened, worried, Nicola rose to her feet. She looked around for help, but none was forthcoming. Evan, as usual, had had the last word. She noticed then, as she stood with her hand on the doorknob, that Matt was still there, half in the shadows, leaning against the dresser. He hadn't moved a muscle the whole time. Nor had he spoken a single word.

Evan, too, must have just realized the same thing. He swiveled his head and glared at his son. "I must say, Matt, you do have a knack for staying calm. Nothing to say?" There was challenge in Evan's voice, and pain.

Slowly Matt unfolded his arms and stepped into the lamplight. His face looked surprisingly old and haggard.

"You're right, Evan," he said, his voice mocking, "why should someone want to kill a nice, harmless old guy like you?" And with that, he pushed past Nicola and strode down the darkened hallway.

Nicola made her way downstairs and stood in the middle of the kitchen feeling restless and afraid. Something was terribly wrong. It wasn't just Evan's predicament, either. Oh, that was a nightmare all by itself, but there was something else. It had been in that room, in Evan's room, an unseen entity, a disquieting force. Everyone had seemed himself, of course, and they'd all been genuinely concerned, but underlying that concern had been a sense of loss, as if at one time they had truly cared for Evan, but now they were just going through the motions. What had Evan done to them through the years? Why was there this holding back, this fear of loving, of being hurt? Didn't he see what this ruthless, stubborn attitude of his had done?

Standing there, lost in her troubled thoughts, Nicola had not heard Matt enter the room. It was only his shadow falling across the tiled floor that alerted her and made her spin around, startled.

"Oh," she breathed, "it's you."

He stood there, looking tall and handsome, yet strangely like a man who no longer found life's bad joke so amusing.

Another side to Matt, she thought, a distressing side. Her heart squeezed unaccountably, and she was almost overpowered by a need to rush to him and comfort him.

"I want to talk to you," he said, "away from here."

Something in his voice told her this was no game. He was in deadly earnest. She nodded, took her parka off the peg by the back door and followed him out.

The night sky was brilliant, crystal clear and diamond sharp. But on those perfect winter nights, it was always cold, a dry, biting cold that groped at her face and numbed it instantly.

Yet Nicola barely noticed. She knew only that something was awfully wrong with Matt, and she sensed, too, that he was not going to share it with her. *Who are you, Matt Cavanaugh? Who are you, really?*

They strode side by side in silence, out across the shadowed field of snow toward the helicopter pad. Their feet crunched in the white stuff, and their breath froze on their lips. She shoved her hands deeper into her pockets but thought only of this man walking close by her, this man whose body had filled hers and made her cry out in a fevered frenzy, this man who calculatingly kept himself from her, who lied to her, this man whom she loved despite it all.

"Nicola," he said softly, so softly that she wasn't certain she'd heard. "I don't know what to say to you. All I know is that you had to go it alone upstairs tonight, and I couldn't be there to help."

"You were sarcastic enough," she said.

"I know. Evan does that to me. He gets to every one of us, I guess."

"Then you are worried."

"Sure, I'm worried. I just can't find it in myself to let him see it."

"Afraid it will weaken you in his eyes?"

Matt smiled crookedly. "Something like that."

They'd reached the pad, and Nicola stopped, leaned against the cold metal of the big machine and faced him squarely. It hurt to be alone with him, to want to reach out and touch his face but not to have the time and permission to love him. How could she have let herself care so deeply?

"Nicola," he said, and leaned against the chopper, too, his body so close to hers that she could almost feel its warmth. "Look, I know I've hurt you."

Oh, how she wanted to deny it!

"And I'm sorry. It's partly my fault, but not all of it. I just don't know what words I can use to convince you that I care, kid. There *aren't* words to tell you how much."

"Really?" she said airily, her stomach wrenching. "I think you know the words, Matt. I just don't think you're capable of feeling them."

"So smart, aren't you?" He laughed lightly. "Maybe you're right. Maybe I knew at one time." He shrugged. "I guess I'm getting old and jaded."

"You could try," she whispered, looking up at his face. "You could let yourself feel. You could try being honest."

"Right. And I could tell you everything, Nicky, and get myself in a whole lot of trouble."

"There you go again."

"Yes, here I go again." Abruptly he moved and took her shoulders in his hands, fixing her with those eyes. "I'm asking you to trust me, Nicky, for a little while longer. Call it blind faith, I don't care. I can't answer your questions, not yet. But I swear I will, and you'll understand."

"Damn you," she breathed, uncertain, knowing that if he didn't let her go in a moment, she'd come apart at the seams. But paradoxically if he did let her go, she'd cry. "I don't know what to think or do or say. You keep talking in riddles. Oh, Matt," she said with a sigh, unable to look him in the face, "I want to trust you. I do. But for me it's so hard. I've been burned so bad."

"I know. Went."

"Yes. I have to protect myself. You see that, don't you?"

"Yes."

"Then how can you ask me to trust you? You sleep with me, lie to me, I don't even know who or what you are."

"I'm the man who cares about you very much, who'd kill any other guy who even looked at you. You believe that much, don't you?"

"Yes...no...I don't know. Oh, Matt, you've really torn my walls down, haven't you? And I don't even know if you care at all that I . . . that I love you."

Suddenly the world seemed to close in on her as if the night sky had fallen and the earth were swallowing her up.

She felt the blood rush into her cold cheeks, and her knees were about to buckle. If he didn't say something, do something, in a moment she was going to scream. How could she have admitted her love to him?

Carefully he put a finger under her chin and lifted her head. "Nicky," he said, his voice deep and concerned, "I don't have the right to take your love, not yet. But maybe someday, someday soon, I can give you back as much." He bowed his head toward her, his mouth so close she could feel his warm breath fanning her lips. "Is it enough, for now?" he whispered.

"Oh, Matt, oh yes, as long as you do care." She felt his mouth cover hers, tenderly at first, and then with force, parting her lips, his arms encircling her, molding them together. She wanted to cry and laugh and pull his parka open right there and feel the hard corded muscles of his back against her fingers. She wanted him, all of him, and in any way she could have him. It no longer mattered that she knew nothing about him; she knew everything she needed to know, and strangely she *did* trust him—she had to, she was out of choices and wholly head over heels in love.

They went to the bunkhouse, tiptoeing down the hall so that none of the staff heard them. Then in her tiny room, he pulled her around to him and his mouth closed over hers hungrily, and she could feel his urgent arousal pressed into her belly.

Breathless, he lifted his head up and whispered, "Are you sure? I never want to hurt you again."

She could only nod, closing her eyes. Yes, she was very sure.

Parkas fell to the hard floor, and boots were tugged off. Then she was lying on her narrow bed and he was pushing up her black turtleneck, unsnapping her bra, lowering his head until his lips brushed her breasts. Their passions awakened like the wildness of a winter storm.

Nicola gasped at the instant warmth that coiled in her stomach and spread downward. She twisted her fingers in his thick, curling hair, along the soft skin at the back of his neck, and then she was pressing his head to her bosom, impatient, yet wanting his caresses to go on forever.

Matt responded with equal need, tasting her nipples, his head coming up to trace the line of her collarbone with his tongue, their eyes meeting briefly before he took her mouth in a hard, greedy kiss.

They shed their clothes hastily, all quick movements, their breathing sharp and shallow. And then he was next to her on the bed, his nakedness brushing hers, playing with her, teasing, tantalizing. She ran her hands along the steel hardness of his thighs and buttocks and up his spine, touching all the vertebrae, glorying in the feel of his tight muscles, his maleness.

While Nicola boldly explored his body, Matt had the leisure to move his hands along the curves of her thighs and hips, the swell of her stomach. He kissed her, running his lips across her shoulders, down her arms, tasting her flesh. He ran his tongue down her side, over her ribs to her waist, and shock waves darted into her hips and she laughed, pulling his head away. He seemed to know all the little places on her body that, once touched by artful hands, sent pulses of white-hot pleasure coursing through her.

"Oh, Matt," she breathed, "make love to me."

Smiling, his eyes heavy lidded, purposeful, he poised himself above Nicola and entered her slowly, moving his hips in a circular pattern until her movements beneath him quickened, became wild, impatient, their bellies slapping together in the age-old ritual of fulfillment.

When it was over and they lay side by side, their breathing becoming even again, he reached up and ran his fingers through her damp hair. "Thank you," he said, his voice wholly sincere, "thank you for putting your faith in me."

She lay there for a long moment, her head turned to him, her eyes fastened on his. She could tell that love did that to a person, it took over all reason and logic and led a soul down an unknown path. She could tell him that, but Nicola sensed he already knew how deep her commitment was. She merely smiled instead, contentedly, and said, "You're welcome, Matt Cavanaugh."

## CHAPTER FIFTEEN

"I SUPPOSE I'LL GET chicken soup and Jell-O for lunch!" Evan said truculently the next morning.

"Now, Dad," T.J. said soothingly.

"Damn it, I want to go skiing! I'm on vacation!"

"Darling, you know you don't feel well enough to do that. There's always tomorrow," Maureen said.

Evan subsided, muttering angrily, like a child denied a treat. He sure could be a pain in the neck, Matt thought once again. But the fact that Evan hadn't gotten up, dressed and gone skiing meant that he really didn't feel very strong. It shook Matt to the core to see his father in bed, circles under his eyes, looking pale and old. Evan had never been sick, never weak, never uncertain, and to watch him in the role of a petulant invalid rattled Matt more than he liked to admit.

*Had* Evan been poisoned? Matt had already considered food poisoning but had instantly rejected the idea. Everyone at the lodge ate the same meals; someone else would certainly have been sick, too, if it was the food.

Poison. Matt was no expert, but there were dozens and dozens of lethal substances available in chemical supply houses, in pharmacies and, horror of horrors, in local grocery stores all over the world. Heck, every woman alive had a ready supply of them under her kitchen sink! He wanted to believe Nicola had leaped to conclusions, but then he'd been thinking the same thing from the moment they'd gotten Evan in the chopper.

Poison. There were so many types—fast acting as well as slow. Two scenarios were possible: either someone had been dosing his father over a long period of time, or that someone had administered a large dose quite recently.

But who had gotten to Evan?

Matt leaned against the wall of his father's room, arms crossed, watching the drama unfold: T.J. was solicitous, Maureen fussy and anxious, Evan irritated.

Evan had been served toast and tea for breakfast and was complaining all the while. "I'll bet Nicola cooked up something delicious for everyone else," he growled. "And I get this." He flicked at his tray contemptuously.

"It was blueberry pancakes and eggs and sausages," T.J. said artlessly.

Dumb, Matt thought.

"See? See what I mean? I love her pancakes!" Evan said.

"But you felt so sick to your stomach," Maureen said. "And we've all been worried about poison."

"Poison! You people *are* crazy. Do you think Nicola's been poisoning me? Why can't I have her pancakes and sausages?"

"Evan, stop giving us a hard time. You know Mom's right," Matt said.

Evan glanced at Matt. "Since when do I need advice from you, wise guy?"

Matt shrugged. *Since I'm responsible for your safety,* he wanted to say. Instead he offered another suggestion. "I really think you ought to be flown to the hospital in Banff, just to be checked out."

"I told you to forget it. I'll feel better tomorrow. It's the last day of skiing, and I'm going up in the chopper come hell or high water," Evan insisted.

Matt had never had such an impossible assignment. He was alone in an isolated ski lodge, trying to protect a man who obstinately refused protection, and he didn't even know who the enemy was. But worse yet, there was Nicola—sweet, worried, innocent Nicola—in the middle of this predicament running around talking about poison and Evan being in danger. Good Lord, how was he supposed to protect her, too? How many people had she voiced her suspicions to? If she'd told the wrong one, or if word got back to that particular guest of the lodge, then she'd be in danger, as well.

And Matt had to stay flippant and carefree and unconcerned to keep his cover intact. He prayed it was holding firm—with everyone else, that was. With Nicola his cover was definitely compromised. Ned would murder him; he'd told her too much already. Nicola Gage knew more about him than his own mother.

"Stop hovering over me," Evan snapped at T.J.

"Sorry, Dad, I'm just worried."

"We're all worried," Maureen said, "aren't we, Matt?"

He nodded dutifully.

"Well, I wish you'd all go worry somewhere else and leave me in peace. Go skiing, all of you. I paid for this farce of a holiday, so you better get your money's worth. Go on, get out of here," Evan said.

"Dad, will you be all right?" T.J. asked. "I think someone should stay with you."

"I'm staying," Maureen said. "I'll go downstairs, and you can take a nice nap."

"You'll check on him, Mom?" T.J. asked.

"Of course."

"Oh, for God's sake!" Evan blustered.

"I, for one, think he's right. If he's too damn stubborn to go to Banff, then we should at least enjoy ourselves," Matt stated easily, but inside his gut churned. How was he supposed to handle this now, with Evan refusing to fly to Banff? And if he hung out in the lodge with Maureen, hovering over his father all day long, everyone was going to notice. Too bad he couldn't come up with a bum knee or a sprained ankle. Too obvious, though.

Okay, Matt thought, he'd go skiing; he'd pretend he couldn't care less about his old man. Maureen was going to watch Evan anyway, and only Helga would be around. Maureen could handle that one, all right; she wouldn't let the woman within fifty yards of her husband.

Maureen. Should he discount his own mother as a suspect? She had plenty of motive to rid herself of a husband who had caused her emotional anguish for years. And who had a better chance to use poison?

He looked at his mother, petite and trim, every inch a lady. He studied her expression and the nervous fluttering of her white fingers. No, it wasn't Maureen; all of his training and instincts for deception told him that.

To be fair, he should consider T.J. Poor T.J. Everything he craved was in his father's hands: money, power, position, the family bank, Maureen. Oh yes, he could see how T.J. adored his mother and tried to protect her, how much he strived for her approval.

Matt studied his brother, too, the expressionless features, the slightly receding hairline, his gawky height and his tenseness. But that was because T.J. needed a cigarette and wouldn't dare light up in Evan's room. It couldn't be T.J., the downtrodden. No, he had no guts at all; they'd been beaten out of him. Maybe, Matt thought fleetingly, he'd think more of T.J. if he stood up on his hind legs and *did* try to kill Evan.

There was a knock on the door. "Can I come in?" Nicola asked.

"Sure, send everyone in, why not?" Evan said caustically.

She went right over to Evan and kissed his cheek. "I'm so glad you're better today." She still had her apron on from breakfast, and her silken black hair was pulled back into a ponytail. Her cheeks were flushed from working in the hot kitchen. She looked beautiful. His palms tingled with the sudden memory of how her skin had felt, smooth and cool, and he recalled with complete clarity the way the soft, dark cloud of her hair had looked drifting on her pillow after they'd made love. He had to blink and force his mind back to reality.

"Did you eat breakfast?" she was asking.

Evan waved his hand. "That baby food. I wanted your blueberry pancakes."

Nicola put her hands on her hips and turned to Maureen and T.J. "Has he been like this all morning?" she asked.

Matt stepped forward. "He sure has been. Cranky as hell."

She couldn't acknowledge him or what had gone on between them, he knew, nor would she ever show her feelings in front of the family. He wanted to put an arm around her and tell them all proudly, "This is my woman and we love each other," but he couldn't do that, either. Not yet. For now, he had to pretend indifference when his body quivered with the awareness of her, and watch her faint awkwardness, her discomfort, which nobody noticed but him.

Studiously she avoided meeting his eyes, turning to his father, instead. "Evan, you're sick. You're supposed to rest and eat lightly. Are you going to behave?"

"Probably not." Evan had a twinkle in his eye. Nicola could always do that to him. It was a talent that the rest of his family, sadly enough, lacked. "What's on the menu for tonight?"

"My lasagna, you know, the northern Italian recipe. You've had it."

"Yes, and I'll have it tonight, Nicola, or else," Evan said sternly.

"We'll see," she replied lightly.

Nicola was untying her apron. "Well, I've left soup and crackers for your lunch. Maureen, you can find everything, can't you?"

Evan groaned.

She ignored him, unperturbed by his grousing, and turned to T.J. "Are you skiing today?"

But Evan answered. "They're both going. I want them out of my hair."

"Oh, good," Nicola said unconvincingly. "I'm going, too."

"Great, get out of here, all of you," Evan said, waving his hand.

"Oh, be quiet, you big grouch. You're just jealous," Nicola teased.

"You bet your bottom I am. Huff is going to top my vertical feet, and it gripes me."

She patted his arm. "I've got to get going now, or else Junior will have to wait. You take care."

"Yes, we better get ready, too," T.J. said, edging toward the door.

"See you this afternoon," Matt said as if he hadn't a care in the world.

"Have fun, all of you," Maureen called after them.

The rest of the guests at the lodge had recovered with astonishing rapidity from the unpleasantry of Evan's sick spell the day before. The group that gathered at the helipad that morning was in the usual high spirits. They all asked after Evan as a courtesy, but they were more intent on their day of skiing. T.J. was there, along with Nicola, Werner, Carlos and Rei. Even Jon was taking a morning off from worrying. Dave and Ruthie Huff and Hans completed the party.

"So, how is he?" Dave asked Matt. "A bear, I bet."

"You got it."

"He's a little better," T.J. added.

"Poor Evan, it must be killing him," Ruthie said.

*Someone hopes so,* Matt thought.

A few minutes later the helicopter shuddered above the peaks, and Matt studied the faces of the people packed shoulder to shoulder on the benches, facing one another. He studied them and matched motivations and used every ounce of experience and instinct he had to try to feel out the guilty party. Surely the man or woman—never forget women, who could be cleverer and more diabolic than men—was in that helicopter, pretending, as Matt was, to be something he or she was not. Rei the enigmatic Oriental, Carlos the volatile Latin, Werner the stolid Aryan, Dave the joker, Ruthie the capable wife, Hans the guide, Jon the old friend, T.J. the put-upon son and Nicola.

Nicola was an innocent, but she was also a catalyst for the evil going on around her. She saw the danger Evan was in, but she couldn't seem to make anyone believe her. Matt wished he could tell her *he* believed her; she must be going half out of her mind, thinking she was crazy or paranoid. She sat in the corner seat, next to Hans, very quiet, a little pale, and beneath her sad, dark eyes were the fingerprints of weariness. He wanted to hug her, to hold her close and kiss each pale, blue-veined eyelid and erase that slightly harried expression she wore. He wanted to feel her long body relax under his hands, to comfort her, to tell her how very much he cared about her.

"Now, listen up," Hans was saying. "The weather reports we got from Banff this morning were not great. There's a front heading our way. It may fizzle out over the West Coast or it may not. But you can see it's windy out." He gestured toward the window of the chopper, and all heads turned to take note. It was overcast, with wind blowing plumes off the high peaks. "So," Hans continued, "we'll be extra careful today. Wind makes the snow unstable, and it can slide. We may end up skiing in the trees lower down, where it's safer."

"Oh, come on," Dave wheedled. "Just one little bowl?"

"*Sí*, this morning, before the wind gets bad," Carlos said.

"What do you think, Jon?" Rei asked.

Jon raised a restraining hand. "I am not the guide. Hans decides vat to do."

They landed at the top of a snowfield. Everyone piled out, collected skis and poles and stood ready while Hans skied a few yards down the slope, checking the snowpack.

"I think it's okay," he called up to them as he side-stepped up the hill. "It's protected from the wind here. Let's have a Skadi check."

They filed by him, one by one, knowing the routine. But today Hans was a little more cautious than usual. He stopped Werner. "Is yours turned up?" he asked. "I'm having trouble hearing it.

Werner unzipped his parka and pulled his Skadi out. He smiled ruefully. "I had it turned to receive," he explained. "Sorry."

They paired off. If it wouldn't have embarrassed Nicola, Matt would have taken her for a partner, but Ruthie was already at her side, jabbering away about men and Evan and how could Werner have been so thick, so he let it lie.

"If it snows tonight, we'll have fresh powder tomorrow," Rei was saying.

"And if it *keeps* snowing, we'll be stuck in the lodge," Matt added. "The helicopter can't fly in the snow. It's happened before."

"Well, then we better get a lot of skiing in today," Werner said. "Just in case."

"I agree," Rei said, shuffling his skis in the knee-deep snow.

Hans tilted his head back and checked the snow blowing off the peaks around them. "Follow me," he said. "Please stay within sight of your partner. Today you really must stick to the rules, or we'll have to return to the lodge."

Groans and hoots met his words, and Matt complained along with everyone, as if he wouldn't like to return to the lodge.

Hans pulled his goggles down and took off, Jon following, skiing in the old-fashioned Austrian style, standing straight up, rotating a shoulder to initiate each turn. The rest followed, two by two, spreading out to find an untracked path in the wide bowl.

"I'd feel better staying behind," T.J. said, "just in case anything happened."

"Sure, fine with me," Matt said. It was common for the strongest skiers in the group to bring up the rear, for safety's sake, and Matt knew T.J. was right. On a marginally safe day, he and his brother were good choices to be the tail gunners.

Matt loved to ski. He loved the freedom of it, the power, the speed, the beauty of using finely tuned equipment to perfection. He'd been brought up skiing, and he wished he was having the fabulous time he was supposed to be having. He wished he could joke and cavort in the snow without care; he wished he could love Nicola without restraint and have a grand old time with his dad. As it was, he had to look as though he was having that grand old time, but he had to be on his guard each second, assessing people, judging whether they were as saturated in deception as he was, deciding who the enemy was.

He followed T.J. down, staying alert to the feel of the snow. He aimed over to his brother's right, toward a slightly steeper pitch than the center of the bowl, traversing to get to it. He felt it then, that sinister hollow whomp of the snow settling under his weight, and froze. He'd felt it before in touchy places. It meant that the snow had released its tension and wouldn't slide—this time. Drawing a deep breath, reveling in the risk and the closeness of the call, Matt made tracks down the steep side of the hill, turning, turning, breathing in the frozen crystals that swirled up around him.

And all the while he watched the skiers below him: Ruthie in purple, Dave in blue, Rei in black, Carlos in yellow, Nicola in bright, cheery red. She was a graceful skier, smooth and controlled. A good all-around athlete. She was good at a lot of things. Unfortunately, trusting was not one of them.

If he wanted Nicola, he'd have to prove himself to her. He'd have to tell her the whole truth; nothing else would suffice.

He came to a stop at the bottom of the open bowl, next to Hans. Everyone was huffing and puffing and talking at once.

"Great run!"

"Did you see that turn?"

"It was *deep* on my side!"

"Damn, but that was good!"

The group wanted to do the bowl again. Hans wasn't sure. Gray clouds were scudding in from the west, blowing steadily toward them as the front pushed in off the Pacific Ocean.

"Sure, once more, before it gets bad out," Dave urged.

There was a chorus of agreement, everyone begging, suggesting, pushing. "Come on. It's safe now, we've already skied it. Then we'll ski lower down."

"Okay, it should be all right for one more run," Hans said, and everyone cheered.

The chopper came in, thudding, causing the snow to foam up around them, and it flew them up to the top once again. Dave wanted to ski with his wife this time, "Just for a change," and the couples rearranged themselves as they flew, T.J. with Carlos, Rei with Hans.

"I'll go with Nicola," Matt said.

She shot him a look that lasted too long, a questioning, probing glance that turned into an uncertain smile. "Sure," was all she said.

Someday he'd explain everything to her, every cruelty, every deception. He'd tell her why they had all been necessary and how he'd gotten himself into this nasty situation in the first place. He'd make her understand. This was the last time, he promised himself fervently, clenching his jaw as he watched Nicola turn her head away to stare out the window, rejecting him. The last job.

Soon the snow lay before them once again, tracked on one side of the bowl, untouched on the other. The group was poised above the clear side, savoring the pleasure to come, picking lines.

"Whoo-eee!" yelled Dave, shoving off behind Hans, Ruthie following. The others started, carving their lines, shouting their joy, racing, crossing one another's tracks to make figure eights. Matt and Nicola went then, and she took a line far over to the left, below the steep chute Matt had done last time. He followed her, aware that Jon and Carlos and some others were behind him. Maybe he should have warned everyone about that unstable steep spot, maybe he should have told Hans. But surely it was safe now; he'd already skied it.

His thought was scarcely completed when it happened. He was watching Nicola's red back one second, then there was a whoosh and a roar and an explosion of snow, and she vanished in the foaming avalanche the next. It happened so fast; he had time only to shout and race after her, panicking, helpless, seeing her head disappear, feeling the stinging pellets of the snow cloud hit his face.

He was there first, kicking his skis off, aware in a corner of his consciousness that utter silence prevailed for a split second before voices were yelling up to him, but he was so out of breath he couldn't answer. He saw a patch of red, a broken ski, a hat lying defenselessly on the churned surface. He ran, scrabbling over the rough avalanche path, reached the red patch. Her suit! He dug with his hands, cursing the hard-packed snow. Voices approached, shouting, but he was too busy to answer, clawing at the snow. Then there were people helping him, and they uncovered her face.

"Thank God!" someone said.

"*Gott in Himmel.*"

"*Gracias a Dios.*"

"Is she alive?"

"How did it happen?"

They pulled her out. She was white-faced but breathing. Her eyes opened, and she stared blankly at Matt as he chafed her hands.

"You're okay," he said softly. "You're safe."

"What . . . ?" she began.

"An avalanche. A small one, luckily, a surface slide. It caught you."

She shut her eyes and shivered.

"Does anything hurt?" Hans asked.

"I . . . I don't know." She moved her shoulders, her legs. "I think I'm all right."

*"Mein Gott!"* Jon shouted. "My partner! Werner! He is not here!"

Hans swore. "Okay. Matt, you stay with her. Everyone else, listen up. Take out your Skadis, turn them to receive. Got it? *Receive.* Put in your earpieces." He did it along with them. "Stay calm. Listen carefully. He's got to be below us. We'll spread out, an arm's distance apart. Walk slowly. When the beeps get louder, we're closer to him. You all know the routine, we've gone over it before. Start right now. I'll radio Junior immediately. The helicopter has rescue equipment. Any questions?"

They started, a line of brightly clad skiers, walking downhill, their heads cocked, listening avidly. Matt turned back to Nicola. She was trying to get up. "I'll help, too. Matt, I'm okay now. They need us."

He pushed her back gently. "Relax, kid. They'll find him."

Her eyes were huge, frightened. She sank back weakly. "I almost... I can't remember... It was so fast. I thought I fell and then... and then...I..."

He put an arm around her shoulders. "You're okay now. It'll pass."

"Oh God. Werner. What if he's . . . you know . . ."

"They'll find him," he repeated.

She turned her face into his shoulder and gave a short sob.

He stroked her dark hair; it was wet and tangled. "It's all right," he soothed. "The helicopter will be here soon. You'll be back at the lodge in no time."

There was a shout from below. Hans was holding up his hand, then everyone converged on the spot, digging with hands and the avalanche shovels that Hans carried in his backpack.

"They've found him," Matt said. "Everything's going to be fine."

She was clinging to him, staring down as they dug Werner out. "Is he . . . ?"

But Dave Huff was making a thumbs-up gesture and calling up to them. "He's alive! He's okay!"

"Thank God," she whispered.

The helicopter flew in then, landing a hundred yards away on a flat spot. The men carried Werner to it, and Matt helped Nicola, supporting her as she walked, because she was tottering a little.

"Oh, honey," cried Ruthie, hugging Nicola, "I was so scared!"

"We were all lucky," T.J. said. "It could have been any of us. Thank heavens it was only a small slide."

Werner was coming to, pale, his face scraped and bleeding. "What . . . ?" he mumbled.

Then they were all in the helicopter, and Junior was on the radio to the lodge, reporting to the group of skiers that had been waiting on the helipad what had happened. Matt sat next to Nicola, still grasping her cold hand. Everyone talked at once, relieved, guilty it had not been him, scared or exhilarated by the danger, each according to his own inner voice.

"How did that happen?" Hans kept saying. "I figured it was safe."

"Fate," Carlos said. "It was not their time."

"Never again," Ruthie breathed.

"Poor kids," Dave mumbled, sober for once.

"Ach, everyone will cancel their reservations," Jon muttered. "The newspapers..."

"They're okay, Jon. No one was killed. Hey, it's happened before."

"Yes, and I am grateful no one has ever been killed, so grateful."

"It is the risk we take," Rei said, "for the pleasure of skiing."

"It's always a risk. We know that, Jon," T.J. agreed.

The voices eddied and flowed in Matt's head, keeping him from thinking, from remembering. He leaned back against the vibrating wall of the chopper and shut his eyes for a moment, listening to the whomp-whomp of the blades over his head, trying to clear his thoughts. It came to him grudgingly, the memory of that snow settling under his skis on the first run. It had been stable. Then, too, the fracture line had been off to the side, way above where Nicola had been skiing.... It shouldn't have happened that way. No. Not unless...

His eyes flew open, and his heart felt suddenly like a cold stone beneath his ribs. Slowly his hand tightened on Nicola's, and his gaze came around to meet hers, and in that instant he saw the same question in her eyes. Had someone intentionally set off that slide? And, if so, had it been meant specifically to annihilate her?

## CHAPTER SIXTEEN

NICOLA WRAPPED THE BLANKET around her shoulders more tightly and gazed into the fire. Around her in the living room the guests who had given up skiing for the day were talking, offering her and Werner more hot tea, a bite of lunch, recounting the events of the morning nervously.

But no one was more upset than Hans. "We never should have gone down the slope," he kept saying to the others, with a guilt-ridden expression on his face. "It looked stable, though, honest it did. It *should* have been stable. I just don't get it."

Matt, who was pouring a couple of drinks at the bar, met Nicola's eyes meaningfully for a moment, then went back to the drinks.

The guide shook his bowed head. "It *shouldn't* have slid like that."

It shouldn't have, Nicola thought, but it had.

She shifted on the sofa and readjusted the blanket. Her left ankle hurt, and so did her left hip. And her elbow. She could just imagine the bruise on her upper arm; by tomorrow it would be a doozy. But she was alive. That's what mattered. And so was Werner.

As she sat there she wondered over and over; had the slide been meant for her, and had Werner only been caught in it by accident?

She shouldn't have opened her mouth as she had with her theory about Evan's sudden illness. She'd mentioned it to a couple of the maids and Jon, of course, and who else?

Dave, yes. And when she'd told Dave, there had been others around. Who? But really, it didn't matter. Anyone could have blabbed—the whole lodge had probably known by that morning that she thought Evan had been poisoned.

Nicola dragged her eyes from the mesmerizing flames and glanced around the room. A few of the skiers looked troubled over the slide, especially those gathered around Hans, listening intently. Others had sidled up to the bar and were making hapless jokes. Matt had them well in hand, of course. Amazing how he could put on an indifferent face while her own was a dead giveaway—she knew she looked downright scared.

Over there was Jon, his head bent toward Dave in serious conversation. Were they discussing the slide, her, Werner? Were they talking about Evan?

"I feel much better, and you?" It was Werner, speaking to her from an easy chair where he, too, was wrapped in a blanket.

"Oh," Nicola said, "I'm still a little dazed. I'll be all right by tonight."

"Yes, me, too. Tomorrow I'll be ready for the mountain again, yes?"

"Sure," she said, distracted.

An unfocused fear seemed to fill her, as if she were a child intimidated by a faceless monster in a dark closet. She wondered if there would be another attempt on her life or on Evan's. And if so, from which direction would it come? And when?

Matt was pouring Helga a drink, another drink, Nicola noticed; the woman must have consumed half a dozen in the past hour. And she was showing the effects. One false eyelash was hanging slightly askew, and she was wobbling on her high-heeled boots. She kept tossing her head back, the swath of flaxen hair falling across her nose.

"Oh, my poor Werner! My dahling! What if I had lost you?"

"He's okay," Matt said. "Here, let me refill your glass." He winked at T.J., who, like most of the group of skiers, had given up for the day, disheartened.

Well, Nicola decided, the slide had accomplished one thing: Werner was crossed off her list of suspects. It would have been unbelievably careless of him to have set off that slide and then gotten caught in it. Of course, things like that had been known to happen. Maybe she was discounting too quickly the tall, muscled German with those cold blue eyes. Maybe Helga had more than one reason to be getting drunk: she'd almost lost her lover boy, *and* she'd failed to silence Nicola.

Who else had been above Nicola on that slope? Rei, the smiling, suave Japanese man? His buddy, Carlos? They both skied expertly, and either one of them could have kicked off the slide on purpose. And what was more, they'd gone off skiing again, obviously unconcerned.

Jon had been up there, too. Jon, with his relatives in Central America, who were worried about the repercussions of a bankrupt Costa Plata. And she shouldn't forget, Jon had also been at hunting camp. Even as she mulled over the facts in her head, Jon lit a cigarette, holding the match for a long time, as if lost in thought, until he burned his fingers. Those cigarette butts on that hillside... The trouble was, there were too many people around, and most of them seemed to light at least an occasional cigarette.

Her head was swimming. She looked up and saw a glass of wine being offered to her. "Here," said Matt, "you look like you could use it."

But Nicola shook her head. "What I need is an aspirin, and to get into the kitchen and get my work done."

"You're not cooking this afternoon?"

"Of course I am."

"Come on, Nicky, you've got to rest."

"What for? So I can drive myself bananas trying to figure out who's the bad guy around here? No thanks." She sighed. "I'd rather be busy."

Casually Matt put aside the drink, then squatted in front of her. "Listen," he said quietly, "I don't want to hear another word out of you about poison and hunting accidents. You're to keep quiet." He said it kindly enough, but there was an authoritative edge to his voice.

"I think I've learned my lesson," she said, looking down at her folded hands, all too aware of his scrutinizing gaze. "Matt," she said then, "when are you going to tell me what's really up with you? And what about Evan? I'm really upset."

He said nothing, merely patted her knee, then headed on back to the bar. She felt a spurt of exasperation. *Patience, Nicola, patience,* she told herself.

After a short nap, the routine of cooking dinner did calm her somewhat, and the aspirin she'd taken helped the ache in her muscles. Yet even as she chopped the onions, carrots and celery and diced the smoked ham to make the *soffritto* for the lasagna, her thoughts kept circling back to the guests, one by one, each face imprinting itself on her mind's eye. Which one of them had tried to kill Evan...and *her?*

"I don't know," Jon said, coming up behind her from his office, "you should be in bed, maybe. This is bad business, this avalanche. Only a few still ski today. They are all very nervous."

"I don't blame them," Nicola said. "But things like this happen."

Jon bowed his shoulders. "Yes, yes, it is awful."

Nicola held the knife poised above the ham. Yes, she thought, Jon, of all the skiers up there, would have known how to get a slide moving down that chute. He knew every inch of the mountain, knew every unstable slope, every tree and rock and angle of pitch. And he was a high-strung sort. Intense, worried, perfectly capable of going off the deep end if it involved money. Was Jon going to have to help his relatives financially?

"Be careful there," Jon said, nodding toward the knife, "you'll cut yourself. You should be resting."

"I'm fine," Nicola said, eyeing him.

It was midafternoon when Matt strode into the kitchen looking like a man with a purpose, or perhaps, she thought, a messy task confronting him. His hands were jammed in his trouser pockets, and his face was pulled into tight lines around his mouth and brow. The spark was gone from his blue eyes.

"Look," he said, "I need to see you up in Evan's room for a few minutes."

Nicola glanced at the clutter on the cutting board. "I've got dinner to finish—how about later?" she asked.

"*Now.* I want to see you now. This is a whole lot more important than your noodles there."

"Well, in that case," she said, shrugging, taking off her apron.

She was curious as she followed him out and across the living room. Maureen and Ruthie were the only two there, having wine by the fire. Matt stopped for a moment when his mother waved him over.

"Darling," she said, "what are you two up to? If you're thinking of disturbing your father, he's trying to rest."

"No, no," Matt was quick to say. "We're, ah, headed to my room. There's this ski wax I wanted to give Nicola."

"I see. And Matt, when Evan wakes up, I'd like you to try to talk to him about seeing a doctor. He won't listen to me, and frankly, I don't think he looks any better this afternoon."

"I agree," Ruthie added. "Talk to him, Matt. Dave's already tried." She shrugged. "Men."

"And how are you feeling?" Maureen called to Nicola.

"Oh, fine. Much better," she replied, wondering why Matt had just told his mother a lie. Ski wax?

Evan did not look well. He was pale, and she could see he had left most of his lunch on his tray.

"What d'you want?" Evan asked irritably, putting down the *Powder* magazine he'd been reading.

"Just a little chat," Matt said, taking charge. He made Nicola sit in the rocking chair beside the bed, lifted the magazine from the bedclothes and set it aside.

Why did he want her there? Nicola wondered, and she began to feel a sense of urgency in the room, as if the air had become charged.

"Okay," Matt was saying, "I want you both to listen to me. And what I have to say doesn't leave this room. This is on a need-to-know basis, so Mom and T.J. are to be kept out of it. Is that understood?"

Evan grumbled "most ridiculous thing I ever heard," while Nicola stared at Matt in mute fascination. She'd never seen him like this: determined, commanding, a muscle ticking in his jaw. *He's Evan, younger, but the spitting image....*

Matt walked to the door, opening it and checking the hall before closing it again, and Nicola rubbed at her bruised elbow and felt her heart begin to pound. What was going on?

"Okay," he said, beginning to pace the room, pinning his father with a hard gaze.

"'Okay,' what?" Evan demanded.

Matt stopped abruptly. "Try to listen, Evan," he said. "Just this once, try to listen without interrupting. Will you?"

"Sure, sure." Evan glared at his son suspiciously.

"There *have* been attempts made on your life, Evan. That was no accident at hunting camp, and this isn't any flu you've got."

"Who the hell do you think you're talking to?" Evan began.

Matt ignored him. "I'm breaking the rules telling you two this. I'm breaching security, but you're too damn stubborn to listen otherwise." Matt paced, his face drawn. "I'm an agent of the U.S. Foreign Service, Evan. I'm on a job, right now, here."

"Ridiculous," his father scoffed.

"No, Evan," Nicola said softly, putting a hand on the older man's shoulder. "Listen to him."

Matt glanced at Nicola, then turned his full attention back to Evan. "I'm sure this is not exactly news to you," he said, "but the United States government has a vested interest in protecting the head of the World Bank. You, to be exact. And—"

"Look," Evan interrupted, "this is a pretty bad joke here, boy, and I fail to see any humor in the situation, so why don't you and Nicola just go—"

"I'm dead serious," Matt said.

"He's telling you the truth," Nicola put in, as all the pieces of the puzzle finally came together. "Listen to him. Please."

"Evan," Matt said, "Dad, why do you think I've been hanging around you? Because I like it?"

Evan was silent, his face pale and haggard, old suddenly.

"Do you understand," Matt was saying, his voice softer now, "that you're in grave danger here? You refuse to leave the lodge, and you've left me with no choice whatsoever but to blow my cover."

"Your 'cover,'" Evan said to himself.

"That's right. I've been working on this case since last May. It's in the interests of the service to see those loans called in, Evan, to see the present Costa Platan government topple. And it's in our interests to see that no harm comes to you as the instrument of that downfall. Are you following me?"

"Of course I am," he replied, but gone was the heavy hand; it was almost as if he'd been defeated. "How long?" he asked then. "How *long* have you been with the Foreign Service?"

Matt let out a breath. "Since college."

Evan sat up straighter, his black brows, so like Matt's, drawn together. "All these years? And you never told us? And here you are, without my permission, without consulting the World Bank, *protecting* me?"

"I'd say you need it," Matt replied coolly.

"But you can't do that. You can't just take matters into your own hands like that!"

"It's not my hands. The Foreign Service gets its directives from the secretary of state. I only follow orders. You know that's how governments work."

"My God...."

"I wouldn't be telling you this if there was any other way to get the job done. And now Nicola—" he shot her a glance "—is in danger. Maybe you're not worried about yourself, but think about her. That slide today was no accident."

Evan sat there motionless, trying to assimilate everything, his guard down, while Nicola could only stare in utter wonderment at the man she loved, Matt Cavanaugh, agent of the Foreign Service, a spy, a complete stranger to her.

She watched Matt intently, knowing the truth at last, yet still unable to fit her thoughts around the reality. Matt, footloose, fancy-free Matt, a spy. But then, what else would Evan's son be but some kind of a hard-core professional? Why hadn't she seen it all before? Yet she had; a part of her had sensed the disparate sides of this man.

"Since college?" Evan was asking, the confusion in his face giving way to frustration. "You're telling me that you've been gallivanting around the world as a bartender for damn near twenty years, and it was all a smoke screen?"

"You could put it that way," Matt answered.

*"All these years!"*

Uh-oh, Nicola thought, looking up.

"Yes," Matt said, "that's about it."

"You couldn't have told us?"

"That's right. I'd have been useless to the service if I had told anyone."

"But your mother... and me? We went on hoping, believing, praying, for God's sake, that someday you'd settle down and... and..."

"And come into the family business? Be a yes-man to you, Dad? Sorry, but I had my own route to go."

"Give me a minute," Evan said under his breath, and Nicola could see that he was sweating now, a cold, clammy sweat.

"Matt," she whispered urgently, nodding toward Evan.

*I know,* his eyes told her, *I know.*

"All these years," Evan kept repeating, the anger draining from him, "all this time."

"I am sorry," Matt said, intruding gently on his father's thoughts. "I was young, Dad, and rebellious. The job gave me a way to vent that wild streak in me. What can I say? And then the years just slipped away."

"But you hurt us," Evan breathed. "Oh, brother, did you hurt us! You have no idea what it was like to think that your only... your oldest son," he said, correcting himself, "had turned out to be a spoiled little..." He looked up into Matt's eyes. "I suppose you blame me, don't you, for pushing too hard? Maureen always said I drove you away."

"I don't blame you. I don't blame anyone," Matt replied softly. "We all do the best we can." And then, a mocking smile touching his lips, he said, "Hey, we could write a book together on lousy father-son relationships. We'd make a fortune, Dad."

Nicola caught Matt's eye. "Listen," she said, "you two can hug and make up or tear each other to shreds at a later date. I think, though, that we better concentrate on getting Evan out of here safely."

Matt turned to his father. "She's right, as usual." He gave a short laugh. "You'll agree to fly to Banff, Dad?"

Evan sighed, giving in for once. "I'll go. I don't like it, but I'll go. And Matt," he said, "you've got to tell your mother."

"I can't just yet. But soon. I promise."

"What," Evan said, his old self again, "in *another* twenty years?"

They left Evan to rest, although Nicola doubted he could. She felt sorry for him, only just now discovering that his son was someone else entirely. And could Evan come to terms with that? Could she?

As they stood in the hallway outside Evan's door, Nicola put her hand on Matt's arm tentatively. "You really threw him for a loop in there just now," she said.

"I know."

"What did you expect? Did you think he'd leap for joy and take you right back into the fold?"

"Hey," Matt said, "what about my feelings? That man lying sick in there treated me like an idiot for years. Me, my mother, T.J. He's no saint, Nicky, you know that. He's hard, and he can be ruthless. And ask yourself this—was anyone surprised that someone was trying to kill him? Hell no."

Of course, Matt was right, and his anger was justified. Still, there was hope, wasn't there? And certainly Matt was not without blame. "I saw something in there," she said, "I never would have dreamed it, either. But the two of you are alike, really alike. Oh, I know Evan can be a tough cookie, and he sure has a lot to learn about being a father, but you're hard, too, Matt. I think you enjoyed shocking him like that. It was as if you were throwing those wasted years in his face, saying, "'Here, Dad, if you'd been a better father, you would have seen me for myself.' That's true, isn't it, Matt?"

"Maybe. I don't know." He took her hands in his then, and faced her. "But you saw through me, didn't you, Nicky?"

"I don't know."

"You trusted me. And you gave everything you had, even when it was hard."

"You make me sound like Joan of Arc or something."

"And you aren't even that shocked by what I do," he went on.

"Oh, I'm shocked. I can't even get it all straight right now."

"But you're not mad, are you?"

She shook her head, and that was when he caught her chin in his fingers and tipped her face up to his. He placed his hands on her cheeks then, and his mouth covered hers. It was not a long kiss, nor even a passionate one. Rather, Nicola thought dreamily, it was a kiss of trust, of sharing, of promises to come.

He moved then, slightly, his mouth beginning to leave hers, their lips still trying to cling until the touch was feather light, an ending, a beginning. Her stomach rolled involuntarily as she looked up through half-closed eyes and met his gaze.

"We better get Jon to radio the chopper about Evan," Matt said in a whisper.

"And tell Maureen," she replied.

"About Dad going to Banff," he said, running a finger down her cheek, "not about me."

"Okay."

"Okay." He reached around and gave her fanny a pat. "Let's go. I'll give Mom the good news, and you find Jon."

Happily, feeling as if she could whistle, Nicola headed straight to Jon's office, where the radio was located. The chopper could unload its last skiers and then fly Evan out. And once in Banff, at the hospital there, whatever was wrong with Evan would be discovered. He could mend, and there wouldn't be anyone around to harm him.

"Oh, Jon? You in here?" She opened the door and found him hunched over his cluttered desk, shuffling papers absently. "Listen," she said, "Evan's agreed to fly on into Banff and see a doctor."

"Ah," Jon said, straightening, looking pleased, "good. Ve'll radio Junior and have him come straight here to the lodge. Good, good." He switched on the set, waited for it to warm up, tapping his fingers on the top of the desk. Matt came in then and stood in the doorway.

"He's calling Junior," Nicola told him.

"Jon here. Come in, Junior. Over." He released the button on the hand microphone.

Crackle. "Yeah, Jon, I read you. What's up? Over." Crackle.

"Vat is your status? Over."

"Just picking up the last of group three and bringing them home. Over."

Crackle, sizzle.

"Good. Now, I vant you to vait on the pad and transport Mr. Cavanaugh to Banff. You understand, Junior? Over."

There was a long string of static, and several crackles interrupted Junior's words. "We got . . . problems. Storm moving in . . . west. Winds at . . . forty-two knots and . . . real bad up here, Jon . . . in morning. Over."

"You sure? Over."

"Sure . . . maniac would . . . fly . . . over."

"Over," Jon said, pressing the button, "and out."

Slowly, her heart beginning a rapid beating, Nicola moved to the window and pulled aside the ruffled muslin curtain. She sensed Matt's presence behind her, and she could feel the frustration emanating from him. Outside, the sky was black, there were twisters of snow coming out of the trees, and streaming plumes of white blew off the forbidding spires of the Bugaboos.

# CHAPTER SEVENTEEN

THE *BESCIAMELLA* came to a boil as Nicola whisked it, and she took it off the stove, stirring salt and nutmeg into the rich white sauce. The routine of cooking soothed her; the kitchen was warm and secure, and she had time to consider a new reality while her hands were occupied.

Matt. She would never, never in a million years have thought... But it all made so much sense now. Everything fit together. She was buoyed up with joy, besieged by amazement, pricked by guilt that she hadn't recognized his worth. All those wasted years, all those hard words from Evan and the passive sadness from Maureen. All the disappointment. How had he stood it?

She searched her inner self. Had Matt's revelation changed her love for him? A spy. How did one love a spy? She supposed the same way she'd love anyone else, but wouldn't he always have to keep secrets from her? And, dear Lord, when would she ever see him again?

*Things always work out,* Nicola told herself firmly. Nevertheless, this predicament she'd gotten herself into promised to pose some awfully big problems. She'd just have to talk it all over with Matt; they'd figure something out.

She began to layer the lasagna noodles, the *soffritto*, the *besciamella*, the Parmesan cheese. Until now, she knew, she'd always been so afraid of love, so afraid to sip the magic elixir. But that had all changed. He'd said he loved her....

She stopped short, a long lasagna noodle dangling from her fingers. Was she truly free of fear now? She searched within, searched the hidden crevices of her mind and found a small, noxious shadow still cowering in a corner, asking, Does he mean it? Will he always love me? Can I trust him?

So, she'd have to deal with that; she'd tell Matt, she could tell him anything. But, she suspected, he already knew that about her anyway.

He was upstairs now, with Evan. She wondered what they were saying to each other. How difficult, how awkward. But they were, at least, talking. Suddenly she wanted to tell her mother that she was in love, really in love, and what a fine person her man was. "Mom? You remember Matt, don't you? Yes, Maureen's son. We're in love, Mom. I'm so happy. And do you know what he's been doing all these years? You won't *believe* it." She wanted to share it. She wanted her mother to be happy for her, to laugh and cry and tell her not to rush into anything.

And Went. Well, he would say something polite if she told him, but he wouldn't really care. He'd be glad if some man took Nicola off his hands—not that she'd ever been on his hands, not really.

Maureen would be thrilled, more a mother to her than her own. And Evan... How would Evan react? She grimaced, wondering as she slipped the two large trays of lasagna into the oven. Would he be thrilled, furious? She just didn't know.

Snow tapped against the kitchen window, begging entrance. The storm had come roaring in, a full-blown blizzard, with howling winds and snow so thick that from the lodge you couldn't even see the helicopter tied down on the landing pad. Jon had called Banff on the radio, telling them of Evan's condition and asking for a doctor to be kept handy in case his situation deteriorated. It wouldn't be much help, but a doctor might be able to give some advice over the radio.

Nicola felt the isolation of the lodge, a fragile island in a whirling white ocean. No one could get out, no one could get in. And Banff had reported that the weather service was calling for at least twelve hours of heavy snowfall.

Nicola thought about tomorrow; if the storm held fast in the mountains, the lodge would be full of frustrated, restless skiers, playing checkers and ruing the waste of their last precious day. It had happened before, and it always made Jon doubly nervous, but somehow everyone survived. *What an odd choice of words,* she mused.

Dinner was a success, despite Werner's obvious discomfort from his ordeal and Helga's drunken doting on him. The college boys, each paired up with a lady now, couldn't hear enough about the avalanche. "What a rush!" one of them commented with fervor.

When everything in the kitchen was tidied up, Nicola sat by the fire talking to Maureen, worrying about Evan and the fact that he was still complaining of nausea.

"If only we could fly him to Banff," Maureen said more than once.

Nicola sipped on a blackberry brandy provided by Jon. She tasted the strong, fruity alcohol and wondered, before dismissing it as ridiculous, if Jon had slipped something into her drink. A person could go nuts thinking about the whole crazy situation.

Finally T.J., who'd been talking at the bar, went up to Evan's room to spell Matt, and Nicola couldn't help but train her eyes on the staircase, waiting for Matt to appear, knowing that he'd come over to them and say something reassuring. If only she could tell Maureen how she felt, share the wonderful news. And she would, soon, when all this terrible business with Evan was behind them.

Matt did appear, and he did crack a joke or two, taking Maureen's hand and squeezing it while his gaze held Nicola's.

"Well, Evan tried to eat some dinner," he told his mother, "and I think he's looking much better." But Nicola wondered. Evan's plate had been returned to the kitchen, his favorite lasagna all but untouched.

And then Matt turned to her. "Say, I wonder if you wouldn't run on up to my room for a sec," he said. "I'll find that *Powder* magazine I promised."

Of course, he'd promised no such thing, but Nicola got the hint. "Oh, sure, thanks."

Maureen seemed not to notice their departure, nor did anyone else, yet Nicola climbed the steps feeling every muscle in her body ache and was certain that all eyes in the room were watching them. She wondered what he wanted.

Upstairs the hallway was dim and silent. Matt stopped her short and held a finger to his lips. "Sorry about that," he whispered, "but I wanted to see you alone. I've been going over and over that slide today in my head," he said, "and I just can't figure it."

"*You* can't."

"Then you haven't any idea who might have set it off?"

Nicola shook her head. "I just can't believe someone would try to . . . to kill me." She shivered, hugging herself.

"Poor Nicky." He reached out and tucked her loose hair behind an ear. "It's been hard on you, I know. I just wish I had a clue to go on."

"I just wish Evan was out of here," she said.

"Yes."

"You know," Nicola said, "I'd search every inch of every room in this place if I thought I'd find anything."

"You mean poison?"

"Exactly. And I did think of doing it, but I really doubt if anyone would have a bottle with a skull and crossbones on it just lying around." She looked up into his eyes. "I mean, do you think we should?"

"Search the rooms?"

"Well, yes."

He shook his head. "I'm embarrassed to say that I don't know the first thing about poison. I wouldn't even know where to begin."

"I thought you were a spy."

"This is the first job like this I've ever had, and I'm only doing it because I was the obvious choice to stay close to Evan."

"So we're at a dead end."

"Until someone tries again, I'm afraid."

"Oh God," Nicola said, "you're right. We're all stuck here in this storm, and—"

"Hey, don't think like that, Nicky. Evan's being watched every second of every minute, and I'm not about to let you out of my sight, either."

"Really?"

"Really." He ran a finger along her jaw. "I don't give a damn what people think. Do you?"

"No. Not if you're here with me. Oh, Matt," she said, but suddenly the door to Evan's room opened and T.J. came out. He saw them down the hall and seemed a bit surprised.

"Oh," he said, "I thought I heard something. I'm glad it's just you two. I'll tell you, I don't like this whole thing."

"Neither do I," Nicola said. "How is Evan, anyway?"

"Okay. He keeps asking for a cup of tea, but I told him I wasn't leaving until someone came up to spell me."

"I can get it," she offered.

"Oh no, that's okay. I know my way around the kitchen. If you'll just sit with Dad..."

They found Evan dozing fitfully, licking dry lips. Nicola sat by the bed on a rocker, watching him, fretting, wondering if they shouldn't radio that doctor in Banff and see if there wasn't something, *anything*, that could be done here at the lodge.

"Oh," Evan said, opening his eyes, disoriented, "where's T.J.? I didn't hear you two come in."

"He went to get you your tea," Nicola replied, and she rose and began straightening Evan's pillows.

"Where's Maureen?"

"Downstairs."

"Is it still snowing?"

"Like crazy," Nicola said.

"Good. Old Huff won't be able to get in his vertical feet tomorrow."

"That's mean," Nicola put in.

"But honest," Evan said, turning his head to study Matt, who was standing, looking out the window. "Don't you think honesty is important, Matt?"

"What?"

"I said, don't you—"

But T.J. came in then and set the cup down by the bedside. "Here you go, Sleepy Time. I hope that's okay."

"Sleepy Time. How clever of you," Evan said, pushing himself up, grumpy.

"Sorry, Dad," T.J. said. "I only meant to be cheerful."

"Well, I don't feel cheerful."

"Evan," Nicola admonished.

"Hell," he said, "I hate being fussed over."

"I know. Well," she said, "I'll say good night. I can see you're in good hands now. I hope you feel better in the morning."

"And by the way," Evan said, his brow creasing, "are *you* all right?"

"Just sore." She smiled crookedly, shrugging.

"You take it easy, Nicola," he said, and she left, catching Matt's glance, knowing that in a few minutes he'd come downstairs again, looking for her.

She went through the bar, where Bernie was playing his guitar for the assemblage, and headed toward the kitchen, intending to take out the loaves of banana bread from the freezer to thaw for morning. The room was spotless, reflecting back to her a dull gleam of stainless steel. There was a tea bag lying on the counter by the stove, though. T.J. He always had been sloppy. Maureen spoiled him. Maureen and Lydia.

She picked the damp, limp thing up and threw it into the trash can, then automatically reached for the sponge to clean the counter. Out in the bar the guitar was twanging, and everyone was singing the chorus to "Ramblin' Rose." Nicola hummed along as she wiped at the counter. Wind-driven snow rattled the window. Idly she wondered if Matt would appear soon, and would he want to go to her room? She hoped so. It was awfully cold out, though, and they'd have to run, but then they'd be warm soon....

The sponge grated against some granules on the counter. Oh, that T.J. He'd spilled sugar all over.

Sugar. Boy, was Evan going to be furious when he tasted sugar instead of honey. T.J. knew better than that....

It came to her reluctantly. It didn't want to come, but it did, a suspicion bordering on knowledge, oozing up out of the mire. Slowly, barely in control of her actions, Nicola wet a finger with her tongue and pressed it into the granules, raising her finger back to her mouth. The stuff was taste-less. Utterly tasteless....

Abruptly the blood left her head. She reached for the counter, faint with horror. A thousand wild thoughts whirled through her head, circling like bats, flitting, terri-fying. T.J. Sugar. Poison. T.J.! As if she were awakening from a nightmare, the room began to come back into fo-cus, and finally a rush of adrenaline surged through her veins. She raced out of the kitchen, mindless of her stiff muscles, and pounded up the stairs, her heart thumping, her chest sucking in air. She flung herself against Evan's door, fumbling at the knob, twisting it, bursting through into his room.

"No!" she cried. "No!"

She lunged for the teacup that Evan held, lunged and knocked it aside, flinging hot tea everywhere, still crying, "No, no!"

"What the...?" Evan gasped.

But she couldn't explain. Horror fueled her body. "It's you!" she breathed, whirling on T.J. "Oh God, it's *you*!"

"Nicky..." Matt began, stepping toward her, looking from her to T.J., bewildered.

But T.J. was backing toward the open door, his face frozen, drained of color, backing away stealthily, slowly.

Comprehension was dawning on Matt. He stepped toward his brother, held a hand out. "Wait, T.J.," he started to say, but his brother lashed out, lizard quick, and knocked Matt aside. Then, with an inhuman wail of anguish, T.J. turned and fled.

Matt stumbled, holding his jaw. Evan was climbing out of bed, his face a mask of pain, of knowledge. "Nicola, is Matt all right?" he asked first, reaching shakily for her.

"I'm okay," Matt said. "Nick, how did you...?"

"It was the sugar," she breathed. "There was sugar on the counter, but it wasn't sweet, and then I knew!"

"Oh no, oh no," Evan whispered, sinking back onto the bed. "Not T.J."

"Take it easy, Dad," Matt said, sitting on the side of the bed, holding his head. "He can't go anywhere."

But Evan shook his head. "Go after him. Matt, go after him. Help him."

Nicola was frozen, paralyzed. T.J. a murderer. Evan...her... Oh God, he *had* been above her today. Poison. He could have been giving Evan poison all along. Why? Why?

"It's my fault," Evan whispered, white-faced. "I pushed him too far. I knew he was weak. I knew."

"Evan." Nicola put a hand on his back. "He can't go anywhere in this storm. We'll find him. There must be some explanation—there must."

Matt stood, carefully working his jaw, feeling out the damage. "Let's go, Nicky. We better look for him. There's no telling what T.J. will do."

She glanced at him, alarmed. What? What did Matt mean? Their gazes locked, and Matt made a quick movement with his head toward Evan, a negative gesture, as if to tell her, *Don't worry Evan about this. He's too weak.*

She followed Matt out and down the stairs. What did he plan to do? Talk to T.J.? Reason with him? Murder. T.J. had tried to murder his father and her. The shot at hunting camp. T.J. knew exactly where Evan would be that week. Oh no, the cigarette butts, the Marlboros.

Matt was cursing under his breath. "I should have known," he said harshly. "I should have seen it."

"You couldn't have," she replied. "He's your brother."

"I should have seen it," he repeated.

The fire was crackling cheerily in the bar, and everyone sat around singing while Bernie played his guitar. It was a scene from a brochure for a ski lodge: comfortable, happy, fun, full of camaraderie. A few guests looked up as Matt and Nicola came into the room.

"Have you seen T.J.?" Matt asked casually.

"Yeah, he went out. Thataway." One of the college boys stabbed a thumb toward the front door, then put his hand back on the knee of his lady friend.

"In this storm? He must be nuts," Nicola remarked.

"He must have a hot date with one of the maids," the boy said, winking.

"Thanks," Matt said.

"Where could he be going?" Nicola asked as they hurried out of the room. "There's no place. The storm—"

"We need our parkas and a flashlight," Matt said tightly. "God knows what he's thinking."

"The kitchen."

While Matt fetched his jacket, she grabbed her own coat off its hook and found the flashlight, then opened the back door. The cold hit her face, and the wind howled in her ears. Snow filled the air, thick and cloying, an impenetrable white veil in the narrow beam of the flashlight, melting into slush on her skin instantly.

Matt was alongside her shortly and pulled at her arm, trying to tell her something, but the wind snatched his words away.

"Tracks!" he yelled louder. "We've got to find T.J.'s tracks!"

Six inches of new snow had already piled up; it had been falling more than an inch an hour. Prime conditions for avalanches, Nicola thought as Matt led her through the snow and darkness toward the front of the lodge.

The light over the door showed shallow dimples in the snow, nearly filled in already. They followed them with the flashlight through the roaring blackness toward the maintenance shed. The doors of the shed were open, yawning like a gaping mouth in the face of the blizzard. And there were tracks, much clearer than the footprints, leading out of the shed.

"The snowmobile!" Nicola shouted so that Matt could hear her. "He took one of the snowmobiles!"

Matt tugged her into the shed, and together they yanked the doors shut. Nicola pulled the light cord, and abruptly there was quiet and illumination and they could talk.

"He's taken the snowmobile," she panted.

"Where? What's he thinking?"

"The tracks went toward the old logging road. That's the only possible way out of here, but it's—"

"He's crazy," Matt said grimly. "He can't think straight."

"Matt, he'll freeze to death! He can't get away. It's miles, I don't know how far. He doesn't have enough gas to get anywhere. And, oh my God. The road crosses avalanche paths, dozens of them. In this storm, they'll slide. Matt."

"We'll have to follow him. Can you drive one of those things?"

"Yes, but—"

"Let's go. He's already got a head start."

"Wait." She grabbed his arm. "We have to wear suits. We'll freeze otherwise. We won't do T.J. any good, then."

The padded snowmobile suits, bright orange and stained with grease, hung on hooks on the wall. They dressed, pulling on thick gloves and helmets and goggles. Then, with Matt's help, she lifted the lighter back end of the machine, and they swung it around to point out of the shed. Nicola pulled the hand starter, a lawn-mower-type cable, once, twice, three times until the engine sputtered and roared to life. Quickly she pushed the choke knob back in so it wouldn't flood, then depressed the accelerator on the handlebars until she was sure the growling machine wasn't going to stall.

"Open the doors," she called, swinging herself onto the seat, pulling down her goggles.

Snow blew into the shed in fitful gusts as Matt pushed open the doors. The snowmobile's single light pierced the darkness, cutting a hole in the night, a hole filled with thick, swirling snowflakes that reflected back to Nicola's eyes like a blank wall. Matt got on behind her; she felt his hands at her waist, holding on to the quilted fabric of her suit. The rapidly vanishing groove that T.J.'s machine had made lay in front of her, but only to the extent of the reach of the headlight. What lay beyond? Only darkness and cold and wind and a sad, crazed human being running for his life.

"Ready?" she shouted.

"Ready!" Matt said into her ear.

She gave the machine gas, and the engine screamed and lurched forward. She followed the line in the snow as fast as she could, bouncing and sliding, her ears filled with the engine noise, her body tense, her hand controlling the gas feed. The snow was piling up, ever faster, splatting onto the windshield, sticking there, making it hard to see. She was afraid to go too fast, even more afraid to go too slow and get bogged down in the deepening snow. There were drifts across the logging road, and when she hit them too fast with the two front skis, the machine skewed sideways, trying to rip the handlebars out of her grasp.

T.J. was up ahead somewhere. How far? The mountain loomed to her right, a dark, unseen bulk. She was aware of Matt, his body pressed against hers, and his very presence steadied her.

How far had T.J. gone? He wasn't even dressed warmly. He'd freeze or he'd get stuck in the snow or run off the road or get lost in the trackless wilderness or be buried in an avalanche.

The headlight threw crazy shafts of light ahead into the driving snow and against the dark tree trunks that popped up at her like ghostly sentinels. She had to catch up—she had to.

She hit a snowdrift then, at the wrong angle, and the handlebars were wrenched out of her hands. The snowmobile flopped onto its side, the track still moving, and tossed them in the deep snow. It was a nightmare, then, of heaving and gasping and sinking to their hips in the snow, to right the machine. Thank goodness Matt was there. Wrapped in a cocoon of whipping snow, they stood for a minute to catch their breaths before getting back on the snowmobile. He grasped her arm, and she knew there was so much they had to say to each other, but they couldn't, not then.

They must have traveled five miles along the old logging road, the extent to which it was safe for cross-country skiing from the lodge. Beyond that there was acute danger of slides, and even one place where there was a permanent pile of avalanche debris that blocked the road all winter, she suddenly recalled. T.J. wouldn't know about it. He would be barreling along at top speed, half out of his mind, and there would be this wall of snow in front of him . . .

She felt her heart leap in fright, and she wanted desperately to tell Matt about it, but when she turned her head and shouted, the wind whipped her words away, sucking them out of her throat and flailing them on the storm. And then she could only hope and pray and depress the throttle as hard as she could.

Suddenly there it was, the solid barricade of snow across the road, faintly seen through the blizzard. But then, she had been looking for it. T.J. would never have. . . .

Simultaneously Matt stiffened against her back, and she saw T.J.'s machine, a shadowy blur on the snow. It was on its side, and a dark hump, almost covered with snow, lay motionless beside it.

## CHAPTER EIGHTEEN

EVERYTHING HAPPENED QUICKLY during the next few days, so quickly that Nicola wondered if she was still in charge of her own destiny.

Jon had come to her the morning following T.J.'s accident and insisted that Nicola go with the Cavanaughs to help them through this difficult time. He'd get his former cook to fly in right away. She'd agreed on the spot, relieved, thankful that she wasn't leaving Jon in the lurch. She'd flown home to New York with the family, the *whole* family, and she'd been glad to be there, ready to share the bad with the good, ready to sit between Matt and his silent, withdrawn brother, ready to give what comfort she could.

Everything had gone smoothly under the circumstances, yet she felt as if her life was in the hands of a puppeteer. Despite the fact that she wanted to be with the Cavanaughs, she couldn't help but wonder where she would be going from there. She'd cook, of course, but where? Nicola hadn't changed, but everything and everyone around her had.

Upon returning to New York, Evan had refused to press charges against his son. He'd accepted full blame for T.J.'s aberrant behavior, an uncharacteristically humbled man. They'd quietly driven T.J., who had only a dislocated shoulder from his accident, to an upstate New York mental hospital, a very exclusive hospital, where only the wealthy could afford the long healing process.

And Evan. He, too, had entered a local Westchester hospital and been given a clean bill of health with mild reservations: no overexertion for several weeks, watch the alcohol and caffeine. The remnants of the arsenic would be in his system for a while yet, although recovery eventually would be complete. T.J. had come clean immediately, admitting that he'd purchased the poison through a chemical supply house in New York and had only begun to slip the tasteless arsenic into Evan's tea just before the trip to the Bugaboos.

Evan had grumbled royally over the doctor's advice, especially the taking-it-easy end of things. "What am I supposed to do all day long," he'd said, "lie around in bed?"

But Maureen had stepped in. "I think," she'd replied, "you could afford to take a few months' leave from the World Bank. You *should* do it, dear, and maybe this family can pull the shreds of our lives together."

There hadn't been much Evan could say to that.

So now Nicola sat at the dinner table with Maureen and Evan and Matt, a part of the troubled family, each member of which was trying in his own way to make the necessary adjustments.

T.J. had inadvertently brought them together, given them this chance to open all the old wounds and let them finally heal. What a devastating shock it had been to Evan to find out that neither of his sons was what he appeared—and it had all happened in the space of a day. The strange thing was, Evan held no malice toward T.J., none whatsoever. Oddly he almost respected his younger son for the attempts on his life, although Evan was well aware of just how disturbed T.J. was.

Yes, Nicola had made the decision to be there with her adopted family. So why, then, was she still feeling as if someone else were pulling her strings?

The answer should have been obvious. It was Matt, naturally, trying to manipulate those strings. Matt, the man who was finally showing his true colors—Evan's colors—and who was gently but firmly trying to run Nicola's life. She wanted to be with him every second of every day, and it was clear to Maureen and Evan what was going on even if Nicola and Matt kept separate bedrooms. The Cavanaughs approved, and underlying the anguish and recriminations there was happiness for the love that had blossomed in the midst of so much turmoil.

But Matt had become, well, not pushy exactly, Nicola decided, but intent upon getting his own way.

"Matt tells me you're going to Washington with him," Evan said to her during the meal.

"Well, I don't now if I—"

"Of course you're going," Matt said, interrupting. "Don't you want to go? It's only for a few days."

"I wish someone would clue me in," Maureen interjected.

"We will, Mom, on everything, just as soon as I get the go-ahead from my boss."

Maureen frowned. "Your boss. You won't even tell me who you work for." She looked at Evan. "But you know, don't you? It makes me so angry...."

He gazed at his wife with understanding. Amazing what a terrible shock could do to a person, Nicola thought. "Listen," he said, "in a few days Matt will tell you everything and you'll understand. Right, Matt?"

"Right, Evan."

"So are you going to Washington, dear?" Maureen asked Nicola.

But Nicola couldn't decide. She wanted to go; she wanted to be there when Matt told his boss he was through with fieldwork and wished to be stationed in the home office. She wanted to support Matt in this decision and be there for him if his boss gave him any trouble. But she also knew in her heart that Matt, given an inch, would snatch away her independence. By not going, she would be making a statement. *Give me room to breathe.* Oh yes, Matt was definitely Evan's son.

There was another matter, too. Marriage. Maureen had hinted at it to Nicola in private; Evan expected it. But no one had told Matt. And somehow Nicola couldn't see herself traipsing around Washington, or wherever, for the rest of her days as Matt's doting mistress. Besides, she couldn't afford to sit around forever, sponging off the Cavanaughs. She needed to find a job and keep busy, but she was so uncertain about the future that she just kept hesitating, unable to make a commitment to an employer.

"I think I better stay here," she finally said, catching Matt's sharp glance. "Maureen wants me to drive her up to see T.J.'s doctor."

So, angry and disappointed, Matt took off for Washington, and Nicola drove Maureen north to visit the doctor; even though she ached for Matt's company, she at least felt free to think again and to make her own choices. And then, too, she could be there for Maureen.

T.J.'s doctor didn't look anything like Nicola had expected; he wasn't white haired and bearded and stooped like Sigmund Freud. He was tall and freckled and strongly built and young.

"Call me Dr. Stan. Everyone does. My last name is unpronounceable. So good to meet you, Mrs. Cavanaugh, and I'll bet you're Nicola. Thomas has told me about you."

"Thomas?"

"When we make a complete, therapeutic break with past behavior, we often change our names. So he's no longer T.J., he's Thomas," Dr. Stan explained.

"How is he?" Maureen asked shakily.

"Physically he's fine. Mentally he has a ways to go. But then, that's what he's here for."

"Can I...can I see him?" Maureen asked.

Dr. Stan put a hand on hers. "Mrs. Cavanaugh, I'm afraid that would be counterproductive to Thomas's well-being. He first has to learn to live with himself, then he may be able to move back into society."

"May?" Maureen asked faintly.

"Mrs. Cavanaugh, I won't lie to you or jolly you along. Your son has severe problems with self-esteem and with repressed rage. There's no magical cure, no pills. It will take time and hard work, and Thomas may never be able to live with you again."

"Never, oh God...."

"We have a forty percent cure rate here. That's very high, so his chances are excellent."

"Is there anything I can do...we can do?"

"I'll let you know when it's time to see him. There may be some family therapy called for."

"Anything, Doctor, anything. We love T.J.... I mean Thomas."

"You *keep* loving him. That's vitally important, Mrs. Cavanaugh."

They drove home in a thoughtful mood. Maureen cried a little and dabbed at her eyes and then said, in an uncharacteristically forceful voice, "If we need to go to family therapy, Evan will go, Nicola. I don't care what he says."

And Nicola believed her.

The new, if unspoken, rule around the house was openness and honesty, a difficult goal for the Cavanaughs to achieve, but they tried—even Evan.

But was *she* being open? She wanted Matt, she loved him, her whole being ached for him, yet she didn't quite have the guts to tell him that the bottom line was marriage and kids and her own career. She was afraid he'd buck her at every turn.

Matt came home on a weekend in early February, rocking the house with his presence, grinning from ear to ear. He announced to the family that Ned had given him a post in the home office and that his Section C days were history. "Hell, I even got a raise!"

Evan put down his Sunday newspaper and took off his reading glasses. "I want you to come into the family bank," he said. "I need you there, Matt."

Matt put his arm around Nicola's shoulders. "Not a chance, Evan. I've got my own gig going, and I'm happy as a lark."

"I'd give you a free hand."

"Easy to say now. But face it, Dad, you're no more capable of that than I am of pushing pencils in a bank every day."

"But won't you be in an office with the Foreign Service?" Maureen asked, looking up from her book.

"Most of the time, I will. But there'll still be trips to Paris, Rome, you know." He squeezed Nicola's shoulder. "Come on outside," he said, winking at her. "I want to talk."

It was a cold day, gray and blustery, the wind soughing in the bare tree branches, dead leaves stirring on the tarp over the swimming pool. Nicola felt her cheeks sting with the raw dampness as they walked, bundled close together, along Maureen's garden path.

"How was T.J.?" Matt asked, looking straight ahead.

"The doctor was guarded. Optimistic but guarded."

"I wonder if he'll ever be well again."

"Who knows?" she said. "He spent so much of his life hating Evan. I guess all he ever thought about was being left out of the family business and worrying that you'd inherit everything."

"Crazy."

"Yes, it is. But if he can get over that hatred, if he and Evan can ever talk, really talk, that is . . ."

"How is Evan doing?"

"Oh," she said, "good, considering everything. He talks a lot to Maureen about what a fool he was trying to run his sons' lives. He's beginning to get it, anyway. And Maureen's been the Rock of Gibraltar. I think she's reveling in the role of Evan's sounding board."

"I guess we'll all make it through," he said. "It's been hard, though."

"Worse," Nicola said, pulling the open collar of her sweater closed while they walked, each thinking separate but oddly similar thoughts as the wind whirled dead leaves up into a spiral, then let them drop.

"I did some thinking," Matt said then, "while I was gone. I guess you were right to stay here."

"I thought so."

"Look, I know I've got a crazy life-style, and Lord only knows, I'm too much like my dad for comfort. But, Nicky, I can learn. You only have to tell me to back off, and I will."

"What're you trying to say, Matt?"

"I'm saying that I love you so damn much I'm willing to do anything to have you. I was scared half out of my mind that I'd get back here and find you gone off to some wilderness somewhere."

"Me?" She laughed. Was he kidding? Surely he must realize that she'd been putting off going back to work, halfheartedly reading the want ads, because she knew there had to be a confrontation between them, an honest examination of their feelings. "No wilderness for me," she said. "It's the wrong season, anyway."

He stopped and pulled her around to him roughly, playfully, his mouth searching for hers. "Oh God, Nicky, you taste so good. I swear, I'll turn into a lap dog if you'll let me."

"I doubt *that*."

"You're probably right." He grinned that old, wicked grin of his, and his blue eyes danced in the gray winter light. "I don't know how good I'll be at settling down, kid. But I'm getting old, and nature is starting to do the trick for me. I want you, I do know that, and I want kids and dogs and cats and all that stuff."

"Are you ... proposing?" She felt her stomach roll over, and her knees were threatening to give out on her.

"I guess I am. You wouldn't consider living in sin, would you?"

"Stop teasing."

"Okay. But will you marry me, Nicky?"

"There'll be rules," she said, hardly believing her own temerity.

"Oh?" He brushed her hair off her shoulders and put his hands on her arms.

"Yes. I've had to be too self-sufficient, Matt, you know that."

"Still don't trust men."

"Not entirely, I don't. I'll be honest."

"But I already knew that. And it's a part of what makes me love you so much. I want to spend my life with you. I want to be the man you trust the most."

He kissed her thoroughly then, pressing the length of her body to his, a long, white-hot kiss that made her feel as if her life force were draining right out of her toes and pooling at their feet.

Breathless, she wedged her hands between them and laughed. "Wow," she said, "I guess we *better* get married."

"You mean it?"

"Absolutely. But we're equals in this, buddy, and none of this Evan-style bulldozing. Okay?"

"I'll put it in writing."

THE DAYS OF FEBRUARY slipped away. There was so much to be done, arrangements to be made, invitations to be sent out, a larger apartment to be found in Washington—not an easy task. And then there were the weekends when Nicola insisted on going skiing or hiking or something. Living in the city was certainly going to have its drawbacks, but if she was going to be with Matt, then that was okay.

They'd just gotten back from Washington, having found an adorable, if expensive, Georgetown apartment, when Maureen tapped on her door. "You'll probably be furious with me," she began, then went on to tell Nicola that Went was going to cater the March wedding and that he insisted on seeing Nicola immediately about the arrangements. So Nicola had to turn around, after just driving up from Washington, and head into the city.

What Maureen had not told her, though, was that good old Went had a surprise for her.

They sat in his hot, cramped office behind the kitchen. In the background, pots and pans clanged furiously as the dinner hour approached. Matt had offered to come along with her, but Nicola had known in her heart that she had to go this alone. It was time to tell Went the truth, time to be honest with him and herself. She sat there readying her speech in her head, prepared to tell him what a jerk of a father he'd been, and how, because of his neglect, he'd botched up her life, made her angry and insecure, darn near made her run from Matt. Oh yes, she was all ready—no more games.

But then Went popped his surprise on her.

"I've been thinking," he began, nervously folding and refolding a kitchen towel. "I'd like to open another restaurant."

"Oh, really," Nicola said. He didn't have time for anyone but himself—and a woman or two—as it was.

"Yes, Nicola, another French restaurant. And I've been thinking about Washington."

"Washington?" A faint bell rang in her head.

"Another one like Sansouci, but smaller, more intimate. There's a spot for sale, in fact, not far from where you and Matt will be living."

"How do you know where I'll be living?" Nicola was beginning to smell a rat.

He waved a hand eloquently. "Oh, I had a chat with Evan the other day."

"I see."

"Well, yes, and you know, I'll need a right-hand man in Washington, a good manager, and a good chef, too."

"Dad..."

"And I was thinking... Here I have this beautiful daughter, family, you know, and she's always working for someone else."

"Are you suggesting...?" She couldn't believe it. This *wasn't* happening.

"If you say yes," he said, shifting his eyes away uncomfortably, "then we could see each other once in a while, Nicola. Look, I haven't been much of a father, have I? And if I can do this one small thing, well, maybe we could get together from time to time."

"Yes," Nicola said, her resentment melted, barely able to hold in her joy, "oh yes, Dad! It'll be the best restaurant in Washington! You'll see!"

"I'm sure it will." He smiled, embarrassed, happy, proud of himself. "There's one other thing, though. When I have grandchildren, I want to visit often. I missed so much of your growing up. Anyhow, we'll make it a great success, you and me. We'll call it Sansouci et Fille."

Nicola wanted to laugh and cry and hug him. Oh, she wasn't so blind as to think he was going to change overnight—no doubt he'd only make it to Washington a couple of times a year at best—but it was a start. And Went had gone the whole nine yards for her this time. Incredible.

"Thanks," she said, choking on the word despite herself. "Thank you, Dad."

The house in Westchester began to swell with expectancy as the date of the wedding neared. Matt was gone a lot, getting acclimated to his new work, flying to London once on the Concorde for an overnight. But when he was home, it was heaven between them, laughter and kisses and breathless long nights stolen in her room. They took the time to visit Suzanne and invited her to the wedding. Surprisingly Suzanne was delighted, nervously putting aside her depression for once and declaring that she would be there, and was there anything she could do to help Maureen?

When they were outside in Matt's car, however, Nicola frowned. "She won't make it. I already know that. Oh, she'll send a lovely gift, but it will be too much for her to actually come. And then she'll get depressed because she can't."

"Maybe she'll make it," Matt said softly.

Suzanne sent her regrets that March morning as the house in Westchester was turning inside out for the affair. Nicola clenched her teeth and stood it, though, because life couldn't always be perfect. She'd accept her mother's condition, and she'd try only to think of the good times and never the unhappy moments with her mother.

The house looked beautiful. Flowers rose from delicate vases everywhere, and the air was scented with hothouse blossoms and the singular musk of old lace. Went gave the bride away, and Nicola stood next to Matt in front of the minister and repeated the solemn vows. When it was done, and he lifted the veil, there was a moment, a pause, and a reverent hush filled the room.

"We'll go see Suzanne tomorrow," Matt whispered, his eyes holding hers. "We'll tell her all about it, and she'll be happy. Okay?"

"Okay," Nicola breathed, her heart filling with love, "but now it's time for us."

"For us," Matt said as his head descended toward hers, and the first moment of the rest of their lives began.

# *Harlequin*
# *Superromance.*

## COMING NEXT MONTH

#### #374 SILKEN THREADS • Connie Rinehold
At age thirty-two, fashion designer Sabrina Haddon
finally met the daughter she'd given up sixteen years
earlier—and the girl's irate adoptive father. The sparks
between Sabrina and Ramsey Jordan were instant, but a
relationship was impossible. Sabrina could only hope
that in time the delicate threads of their individual lives
could be woven together....

#### #375 HANDLE WITH CARE • Jane Silverwood
Dr. Jim Gordon barely made it back alive to Maryland
after being held hostage overseas. Wounded in spirit,
he felt rejuvenated when he met Dory Barker and
her teenage daughter. But he failed to realize that
the pretty pottery instructor was also one of the
walking wounded....

#### #376 REMEMBER ME • Bobby Hutchinson
While researching a children's book, Annie Pendleton
met ambitious pediatrician David Roswell, and before
she knew it Annie was as hard-pressed to balance the
duties of single parenthood as her lover was to balance
his work load. Perhaps this stress explained Annie's
chronic physical pain, but maybe it was David's
opposition to decisions she'd made—decisions that
dramatically affected them both.

#### #377 WORDS OF WISDOM • Megan Alexander
He'd broken their engagement, and he hadn't said why.
All Jenny Valentine knew for sure was that men like
Luke Beaumont ought to come with warnings tattooed
on their foreheads. Luke thought he'd done the noble
thing by breaking their engagement. Well, he'd had
enough of being noble. Only now it seemed that Jenny
had had enough of *him*....

# JAYNE ANN KRENTZ WINS HARLEQUIN'S AWARD OF EXCELLENCE

With her October Temptation, *Lady's Choice*, Jayne Ann Krentz marks more than a decade in romance publishing. We thought it was about time she got our *official* seal of approval—the Harlequin Award of Excellence.

Since she began writing for Temptation in 1984, Ms Krentz's novels have been a hallmark of this lively, sexy series—and a benchmark for all writers in the genre. *Lady's Choice*, her eighteenth Temptation, is as stirring as her first, thanks to a tough and sexy hero, and a heroine who is tough when she has to be, tender when she chooses. . . .

The winner of numerous booksellers' awards, Ms Krentz has also consistently ranked as a bestseller with readers, on both romance and mass market lists. *Lady's Choice* will do it for her again!

This lady is *Harlequin's* choice in October.

*Available where Harlequin books are sold.*        AE-LC-1

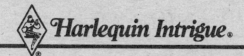

## *Harlequin Intrigue*®

## High adventure and romance— with three sisters on a search ...

Linsey Deane uses clues left by their father to search the Colorado Rockies for a legendary wagonload of Confederate gold, in #120 *Treasure Hunt* by Leona Karr (August 1989).

Kate Deane picks up the trail in a mad chase to the Deep South and glitzy Las Vegas, with menace and romance at her heels, in #122 *Hide and Seek* by Cassie Miles (September 1989).

Abigail Deane matches wits with a murderer and hunts for the people behind the threat to the Deane family fortune, in #124 *Charades* by Jasmine Crasswell (October 1989).

*Don't miss Harlequin Intrigue's three-book series The Deane Trilogy. Available where Harlequin books are sold.*

DEA-G

# The series that started it all has a fresh new look!

HARLEQUIN *Romance*

The tender stories you've always loved now feature a brand-new cover you'll be sure to notice. Each title in the Harlequin Romance series will sweep you away to romantic places and delight you with the special allure and magic of love.

Look for our new cover wherever you buy Harlequin books.